HOLLYWOOD HIT MEN

OTHER TITLES BY MICHELE DOMÍNGUEZ GREENE

Martika's Magic

Keep Sweet

Special Agent Emily Ray

My Name Is Emily Ray

Hayley Hope Is Gone

HOLLYWOOD HIT MEN

CASSIDY CLARKE BOOK 1

MICHELE DOMÍNGUEZ GREENE

This is a work of fiction. Names, characters, organizations, places, events, and incidents are either products of the author's imagination or are used fictitiously. Otherwise, any resemblance to actual persons, living or dead, is purely coincidental.

Published by Thomas & Mercer, Seattle
www.apub.com

EU product safety contact:
Amazon Media EU S. à r.l.
38, avenue John F. Kennedy, L-1855 Luxembourg
amazonpublishing-gpsr@amazon.com

ISBN-13: 9781662531699 (paperback)
ISBN-13: 9781662531705 (digital)

Cover design by Caroline Johnson
Cover image: © Joseph Sohm / Getty

Printed in the United States of America

HOLLYWOOD HIT MEN

CHAPTER ONE

Geronima Velasquez tapped lightly on the door to the guesthouse. Jennifer was usually up early to go to her Pilates class. Her car was still there—maybe she overslept? Geronima waited. She had arrived early to clean the big house because Mr. and Mrs. Wallace were away on a trip. The sky had still been lavender when she'd trudged up from the bus stop at Cahuenga. It was so quiet that she worried as she walked through the tunnel on Holly Drive; homeless people slept there sometimes. She passed under the big jacaranda trees whose roots pushed up the pavement, leaving their sticky, candy-like petals to form a purple carpet on the pavement. She enjoyed working early. The California sun always cast a rose gold tint on the houses as the pale blue of the dawn dissipated.

Usually, Mr. and Mrs. Wallace were home. He was on the phone, and she was in her home office making dinner reservations or scheduling the never-ending house upgrades. There was always something to do: Marfa kitchen cabinets, new seats for the home theater, drought-resistant flowers, and huge cactus plants that were delivered with a crane. Mrs. Wallace said the plants cost $5,000 each. Geronima and Jennifer had laughed at that. There were plenty of cacti growing in Arizona, where Jennifer was from, and even more in Geronima's village in Guanajuato. Who would pay $5,000 for one?

She liked that Jennifer was easygoing and down to earth, even if she always looked stylish and worked for famous people. Geronima knocked again on the guesthouse door. No answer. She noticed that it wasn't fully shut, so she nudged it. The door swung open slowly, and she stepped inside. The small living room was a mess. The couch cushions were strewn across the floor, the arrangement of glass spheres on the coffee table was upended, broken shards scattered across the carpet. The white linen curtains were stained, one of them half torn from the rod as if someone had grabbed them and pulled hard.

"Miss Jennifer?" she called out. Then she saw her.

Then she screamed.

Cassidy Clarke moved the maple breakfast sausages around the skillet with precision, wielding the spatula like a surgeon, moving the scrambled eggs to one side of the pan. She'd added Boursin cheese and green onions today, and in the toaster was some of the kalamata-olive bread she'd picked up at Panos in Hollywood. She glanced at her navy blue LAPD uniform hanging on the coatrack, covered in a plastic sheath. Today was an auspicious day in the Clarke household. It was Cassidy's first day as a new boot in the LAPD, the day she'd be assigned a patrol partner and a beat.

Her father, Bill, was getting dressed for his final day of duty as a homicide detective after forty-one years with the department. She could hear him singing Springsteen's "Glory Days" through his bedroom door, the familiar smell of Old Spice wafting down the hallway from the steamy bathroom. No CHANEL or Clinique cologne for him, not even Drakkar Noir. He was old school, with a closet full of ill-fitting brown and gray suits from the Men's Wearhouse and a tie clip from Knott's Berry Farm that he'd worn for years.

His phone rang where it was charging on the kitchen counter. She saw that it was from his longtime partner, Pete Barrera, another veteran homicide detective, who'd be retiring next year. Bill hurried down the hallway with the agility of a man ten years younger and grabbed the phone.

"What's up, brother?" he asked.

With a sidelong glance, Cassidy saw him grimace and hang his head for a moment before continuing, "Where? That's the Hollywood Dell?"

There was a pause, and then he said, "Another one, right?"

He grabbed a plate and slid it across the counter to Cassidy, who served up the sausages and eggs while he poured a steaming cup of black coffee from the 1980s-era percolator he insisted on using. He hung up and jammed the phone into the pocket of his jacket.

"Did Pete say it's the same guys who did the other two?" she asked.

"Looks like it. The victim is early thirties, found at home, strangled. Posed on a chair this time, with the same lipstick heart drawn on her cheek," he replied wearily.

Two earlier victims had been posed as well, a particular kink of a certain kind of performative killer. The lipstick heart was a macabre touch. The first victim was Christy Cline, a social media manager for several A- and B-list celebrities. She'd been found in her courtyard apartment on Los Feliz Boulevard, strangled and propped up in her bed with an open newspaper spread across her lap.

The second victim was Elise Mannard, a personal assistant to a fading TV ingenue who was now well past forty, still doing rom-coms with her carefully curated beach-girl aesthetic and lots of camera filters. Elise had been her long-suffering girl Friday, on call twenty-four seven to handle any crisis, from a late-night breakup to a craving for salted seaweed stems from Koreatown on a Sunday morning. Elise lived in a classic 1920s apartment building called the Soñador, once home to silent-film star Pola Negri on her rise to fame and later to Dayna Delaurie, the troubled teen star who overdosed on Soma and Lortab in the '90s. Elise was found by a neighbor in her living room, seated on a pale-leather couch, dressed in an evening gown. On her cheek, a bloodred lipstick heart.

"You're going straight to the scene, right?" Cassidy asked her dad.

"Yep, I won't be there to watch you step out in uniform. Tell me who your partner is so I know who to harass when I get back," he said. He bolted down his food and drained the last bitter drop from his coffee cup, then took his gun from a kitchen drawer and slid it into his shoulder holster.

"You really should lock that thing up," she said.

"It's just you and me here, and we're both cops, so what's going to happen? I'm going to mistake you for an intruder?"

"Anything could happen. You could freak out and accidentally shoot the gardener," she said.

"I would only shoot someone breaking in here in the middle of the night. Why would the gardener be in our house at that hour?"

"It's no use—you always say the same thing." She laughed.

"This thirty-eight sat in the kitchen drawer all through your childhood, and nothing ever happened," he said.

"Right. I know you boomers love to glorify those reckless days before motorcycle helmets and you just ran around the streets until dark when you were in elementary school. Isn't it amazing how social progress works, Dad? We know so much more with the passage of time!"

"I don't have to put up with this from a scrawny new boot like you!" He grabbed her shoulder and planted a kiss on her cheek. "You'll be home for dinner? Should I pick up Zankou Chicken?"

"I'm not sure. I may meet up with Carter after his classes let out."

Carter Sims was Cassidy's boyfriend, a second-year law student at USC. He was clean cut, polite and came from a wealthy Pasadena family. Most fathers would have considered him a catch. Not Bill.

"Okay, give Howdy Doody my best and tell him not to give his trust fund account number to any of the thugs down by USC. They might steal some of his unearned cash," Bill said as he headed out the door.

"Love you, Dad."

"Love you, too, Binkie."

Cassidy bit back a smile. Carter did resemble a modern-day Howdy Doody. She sent him a text.

off 2 work ur gf is officially a cop watch out!

She had lived with her dad since her parents' divorce when she was fifteen. Her mother, Cathy, had hung in as long as she could with Bill's crazy schedule, his gruff machismo, his throwback mentality. She had fallen for that as a twenty-seven-year-old store clerk with no big plans in life. Bill was a detective, which had seemed kind of glamorous. He had a bigger-than-life personality to complement her natural shyness. They'd bought the ranch house in Chatsworth before shacks cost a million-five in the bad part of Reseda.

Then came the sorrow of the miscarriages and the stillbirth of their son, Jamie. When Cassidy arrived after years of trying, she was their miracle child. But even with her sweet disposition and tomboy drive to be just like her dad, she couldn't save a failing marriage that had seen too many illusions go down in flames.

The divorce was easy, and given Cassidy's age, the judge let her decide who to live with. She chose Bill, of course. Cathy stayed in town for weekend visits and holiday vacations until Cassidy graduated from high school. Then she moved to Wyoming, met a quiet, kind cattle farmer, and lived her best life on eleven acres. At twenty-three, Cassidy was beginning to have a better understanding of what her mom had gone through.

Bill was charismatic, always the center of attention, certain that he was right and knew best about everything, for everyone. He'd spent his life boxing at various gyms—it was his stress release with the pressure of working homicide. He'd started as a young man and stayed with it; it gave him a place to safely vent his anger and built-up frustrations, but it came with a price. Always ready to play the tough guy, he shrugged off headgear until it was required to get into the sparring ring. He'd been hit in the head countless times, busted teeth out and suffered more than one broken nose over the years. A serious motorcycle accident ten years earlier had been the game changer, delivering the most severe head trauma of his life. He'd been off work for six weeks, and his short-term memory had taken several months to return to normal.

That injury, combined with his many years working out in the ring, had changed his temperament. He had less impulse control and bigger mood swings, and Cassidy knew that had been hard on her mom. She could understand the many ways that her father had been a difficult man to be married to. And how much it must've hurt when Cassidy chose to stay with him. Now that she had grown up, gotten her criminal-justice degree, and traveled for a year, she understood more of the nuances of life. The gray areas where there was no clear distinction between right and wrong. That people could hurt those they loved without meaning to. She made a mental note to call her mom when she got home, to fill her in on her first day as a cop.

Her phone pinged. It was Carter.

be careful out there can u bring ur handcuffs over later?

She sighed, then smiled, wondering what he would do if she whipped out a pair of cuffs next time they were in bed. Would he blush and stammer, or would he slap them on her wrists and get to work? Maybe she'd just have to find out.

Across town, in the Hollywood Dell neighborhood, east of Cahuenga, where the homeless parked their broken-down trailers and limping Winnebagos, Pete Barrera and Bill stood in the bedroom of Jennifer Dale's guesthouse, situated behind a Mediterranean-style mansion from the '40s. The forensic techs and the photographer were silent as they documented the scene and gathered evidence. It felt wrong and somehow offensive to talk loudly in such a place.

Jennifer had been strangled, the ligature marks clear around her neck, her eyes bloodshot from broken vessels that had ruptured under the pressure that had choked her life out. She was posed in her nightgown, seated at her vanity table, staring lifelessly at her reflection in the mirror. The lipstick heart drawn on her cheek was a perverse provocation.

"No wonder the cleaning lady lost her shit," Bill whispered. "This is like something from a horror movie."

Geronima Velasquez was seated in the driveway with a female officer, wrapped in a blanket despite the warming weather. She was shaking, and her eyes were swollen from crying. She struggled to speak to the officer who took notes.

"It's the same two guys. The posing is too weird. The lipstick heart," Pete said. "And there are two sets of footprints. She put up a fight, but she couldn't handle two of them. The housekeeper said she's a personal chef for celebrities, so we're going to have to talk to them. Said she worked a circuit doing parties and daily cooking for the ones that require those special keto, gluten-free, vegan meals, the ones who pay ten bucks for a single roll of toilet paper at Erewhon."

"Oh, fuck me . . ." Bill said, stepping over the busted furniture to look at Jennifer's bruised face, her skin losing color and settling into the gray pallor of the dead.

"I'm just about done here, Bill," said the forensic tech.

"Anything left this time, or is it the usual clean sweep?" Bill asked.

Bill and Pete knew there were two killers. At each scene they had found two pairs of bloodied footprints in different sizes with different shoe brands, based on the treads. But that was all they had found; the clues seemed almost deliberate. The killers left nothing that could be run through CODIS. They had been calculated and careful. The security cameras at all three locations were not working; the internet connection they relied on was down. At the two previous crime scenes, the internet service providers did not report a company outage. The signals were jammed, which was easy to do with a laptop and the correct software. The scenes showed a brazen level of planning and confidence, to hang around and pose the victims after killing them. All the women had been sexually assaulted as well, but there was no semen left behind. The killers used condoms assiduously, like an NBA player with a hoop groupie after an away game. Bill presumed it would be the same this time.

"I've got two sets of footprints; the sizes are different from each other but also from the previous cases. They're using different shoes each time. The coroner said the time of death is about three a.m.," the tech said. The air in the room felt heavy, the metallic smell of blood permeating everything in the rising temperature. It was going to be a hot day.

"The owners of the house are on vacation. He's some kind of real estate investor, rich housewife. The housekeeper said they've gone to Napa," Pete said.

"There's no forced entry. What single woman lets two strange guys into her house at three a.m.? They had to know the place, and they were here when she got home," Bill said.

Pete went to speak to the gardening staff while Bill texted Cassidy.

Its another one, be careful coming and going from the house or anywhere else

Will do thx 4 letting me know fill me in at home?

Yep, stay safe binkie

Outside, neighbors had started to gather behind the police tape. A guy wearing a fedora and holding a dachshund sporting sunglasses stood on the hood of a car, taking photos with his phone. An officer yanked him down and pushed him back to the sidewalk.

"I'm an influencer! I cover crime in the city!" he protested.

The cop ignored him and resumed her guard position. Several reporters had arrived from newspapers, and local news vans had pulled up. This was the third murder in the area with similar victim profiles. Police Commander Joyce Ramsey rolled up in her blue sedan and pushed her way past the gawkers and the press. She was dressed in a severe gray suit, her blond hair in her signature style that looked as if it were shellacked in place. As she approached the guesthouse, she nodded to Bill and Pete and slipped on protective booties. Then she stepped into the crime scene. The coroner's office personnel were zipping Jennifer Dale's body into a black plastic bag for transport to the coroner's forensic science center on Mission Road. Ramsey surveyed the aftermath of the murder with disgust.

"We're asking the press for restraint, and we're not revealing anything about the way the bodies are found."

"Three victims in five weeks, same profile, same perps. They're going to jump all over this," Pete said.

"We can hold back the information on the clues—they don't need to know any of that. We don't want to create a panic," she said. "The bizarre posing of the bodies, the heart drawn in lipstick on their faces. What the hell does this insanity mean?"

Bill shook his head and popped a piece of Trident gum into his mouth.

"It means we've got two sick-fuck serial killers in Hollywood," he said.

CHAPTER TWO

Cassidy stepped out of the house, carrying her duty bag and uniform over her shoulder. She had done an extra safety check of the windows and doors and set the alarm. Whoever was killing women in Hollywood could easily get on the 101 freeway and come to the Valley. It had rained heavily over the weekend; now the hills surrounding their neighborhood were brilliant green like an ad for travel to Scotland. She knew in a week they would be dry, brown, and dusty, like they always were in the arid California heat. Across the cul-de-sac, her eyes once again stopped on the Keyes house, with its 1970s Swiss-chalet detailing and a circular driveway. It belonged to different people now; the house was sold within a year of the incident. Cassidy stood rooted to the ground, staring at the front door the way she had years earlier, remembering the day fourteen years ago that had led to this moment in her life.

The police cars were parked strategically in a circle, blocking both ends of the driveway. A SWAT team had been sent out; a sniper was on the roof of the nearby Fowler home. Inside the Keyes house, Marvin Keyes, her best friend's father, had shot his wife and two of his children. He now held the third child hostage against the growing police presence. Mrs. Keyes had managed to call 911 from the wall phone in the kitchen before she died.

The neighbors watched from windows, from driveways, picking up snippets of information. Marvin Keyes had spoken to the police lieutenant, confirming that his wife and one of his children were dead. Nine-year-old Cassidy Clarke watched in terror from behind her mother's

Chevy Malibu parked in the driveway. Kylie Keyes had been her best friend since kindergarten. They had started in Mrs. Rubino's class at Chatsworth Park Elementary. They did everything together—they matched outfits on Twins Day, they joined Brownies in the same troop. She had stayed at Kylie's house countless times for sleepovers, sneaking Easy Cheese and RITZ crackers under the covers of the bunk beds in Kylie's room.

Kylie's older brothers, Brad and Kevin, were three years ahead of them in school. Mrs. Keyes was pretty and vivacious, putting up the most elaborate decorations at Christmas and Halloween. And how many times had Mr. Keyes tossed them high into the air while playing in the pool? How many barbecues had she and her parents had with them, cooking burgers and hot dogs, drinking sodas and Capri-Sun?

Cassidy gripped her small hands together, her fingers interlocked. She could feel her teeth clenching, and her breathing was shallow. Her mother had gone to the supermarket with Mrs. Fuller and left her at Kylie's for the half hour it would take to pick up the makings for French toast. Mr. Keyes had come home, sweating, with dirty hands. When she and Kylie greeted him at the door, he pushed Cassidy outside with one shove and slammed the door behind her. Uncertain, she had crossed the cul-de-sac to go home. Then she heard the first gunshots, followed by several more in quick succession. The police arrived, and then ambulances. Then more police and SWAT, telling everyone to stay inside. No one had noticed her behind the Chevy. She saw her mother, up the street, behind the police cordon, arguing, trying to get through. Cassidy ran from behind the Chevy just as gunfire erupted inside the Keyes house and from police outside. It seemed to come from everywhere. Through the cars, the uniformed cops, the paramedics, she ran and ran and ran toward her mother . . .

Cassidy had relived that day too many times. Her parents had taken her to therapy, which helped, but it didn't make the memories go away. Mr. Keyes was killed by the SWAT officers that day. He had been unraveling mentally for several months, but no one knew, except his wife, who had tried to get him help many times. An accountant for a large real estate company, he was quiet, unassuming, a family man.

But he had lost his job, and their house was heading to foreclosure. His wife's new minivan was about to be repossessed. He had been drinking and smoking methamphetamine to escape a life that had become unbearable. If he couldn't provide for his family, who was he? What would happen to them when they discovered his failure?

Kylie Keyes had been the second child shot that day, and she had survived, but with serious brain damage. She would never walk again; she struggled with involuntary movements. Her speech was garbled and halting. She lived in a residential rehabilitation center in Northridge. Her brother, Brad, died with their mother that afternoon, in the kitchen of their ranch house. The police found them next to a fridge covered with school award certificates, photos, and a chore chart that determined who loaded the dishwasher and took out the trash. A funny magnet showed a police officer holding a sign that said **STOP! YOU DON'T NEED THAT COOKIE!**

Brad's twin, Kevin, had moved away to a small town in Indiana and worked as a schoolteacher. He withdrew, lost contact with everyone. The family home was sold several times. New people came, then left. But Kylie remained trapped in a body that she could not escape, her family scattered, erased. Except for Cassidy, who had gone to see her in those early days at Northridge Medical Center, when she was connected to tubes and in an induced coma to help her brain heal. She had been there when Kylie opened her eyes, moved her fingers for the first time. Cassidy and her mom had brought Kylie's artwork from school, her stuffed animals to decorate her hospital room. She had been visiting Kylie regularly ever since, keeping alive that childhood connection like an IV, letting her friend know that she was not forgotten or alone. She had a standing visitor's appointment twice a week at West Valley Residential Care. The staff all knew her; they called her Kylie's twin.

At nine years old, Cassidy Clarke had grown up. She had learned that everything could be taken away without warning, on a sunny day in April, when your mom ran to the supermarket for milk. That people can suffer in silence, without knowing how far they've fallen until it is too late. That a moment of clarity in a man spiraling into madness can make him push the neighbor child out the door, sparing her life. That good people can do bad things without meaning to. That was why she became a cop. Why she wanted to put herself on that line between life and death, where she might make a difference. Today was the day that journey began. She climbed into her MINI Cooper and backed out into the cul-de-sac, watching the Keyes house disappear as she drove away. Today, she chose happiness. She chose moving on and doing her best. It would be a good day.

Bill and Pete stood outside the medical examiner's office, waiting for the autopsy on Jennifer Dale. They had called her family in Arizona; her sister was catching an afternoon flight. Her ex-boyfriend was coming in for an interview at three o'clock. Bill and Pete had put in requests to speak with her celebrity clients but were awaiting replies. Famous people in Hollywood never wanted to talk when something like this happened, as if the violence and tragedy would somehow dim the sparkle they worked so hard to cultivate.

The medical examiner, Gil Mendoza, opened the door and signaled them to come in. Bill pulled a small jar of Vicks VapoRub from his pocket and dabbed it under his nostrils.

"We use NeutrOlene right on the body. You don't need that," Mendoza said.

"It's his last day, Gil. Let him stick to his old habits," Pete said.

Mendoza smiled and gave Bill a fist bump before he scrubbed and pulled on his plastic gloves. "How many years?" he asked.

"Forty-one," Bill replied proudly.

"How many of these have you attended? A rough guess?" Mendoza asked.

Bill shook his head. "I can't even begin to count. I've worked Robbery-Homicide for half my life. But there are some you always remember, like this one. She was posed, like the others. Really psycho."

"What a case for your last day. Couldn't be an easy gang shooting or a domestic that goes too far," Mendoza said.

Pete shot Bill a quick look. Mendoza was young, just thirty-four, and he hadn't been on the job that long. There was nothing easy about a domestic that ends in murder.

Mendoza was checking Jennifer's mouth, taking swabs of her nasal and oral membranes.

"Looks like she bit her tongue," he said, "and with the petechial hemorrhage and the nasty ligature, I'm pretty sure cause of death is strangulation. The hyoid bone is broken, also."

"Like the other two," Pete said. Jennifer also had a series of lacerations on her hands and arms, clearly defensive wounds. Mendoza was clipping and scraping under her fingernails.

"We might get DNA here," he said. "She fought back pretty hard."

"I hope so," Bill said.

He wanted the lucky break that led to a quick resolution to the case. He wanted the murderers caught and behind bars. He wanted his final homicide to be closed, not to have it lingering on the books, like an accusation staring at him every day that he was home, living the quiet life. He told himself that he was ready to retire and put it all behind him. But all this—the autopsies, the interrogations, that moment when the clues finally connected—had defined his life for so long. He was secretly afraid of what his days would be like without it. The familiar pressure of a headache was starting at the base of his skull. He had them regularly, for years now, worse since the motorcycle accident. He popped open the ever-present bottle of Aleve in his coat pocket and swallowed two pills, dry. Retirement was the start of a new chapter—that's what Cassidy said. But he wondered, How does a new chapter fit into an old book?

In the bullpen of the Hollywood station, Watch Commander Steven Kriss had just finished the partner assignments for the new boots. Cassidy was paired with Sean Riley, a five-year veteran patrol cop who had worked with Bill on a homicide case earlier that year.

"We've got a lot going on today, everyone. Demonstrations scheduled and permitted near the Hollywood Bowl—those streets are a nightmare on a good day. The homicide team is dealing with a repeat offender, possibly a serial-killer team in the Hollywood area—we'll have more details later from Detectives Barrera and Clarke. And for those who don't yet know, Detective Bill Clarke is retiring today after forty-one years on the force. Barrera will be posting flyers with information about his retirement party tonight, or you can ask his daughter, new boot Cassidy Clarke," Kriss said with a flourish.

There was some scattered applause, and Cassidy smiled self-consciously. She'd already heard some nasty comments from Landon Dykstra, a police captain, who had referred to her as a *nepo-hire*; she didn't want any more blowback from being Bill's daughter.

Pete Barrera and Bill were at his desk, entering their notes from the most recent Hollywood murder. Bill's replacement, Detective Judson Postiff, stood at attention, ready to step in or help in any way he could.

Bill waved to the assembled officers and shouted, "The party's at the Smoke House, across from Warner Brothers in Burbank tonight! Be there or be square!"

Barrera handed Cassidy a stack of flyers for Bill's party.

"Make sure the blue suits get these, kid. We want a big turnout for your dad's party. I'm dropping a bunch off at Rampart, Hollenbeck, and at Parker Center."

"My dad said you got another one today, same MO as the others," she said.

"Yeah, it's bad. We just came from the autopsy. But that's not your problem on your first day. Riley, take good care of her. Clarke and I will be watching," Barrera said.

"Don't I know." Riley sighed, signaling Cassidy to follow him.

Ten minutes later they pulled out of the station parking lot. Hollywood had changed in the last decade. Gone were the weird storefronts that had barely hung on for years, the seedy strip malls that used to house greasy spoon restaurants where anything from weed to *bombita* could be bought. Everything was gentrifying: The old, neglected apartment buildings had been turned into fashionable lofts, and nightclubs thrived on streets that used to be too dangerous to walk after dark. The niche clothing stores on Hollywood Boulevard that had catered to exotic dancers for decades had found a new mainstream clientele in the advent of the Kardashian blow-up doll aesthetic.

Cassidy was familiar with her new partner. He was on Bill's short list of cops he hoped she would get paired with. Riley had a reputation as a reliable, straightforward officer, with no drama. He'd grown up in the Valley, his dad was a plumber, his mother, a kindergarten teacher. One of three boys, he'd joined the police academy after two years at Valley junior college. He was attractive, with black hair and hazel eyes, built like a swimmer, which had been his sport at Saint Finbar Parish School.

"Did your dad ever take you to see Thai Elvis at Palms restaurant?" Riley asked as they crossed Western Avenue and headed into Thai Town.

"Yeah, I went years ago when I was in middle school," Cassidy said with a laugh. Thai Elvis was a Hollywood institution. He was a small, middle-aged Thai man who impersonated Elvis Presley, complete with the black pompadour, the elaborate costumes and capes, the patent leather white boots. He did a good Elvis impression, knew all the vocal licks and stylings of every hit. His music tracks included the Jordanaires on backing vocals. Thai Elvis entered the Palms restaurant on Friday and Saturday evenings like a rock star, doing all the signature moves. No one knew his real name. He was simply Thai Elvis.

"I heard he had a stroke, just before Covid hit," Riley said. "It's too bad. I used to like his show. And it was a great first-date place to let you know if a girl has any sense of fun or if she's wanting you to take her to Soho House."

"Don't you have to be a member to go there just to have a drink?" Cassidy asked.

"Yeah, a drink that costs thirty-five dollars!"

They made a loop through Thai Town, which butted up against Little Armenia. They were the same neighborhood. The signs that designated each area were just a few feet apart, and over the years the residents had learned to appreciate their differences and similarities. The neighborhood retained a scrappy East Hollywood feel, despite being just below the high-dollar homes of Los Feliz.

"You want to be a homicide detective like your dad?" Riley asked.

Before Cassidy could answer, their radio crackled with a call from dispatch. A 911 call from a public bathroom in Griffith Park, a man in distress, stuck inside the stall. Riley swung the car into a U-turn and headed toward Vermont Avenue, one of the main thoroughfares running through the park. It had been a well-known gay cruising area for decades.

"I'll go inside, you stand guard. It's probably a hookup gone wrong," Riley said.

"I'm fine to go in. I'm not going to be shocked, you know," Cassidy said.

"I know, but I've been given notice to take good care of you, especially on your first day."

"I don't need any special treatment," Cassidy said, "but you can do it. Men's public restrooms are disgusting."

They arrived at the Vermont Canyon Tennis Courts. No one was outside; the parking lot and the courts were empty. In the small office, an annoyed clerk nodded toward the bathrooms. Riley went in while Cassidy scanned the area for any activity. Riley emerged a moment later and leaned in the squad car window to the radio.

"EMT needed at Vermont Canyon Tennis Courts in Griffith Park," he said, with a lack of urgency.

"Is the guy hurt?" Cassidy asked.

"No, he got his dick stuck in a glory hole drilled into the bathroom stall. Someone on the other side put a bulldog clip onto it, and he can't get it out," he said.

"Do we need an EMT for that? Can't we just unclip it?"

"I don't want to touch it! Just let the EMTs do it. He might sue us if something goes wrong."

"What can go more wrong than being stuck in a glory hole with a bulldog clip on your little buddy? It must hurt like hell," Cassidy said.

"Did you just call it a little buddy . . . ?" Riley asked, horrified.

Cassidy slipped on a pair of plastic gloves and went into the bathroom. A moment later she came out with the clip wrapped in a paper towel. She put it into a plastic evidence bag. A skinny guy with a goatee and a man bun skulked out, looking sheepish.

"I think I still need the paramedics. My knob was in that clip half an hour! It might be damaged," Man-Bun whined.

"Do you want to press charges, sir?" Riley asked.

"I don't know the guy's real name. We hooked up on Grindr. I've never had anything like this happen before." He looked like he was about to cry.

"That bulldog clip was on pretty tight. You could have lacerations or tissue damage," Cassidy said, with a serious glance to Riley, who was trying not to laugh openly.

They waited until the EMTs arrived and checked Man-Bun's penis, which did not require treatment beyond a cold pack and some Neosporin ointment. Man-Bun climbed onto a ten-speed bike and gingerly rode away.

"He didn't even say 'thank you,'" Cassidy said, watching him disappear into the park.

"And you win for most memorable first call of patrol!" Riley said, giving her a high five.

Just four minutes away from the Vermont Canyon Tennis Courts, on a leafy, quiet street in Bronson Canyon, Millie Grace, a retail clerk at Nordstrom and part-time Uber driver, fought against the nylon cord wrapped around her neck while staring into the grinning, watery eyes of the attacker who straddled her. She had managed to grab at his mask and pull it upward. She kicked hard as his accomplice held her lower body tight against the rough, jute carpet. Her bladder released; she felt the warm urine running down her leg onto her expensive new rug. She lurched her knee upward in one final, desperate push. The man with the rope shrieked in pain and rolled off her just before she blacked out.

CHAPTER THREE

Bill sat at his desk, swallowing down the last dregs of his black coffee. He popped several TUMS from the ever-present bottle in his drawer. He was tired even though he'd slept well. He waited on hold to speak to the assistant of a once-hot-but-now-fading musician who employed Jennifer Dale as his personal chef several days a week. He knew the guy would try to dodge the conversation and he might well have to drive out to his place on Mulholland to pin him down. Bill needed information to build a clear picture of Jennifer's life and daily schedule to understand how the killers targeted her and why. He didn't think the murders were random and opportunistic. Bill and Barrera had talked to Jennifer's neighbors, Postiff had tracked down her friends, past and present lovers, but they were still in the early days, building the victimology and a profile for the killers. He could see Barrera and Postiff bringing Lieutenant Lisa Carbone up to date on the case.

Watching Postiff filling his shoes was not easy. Bill wasn't one to go softly into that good night or good day or good anything. He wanted nothing more than to be in Carbone's office, but he had to step back and pass the baton. Postiff was a good cop and an even better detective. Bill knew the big dogs wanted him gone and forgotten, no matter how splashy a send-off they gave him. That was just public relations. The TUMS tablet dissolved on his tongue, leaving a chalky, candy-flavored residue that was mildly disgusting and comforting at the same time.

Forty-one years on the force and the world had changed. Cops couldn't do their jobs the way they used to; everyone had a phone to record every interaction. He remembered his days on patrol when he could pull a guy over because he didn't look right, because he didn't fit with the neighborhood he was in. Now it was racial profiling; it was a civil rights violation. Back in his day, it was just doing his job, but cops like him were on the way out. The higher-ups considered him a liability, and he knew it. He had become a man out of step and out of time; it was like Cassidy said, a new chapter. Maybe he'd find a passion for gardening or welding or improving his shitty golf game.

"Detective Clarke? Are you still there?" the young female assistant asked.

"Yes, I am," Bill said.

"Mr. Sparks will not be able to take the call right now. I can verify that Ms. Dale worked for Mr. Sparks as a personal chef for the past two years. She also provided services when he was working on a video or photo shoot—"

"How long have you worked for Mr. Sparks? Miss . . . I didn't catch your last name?" Bill asked, cutting her off.

"Hughes. I'm Laci Hughes. I've worked for Mr. Sparks for the past three months," she said proudly.

"No offense, but you haven't been in Mr. Sparks's employ long enough to give me the information I need. I can come by his home to speak to him directly, or he can come down to the Hollywood station if that's easier for him," Bill said, knowing full well that no celebrity—even one on the waning curve of fame—wanted to pull up at the police station, not with the ever-present paparazzi parked outside.

"I'll pass that on to Mr. Sparks," Laci Hughes said nervously.

"I'll call before I swing by," Bill said, then hung up. He had no intention of calling first.

The energy in the station shifted as Joyce Ramsey arrived; it was the second time that day Bill had to deal with her. Not the final hurrah he had hoped for on his last day. Ramsey was a political hyena, always jockeying for position and ready to throw anyone under the bus for her own advancement. Lieutenant Carbone signaled Bill, Barrera, and Postiff to join them in her office.

"I've just come from Parker Center, where the deputy chief and I met with the press to ask them for restraint on these Hollywood murders. We said no monikers, no catchy names, as it only emboldens them. They pushed hard for details; we let them know that we suspect two assailants working together. Where are we at with the third victim?" Ramsey asked.

"We're waiting to interview her employers. The boyfriend is cooperating fully. He's coming in for a polygraph tomorrow. We've pulled her phone and bank records. She lived a quiet life, no online dating recently, not a club hopper. Very similar to the other victims, providing services to wealthy celebrities and the like," Barrera said.

"We're waiting to hear back on the security camera footage, but I'll bet the signal was jammed and there's nothing, like with the first two," Bill added.

Ramsey looked to Bill. "A big case to catch in your final days, huh?"

"I'm leaving it in young Postiff's very capable hands, commander. I'm looking forward to days of leisure and no dead bodies," he lied with a smile.

"Looks like the *LA Times* didn't heed your request, commander," Postiff said, scrolling through his phone.

"What do you mean?" she asked.

"I just checked their online edition. They're calling these guys the Hollywood Hit Men."

The rest of the day for Cassidy and Riley was routine: two domestics, a suspected elder-abuse call, a homeless guy who stole cash from a woman at an ATM on Sunset and Wilton, disappearing into a homeless encampment that they spent two hours searching. They provided backup for officers dealing with an ex-military ex-husband in violation of a protection order for his wife and young son. He had to be tased into submission, and the other officers arrested and transported him.

When Cassidy and Riley pulled into the station parking lot, Riley grabbed a plastic grocery bag from the back seat and handed it to her.

"Just a little first-day-on-the-job welcoming gift," he said.

"Thank you," Cassidy said, cautiously opening the bag to find a bento box–style clamshell filled with small, brightly colored, fruit-like candy.

"Is it marzipan?" she asked.

"It's a Thai dessert called *luk chup*. I get them from a friend who runs a Thai massage place on Hollywood."

"They look so pretty. I hate to eat them," Cassidy protested. The *luk chup* was indeed gorgeous to behold; each tiny fruit shape was perfect, from the green calyx of the eggplant to the mottled rind of the cantaloupe. They were so shiny; they looked as if they were made of plastic.

"Try one. They're delicious," Riley said.

Cassidy popped the carrot-shaped *luk chup* into her mouth, and it dissolved into a rich, sweet bean paste, unlike anything she had ever tasted. She sat up, her eyes wide as the flavor complexity developed.

"This is the best thing I've ever eaten!" Cassidy exclaimed. "Thank you. That was really nice of you," Cassidy said.

"Sure, just a little first-day-of-patrol treat."

"You said you get them at a massage place?" she asked.

"It's completely legit—a lady I've known for years runs it," he said, somewhat defensively.

"I was just asking. You know, a lot of massage places in Hollywood are for more than just . . . massage."

"What do you take me for? Those happy-ending places are for pigs like Acevedo. I was an Eagle Scout, for god's sake!" Riley said.

Ethan Acevedo was a member of the Metropolitan Division, an elite squad of officers who took on the most challenging assignments. They considered themselves at the front of the thin blue line, often justifying their abuse of police power against the risks of their work. Acevedo was known for skirting the razor-thin edge of legality and was suspected of a wide range of dirty activities. There had been stalking complaints against him, harassment lawsuits, and one incident involving a victim who ended up in a coma at Saint Joseph's after a suspicious beatdown, but nothing ever seemed to stick.

The rumor was that Acevedo buried evidence on an attempted murder charge against the son of a state legislator and thus began a tight relationship between Acevedo's wealthy parents and Sacramento. He held a mythic kind of control over other Metro cops, who always covered for his transgressions, creating an aura of invincibility around him. If a bad cop was hitting up prostitution massage parlors, it would likely be Acevedo. Riley hated him, as did Bill Clarke and several other rank-and-file cops.

"I didn't mean anything. Please thank your friend for getting these for me."

"Her name is Boon Nam. Her place is Nam's Thai Massage, right next to the Carousel Restaurant."

"Thanks. Maybe I'll go there."

"You should. Speaking of relationships, how's your USC-frat boyfriend?"

"Were we speaking of relationships?" Cassidy asked, and Riley blushed tomato red.

"Doesn't he have a first name that's actually a last name?" he asked, recovering.

"His name is Carter, and he's not a frat boy—he's a law student. Does everyone know everything about me on my first day?"

"Yep, when you're Bill Clarke's daughter and he's warned us all that you're out of our league with Richie Rich," Riley replied with a grin.

"Fuck me," Cassidy muttered.

Bill took Laurel Canyon to Mulholland on his way home to Chatsworth. In the back seat of his Chevy SS, a cardboard box held the contents of his desk at the Hollywood station. He had emptied it out while the other detectives kept a silent vigil. By the next day, they would fall into step with Judson Postiff, who diplomatically refrained from setting the desk up with his own photos and case files. Bill smiled bravely as they each shook his hand on the way out. He'd see many of them at the party that evening, but leaving on his final day was harder than he expected.

Now he swung west onto Mulholland, to show up at Paxton Sparks's house to discuss Jennifer Dale. Sparks was a country singer who had seen his heyday in the early '90s, an Eddy Arnold–style crooner in an era of bad pop music passing as country, all about trains and trucks, with a pedal steel guitar slapped on in the studio. Gone were the headlining tours at big venues, the awards and splashy tabloid romances. Sparks had sold several of his songs to be used in car-insurance jingles and fast-food advertisements. He played midsize casinos in the Southwest and the occasional private parties for jowly, sixty-year-old Realtors in Yuma, Arizona, or Tyler, Texas. Bill pulled up to the gates of Sparks's Mediterranean-style villa and rang the bell.

A moment later, a man's hushed, nasal voice came over the intercom. "Who's there?"

"Detective Bill Clarke from the LAPD. I'm here to speak to Paxton Sparks about his employee Jennifer Dale."

"Oh fuck . . ." the man grumbled. "Okay, I'll buzz you in. Park behind the golf cart."

The gates swung open, and Bill pulled into the parking area outside a four-car garage. A shiny black F-250 King Ranch with oversize tires was parked alongside a red Corvette, a cable utility truck, a gardener's van, and a golf cart. Bill squeezed his car behind the cart, with barely enough room to step out. The house was huge, with French doors and a perfectly tended cactus garden out front. Through the glass, Bill could see the inside looked as if no one lived there; it was like a page from an interior design magazine.

As he walked to the door, Paxton Sparks opened it and extended his hand. "I'm Paxton. I thought you were gonna call first?"

He was taller than Bill expected, wearing a Prada tracksuit and a $600 John Dutton buckskin cowboy hat. On his feet, he wore rubber drugstore sandals with white athletic socks.

"I planned to, but my phone died," Bill fibbed.

"Guess you don't have a charger in your car," Sparks said pointedly.

"I guess those Taco Bell commercials pay pretty well," Bill shot back with a smile.

Sparks turned to face him, taking Bill's measure, deciding that it wouldn't do any good to play the impatient, testy pop star with an old barracuda like Clarke. With a weary sigh, Sparks shuffled to the kitchen. Bill followed. It was a large modern affair, all-white marble and wood. There was nothing on the counters, except a glass cylinder holding stainless steel utensils that had never been used. The stove was spotless, no signs that any cooking or eating took place in this oversize room. A huge Plexiglas doghouse stood in the corner. Inside, a nervous face peered out, its ghostlike eyes glued to Sparks's every move. A large Jasper Johns neo-Dada painting took up an entire wall.

"Nice-looking dog," Clarke commented.

"German shorthaired pointer, good hunting dog," Sparks replied.

"You do much hunting out here in Hollywood?"

Sparks fixed Bill with a flat stare and filled a glass from the tap, which had a giant water filter installed on it. "Would you like a coffee? A bottle of water? Some matcha tea?"

Bill noticed how he meticulously wiped the water spots from the faucet and sink to erase any signs of use. Or life.

"No, I'm fine. I want to know about Jennifer Dale," Bill said.

Sparks led him back into the living room and motioned for Bill to sit on a blue mohair couch. He rubbed his hand over his face with a sigh. "She was a nice girl. She cooked for me a few times a week, and if I was on a shoot 'cause I eat a very restricted diet and I needed someone who could handle my specifications. No meat, no dairy, no sugar, no carbohydrates, no wheat, no gluten, no fat."

"What does that leave?" Bill asked. "Not trying to be rude—I'm just wondering what she cooked for you."

"Edamame, miso paste for soups, with vegetables. She made a really good sundubu something or other. It was a spicy Korean soup but without the spice. I don't do spice," Sparks said with a shake of his head.

Bill figured Sparks didn't eat much of anything. He was tall and rail thin; his flaccid skin was the color of skim milk. His pale, hooded eyes gave him the appearance of being half asleep, which had been sexy and mysterious when he was twenty-five; now he just looked like he needed a nap. A young, blond woman who Bill assumed was Sparks's daughter came in, wearing a beach cover-up over a bathing suit, looking at her phone.

"Babe, did you order the lion's mane–mushroom gummies?"

"Detective Clarke, this is my wife, Kellie."

Bill nodded stiffly in greeting. Kellie looked barely legal, with an open, unsuspecting face and the svelte body of a girl, except for the obvious, eye-catching breast enhancement.

"Oh, hi. Is he here about the pet sitter?" she asked.

"Not the pet sitter, honey. The cook, remember? Jennifer?"

"Yeah, I remember. She was nice. She made really good spinach," Kellie said.

"Did you ever have any issues with Ms. Dale? Disagreements, work disputes, with other people on your staff? Any mention of a crazy ex-boyfriend or anything?" Bill asked.

Sparks shook his head. "No, I never have any problems with my people. I'm very clear about my boundaries, and if they screw up, I fire them. No personal issues at work. I don't want to hear about it, you know? Their drama isn't my problem."

"She said she was getting some weird phone calls a few weeks ago," Kellie said, settling on the arm of the mohair couch. Sparks gave her a gentle push off.

"Don't sit there, honey. That part's not for sitting."

Kellie dutifully stood up.

"Did she tell you that specifically?" Bill asked.

"She told me when she was making Pax's edamame. You know, I didn't even know what that was when I came here. I thought they were a plant from the yard!" She giggled.

"What'd she say, exactly?"

"Just that she was getting some weird calls late at night. No one said anything, but she could tell there was someone on the line."

"Do you remember the date she spoke to you about it?"

"Not exactly . . . wait! It was the day that the dog arrived from Missouri! We got a new Weimaraner, but we had to send him back 'cause Pax didn't like his eyes," Kellie explained.

"That dog had weird eyes, like he was reading my mind," Sparks said to no one in particular, cracking his knuckles.

Kellie scrolled through her phone. "It was the tenth of March! That was the day we talked about it."

"Honey, I've told you again and again, I don't want you getting friendly with the help. They get to thinking you're their pal, and it gets too complicated," Sparks admonished her.

"Sorry, I was just getting something from the fridge, and we started chatting . . ." Her voice trailed off.

"She doesn't know anything about this," Sparks said dismissively.

"Mr. Sparks, your wife has mentioned something that could be of value to the investigation. Please let her tell me what she knows," Bill said. Sparks scowled and nodded for Kellie to continue.

"She said that she was getting weird calls sometimes at night and sometimes during the day. She said it felt like someone was checking to see if she was home or not," Kellie said with satisfaction.

Bill felt sorry for her, married to a guy who could be her father, who didn't want her to sit on the couch or talk to people. He wondered what other bizarre rules Paxton Sparks had for his young wife and if the money and the backstage passes at Morongo Casino were worth it. The information that someone may have been stalking Jennifer's schedule was significant. Her phone records could reveal a number and a name.

"I'll need the names of your other employees here at the house, all the people Jennifer might've come in contact with," Bill said.

"Oh man, really? I have the gardening staff, the pet sitter, a handyman, a girl who waters the houseplants, the pool guy; the housekeeper is here twice a week; my assistant, Laci, is on call all the time. You need to talk to all of them?" Sparks complained.

"Yes, I do. We're talking to all of her clients and the people she worked with."

"Fucking hell. This isn't going to get out, is it? I mean, my name isn't going to be dragged into it? This is not a good time for me to have any negative press. I have a greatest-hits compilation coming out for the holidays."

"Isn't this going to be the fifth one of those greatest-hits albums?" Bill asked with feigned innocence. Sparks fixed him with an icy glare.

"We'll only follow up if something related to you is connected in some way to her death," Bill said, emphasizing the word *death* to remind Sparks that a young woman had just lost her life. It didn't register and Sparks stood up.

"I've got to get back to work. I'll have Laci get you all their names and contact information. I don't know how anyone here would've been involved. I do a background check on everyone; I don't let them hang out together or anything like that."

Bill figured that Sparks didn't allow anyone in his circle to do much that he didn't control. He didn't want to get involved with an investigation into the unsavory death of a mere employee, one of the many anonymous worker bees who supplied services to the rich and famous. Bill handed both Sparks and Kellie a business card. Without a word, Sparks took the card from his wife and pocketed it.

"This is the contact information for my partner, Detective Pete Barrera, and Detective Judson Postiff. They'll be following up with you on this," Bill said.

"Not you?" Sparks asked, his eyes narrowing in suspicion.

"No, I'm retired at five p.m. You're the last interview of my career," Bill said.

Sparks's eyes lit up. "No fucking way! Then I guess you'll always remember me, right?"

"Oh, yes. I will definitely remember you, Mr. Sparks."

Bill walked out to his car, passing a woman he assumed was Laci Hughes arriving with a stack of files, shopping bags, and a cup holder with three giant Starbucks drinks in it. Two uniformed gardening staff were gathering yard debris into plastic trash bags. A cable technician was on the roof of the pool house. Paxton Sparks had a lot of people at his house on a regular basis. Any one of them could've taken notice of Jennifer Dale, and finding out her name and address would've been easy. Every week young women were targeted by unhappy or maladjusted men who fixated on them for no reason. Bill was relieved that he wouldn't have to deal with Paxton Sparks and his child bride again. Despite the wealth and the big house, the interview had been depressing.

They were two people living in a bizarre bubble of their own making, revolving around Sparks's inflated idea of himself and his currency as a celebrity. The city was filled with similar people living hollow lives, running a relentless race to remain relevant, to escape the black hole of death that came the same way for everyone, that wiped out everything. In fifty years, no one would remember Paxton Sparks or Bill Clarke or anyone else.

It wore him out. He drove down Laurel Canyon, toward his ranch property on that quiet cul-de-sac deep in the Valley. Perhaps he'd finally get some horses for the corrals. He'd never have to talk to a self-important ass like Paxton Sparks again. Maybe retirement wouldn't be so bad, after all.

His phone pinged. It was Barrera.

We got another one, just wanted to let you know. But guess what? This one survived.

CHAPTER FOUR

Barrera and Postiff waited in the hallway of Kaiser Permanente hospital on Sunset Boulevard. Millie Grace, the newest victim of the Hollywood Hit Men, was still being attended to by medical staff. She had been there for two hours after being found unconscious by her roommate, Rosalie McTeer, in their Bronson Canyon home. Millie had been beaten by her assailants, and they had tried to strangle her, but she had fought them off. Once the doctors gave them an all clear, Barrera and Postiff would take her statement.

Barrera waited calmly, taking a foil-wrapped, full-size piece of chewing gum from his pocket. With his plain gray suit—cut loose to accommodate his growing girth—his military haircut, and his pockmarked skin, Pete Barrera was a relic from the golden days of Robbery-Homicide in Los Angeles. He'd been a new detective when Richard Ramirez, the Night Stalker, held the city in abject terror, crisscrossing the region, violently killing random people with no common victimology. Barrera had been on the team that caught William Lester Suff and Chester D. Turner, both prolific serial killers that were part of the Los Angeles murder lore that began decades earlier with the Black Dahlia and the Georgette Bauerdorf killings.

Barrera planned to take his retirement in seven months, and until then he was paired with Postiff, who was what Barrera would refer to as a *whippersnapper*, with his slim-fit monochrome blue suit and his flashy Belvedere Astor shoes. His black hair was cut short and styled with a dollop of gel that kept it in place, even in the Santa Ana winds.

He was as different from Barrera as a Ferrari was from a Dodge van, but he knew Postiff was a smart pit bull of a detective under that polished exterior. Barrera could handle seven months with him.

When the doctors emerged from Millie's room, a young physician approached the detectives.

"She's fine to talk to you. She's pretty badly beaten up—she fought back. Her internal injuries aren't life threatening, but she has three broken ribs, a shattered kneecap, and her left ear is practically torn off. She has a concussion as well from blunt force trauma. They didn't rape her. The guy who tried to strangle her almost broke the hyoid bone, but I guess she kicked him in the balls before she blacked out. She's lucky they left instead of finishing her off. She's drugged up but coherent. Tough girl," he said, waving them into her room.

They found Millie Grace, once a smiling, bouncy blond with dimples, sitting up stiffly in bed, her head wrapped in bandages. One eye was covered in gauze, the other one swelled shut with an oozing purple-red laceration that looked like someone had attached a chunk of ground beef to her face. The injury was so big and raw that it hurt Postiff just to look at it. Her lips were swollen and cut; her neck had dark bruising all around it. The bruises continued down her neck and clavicle; Barrera and Postiff could only imagine what the rest of her body looked like. She had a plaster cast on her left wrist and raised the other one slightly in a small wave.

"Hi! Are you the detectives?" she asked, trying not to move her busted lips.

"Yes, I'm Pete Barrera. This is my partner, Judson Postiff. You're one brave young lady, Ms. Grace."

"I wasn't ready to die yet," she said, her voice raspy.

"We think whoever attacked you is responsible for several murders in the area. And we've been suspecting it is two men working together," Postiff said, and Millie nodded in agreement.

"There were two of them. They came in through the laundry-room window, I think. I left it open while the clothes were drying. It gets so hot in the house if it's closed . . . they were waiting in the hallway. They both came at me . . . they wore masks. One was a ski mask, and the other one was like a Halloween mask, the rubber kind . . ." Her voice faltered; the effort to speak was hard for her. "It looked like a wolf or a dog . . . he's the one who got on top of me. I pulled the mask up when I broke one of my hands free. That one was in his late thirties, maybe forties, for sure. I don't know about the other one . . ."

"How did you manage to fight them both off?" Barrera asked. "No offense, but you're pretty tiny."

She tried to smile, but the skin of her lips was too tight and swollen.

"I was a state champion in martial arts. Tae kwon do, Muay Thai, even some Krav Maga."

"We got some really good DNA evidence from under your fingernails, and we'll know in a few hours if it's a match to the DNA we found on the previous victim," Postiff said.

"He had that cord around my neck, and I knew I had to do something . . . so I kneed him in the balls as hard as I could. That's all I remember."

"Do you think you could remember the face of the one you saw?" Barrera asked.

Millie Grace tilted her head, fixing her unbandaged eye on Barrera's face; just a sliver of light was visible through the swelling.

"I'll remember his face for the rest of my life," she said.

Barrera called the police sketch artist to come out to Kaiser immediately. By midnight they'd have an image to put out to the public.

The beat-up Ford Ranger truck turned right from Franklin Avenue onto Bronson, past the Gelson's Market and the trendy mini mall across the street. The driver had noticed a girl in the Barks and Bones store there a few weeks ago. Something about her voluptuous form, straining at the little pearl buttons of her vintage print dress, had sparked an inexplicable rage in him as he perused the fashionable dog collars hanging against one wall. He didn't have a dog; he had seen her going into the store on his way to work, and he wanted a closer look. She wore her shiny black hair like retro pinup girl Bettie Page with short, saucy bangs. Her lips were painted bright red. Her body was more Marilyn Monroe than Gisele Bündchen, with a soft, squishy layer of flesh over her bones. Bones that could so easily be broken in his grip. He loved that feeling—the building tension under the muscle that gave way as it snapped, the contortions of pain that overcame his victims.

He'd gotten her name from business cards on the counter of the pet store. Rosalie McTeer. She was a pet sitter as well as a store clerk. The cards showed her smiling face posed with a black Labrador. She fit with the others, engaged in a ridiculous kind of job for people who didn't know the meaning of real work. Parasites, taking advantage of the rich and undisciplined, who couldn't walk their own dogs or cook their own food. Who needed someone to curate their image and profile for public consumption. His raging thoughts swirled in his head, steadily taking him under, like a powerful riptide.

How had the world spun so far off its axis, from a time when men were strong and women respected that strength? Now they dumped you if you had a quick fuck with some bar slut after a few drinks. They didn't understand that a man needed his little vices to blow off the pressure building inside his head, the spinning thoughts that disturbed his sleep. He longed for a time when women couldn't ghost you or block you; they felt obligated to speak nicely to you if you approached them out in public, flattered if you asked for their number. He hated that things had changed and the world was worse for it. That was why he posed them, in nice clothes and makeup. He was the one who decided if they looked pretty or not. He put them in a negligee or at a vanity table. Or he could leave them broken and bloodied on the floor. The lipstick heart he drew on their faces was an ode to the beauty marks popularized by the vintage pinup models. Those were the days he longed for.

He felt her eyes on him as he moved through the store. He imagined her approving gaze, taking in his muscular body and thick, curly hair. He knew women wanted him; he could see it in their eyes as they watched him at work, or in the admiring glances of the exotic dancers when he visited Cheeta's. Every day he saw how they responded to him; they knew that he could give them what they wanted and needed. They were just too afraid to ask.

On that visit to Barks and Bones, he had intended to speak to Rosalie McTeer, but when he turned to face her, he found she was indeed staring at him. But not with the admiration he expected. She looked at him, unimpressed and suspicious, as if she could see his darkest thoughts and every twisted thing he had ever done. As if she knew about the teenager in Santa Cruz and the pretty redhead in Lompoc. And the girls in the hills. Her dark eyes bored into him without flinching, unafraid, with an undisguised distaste, which triggered his internal fury. She should be afraid; they all had to be afraid. He had been the first to look away that day, his masculinity further denigrated by her audacity.

He'd followed Rosalie McTeer home to the yellow-and-white ranch house on the shady side of the street. He'd watched as she went inside, without a thought to close the drapes of the big front windows. He had seen her drop her things on the couch, disappear down a hallway, and return in sweatpants and a T-shirt, her ample breasts undulating freely, pushing against the thin fabric. She had no business moving through the world with such ease and confidence. She was like the others, so assured of their place in life, with their own money, their own cars. Surrounded by the kind of nice things that a man should be able to give them and take away as he deemed fit. He hated her. Like he had hated the others.

The next day he'd driven by the store with Vithu, who was less provoked by the flippant little hitch in her gait as she walked. But he was always less discerning in his hunting; Vithu was an opportunist, lazy and undisciplined. He'd go after any low-hanging fruit that made itself available rather than choosing his prey. He was only good at the computer stuff; everyone from his country was good at that. Vithu could never be the leader. That was okay. One leader was enough.

As the truck approached the low-slung ranch house on Bronson, his hopes of doubling back to clean up after himself were dashed when he saw a crush of police activity. The street was cordoned off, frightened neighbors gathered on the corners. They had found the girl faster than he had imagined. He and Vithu had gone to the house earlier that day, expecting to find little Miss Saucy Walk McTeer inside. But instead, they ran headlong into that blond Kewpie doll, doing her laundry and household chores. He had never seen her, but there she was, screaming when they jumped out and took her down. The bitch was small and petite but as tough as fuck.

She fought back hard. She had more power and control than he expected. With two of them, it should've been easy to overpower her, but it wasn't. And she wasn't afraid—she was as mad as hell. She had twisted and torqued her body to get free; she had snagged her nails into his mask and pulled it up. She had looked straight at him. Her pretty blue eyes were like flint stones sparking with rage. She had cursed him in language no lady should ever use. The little bitch wasn't following the script in his head, and he was going to teach her the hard way that he was to be respected, but she had hit him in the balls so hard he almost blacked out. He'd lost his grip on her throat, and they'd panicked, bolting out of the house like scalded dogs running from a fire. She must've been dead. He'd choked the life out of her tiny body before he rolled off her in gut-wrenching pain, hadn't he? Her lips had started to turn blue. He had felt the fight leaving her. But she had managed to kick him with such force, she could still be alive. His balls were still sore and swollen; he shifted his weight to ease them in the cab of the truck.

He had planned to go back in and make sure the job was done right, just in case she'd survived. It had been several hours—it was risky and messy, but he had to be certain. He was going to sneak in and see her lifeless body on the floor of the hallway, where he had left her. But someone else had found her first. He didn't see a coroner's truck, just the forensics vans. They'd probably taken her body away by the time he circled back. She had to be dead. Unless she made it and was alive somewhere telling them what he looked like. He made a U-turn as he pulled into the Bronson Caves recreation area. He drove back down without slowing; he didn't need to attract any attention from the cops stationed outside.

The truck passed the house. No one noticed him. As he drove toward the ever-present traffic jammed up on Franklin Avenue, he glanced in the rearview mirror, where the flashing yellow lights of the police cars grew smaller with each rotation of his tires, taking him away from the place he had killed an unknown girl a few hours earlier. His palms were wet with sweat. Why had the blond been in the wrong place at the wrong time? He had no choice but to do what he did. And where the hell was Rosalie McTeer?

CHAPTER FIVE

The crowd at the Smoke House was relaxed and celebratory. Cops and detectives sat at the red vinyl booths while career waitresses balanced multiple plates of ribs, roast chicken, and baked potatoes on their forearms, moving deftly through the throng of people. Bill stood with the band, already tipsy, belting out "Like a Rock" by Bob Seger. The bartender had a fresh cocktail waiting for him after his floor show.

Cassidy sat in a booth with Riley and Diana Montoya, another patrol cop who had graduated from the academy a year prior. Montoya watched Bill with amusement. She had to shout to be heard over the din in the room.

"Your dad is having the time of his life up there!"

"Oh yeah, this is his big day. The band is going to play all his favorites. Bob Seger, Bruce Springsteen, Mellencamp. All those anthems of working-class discontent. That's my dad," Cassidy said, raising her Corona in a toast.

"Do you think he's excited to be done? Or is he going to miss it?" Riley asked.

Cassidy watched Bill for a moment; now he was straddling the microphone, singing "We Are the Champions" by Queen.

"He's going to miss every minute of it. The bad coffee, the stress, the adrenaline. He's going to go stir crazy, I fear."

"You gotta get plans in place for him. I had to do it for my mom when she retired from teaching. I got her signed up to read to kids at the library, to volunteer at the free clinic. I even got her started on pickleball," Montoya said. "Now she kicks my ass when we play."

Cassidy knew it would be a hard sell to get Bill involved in any of those activities, the things that normal, well-adjusted retired people did to fill their time. He would brood and obsess over things he couldn't control; he'd remember a grievance he had with someone ten years earlier. Maybe she could get him interested in fixing up the horse corrals or adopting a pet from the shelter.

"I'll try anything. I'm a little worried about keeping him on an even keel. He's kind of a wild man," Cassidy said.

"Just don't let him back on a motorcycle!" Montoya added.

Cassidy always suspected that his accident was her dad's weird, dysfunctional way of trying to stop the divorce from happening. If he got hurt, time might stand still and there would be some way to fix the things he didn't even understand were broken. Everything about the crash was pure Bill Clarke: driving too fast without a helmet, showboating his daredevil antics for his buddies, hitting a concrete wall to stand up and walk away with a sassy quip, blood spurting from his nose, his forehead split open to the bone. He collapsed and lost consciousness a few feet away and woke up in the Providence Medical Center ICU.

Cassidy—as well as her mother—had long suspected he suffered from CTE, but Bill dismissed their concerns with a joke. Now, with Bill in retirement, Cassidy had scheduled an appointment with a neurologist for the following week. Bill had refreshed his drink but still had not relinquished the microphone, ready to break into "The Wall" by Pink Floyd.

"Excuse me, I'm going to go save the singer," Cassidy said, moving out onto the crowded dance floor. She pried Bill away from the stage and directed him to a table filled with other homicide detectives, some of them retired.

"Here, tell your war stories and make sure you eat. Did you get your food yet?" she asked, guiding Bill into the booth.

"I had the appetizers but not the steak. Can we get more cheese bread?" Bill asked.

"I'll check with your waitress. Don't let him escape, gentlemen!" she said to the assembled group, who were backslapping Bill and congratulating him. As she moved through the room, she noticed that Commander Ramsey and Chief Charlie McCall were notably absent. It was a subtle signal that they weren't going to miss Bill Clarke, after all the issues he had created for the department over the years. She saw several lawyers who always defended police in misconduct cases, including Andrew Nishikawa and John Safran. They were well acquainted with Bill and would not miss having his file land on their desks again. Postiff hadn't showed up yet, but she knew he and Barrera were dealing with the surviving victim of the Hollywood Hit Men. When they arrived, Bill would be stuck to them like gum, dissecting the case over a whiskey and Coke in a booth at the back of the bar.

A group of intoxicated guests formed a conga line and moved through the restaurant like a giant caterpillar. As she passed, a woman in the line knocked into Cassidy, sending her careening into the uniformed chest of Ethan Acevedo, who was holding court with a cabal of Metro cops.

"Excuse me," Cassidy said, pulling back.

"No problem. You're Clarke's daughter, aren't you?" Acevedo asked, his hand still on her arm to steady her.

He looked down at her with an appraising eye, a playful smirk on his face. He was Filipino, attractive in a boyish way with his close-cropped Catholic-school haircut and wide cheekbones. Only his eyes betrayed the flat, emotionless quality of his character. Colliding with him felt like she had run into a cement wall, so muscular and rigid was his body.

"Yes, I am," she said.

"I heard you're good. We might need to recruit you into Metro!" He laughed, still holding tight to her arm but giving it small squeezes, like someone testing the firmness of a sausage at a delicatessen. It was too familiar, but Cassidy knew that was his style, to cross boundaries and make people just uncomfortable enough to pull away, then gaslight them with claims of innocence. Acevedo was the kind of man any woman would instinctively fear if she encountered him alone on a dark street, and the fact that he was an elite cop in a specialized unit made it even more unnerving.

"Excuse me," she said, pulling away and moving past him. She could feel him watching her go. Back at the table, Police Captain Landon Dykstra was hovering, nursing a double scotch.

As Cassidy slid into the booth next to Montoya, Dykstra announced, "She's back! Top one percent of this class at the academy. She would've been hired even if she didn't have a shoo-in to the department!"

Montoya, Riley, and Cassidy shared an uncomfortable look, but no one said anything. Dykstra continued, clearly in the early stages of intoxication.

"Being a nepo-hire can be a drag, but you didn't need that, did you, Clarke? You were at the top!"

"Why don't you have a cup of coffee, Landon? You should start sobering up," Riley suggested, standing up to lead him toward the bar.

Cassidy and Montoya sat in awkward silence; then Montoya said, "Don't pay any attention to him. He's an asshole, and everyone hates him anyway."

Suddenly a shrill woman's voice carried over the music.

"I can't believe you're here! Vaaaa-leriee!"

It was Eden Balcomb, a former girlfriend of Bill's. She was loudly greeting another police groupie who never missed a chance to hang out with cops. Cassidy shifted her weight to turn away, hoping to avoid Eden pulling her in for a crushing hug amid a cloud of Fancy Love perfume.

Eden's real name was Elaine, but she'd started calling herself Eden at some point, thinking it sounded more exotic and girlish. She was somewhere between forty and sixty. Her true age was hard to tell under her mane of thick, tricolored blond hair that was precisely cut to frame her face and give a youthful look. She was fit and trim, she dressed like she was twenty-two and saved money to make biannual trips to Baja to see her plastic surgeon, Dr. Macario, for an array of antiaging miracle treatments: Sculptra, sermorelin injections, DAXXIFY, NAD intravenous infusions. She had met Bill while volunteering at the police station, part of the gaggle of women who happily donated their time, so impressed by men in uniform and the possibility of dating a cop. Cassidy tolerated her presence in Bill's life, but Eden's pick-me personality and desperate fawning over men grated on Cassidy's nerves.

After their breakup, Eden hung on to become a friend with benefits, hoping to revive their relationship. Cassidy knew that for her father, it was simply about convenience and a buffer against the loneliness of detective work. Montoya noticed the shift in Cassidy's body language.

"Isn't she one of the groupies?" Montoya asked.

"Yes, my dad's ex. I figured she'd show up," Cassidy said, stealing a glance to see Eden sidling up to Bill and the other homicide detectives.

"I don't get why any woman would want to date a cop—a male cop, I mean. Not us, of course; we're queens," Montoya said. Dykstra started toward their table, visibly more drunk and belligerent. Riley pushed past him and grabbed Cassidy's hand, pulling her toward the dance floor.

"Riley, stop. I don't dance," Cassidy objected.

"I don't, either, but Dykstra is drunk, and he'll try to provoke you again. I'm doing him a favor; you might lay him out if he comes around."

Riley was a liar—he was an exceptional dancer. Cassidy shuffled her feet self-consciously.

"I dance like such a white girl," she complained.

"You do move like someone in a church service in Missouri," Riley replied.

"Fuck you." Cassidy laughed.

"And you talk like a sailor. It's rather attractive and against type." He executed an impressive spin and locking move.

"By golly, you flatter me," she replied.

"And you always have to have the last word."

"I'm my father's daughter."

Across the room, she saw her boyfriend, Carter Sims, at the entrance, scanning the crowd for her. She waved, and he gave Riley a pointed look, then moved to the bar.

"Is that frat boy?" Riley asked, eyeing Carter as he ordered a drink.

"He's not a frat boy. His name is Carter."

"I bet he drinks Macallan, single malt aged for five hundred years or something. You know, a rich white boy drink," Riley said.

"Careful. You're sounding like my dad."

"Go attend to him; he looks out of place with this bunch," Riley said, spinning over to grab Montoya from the booth. Cassidy moved to Carter at the bar, and he pulled her in for a quick kiss as the bartender slid his Macallan single malt across the bar to him. He was handsome in a timeless way, with wavy reddish-blond hair and clear, uncomplicated blue eyes. He had a pleasant, bland smile and square jawline.

"This is a retro place. It's like something from the 1960s," he said.

"How's school?"

"So dull! Administrative law, evidence, trust and estates, civil procedure. It's deadly. How was the first day?" he asked. A woman at the bar threw her arm over his shoulder in drunken confusion. Carter recoiled and gave her a withering look as she retreated.

"Good. Uneventful. Nothing too dangerous," she said, deciding not to tell him about Man-Bun in the Griffith Park bathroom.

"I saw on the news that we have new serial killers, the Hollywood Hit Men. Did your dad get that case?"

"Yeah, but it's not his problem any longer. He's a free man now."

"And you're a free woman! No more worrying over Bill, making sure the kitchen is stocked, that there's toilet paper in the bathroom. He can do all of those things himself from here on out."

Cassidy laughed weakly. She knew her dad would never stay on top of any household necessities, and it was easy for her. She had to do it anyway. She saw Eden weaving her way to the bar, blowing Cassidy a kiss.

"Cass! Isn't this amazing? Your dad is having a great time! Hi, Carter the smarter!" She giggled, squeezing his thigh as she landed on a barstool. Cassidy cringed. Eden had flirtatious, idiotic nicknames for any man she encountered.

"I'm getting Bill another round. I had a cosmo before I got here, but there's always room for one more at a party!"

"Hi, Eden. I'm guessing you didn't drive here?" Cassidy asked.

"No, I took an Uber. I can always get a ride with Valerie, unless something else develops," she said, with a wink at Bill, as she carried the two cocktails back to his table. On the way, she collided with Acevedo, who had put himself in her path deliberately. He took Eden's arm and whispered something in her ear. She looked at him in shock and pulled back. She shook her head and laughed nervously. He stepped closer to her until his groin was pressed up against her torso. She looked like a skinny rag doll next to him. The cosmo sloshed over the rim of the glass, spilling onto the floor as she extricated herself. Cassidy had no idea what the relationship was between them, but it didn't look like much fun for Eden. Carter put his arm around Cassidy's waist and nuzzled her neck. She gave him a quick kiss; she didn't like public displays of affection.

"That tickles," she deflected, with a smile.

"Maybe you should stay at my place tonight? You might wake up with that nutty Eden in your kitchen tomorrow morning," Carter said.

"I have to be at work early. First-week jitters. I should be in my own place," Cassidy said.

"Well, my place could be your place as well, you know. You just have to leave Bonanza behind," Carter said. He thought it was funny to refer to the Chatsworth ranch house as Bonanza. Cassidy liked his place—to visit. It was sleek and modern, with every newest gadget, all done in white, beige, and gray. He had hired an interior designer to furnish the Brentwood condo when he bought it the previous year—or rather his mother, June, had hired her.

"Maybe," Cassidy said, putting off the cohabitation conversation once again.

She surveyed the room. The party was a success. She was happy that so many of her dad's friends and colleagues had come. He acted as if he didn't care, but she knew it meant a lot to him. They had been his family for years, the center of his life, in many ways, even more than she and her mother had ever been. As problematic as his old-school techniques seemed today, he had been a wildly successful homicide detective, and he deserved a big send-off. Cassidy saw that Eden had settled onto Bill's lap. Riley and Montoya were still burning up the dance floor.

Cassidy watched everyone with a sense of detachment; despite the crowd, she felt singularly alone. She always did, ever since the day Marvin Keyes killed his family and shifted her world. She wondered if other people felt the same way, if they carried a yawning place of emptiness inside like she did. Maybe it was everyone. Maybe it was just her. But it didn't bother her at all. She felt it like a comfortable presence, an old friend, always by her side. Giving her a safe place to retreat to. She smiled at Carter, who was knocking back his second scotch, his hand resting easily on her thigh. He had no idea that inside her head, she was a million miles away.

The bartender gave the last call to the dwindling party guests. Carter left, unable to extract a promise that Cassidy would come to his place for the evening. Riley and Montoya were gone. Eden had caught a ride with Valerie after Bill dumped her and made a beeline for Barrera and Postiff when they arrived, fresh from Kaiser Permanente with the sketch of Millie's attacker.

Now a detailed drawing of one of the assailants had been distributed to police departments throughout the city. It would be on the morning news programs as well as all official social media accounts. He was a nondescript white guy in his late thirties, with a fleshy face and shoe-button eyes that seemed too small under the jutting brow ridge of his low forehead. He wore his hair long. Millie Grace had said he was tall and well built, with broad shoulders and a slim waist. He had a scar under his right eye.

Bill signaled for another drink, but the bartender shut him down. Cassidy crossed to his booth and tapped his arm.

"Hey, big man. Time to go home. I'm calling you an Uber," she said.

"Why can't I go with you?" he asked.

"I may go to Carter's. I haven't decided yet."

"It's not that late! We've got more to talk about," Bill protested, looking for support from Barrera and Postiff, who were exhausted. Postiff shook his head and stood up.

"We're going to be back at it first thing. I've got to get home," he said, putting on his suit jacket, which was folded neatly beside him.

"Don't rub it in, young pup!" Bill said, stepping out from the booth and losing his balance momentarily. Cassidy caught his arm to steady him.

"They got a sketch of one of the guys, did you see it? He looks like B. J. Thomas," Bill said.

"Who is that?" she asked.

"B. J. Thomas? You don't know who B. J. Thomas is? 'Hooked on a Feeling'?"

Cassidy and Postiff looked at each other blankly.

"Jesus! How do you not know these things?" Bill scoffed. "But it's a good drawing—someone will recognize this son of a bitch. They said the girl fought him off. She looks like shit, but she survived!"

Cassidy looped her arm through his and steered him toward the doors of the restaurant.

"I'm fine to drive," Bill said, drawing his key ring from his pocket.

"No, you're not. You've been knocking back whiskey all night," Cassidy said.

"I can hold my liquor," Bill insisted.

"Not tonight you can't, partner," Barrera said. "Listen to the kid. Get home without killing yourself or someone else."

"Traitor," Bill muttered.

The Uber arrived. Cassidy waved as the car pulled away from the curb. She turned to Barrera and Postiff.

"Thanks for helping with that."

"It's the end of an era. No offense, Postiff," Barrera said.

"None taken. See you all tomorrow," Postiff said, hitting his key fob as he walked to his Audi, whose headlights and engine turned on automatically.

"Technology is amazing," Barrera said. "Your dad told me he's gonna work on the house, get some projects done. That'll be good for him."

His words hung heavily in the air. They both knew Bill would not be doing any house projects. They were thinking the same thing until Barrera said it out loud.

"What the hell is he going to do now?"

CHAPTER SIX

Bill was still sleeping off a hangover when Cassidy left for work in the morning. When it had been time to choose a freeway the previous evening, she decided to head home instead of the forty-five-minute commute to Carter's place. Now she'd started the coffee brewing and left scrambled eggs and bacon on a foil-covered plate sitting in the oven with a Post-it note for her dad on the kitchen counter. And a bottle of Advil next to a tall glass of water. Despite Carter's jokes, she didn't mind doing these small things for her dad. She didn't feel obligated or resentful; she liked knowing that she was the one who kept things running smoothly in their house.

It was better that she did it than to rely on her dad; otherwise they'd be using napkins for toilet paper and having cereal with apple juice that had been in the back of the fridge for six months. Cassidy had been the de facto house manager since her parents divorced eight years earlier, and it made her feel important and necessary. At fifteen, she'd felt all grown up, making chicken casseroles with condensed soup for dinner and Jell-O with canned fruit for dessert.

As Cassidy pulled out of the driveway, she saw a moving pod being delivered to the Keyes house, which had been empty for the past two months. The pod meant new neighbors; she hoped they'd be better than the last ones, who had drunken barbecues in the front yard and filled the cul-de-sac with ATVs and dirt bikes. More than once she'd gone to retrieve something from her car only to hear one of them shout, "I'd hit that!" when she turned to go inside. When she told her dad, he put a stop to it right away, flashing his badge and telling them that if they did it again, he'd get the Devonshire-station cops so far up their asses they wouldn't walk right for a month.

She had a flyer on the passenger seat with the image of one of the Hollywood Hit Men attackers. She was curious to know how the interview with the victim had gone, what they knew but weren't releasing to the public. She was so accustomed to her dad discussing his cases with her, it felt strange not to know everything that was going on. She could only imagine how her dad felt. She decided to pick up his favorite, a whole Zankou chicken, on the way home. And a clamshell of *luk chup* from Thai Town. She got onto the 405 freeway, not yet crawling with traffic because of the early hour. She wanted to arrive early at the station. She always liked being early and prepared, ready to get out in front of whatever the day might throw at her.

Two hours later, Cassidy and Riley were out on Santa Monica Boulevard as the remaining sex workers made their way home. They looked out of place in their crotch-baring miniskirts and see-through mesh tunics over bike shorts. These were the young men and women who'd spent the evening flagging down the passing cars that prowled the area late at night. The older gay queens in luxury Teslas and Mercedes coupes, the pudgy husbands from Sherman Oaks in SUVs with stickers that read **My Child Is an Honor Student** at whatever suburban school his wife volunteered at every Wednesday.

Riley had picked up a call for backup to a disturbing-the-peace incident off Cahuenga and Fountain, in a scrappy area that had thus far defied gentrification. They pulled up on a pair of cops with their guns trained on a twentysomething Black man with messy dreadlocks, shouting and waving a rope like a rodeo lariat. He was in the grip of mental illness or deep in a state of drug-induced psychosis. His eyes were wide and wild; he looked as if he would explode into smoke and flames at any moment. The two cops on the scene were Derek Mentone and Kyle Teachout, both older, plodding patrol cops who were never going to make detective or rise in the ranks of the department.

"That guy's totally unstable. He needs mental health support," Cassidy said.

"Yeah, but these two aren't going to call that in. They just want someone here when they move in on him," Riley said, getting out.

"Then I'll call it," Cassidy said, grabbing the police radio.

"Don't make any waves, Clarke. Just let it go, okay?" Riley said.

"And what if they kill him? He's holding a rope, not a gun! You know these two—they'll open fire and ask questions later."

The dispatcher's voice came over the radio. Cassidy requested CIRCLE support at the address; then she and Riley got out and took backup positions. The CIRCLE program provided unarmed mental health support to the LAPD when dealing with nonviolent offenders.

"I swear, man, I'm ready to drop this motherfucker!" Mentone shouted to Riley, with a terse nod to Cassidy.

"He's not armed—it's just a length of rope. I'm sure we can talk him down," Riley said.

"My ass! Look at him! He's been carrying on like this for the past fifteen minutes. He lunged at us when we approached him," Teachout said.

"CIRCLE is on the way to deal with it. Let's just keep him contained until they arrive," Cassidy said.

Mentone's face contorted into a disgusted grimace. "Who the fuck called them? We can handle this!"

"I did," Riley said. "That's what they're for. This guy is more crazy than dangerous."

"Oh, for fuck's sake, Riley!" Teachout spit on the pavement.

Cassidy shot a warning glance at Riley, which he disregarded, keeping his gun trained on the dreadlocked man who was now in full meltdown mode, jumping and spinning as he struck out at imaginary adversaries. Twenty minutes later, two social workers arrived to help subdue the man without force. The police could book him on an involuntary psychiatric hold that would allow him to be evaluated for seventy-two hours. Cassidy knew it was probable that he was a drug addict and would end up back on the streets within the week, but at least she had taken the right steps.

Mentone and Teachout huddled by their car and sulked. They were old-school cops who believed that mental health was just a fancy way of excusing criminals, and the nutcases on the street needed to be brought to heel, not coddled with doctors and treatment plans. Cassidy knew they weren't fooled by Riley taking responsibility for calling in CIRCLE, but she didn't care. She was a new and different kind of cop, and the sooner they knew it, the better.

Bill puttered around the sunny living room in his slippers and bathrobe, looking out at the horse corrals as if he were seeing them for the first time. It would be nice to get them cleaned up, maybe take Cassidy shopping for livestock. She'd wanted a horse when she was younger, but Cathy had been against it. She worried about head injuries and who would do the cleanup and how to keep animals safe with the pack of coyotes that prowled the foothills every day and night. She worried about the long nights alone when she'd have to keep an eye on everything by herself. She worried about a lot of things, being married to him. She was right, in the end. All the work would've fallen to her. Cassidy got a dog instead and didn't seem any worse for it. Bill texted Barrera for an update on the Hit Men.

In the kitchen, he found his breakfast and the note from Cassidy; the coffee was warm and waiting. He smiled. They'd raised a good kid even if they couldn't make it work between them. He looked around the blue-and-yellow kitchen and could still see Cathy at the stove, her curly blond hair pulled back into a messy ponytail, smiling and telling him a story he only half listened to, him mumbling distracted replies until she stopped telling stories at all.

He ate his breakfast leisurely, something he hadn't done in years. He leafed through the junk mailers that insisted he purchase new solar panels or rain gutters in a city under perpetual drought restrictions. He checked his phone. No update from Pete yet. He took his cup of coffee and walked to the front windows, where he saw the new pod waiting outside the Keyes house. A gray SUV was in the driveway, and a tall, scraggly-looking guy with long hair was unloading boxes.

Something about his gait bothered Bill, reminding him of someone from his past. A suspect in an unsolved murder of a teenager from down near Olympic and Western. Her name was Min Sun-Hee. The guy across the street looked so much like one of the neighbors of Sun-Hee, a welder named Tom Britt who lived in the same shabby K-Town apartment building as the Min family. Bill remembered Tom Britt; he had always doubted his alibi. Now he watched his new neighbor. They never found Min Sun-Hee's killer. Maybe he was right here, right now.

Bill opened the front door and sauntered up to the man, who was carrying a large box.

"Hey, neighbor!" Bill shouted, a big smile plastered across his face.

"Uh . . . hello. I'm just moving in," the man replied, setting the box on the porch and retrieving another one from the SUV. Bill gave him the once-over—he looked to be in his mid-thirties, making him a solid ten to fifteen years younger than Britt. But some people didn't age that quickly. Maybe he was older.

"So, you're the new renter. We live just over there, two houses down. It's my daughter and me. Bill Clarke," he said, extending his hand to the man, who had to set his box down to take it.

"Alan Musselman. Nice to meet you."

"What do you do for a living, Alan?" Bill asked abruptly.

"I'm . . . a writer. I write novels," Alan replied, picking up his box.

"Wow. A book writer. Solitary. Spend a lot of time alone, I guess," Bill said.

"Yeah, usually," Alan said politely.

He and Bill smiled at each other awkwardly for a beat; then Bill said, "Well, if you need anything, don't hesitate to ask. I'm retired now, as of today! So, I'm around all the time. My daughter's a cop, I'm a detective, so you're well protected."

Alan nodded. "Good to know. Well, I'll see you around, Mr. Clarke."

"No, Bill. Call me Bill."

Musselman went inside, and Bill watched him from the curb, swirling his coffee in its mug. There was something about Musselman he didn't like. Something furtive. Something not right. He couldn't put his finger on it, but it was there. He texted Barrera again, his impatience simmering. He'd started on the Hollywood Hit Men case; it only made sense to keep him in the loop. It was still his case, in a way.

Barrera and Postiff sat at the kitchen table with Rosalie McTeer, who looked ragged after a sleepless night. She'd found Millie on the floor in the hallway, and everything had been like a manic roller coaster since then. The detectives taking her statement, the paramedics, the press hovering on the sidewalk, the police officer posted at her front door. When they showed her the police sketch of Millie's assailant, she recognized him immediately.

"This guy was in the store a couple of weeks ago. I remember the hair and the scar. He gave me the creeps. There was something about him . . . he was bad news. You know sometimes you can just feel that?" she asked, dabbing at her eyes with a wet, crumpled tissue.

"Did you ever see him again?" Barrera asked.

"No, but I had the sense that I was being . . . watched. Sometimes I just . . . feel things. I don't know. I wonder if he meant to get me, and instead he found poor Millie!" she said, her voice shaking.

"That might be the case, if you crossed paths with him previously. Now that we have a good image of him, something should shake loose," Postiff said.

"And he didn't buy anything or use a debit card?" Barrera asked.

"No, but . . . he took one of my business cards. I'm a pet sitter in this area. It freaks me out to think that he had that with my picture and phone number on it!" she wailed.

Postiff had already figured that her job as a pet sitter put her right in line with the previous victims, who all had service-oriented jobs for people with expendable income for lifestyle luxuries. A personal chef, a social media manager, and now a personal dog walker. She fit the victim profile, but she wasn't the victim. It was Millie Grace, innocently doing her laundry on her day off. He didn't want to scare Rosalie, but he was sure she was the intended target of the Hit Men, which meant she'd have police protection until they were caught. He knew Joyce Ramsey was going to be jumping down their throats over this one. They excused themselves and left, promising to check in with Rosalie later in the day.

They had just climbed into their Dodge Charger when Barrera's phone rang. It was Bill Clarke. He set the phone on the dashboard as he pulled away from the curb.

"You aren't going to answer it?" Postiff asked.

"Nah, what can I tell him? He's gonna want the updates, to know what's going on, and I can't give him that information now. You know how he is," Barrera said.

Part of him wanted to include Bill, to get his input on the case. After so many years together, it was second nature, and Bill was a great detective. But Barrera had to admit, if only to himself on the long trek to Simi Valley at the end of the day, that Bill Clarke had always overshadowed him, and he didn't always like it. It made him feel petty and cheap, and he'd swing into remorse right away, but still the feeling lingered. They broke those cases together, through teamwork, but Bill's big personality seemed to pull all the attention his way.

Chief McCall had once said that Bill Clarke used all the oxygen in the room, and it was true. Barrera was every bit as sharp—he just moved through the world more quietly. He liked watching people more than he liked them watching him. Seven months with Postiff would be good for him, give him a chance to shine in his own right. And what he didn't need was Bill Clarke pushing his way into the case now that he was a civilian. It was hard, but it was true. If you stepped out of the river, it kept moving and you couldn't step back in at the same place.

That water didn't slow down or stop for anyone. Once you were out of the game, you were out.

The silence in the patrol car lay like heavy, wet plaster; there was no pushing through it or ignoring it, despite Riley's attempts at small talk.

Finally, Cassidy blurted out, "You don't need to cover for me. I'm a grown-up; I can take responsibility for my own actions at work and everywhere else."

"I know that," Riley replied evenly.

"So, why'd you say it was you who called CIRCLE in? It made me look like an idiot!"

"No, it didn't. You're the only one who thought that. I did it because I get how you want to come in and be part of the new LAPD. Your dad's style of doing shit doesn't work anymore; there's a big push in the department to phase those guys out and get people like you who bring a different skill set to the party. But this department also runs a certain way. And you're setting yourself up for trouble if you come busting in with new tactics right out of the gate."

"They were ready to shoot that guy who was clearly nuts! He didn't even know what he was doing!" she protested.

"Do you have any idea how many times cops have shot people like that? For holding a pencil? Reaching for a tissue? They do it all the time, and it's always ruled in policy. Having the mental health workers is great, but it's going to take time to get everyone up to speed with it. I'm all for change—a lot of us are—but this force is like a paramilitary unit, okay? That's the mentality, and it's very hard to change. I don't want you getting tagged as a troublemaker among the rank-and-file street cops, that's all."

Cassidy didn't reply. She felt her anger subsiding; Riley was right. She was so excited about coming in and changing things that she missed the day-to-day reality of her workplace. Change comes slowly, and the ones who need to change never do it willingly. They dig in and push back and fight until they either adapt or get left behind. As a street cop, she couldn't risk alienating the other cops who had to watch her back out on patrol. In the end, the mental health workers showed up, and the man having a psychotic break was taken to a nearby hospital. Mentone and Teachout hadn't added another lethal shooting to their records. It was a win. Riley was a good partner, and he'd saved her from herself.

"Okay, I get it. Thank you," she said quietly.

"No problem."

They were driving down Hollywood Boulevard into Thai Town when they saw a woman flagging their car down from the sidewalk.

Riley slowed, then said, "That girl works with Boon Nam!"

Riley hung a U-turn and pulled up with screeching tires in front of a young Thai woman who was shaking and fighting back tears.

"What happened?" Riley asked, taking her by the shoulders to steady her.

"That man! He came to our place, wanted a massage, but he went crazy. He grabbed Kulap and tried to put her face in the pillow! We all hit him and pulled him off her, but he ran. Down that alley!" She pointed to a narrow passageway behind the businesses on that stretch of the boulevard.

"I'm going!" Cassidy shouted as she took off toward the alleyway.

"I'll circle from the other side," Riley called out, heading in the opposite direction.

Cassidy ran down the alley, dodging big cans used for cooking oil stacked up next to cardboard produce boxes and trash bags. The area stank of rotted food and fermenting garbage. Homeless people camped out here after closing time, and they left their mark with piles of human waste. Cassidy scanned the area as she skirted her way along the passage, peering into every doorway and hiding place. Suddenly, a tall man bolted past, pushing a pile of boxes onto her. She batted them away and followed him, closing the distance between them as he neared the opening of the alley that would drop them out onto Alexandria Avenue and into a sea of civilians, where it would be harder to get him. She heard Riley's voice calling out to her.

"He's over here! Heading east toward Alexandria!" she shouted back.

The tall man lurched forward, slipping on a pile of wet vegetable cuttings that had spilled from a large plastic bag. His feet went up behind him, and he hit the ground hard, momentarily stunned, which gave Cassidy the opportunity to jump onto him and pin him with her knee in his back. He struggled against her as Riley came around the corner with his gun drawn. He grabbed one of the man's flailing arms, twisting it against his back as he spat and cursed at them, wriggling his body against the concrete. Cassidy pushed his head down as she snapped handcuffs on him. He stopped fighting, the breath leaving his body in defeat as he fell limp.

Cassidy and Riley turned him over onto his back. He laughed and grinned at Cassidy as she leaned over him, his clothing stained and smelling of the fetid mash of rotting food that he'd fallen on. Her breathing came fast and shallow; it had taken all her strength to bring this guy down. He winked at her and chuckled. She recognized him. It was the man in the police sketch. They had just caught one of the Hollywood Hit Men.

CHAPTER SEVEN

Postiff and Barrera sat beside Millie Grace's hospital bed with a photo lineup spread out before her.

"Look at each man carefully. Let us know if you recognize the man who attacked you," Barrera said.

Without hesitation, Millie pointed out Ronald Whitty, the man Cassidy and Riley had brought in earlier.

"That's him," she said.

"He was arrested earlier for an assault and attempted murder of a young woman in a Thai massage spa in Hollywood. He tried to suffocate her into a pillow, but the other employees intervened, and he fled. Two of our officers caught him. We've taken his DNA to see if it matches what we got from you and the previous victim," Postiff said.

"Did the DNA from me match what you found on her?"

"Yes, it did. The man who attacked you also killed Jennifer Dale, so if this Whitty guy comes back with a DNA match, we've got one of them locked up, and we'll charge him for your case also," Barrera said.

"Rosie came by to see me. She said that she'd seen the guy in the store. I remember her mentioning him, that he gave her the creeps. She thinks he might've been after her."

"That's a possibility," Postiff said.

"I'm glad it was me he found, then. Because Rosie hates to work out or exercise. She wouldn't have been able to fight them off," Millie said simply.

Postiff was surprised at her courage and perspective; a lot of victims in her place would've felt angry that someone else had been the target and they were the unfortunate victim.

"We'll keep you posted as the case progresses. We'll be getting everything over to the DA this afternoon. You're willing to testify in court, correct?" Barrera asked.

"I'll be there with six white horses, believe me. I can't wait to look that asshole in the eye and see him found guilty," Millie said with fiery determination that didn't match her damaged, fragile exterior.

On the way out, Barrera turned to Postiff. "She's quite a firecracker, isn't she?"

"That's the kind of girl a guy should marry, not some frilly princess type who loses it when her nail appointment is canceled," Postiff said.

Barrera gave him a sideways smile. "How about you? Once the case is over, you have no conflict of interest. You could always check up on her, being a good detective and all, right?"

"I just might, Barrera. She's my type."

"Let's go see if Whitty is ready to talk to us yet," Barrera said.

Since his arrest, Ronald Whitty had refused to speak to any of the detectives. He insisted on talking to "the pretty strawberry blond who took him down," referring to Cassidy. Given that he was charged with the attempted murder of Kulap Sombat at Nam's Thai Massage spa, and he could well be one of the Hollywood Hit Men, it was the homicide detectives on that case who should interview him, not a rookie cop in her first week on the force. Barrera doubted that Cassidy even wanted to do the interview; she had no experience and was bound to feel overwhelmed at the idea of dealing with a seasoned criminal like Whitty. He hoped the jerk had chilled out and had come to his senses. At least he hadn't lawyered up yet. Usually, these guys pulled the attorney card right away, but Whitty was playing a different game. Barrera just had to figure out what it was.

When Ronald Whitty was booked into the Hollywood station, everyone saw the resemblance to the police sketch of one of the Hollywood Hit

Men. The place was abuzz with speculation that Cassidy Clarke may have collared one of the serial killers on her second day of work. For her part, Cassidy wasn't jumping to any conclusions prematurely. They took Whitty's DNA, and Boon and the other employees who had fought him off had positively identified him, so at the very least they had him for assault and attempted murder. There was a rush on his DNA, and if it matched the sample from Millie Grace and Jennifer Dale, then she had indeed brought in one of the Hit Men.

She hadn't texted her dad with any news yet; she knew he'd be over the moon about it, and she didn't want to set him off into a euphoric high. She was careful these days, now that he was retiring, and in recent months his headaches and volatility had gotten worse. She hadn't even texted Carter. As far as she was concerned, even if Whitty was one of the Hit Men, catching him hadn't required any great skill on her part. It was a routine bust: A guy committed assault and fled the scene. She and Riley chased him down and caught him. If he was responsible for other, bigger crimes beyond that, it had nothing to do with her. She had done her job as a patrol cop, and that was it.

When she heard that Whitty would only speak to her, she declined. She didn't need to be in some power play with the detective squad. They had years of experience in dealing with murderers, and she wasn't interested in stepping on their toes. Captain Dykstra had already given her a big dose of sarcastic praise for the arrest, acting as if she had been on a mission to find the Hit Men, to grandstand and promote herself. She'd taken Montoya's advice and ignored him, but she could feel the attention she was getting from the patrol officers, and she didn't get the sense it was all positive.

After booking Whitty, Cassidy and Riley returned to patrol until the end of their shift. They drove up Cahuenga toward the Hollywood Reservoir, passing the stately homes built by silent-film stars in the 1920s.

"Do you think it's really him?" Riley asked.

"I don't know. A million guys look like that, but his reaction is really weird. This crap about wanting to talk only to me . . . it's not cool," Cassidy responded.

"He's got some bigger plan; it was good you didn't buy into his game. It may not even be the guy, you know?"

"Yeah. If it is, what a break! What did the girl from the spa say?"

"The guy thought it was a sex massage place. When the girl refused and said it was just massage, he went nuts. If it is one of the Hit Men, he had to be sweating bullets knowing his face was out there, so he was probably on edge."

They had arrived at the parking area of the Hollywood Reservoir, known as Lake Hollywood. It was fenced with chain link all around the three-mile perimeter, protecting the water and creating a jogging and biking loop. It was popular with the locals, who met up regularly in the mornings to work out. The original concrete bridge built by William Mulholland in 1923 still stood, offering a vista across the lake straight to the famed Hollywood Sign. The lake itself was closed to the public; only the walking path above the shoreline was open. Two guys on ten-speed racing bikes whizzed by Cassidy and Riley, who stood on the bridge looking out over the placid water.

"Did you know there's a park ranger guy who lives here on the property? He has this whole lake as his backyard. He told me he used to take girls out in his rowboat on dates. Pretty romantic," Riley said.

"That'd be kind of cool, but it must attract mountain lions."

"At least we don't have bears," Riley said, crossing the bridge. "Sometimes I come up here just to stroll around, to see and be seen. It can get deserted, especially at off-hours."

"I wouldn't run here by myself," Cassidy said. "I listen to music when I exercise, so I do it on the track at the gym. Way too quiet up here."

"I forget sometimes. I never worry that some guy is going to attack me when I'm out, but it's different for you."

"It's every single day, every place you go. Where did you park? Is it too isolated? Is there a weird guy in the garage? Did anyone follow you home? Even pumping gas, there's always some asshole wanting to talk to you who gets pissed if you don't play along. That's kind of how I feel about this Whitty guy. Like, he thinks I owe it to him to talk to him or something, just because that's what he wants. I hate that," Cassidy said.

"However this all goes down, I know it's hard being a new cop with your dad being a living legend in the department. I know Dykstra is an ass and I'm sure some of the new boots share his way of thinking, but they're just jealous, okay? Just so you know, I've got your back in all of this."

Cassidy nodded, unsure of how to respond. She felt oddly emotional at his show of support. She wasn't accustomed to depending on anyone else; she had been Little Miss Fix-It since she was a kid, trying to soothe the tensions between her parents and then taking on adult responsibilities after their divorce. Riley was proving to be a partner who was thinking ahead and putting himself out in front to help her and protect her. It made her vaguely uncomfortable. She had never known a man to do that. She realized she was waiting for the other shoe to drop. But what if there was no other shoe?

She found her voice and replied, "I appreciate that, Riley. I really do. I'm just starting out, and I'm already seeing that this is more complicated than I thought."

Riley's phone rang. He answered, and Cassidy saw his expression tighten as he nodded in acknowledgment.

He hung up and said, "The DNA is a match. Whitty's one of the guys who killed Jennifer Dale. And he still won't talk to anyone but you. Chief McCall and Commander Ramsey want to meet with you at Parker Center in an hour. Be prepared—the press is going to go apeshit over this, and your name might be revealed."

Cassidy felt her stomach tighten. It was her second day of work, and it was turning into everything she didn't want.

Postiff texted Bill with the information about Cassidy bringing in one of the Hit Men. After he read the news, Bill jumped in the air, pumping his fist. He texted Cassidy immediately, but she hadn't gotten back to him yet. He moved through the house, unable to settle, his excitement was so great. He was mildly pissed at Barrera, who had still not responded to his texts for updates.

"She did it. She did it right out of the gate, not even a week on the job," Bill muttered to himself as he walked up and down the hallway. He wanted to tell someone, anyone, but all his buddies were at work or had retired to some beach in Mexico. He decided to call Jayce Hendry, a retired detective he'd worked with for years, to give him the news. He dialed the number; it was answered by a woman.

"Hi, this is Bill Clarke. I'm looking for Jayce?"

"Oh, Bill. This is Melanie, Jayce's wife. You didn't hear about Jayce?"

"No, did something happen?"

"He had a stroke. He's in a rehab center right now over in the East Valley. He has to learn to walk and talk again. It's been a few weeks now."

"Damn, I hadn't heard anything about it. I'm sorry," Bill said.

"That's okay. Everyone loses contact when they retire. You know they all say they're going to keep in touch, but they never do. Especially the ones who're still working. He's only had one visitor from work, his old partner. But I'll give him your best," Melanie said.

"Text me the place he's at. I'll go visit him," Bill said.

He hung up, sobered by their brief conversation.

Everyone loses contact when they retire. They all say they're going to keep in touch, but they never do . . .

Jayce was in pretty good shape; he hit the gym several times a week. He was a smoker, but Bill remembered him as a light drinker, often opting to be the designated driver when the group hit one of the local Hollywood bars. Now he had to learn to walk and talk again, out in some rehab center. Was that what he had to look forward to? He'd get back into his fighting shape, now that he had time. His phone buzzed. It was Barrera.

"Hey, brother, what's up?" Pete asked.

"Just checking on the Hit Men case. I wanted to see how things are going. Postiff told me Cassidy collared one of them today with Riley!"

"Yeah, it looks like it. It was crazy good luck," Barrera said.

"So, what's going on?"

There was a pause. Bill waited. Finally, Barrera spoke. "You know how it is, man. I can't tell you anything now that you've retired."

"Whaddya mean? I found the first three victims with you!" Bill protested, offended.

"Yeah, but it's an open case, and now you're a civilian. I can't give you any details—it's against policy."

"Pete! It's me, okay? I'm not some civilian like the cashier at Vons," Bill said.

"I know, but Ramsey and the rest are cracking down on everyone," Barrera lied.

Bill was silent. He knew Barrera was full of shit. He could easily fill him in on the case—they had done it with other retired detectives many times. Bill figured it was because Cassidy had brought in one of the suspects, a guy Barrera hadn't been able to catch. Bill had been retired only one day, and he was already learning who his real friends were.

"No problem, Pete. I get it," Bill said, hanging up. He dialed Cassidy again.

"Hey, Dad. What's up? Everything okay?" she asked.

"Sure. I'm home. I heard you brought in one of the Hit Men!" he said.

"Yeah. It was a lucky break. I'm at Parker Center now."

Bill whistled. "Look at you! New boot, second day on the job, and you're meeting with the big boys downtown! Even your old man never did that!"

"The guy, Whitty, says he only wants me to interview him, but I don't want to. I hope this meeting isn't about that," she confided.

"That's a big step for a new patrol cop. So, the DNA matched, right? What else do you guys have?" Bill asked.

"I don't know. I'm not on the case. And I don't think I'm supposed to talk to you about it now that you're retired," Cassidy said, clearly uncomfortable.

"Pete just told me the same thing! What the hell? Is this some new rule or something?" Bill asked, annoyed.

"I have no idea! I just got pulled into this. I don't know how I'm supposed to handle it."

"Okay, no problem, Binkie. You're not to blame. Pete's being a dick, that's all. Like I can't be trusted with any updates after all the years I spent in homicide," Bill grumbled.

"I gotta go, Dad. I'll see you later?"

"Sure. I might go out for drinks, but that could change."

"With who?" she asked.

Bill laughed. "What're you? My mother? With a friend."

"I just asked who."

"You're not the boss of me. Remember when you used to say that to your mom?" Bill asked, still laughing.

"Okay, okay. Goodbye!" Cassidy said and hung up.

Bill looked around the den, perfectly set up for him to watch sports all day on the wide-screen television, with a pool table gathering dust. He was pissed off that Pete was stonewalling him, and he could see how things were going to be from now on. He'd become like Jayce Hendry, forgotten and irrelevant. He was happy that Cassidy had caught one of the Hit Men and amazed that the guy only wanted her to interview him. But he felt a pang of jealousy also. He hadn't wanted to retire; he would've stayed on the job until he dropped dead working a case. Being a detective was his life, and now Ramsey and McCall and the other top dogs had cut him off. They said it was for the good of the department; they had to bring in newer, younger detectives. He knew they didn't like him; he didn't always play by the rules, and he'd been investigated a few times for overstepping. But the job required that. He couldn't just go up to a criminal and politely ask him to give up all the information. They weren't dealing with altar boys. Sometimes, a little extra force was necessary.

He grabbed his gym bag from the closet. He'd hit the Brickhouse Boxing Club. He could use a good sparring session, get some of his stress out. On the shelves in the closet, he saw boxes of his old case files, the cold ones he'd made copies of, hoping to look into them again one day. Maybe that day had come. If he was going to be shut down by his old partner and the department wanted him to disappear quietly, maybe it was time to solve the cases they still had open. It would be like a stick in their eye if he did it. He pulled the boxes down, a cascade of dust falling on him. Inside, there were murder books, crime scene photos, all his notes over the years on the cases that haunted him, like that of Min Sun-Hee.

He wanted to dig up the information on Tom Britt, who bore such a close resemblance to his new neighbor, the mysterious Alan Musselman. Bill walked to the front window and peered out at the edge of the curtain. Musselman's car was still there, the pod almost empty now. He'd watched him moving back and forth all day, unloading his belongings. There was something off about Musselman, but Bill couldn't put his finger on what it was. Something in his gait, in the set of his shoulders.

Bill had taped a photo of Min Sun-Hee to the mantel of the fireplace in the den. It was taken at a Korean New Year celebration, her smiling seventeen-year-old face full of hope and expectation. Someone had cut her life so short there wasn't much to remember her by. A high school honors certificate, a Christmas wreath she made at her church community center, a citizenship award from her tenth-grade teacher. Her parents had moved to Canada after her death, unable to remain in the country that had taken their daughter from them. He heard they lived in Winnipeg, where it was so cold you felt frozen half the year. He guessed her parents felt frozen every day of their lives. Alan Musselman exited his house and got into his car. He drove away, and Bill took his chance to slip out and look around. There was something off about Musselman; he just knew it.

CHAPTER EIGHT

"I know this Whitty character is jockeying for something, and he figures that talking with you will give him the upper hand. But I think you can beat him at his game, Officer Clarke," Joyce Ramsey said, seated across from Cassidy in a conference room at Parker Center in downtown Los Angeles. Police Chief McCall sat at the head of the table, nodding in agreement.

"I've reviewed your time at the academy," he said, "and you were a stellar cadet, second in your class. I know you cut your teeth on police culture—we're of course all very familiar with your dad and his track record. Commander Ramsey and I have discussed this Whitty situation, and if you're the only one he wants to talk to, we have to put you in that room with him. We must find out who his partner is, and we must get justice for these victims. You're a sharp, astute officer. We think you can handle this."

Before Cassidy could respond, Ramsey added, "We'll speak to the homicide detectives on the case. They will give you the questions to ask; they will guide you every step of the way. Of course, they'll be watching the interrogation and listening in, ready to step in to help you. We're going to confirm to the press that Whitty's DNA is a match, but we're going to keep your identity private. They don't need to know that he'll only talk to you."

"We're saying that he was picked up on a routine call, and then it was discovered that he's one of the Hit Men," McCall said.

Cassidy knew this was a big opportunity for her, a chance to show the chief how good she could be, but she was intimidated by the weight of responsibility. To run the interrogation of a high-profile serial-murder suspect was beyond her training and experience. She knew everyone else in her class at the academy couldn't even dream about sitting across from the chief and commander this way. She felt like a kid dressed up as a cop for Halloween.

"I'm concerned about the blowback from the detectives, to be honest. They're very experienced, and I'm a rookie cop. I don't know how willing they'll be to let me take the lead on this," Cassidy explained.

"Let me handle them," Ramsey assured her as McCall stood up to leave.

"Sorry, I must run, ladies. I've got a meeting at city hall in ten minutes. We believe in you, Officer Clarke," he said, shaking her hand and then heading out the door with his assistants and security detail. Cassidy and Ramsey looked at each other across the table for a beat before Ramsey spoke.

"I know how hard it is to be a woman in this department. I was in your shoes once, and it was some time ago. Things were much worse—the harassment, the resentment, all the pushback we had to put up with just to do our jobs. I've paid attention to you. You can see the bigger picture that some people can't. They're just cogs in a wheel, but you're different. I'm not going to send you out there and let you flounder. I'll handle the senior Robbery-Homicide detectives and make sure they give you every bit of support you need."

"Do I have to say yes?"

"No, but it won't help you if you say no. Do you think you could go in and talk to him tonight?"

Cassidy knew she should agree and do it, but she feared messing everything up, taking on more than she could handle.

"Could I wait until tomorrow morning? I want to talk to my dad about it, and I'll have to meet with Postiff and Barrera to be brought up to speed. I don't want to go in unprepared."

Ramsey considered her request for a moment. "Okay. I'll have Barrera and Postiff draw up the questions, and they can lay out their plan to guide you through the process. We can all be fresh and ready to deal with Whitty in the morning. It won't hurt him to stew in his cell overnight."

Cassidy thanked her and left, feeling the full weight of the ball Ramsey had so deftly placed in her court. Her dad didn't care for Joyce Ramsey, but he didn't like anything new or different from what it was like twenty-five years ago, when few women were in the force at all, let alone commanders. She knew she'd have to go in and do the interrogation; she didn't have a choice. She just had to find a way to get her head around it that didn't make her feel like she was walking into a Roman arena of hungry lions with nothing but a wooden stick.

Whitty had been in custody for four hours, and she still hadn't come to talk to him. The pretty cop with the hair color that was his personal favorite, somewhere between red and blond, silky and straight, pulled back into a tidy twist. Some of the strands had escaped when she wrestled with him in that stinking alley. If her partner hadn't arrived, he might've broken free of her. She had to work hard to pin him; when they rolled him over, he saw that her upper lip was wet with beads of sweat, her forehead too.

He liked that look on a woman. Usually it was the flop sweat of terror that he saw up close and personal like that, right before they realized they were going to die. They had a different scent to them than Officer Pretty Tits. He wished that she had put her whole body on him to pin him down. That would've been tasty, to feel her pressed up against him that way. But still, he could tell when they took him to the police car, she was built for real good fun.

He even liked that she wore a uniform that made her look so severe because he knew that deep inside, she wasn't. She wanted someone like him, someone who wouldn't be afraid of her badge and gun, who'd rough her up a little and she'd like it. He'd pull that fancy clip out of her hair and wrap that silky, honey-colored cascade around his fist so tight, she'd ask nicely for him to let go. He preferred them with a little bit of fight in them.

The ones who were stupid and willing, who made doe eyes at him at the Party Doll bar out on Sherman Way, were not the interesting ones. No, he liked the ones who had a little more spunk, who'd give him a bit of a fight to make the winning so much sweeter. Officer Pretty Tits Clarke was just his style, and now he'd drawn the line in the sand. She'd have to talk to him. She'd have to come in and sit across from him, where he'd be able to pick up the smell of her shampoo, maybe even her body lotion. She'd played hard to get, refusing to come, but he knew they were desperate to get him talking, and she was the only one he would speak to. He knew how to play this game. She'd have to show up, and he'd be ready.

Cassidy took surface streets through Hollywood to get to the 101 freeway. Ramsey and Riley were right: The press had exploded with the news of Whitty's arrest. The *Los Angeles Times* as well as all the local news stations were running stories on the victims and fueling the fear about his alleged accomplice, who was still at large. On social media, a true-crime-in-real-time frenzy had blossomed, with amateur sleuths offering their interpretations of the crimes and the suspect. A new serial killer in Los Angeles was always an epic news story, feeding the lore of the city's disturbing criminal history. So far, no one had leaked her name, which was a relief.

She desperately needed her dad's advice, how to walk into that room and get the suspect to talk. With two detectives, they could play good cop / bad cop; they could switch dynamics to build trust. But Whitty had insisted that she talk to him alone, no one else in the room. She knew Barrera and Postiff couldn't be happy about it.

And it complicated everything else at the station, even though Cassidy and Riley had brought him in on a separate charge and Whitty had set the conditions of the interrogation. She knew there were cops who would think she was getting some kind of special treatment as a nepo-hire. Her dad had warned her that the station could be a snake pit—it was not everyone working together for the common good. There were jealousies, power plays, undermining, and gaslighting among the ranks, jockeying for position, a chance to stand out and get noticed. And for female cops it was worse.

He told her flat out that unless she got raped, no good would come from making any kind of sexual harassment complaint. It would be ignored. She'd be retaliated against, and that could threaten her safety out in the field. A high-profile female detective was currently in litigation against the department for that exact situation. If someone messed with her, her dad said he'd handle it personally in a way that they would understand. Maybe he put that word out, because, so far, no one had dared to make so much as a provocative remark to her. She knew other female boots had been dealing with it since the academy.

But now, she had to shift her focus to Whitty and his interrogation. She hated the smug look on his face when he'd stared up at her from the pavement, the way he'd licked his lips as if she were a snack for him to gobble up, even as she was placing him under arrest.

She hung a right turn from Franklin onto Cahuenga, a main artery into the Valley where she could catch the freeway and make the second leg of her journey home. The rich, garlicky smell of the Zankou chicken was filling her car, escaping through the triple bag she had requested. She was anxious to talk to her dad, but she had one stop to make. She had to go to the place that gave her an emotional reset, to forget her own troubles or let go of a bad mood. It had been four days since her last visit to Kylie Keyes, and she knew she'd be missed.

Barrera popped a Los Lobos CD into his car stereo as he passed Van Nuys Boulevard, wishing he and his wife, Gloria, still lived in the little house on Lemona Avenue. He'd be home by now. They had moved there from an apartment in Highland Park when the kids came so close together, two girls and then a boy. It was a quiet, safe neighborhood, with the wide-open feel of the San Fernando Valley but still a short commute to the Hollywood station. Now he had over an hour drive to Simi Valley, where Gloria had insisted they buy a roomy house in one of the cookie-cutter developments that had been popping up all through the '90s. The house was nice, and Gloria did a great job keeping everything company ready every day. There were towels he wasn't allowed to use in the bathrooms, pillows he wasn't allowed to lean against on the couch.

They had a garage full of inflatable holiday decorations that she hooked up on the lawn like strange alien visitors, with big empty eyes and wide smiles, swaying back and forth in even a slight breeze. She came home with the big boxes from Lowe's each year, and he didn't have the heart to tell her that they gave him the heebie-jeebies. There was a Christmas elf who looked like a scary clown from one of his childhood nightmares. There had been a giant neon clown sign outside a neighborhood liquor store on Boyle Heights Boulevard, and that clown had every kid terrified with his weird smile and ruffled collar. He'd never told Gloria, but when she put that Christmas elf up in the yard, it looked so much like the Jumbos Liquor Store clown, he got the shudders.

So, he sat in traffic to get home to a big, beige house that the two of them rambled around in, now that the kids were grown. Just two old married people with a huge kitchen and three extra, empty bedrooms. And a yard he had to hire a guy to take care of and an HOA that told him what he could and couldn't plant. His mother's house had been overflowing with bougainvillea, fig and peach trees, trumpet vines in a riot of color. Now he had to check with a board of uptight white people who he knew were vaguely if not virulently racist against Mexicans, just to plant a fucking boxwood. The Van Nuys exit receded from view; he had another forty minutes in traffic to get to Simi.

Ramsey had called Postiff and him in at the station to discuss the Cassidy Clarke situation, right after they'd fielded questions from the press, who were like a pack of hyenas. The last thing he needed was the headache of having a rookie involved in his investigation. He'd pushed back, but when he saw that she and the chief were determined to let Whitty have his way, he'd relented. It was about making a show of promoting a new female hire, to show that the department wasn't rampant with sexism. He'd have to draw up all the questions for Cassidy to ask, coach her on how to interact with him, when to give in, when to hold firm. They needed a lot from Whitty, apart from a confession. They needed to figure out his motive, how he chose his victims, and most of all, who he worked with because that guy was still out there, loose on the streets of Hollywood.

Cassidy pulled into the parking lot of the New Day skilled nursing facility in Northridge, which had been Kylie's home for the past seven years. She'd bounced around from one therapy center to another, always hopeful that she would recover the ability to walk until she'd finally given up. Since she'd been so young when she was shot, everyone held out hope that there would be some new treatment, but her father's bullet had torn through her brain stem, causing irreparable damage. The cruelest twist of it all was that her cognition and understanding were just fine. She knew exactly what was going on, and that made it much harder.

Cassidy checked in at the front desk, made her way down the familiar hallway to room 28, and found Kylie sitting up in bed, watching television.

"How was . . . the . . . the . . . first day . . . of . . . work?" she asked with her lopsided smile.

"It was good. I have a really nice partner who's easy to work with. We caught a major suspect in a big case by accident earlier today, and it's gotten kind of wild."

She went on to tell her about her first patrol call with Man-Bun, how Whitty would only speak to her, and all about Bill's retirement party. As usual, Kiley hung on every word, living life through Cassidy's experiences as if they were her own.

Kylie's right arm was locked against her torso, her fists turned in on themselves involuntarily. She squinted her eyes several times, which Cassidy knew was a sign of stress.

"I have . . . a favor to . . . ask," Kylie said finally.

"Sure, what is it?"

"I want you . . . to . . . stop coming . . . so regularly," Kylie said.

Cassidy felt as if she'd been punched. "Why? Does it bother you?"

"No . . . I love . . . seeing . . . you. But . . . your real . . . life is starting . . . now. And . . . you can't . . . be . . . coming here to . . . see me . . . all the . . . time."

"But I like coming here. It's the place where I can relax and just be myself," Cassidy said.

Kylie shook her head. "You have . . . a life . . . with . . . work and . . . friends and you . . . need to do . . . that. Not . . . sit here . . . in this room . . . just because . . . I . . . have to."

"Do you think I come here because I pity you? Like it's an obligation? I want to be here. I want to see you. You're my best friend!" Cassidy said, her voice rising.

She felt an odd surge of emotion overtaking her. She couldn't say what it was, but it hurt, and it was sad and frightening.

"I know . . . but . . . please, just . . . do . . . it for . . . a few . . . weeks. This . . . is a new chapter . . . for . . . both . . . of us. I'll still . . . be . . . here," Kylie said.

"Okay, if that's what you really want," Cassidy said, trying to sound upbeat.

"I . . . do. Now shoo, fly!" Kylie said, repeating the phrase her mother used to say to them as kids when they were underfoot. She kept a smile on her face until Cassidy was out of sight. Her attendant Glennis stuck her head in the room.

"Did you tell her?" Glennis asked.

Kylie nodded. "Yes."

"How'd she take it?"

"Pretty . . . good. She . . . was kind of . . . upset . . . but she . . . agreed. She has . . . to get . . . used to . . . me not . . . being here . . . to me . . . being . . . gone." Kylie struggled to get the words out.

"Did you tell her everything?" Glennis asked cautiously.

Kylie shook her head. "No . . . not . . . yet."

Glennis had been taking care of Kylie for years, and she knew how hard it was for her to hang on to hope, being trapped in a body that didn't work. The pain in her spine and limbs was only getting worse, and she needed stronger drugs to manage it. Kylie didn't want to be a burden any longer, especially to Cassidy. Glennis had helped Kylie look up assisted suicide and the protocols in the states that allowed it, but it broke her heart to see such a young woman facing that difficult decision. It also broke her heart to know how long Kylie had been trapped in that chair with no control over her life.

"Things could change, Kylie. There are medical breakthroughs all the time. You don't have to make any big decisions right now. There's plenty of time," Glennis assured her.

"That's . . . all . . . I have," Kylie said quietly.

Cassidy sat in her car in the New Day parking lot in a daze. She knew Kylie must have a good reason for making her request, but Cassidy couldn't imagine what it was. Seeing Kylie had been a cornerstone of her life since the accident. Each week was built around the time they would spend together, seeing how far she had come, what new progress she had made. With Kylie, Cassidy didn't have to wear any of the masks she needed in her daily life, the emotional armor she put on before stepping out the door. In the outside world, she projected an image of unflappable competency, the girl who could handle anything without losing her cool. But she needed solitude and downtime just to process the debris of daily life. She needed a place where she didn't have to be anything for anyone, and that was what she had with Kylie.

Their lives had been upended the fateful day that Marvin Keyes attacked the wife and children he loved more than anything in the world. That incomprehensible choice hung over both girls as they grew up, coloring their lives in ways that were obvious and invisible. Only they knew how to carry those scars, how to navigate the twisted path to adulthood under that heavy weight. Now, sitting in the dark, Cassidy felt as if she had been locked out of the one place she felt safe, away from the one person who understood her.

CHAPTER NINE

Cassidy drove toward home, not paying attention to the streets, missing her turn twice. She was working out a plan for how to deal with this new adjustment in her life, along with everything else she had to manage. She'd gone to therapy once as an adult, and the nice, understanding psychologist, Dr. Peterson, had explained that she'd been through a life-changing trauma with the Keyeses' tragedy. It had destroyed her sense of safety and trust in the systems that a child relies on. She didn't need a shrink to explain that to her—she felt it every day.

He'd expounded on her being a parentified child, advising that she break free from her overarching relationship with her dad and his issues. That was easy for Peterson to say, sitting in his Toluca Lake office, in a Luca Faloni cable-knit sweater with a quarter zipper. He probably held all his boundaries firm, refused to engage with behavior that raised his cortisol level. She couldn't break free from her dad, even if he could be a pain in the butt. She'd taken on grown-up responsibilities as a kid, so what? Lots of kids did that for reasons a lot more difficult than having a homicide detective for a father.

And she'd chosen a high-octane career that required mental toughness and flexibility beyond what was needed to sit in an office cubicle every day. She willingly stepped into her dad's world of life-and-death decisions, and she wanted that. But she had to admit, she felt worn a lot of the time, and the daily toll of human interaction was sometimes too much for her.

Her phone rang; it was Carter.

"Hey there," she said, trying to sound cheerful.

"Hi, babe, I'm having a late dinner with some friends of my folks who're in town overnight. Doreen and Jim MacDougal. He's in hedge funds. Their plane to Frankfurt was canceled and they can't leave until tomorrow morning, so we're going to go to the Water Grill downtown, and I hope you can join us. They'd love to meet you," he said.

The thought of dinner with Doreen and Jim MacDougal, who was in hedge funds, was perhaps the most unappealing offer Cassidy could've received that evening. That they were close friends with June and Edward Sims told her several things: They were very rich, very stuffy, and had no clue how real people lived in the real world. Dinner with them would be a certain kind of dog and pony show, in which Cassidy, with her middle-class upbringing, her detective father, and her career as a police officer, would be a conduit to the dark, unsavory world they knew nothing about. It would be quite exciting, like having an orangutan at the table. But it wasn't Carter's fault—he'd grown up in that world and didn't know anything different.

"Sorry, sweetie. I just got home, and I have a very big day of work tomorrow. I have to interrogate one of the Hollywood Hit Men suspects."

"They caught him? When?"

"Actually, my partner Sean and I caught him on a routine call. It turned out to be one of them."

"No way! Did you cuff him and everything? Like, you came face to face with him?"

"Yeah, I pinned him down in an alley in Hollywood. He's a creep, and he'll only talk to me, so tomorrow I do the interrogation."

"No fucking way! My girl is such a badass! Doreen and Jim would've loved to hear this story," Carter said.

"Rain check. I'm just about home, so have a good dinner and have a martini for me," she said.

"I'll have two. I'm taking an Uber and staying in San Marino tonight."

She hung up as she turned onto her street, pulling into the driveway to find her dad's car gone. She checked her texts. He'd decided to go for that drink with his mysterious friend; Cassidy knew it had to be Eden Balcomb. She texted her dad.

mcCall and ramsey want me to go in and do the interview with whitty. I need some advice

He replied immediately.

I'll be home early so we can talk about it you'll kick ass Binkie!

She knew her dad; if he was out for drinks with a woman, anything was possible. Sometimes his grandiosity took over and he only saw her as his amazing daughter who could do anything, not as a young woman finding her way who needed help. Of course he thought she would kick ass, the same way he thought she didn't need training wheels when she got her first bike. She hoped he'd be back early enough, but she wasn't going to count on it. So much for the Zankou chicken stinking up the back seat of her car. She wasn't in the mood for it any longer. She'd stick it in the fridge, and her dad could eat it for breakfast.

She took her work duffel from the trunk, looking forward to a hot shower after a quick dinner. As she opened a package of Maruchan ramen and chopped some green onions, the landline of the house rang. She took the receiver off the wall phone, where it had been for decades.

"Hello?"

"Is this Cassidy Clarke?"

"Who's calling?"

"This is Christian Dodge, from the *LA Weekly*. I'd like to speak to you about the arrest of Hollywood Hit Men suspect Ronald Whitty. I understand you're the officer who apprehended him?"

Cassidy froze, then stammered, "I have no comment," before hanging up. She looked at the phone as if it were powdered with poison, then took it off the hook.

Bill sat at the bar of La Popular with Eden, who'd made the drive to Chatsworth from Hollywood, where she lived in Beachwood Canyon. The atmosphere was lively; they'd been there for a couple of hours, drinking margaritas and eating nachos. He'd had a good workout at the Brickhouse; the young guy he sparred with had cleaned his clock pretty hard, and he'd already taken three Aleve tablets. Bill had planned to stay home and have dinner with Cassidy, but after pulling out all his old case files, he'd become restless. He knew that feeling when you bring in a truly bad player, the sense of relief and accomplishment, and he hadn't made peace with the fact that he would never experience that again. But maybe he wouldn't have to give that up just yet. He'd been explaining his plan to Eden, who listened attentively, not quite understanding what he was considering.

"When I was going through the boxes of cold cases, I came across one that we never solved, Stacey Mandel, but I knew who did it. It was a guy who's up in the pen at Coalinga. Tyler Derby. He killed four women back in 2001, and there were more that we couldn't pin on him, but they fit his MO. I know he was good for them," Bill said.

"Are you gonna reopen the cases?" Eden asked.

"I can't reopen them; they're in the deep freeze. No one's even looked at them for years. But now that I have time, I'm going to start going through them and work them on my own. I bet I'll solve a bunch of 'em."

"You're gonna do it with the police department?"

"No, babe. I'm retired. I'll do it on my own. Just a concerned citizen, bringing my expertise and experience to investigate these cases. I have about seven already lined up at home."

"That's amazing. I know you'll be excellent at it. Bill the Drill!" She giggled.

Bill pulled her in for a quick kiss. She was a good listener when he needed an ear to talk into. He didn't know what the hell *Bill the Drill* meant—it was a silly name she used for him, like most things she said. But it didn't matter. She was kind of a dingbat, but she was easy and willing, never too complicated, and ready to accept what he had to give. She was a good cook too. She had a business called Jill of All Trades, where she drove people to appointments, she did their grocery shopping, and she picked up packages. Sometimes she cooked meals and froze them for her clients; she'd make a big batch of lasagna or chicken potpies, and he'd get the extras.

Since they broke up, it was much better for him. No more of her pushing to move in together, no pouty tears if he didn't make plans with her for a Saturday night. Now it was just like his favorite fast-food drive-through, In-N-Out. Food, sex, and a captive audience to listen to his war stories or action-movie reviews or whatever popped into his head. No ties, no commitment—they were both free to do what they wanted with whoever they wanted. And now she was happy to make the drive out to his neighborhood; he used to swing by her place after work for a quick hookup since it was so close to the station. She was slightly drunk, chatting with the bartender about how Brad Pitt and Jennifer Aniston were secretly back together, but no one knew about it.

He was already planning to reach out to Tyler Derby at the Pleasant Valley State Prison in Coalinga first thing in the morning. He'd sought Tyler's input a few times over the years for other cases. They had a quid pro quo arrangement. Bill had a good relationship with the warden out there, Quake Rennison, and if Derby gave him good information, Rennison would give him a few extra perks to make Derby's miserable life easier since he wasn't getting out, ever. Derby wanted desperately to get out of Coalinga. He was the target of a particularly bad group of inmates, and he might be willing to give up information to achieve that transfer. Bill knew Derby was good for the Stacey Mandel murder. Maybe he'd get a confession out of him and some hard corroborating evidence. And if his suspicions about Alan Musselman proved to be right, he'd have two cold cases kicked and off the books. Not too shabby for an old guy they put out to pasture before he was ready to go. He signaled the bartender for another round of margaritas.

Vithu drove through the streets of Hollywood, bustling with nightlife where it used to be a late-night wasteland of hookers and junkies. It was easier in the old days—the girls on the street most likely had no one looking for them, except maybe a pimp who didn't want to call any attention to himself if one of them disappeared.

Brittany must've gone back to Minnesota!

But now, any one of them could be an aspiring actress with a website or what they called social media influencers, which meant someone who would be missed. But again, there were so many of them now, girls who all looked the same with long, streaked hair and faces that were deceptively painted to hide what they truly looked like. Vithu hated that.

He turned onto Wilcox, passing the Hollywood police station, where Whitty was being held after being stupid enough to get caught. Who the hell tried to smoke a massage worker in broad daylight at a place that wasn't even for sex? He knew Whitty wouldn't give him up—he wouldn't admit to anything. Whitty was an asshole, anyway. And like a dumb redneck, he didn't know anything about computers, and needed Vithu to jam the internet signals so the cameras wouldn't work. Without him, Whitty would've been seen and caught weeks ago. But he was always acting the big boss, like Vithu needed him to get action, when he could get it on his own and he didn't have to kill anyone afterward.

Vithu kept his options open; he treated them nice so he could go back for seconds on another day. He preferred a different type of arrangement—he liked to keep them for a while, but Whitty was hot tempered, and he hurt them so much that they had no choice but to kill them. Sometimes it did come to that for him, also, but only after enough time to enjoy their company. He'd pick up some pho and maybe banh mi, and they'd have nice meals together, like he used to back home. They'd talk; he'd learn about their dreams and hopes. He secretly hoped that one of them would want to stay with him, to be a real girlfriend, but that hadn't happened yet. But it could. Maybe even tonight.

He watched a group of girls in high heels make their way across the intersection, toward the Saint Felix. They were already tipsy; in a couple of hours they'd be intoxicated, waiting for an Uber. His car looked like a million other neat, nondescript coupes that trolled the streets looking to pick up a rider, and after a few drinks, the cars all looked the same. He knew a guy in Pico-Union who fabricated false documents, from car-registration tags to US birth certificates. Now Vithu had newly minted Uber and Lyft stickers on his front windshield. He looked legitimate. Even his name, Vithu, meant "wise and intelligent one." Like he always told Whitty, you have to work smarter, not harder.

CHAPTER TEN

Postiff arrived early at the station, waiting for Cassidy. He'd texted her late the previous evening to ask her to come in before Barrera got there. He saw her and pulled her aside, into a conference room.

"I wanted to talk to you before Barrera does. Ramsey told us to help you deal with Whitty. Pete's pissed, as you can imagine."

"Yeah, I've known Pete for years. He's old school all the way."

"For him it's about territory, seniority, all that bullshit. These geezers hate change. All the older homicide guys are bent out of shape over this," Postiff said, confirming her worst fears.

"And you're not?" Cassidy asked.

"I want the best information. I want to catch his partner and get a confession to take to the DA, so we can put this motherfucker away for life. I don't care who gets it. But you have to get Whitty talking. This guy hates women; don't forget that. I have a list of questions and stuff to guide you. The main thing is, get him to talk—the more relaxed he is, the more he'll give away. He thinks he's smart. He's not."

"You've dealt with this type of guy before. I mean, it's not a straight-up thing, like a DV case that escalates. It's random and . . . weird, to be honest," she said.

"This isn't going to be a one-shot deal, where you go in and get what we need. He's playing a game, and we have to figure out what it is and then beat him at it. Just get him to talk, to relax with you.

That's all you need to do today. You've got to build a relationship with these guys."

They left the conference room as Barrera arrived. He took Cassidy back in and handed her two sheets of paper, neatly stapled together.

"Here's a list of questions to ask him. We need this fucker to talk, so don't beat around the bush trying to build a rapport with him. Let him know we have his DNA; it's a match to Millie Grace and Jennifer Dale. If he knows that he doesn't have any wiggle room, he'll stop wiggling and come clean to get a better chance in court. The DA hasn't gotten back to me yet regarding what we could give in exchange for information, but we may be able to work out a plea deal. We'll be listening in on the camera and audio feed in Carbone's office. We'll be right there if you need us."

She took Barrera's notes and put them with Postiff's. They'd given her conflicting instructions, and she had to integrate them. Her dad had come back late the previous night, when she was already asleep, and she'd left before he had gotten up. It had played out just as she had expected. Bill had a long track record of not following through when he was distracted by some new thread he was chasing down. She'd have to figure it out on her own. Whitty would be brought to the interview room in the next fifteen minutes. Cassidy went to the restroom and adjusted her hair and uniform in the mirror. She wanted to give the appearance of strength and control. She had purposely worn minimal makeup today, just a light foundation and a smudge of pale ChapStick. She wished her dad had been home the night before; if she ever needed his input, it was now. When she'd left, he was still fast asleep, and she didn't wake him, knowing he'd be as much use as an angry bear if she had.

She followed Barrera, Lieutenant Carbone, and Postiff toward the interview room, where Commander Ramsey was waiting as well. Carbone didn't look happy about Cassidy doing the interview, barely trying to hide it. She was tall and muscular in her tailored dark suit, with her hair slicked back into a crisp ponytail. She was as by the book as any cop Cassidy had ever met, and this move of pushing a new boot into the Hit Men interview was a major break in protocol, but she had to defer to Ramsey and the chief.

"I'm glad you're doing this, Officer Clarke. You'll be fine. Just know that we've all got your back," Ramsey said, which didn't make Cassidy feel any better. They watched through the glass as Whitty was led into the room and sat in a folding chair. He looked smaller in his orange jumpsuit. His eyes were watery, his skin craggy and dry, and he appeared older than his forty-one years. The room was small, with a table that was too large, taking up so much of the space that it felt cramped. That was by design—they wanted suspects to feel that they were literally up against a wall. Whitty wore handcuffs. He looked around, unfazed, showing no signs of nervousness. Cassidy watched him, wishing he'd display some unease that she could use to her advantage, but he was as cool as a Popsicle, with a smirk on his face as if this game were beneath him.

"Time to go in, Clarke," Ramsey said.

Cassidy entered the interview room alone, and Whitty let out a low whistle. She took a seat stiffly across from him.

"You finally came! I wondered how long it would take you to stop playing hard to get," Whitty said.

"I wasn't playing anything. I was busy," Cassidy replied, as casually as she could. Her heart was beating double time.

"Really? What's more important than me right now? I think you're a little scared to talk to me, right?" he asked in a tone that implied intimacy, like a man cajoling his lover.

"I wasn't scared at all. I had a lot of work, but that's enough about me. What about you?" she asked.

From Carbone's office, Barrera and Postiff watched on the video feed.

"That was a little clumsy," Barrera muttered, "but at least she's taking charge of it."

"She's just warming up, Barrera. Give her time," Postiff said.

In the windowless interview room, the air-conditioning was set low. It was uncomfortably cold.

"What do you want to know about me, Officer Clarke? This will be kind of like a first date," Whitty said with a grin.

Cassidy knew she should shut down his attempts at flirting with her, but she wanted him to start talking, so she ignored his date remark.

"What were you doing at Nam's Thai Massage?" she asked.

"I'll tell you what I thought I was doing. I thought I was getting some action, but there wasn't any of that!" He laughed.

"And you got mad? So, you tried to suffocate Kulap?"

"Was that her name? I just think of them as Asian cunt, you know? They're smaller than white or black girls, tighter fit. And if you get tricked by a ladyboy, man that fit is so tight, you think you've gone to heaven until you realize it's a guy," he said.

"You've been tricked by a ladyboy? Or you knew it, but you didn't want to admit that you liked it?" she asked impulsively.

Whitty's expression changed, his eyes shifting from bemusement to rage in a split second.

"I never said I liked that shit. I've never done that, knowing it was a guy," he said.

"But you just said the fit was so tight, you thought you'd gone to heaven, right? You're a smart guy. You really didn't know? Did you go to Boon Nam's hoping for a piece of that, and it went wrong?"

"No fucking way! When that little gook chick wouldn't do it, I got pissed and messed with her. I was gonna let her up," he said.

"Doesn't look that way from the camera footage. Those little Asian ladies ran your ass out of there, didn't they?" she said with a chuckle.

It felt good, getting under his skin, pushing his macho buttons. She found him repulsive, and now that he was seated across from her, she felt a surge of hostility toward him. She liked the growing fury in his eyes, with him cuffed and unable to do anything. Whitty leaned back in his folding chair, taking time to regain his composure.

"I know what you're trying to do, Officer Clarke. You're trying to piss me off so I say something I shouldn't. I was gonna let her up. They all just freaked out," he explained calmly.

"We've got you on this one—we have camera evidence, witness statements, all of it. The charge is assault and attempted murder. But I want to know about the others, the girls in the hills."

Whitty smiled and leaned in across the table. "I don't know about that. What happened?"

"We have your DNA from Millie Grace and Jennifer Dale. So, we know it's you. What do you want to tell me?"

"You're moving too fast for me, officer. I thought we'd get to know each other a little bit first," he said coyly.

Cassidy stared at him across the table. She wanted nothing more than to grab him by the collar and give him a headbutt so hard he collapsed on the linoleum floor. She wasn't sure what to say to get him talking. She didn't want to get to know him at all, and he was looking at her with expectation, just like he had in the alley behind Boon Nam's. It made her skin crawl. She shifted to adjust her weight in the hard chair and cleared her throat. She knew Whitty could see she was uncomfortable, and he enjoyed it.

"I want to know why you did it, who you work with, because there's someone else involved," she said.

"Man! This is like going straight to the fucking with no kiss and cuddle first! You must be a Nazi in bed! Jawohl, commandant!" he said, making a mock salute with his cuffed hands.

Cassidy was silent, unsure how to respond. In the observation room, Barrera shook his head. "She's getting rattled. He's got the power in this. She needs to get the upper hand!"

Postiff thought she had done well, throwing Whitty off with the *ladyboy* remark. But he could see that she was uncertain going forward. Cassidy glanced at Barrera's list of questions.

"How'd you two pick the girls? They seem random, but I don't think they are," Cassidy said, trying to shift the interview back on topic.

"I don't know what you're talking about, but if I were to do anything with some kind of partner, I'm the one who does the picking, okay? I'm the one who decides how things go. But I don't know anything about any girls in the hills," he insisted with a cagey smile that made her feel as if he were removing her clothing. He leaned back in his chair again, tapping his foot.

"I'm getting tired of this. I'm done talking for today. But let's meet again, officer," he said with a wink.

"We're not done yet."

"Well, I'm done. I like talking to you, unless you think I should get a lawyer?" he asked.

She stared hard at him. He was playing his trump card. She nodded in agreement, standing. If he lawyered up, they'd have no chance of getting any information.

"I'll check with the boss. Maybe they'll keep you here or let you go back to your cell. Not my call."

"Let 'em know that I'm thinking about getting a lawyer, but I'm not sure yet. It'll depend on how our next chat goes."

As Cassidy left, she glanced at the camera mounted in the corner of the room. She knew Ramsey and the rest had to be disappointed in her. She should've been tougher. She should've been more aggressive, but she wasn't sure how to handle a murderer like Whitty. It was all over and done so quickly. Whitty had set the parameters of the whole thing. She'd failed, and it didn't feel good. She didn't know how she'd face her dad when Barrera told him of her dismal performance. She wished the earth would open and swallow her whole.

Bill woke late. His head felt like it had been in a drawer all night. Maybe Cassidy was right—he couldn't handle drinking several nights in a row any longer. Between the Smoke House party and La Popular with Eden, he hadn't fully recovered. He'd missed Cassidy, but he guessed she probably wasn't going in to talk to Whitty yet. Regardless of what the jerk wanted, they'd probably send in a seasoned guy like Pete first.

Bill made a mental note to go over the interrogation with Cassidy when she got back from work. He planned a quick workout at the Brickhouse Boxing gym, and then he'd come back and go over the case files in the den. He had to get them organized by priority, which ones he planned to tackle first. He knew Stacey Mandel was number one; he'd already contacted Quake Rennison in Coalinga to set up a face to face with Tyler Derby. He was pouring coffee when he got Rennison's text.

> Good to go this week, tomorrow if you can make it. Derby is willing.

Bill slapped the kitchen counter in excitement. He'd get a confession out of him for the Stacey Mandel murder; he knew he would. He was searching in the fridge for his hazelnut creamer when he heard a loud thump against the slider to the yard. Outside a swallow had crashed into the glass, breaking her small neck. She lay dead on the pavement. He opened the slider and scooped her up in a paper towel. He thought of Min Sun-Hee, who had her neck broken like this tiny bird. He felt it was a sign.

Bill opened his laptop and ran another background search on Alan Musselman. He hadn't discovered anything significant the day before. Musselman was indeed a writer. He'd had work published in several magazines, and he'd written two picture books for kids. He'd gone between Los Angeles and Sedona for the past decade, and when Sun-Hee was killed, he was in college in Vermont. But he had relatives in Los Angeles, and he could've been in town at that time. But he had never worked as a welder of any kind, and he never had an address in K-Town. He wasn't fitting into the Min Sun-Hee murder, but Bill was certain he was somehow involved.

His head hurt like hell again. He took four Advil and washed them down with black coffee. He was starting to get the headaches several times a week now, used to be once or twice a month. And he was tired all the time. On the fridge, he saw the card for the appointment Cassidy had booked for him with Dr. Baruch, a neurologist over at Saint Joe's. He didn't need a special head doctor, he'd told Cassidy, but she insisted. He just had headaches. He was older; he'd had a very stressful life. Headaches were normal in guys his age.

Bill had looked around Musselman's yard the previous day. He saw boxes stacked inside the house, through the living room windows, which didn't have drapes up yet. In the yard, he'd found a bicycle, a small trampoline, and a treadmill. Bill had tried the back door, but it was locked. He'd reviewed the Min Sun-Hee file and saw that Tom Britt left the area not long after Sun-Hee's death, another suspicious move. Bill couldn't find any trace of him after that, no death certificate, no change of address or work history. It was as if he'd vanished in a cloud. Bill figured that Britt probably changed his name and wiped his record clean. Which meant he could have become Alan Musselman and reinvented himself.

He knew it seemed crazy. But he had been a detective for years, and he had a sixth sense, and it told him that Musselman was a creep. If he hadn't done Min Sun-Hee's murder, he'd probably done something else. They always had. On his way to the gym, Bill would leave the swallow at Musselman's door, just to let him know that someone was onto him.

Ethan Acevedo finished an early lunch at Mario's Peruvian Restaurant, where they always comped his food and gave him an Inca Kola for the road. He'd had the *saltado de camaron*, his favorite dish. Given his status as a Metro Unit cop, he had a patrol car to himself, no partner today. He made sure he always had one or two days a week alone, so no one was around to see what he was up to. He had lingered over his lunch; it was time to work, but he was close to Beachwood Canyon and needed a little stress release.

He pulled up outside Eden Balcomb's apartment, a retro fourplex with a large avocado tree outside. He saw her car and put on his flashing lights and siren, just to startle anyone who might be around on this quiet residential street. Eden's face appeared at the window, and she waved at him. He left the car double-parked and headed inside.

"Hey, baby girl," he said when she opened the door.

"Hi, honey. I didn't know you were coming by," she said with a weak smile.

"I have a little time and wanted to blow off some steam with my favorite lady," he said, stepping in and pushing her up against the wall, his body pinning her like a bug. Her eyes grew wide with surprise—she didn't expect him, and that was the way he preferred it. She was one of several women he kept on a hook, not for real relationships but for sex. He was aware that she had a thing going on with Bill Clarke, but he didn't care who she fucked as long as she fucked him when he wanted it. Like right now. He'd arrested a whacked-out junkie over on Gower earlier, and the guy fought back, getting Acevedo's blood going. The junkie had to be transported to the nearest hospital when it was over, but Acevedo still needed to vent, to release that pent-up fury that pulsed through him, like a jolt of hot electricity from a bad outlet.

He pinned Eden's arms against the wall and felt her going limp, her body falling into his. He kissed her hard and bit her lip just enough to draw a bead of blood. He tasted it on his tongue as it probed her mouth, forcing her lips open. She let out a little whimper, and he reached down to undo his zipper, then under her skirt to pull her panties down. He felt the thin fabric rip in his fingers, and she squirmed to get away.

"Those are new—I just got 'em," she complained, breathing hard as she tried to shove him away.

"I'll get you new ones," he said, pushing her legs apart with his feet, leaning against her.

"C'mon. Not now, baby . . ." she said.

She wasn't wet enough for him to slide in easily, but he pushed hard until she gave in with a yelp of pain. He took her right there, against the wall, with her front door half open. He slammed into her body, her head hitting the wall with each thrust. She said nothing, just rocked against him until he released. He pulled out and felt the warm liquid running down her wobbly legs as she tried to steady herself.

Her lip was starting to swell. She felt sore and raw inside. He'd hurt her, again. She didn't like it this way, but he wasn't a guy she could make date plans with. He wasn't one for concerts at the Hollywood Bowl or dinners out, but he was as hot as hell, in her opinion. She knew he had a lot of women after him, so she felt it counted that he chose her, even for this kind of rough hookup. It was like her mother always said back home in Virginia: *A girl must keep all the balls in play until a fellow puts a ring on her finger, and sometimes the dark horse comes through.* Eden pushed her thick hair out of her eyes, several strands sticking to her damp forehead.

"Have you eaten yet, babe? I made some killer risotto," she said.

CHAPTER ELEVEN

Cassidy was taken off patrol with Riley for the rest of the week, as interviewing Whitty was the priority. Riley was assigned another partner, and after the first interrogation, Cassidy met with the detectives and Joyce Ramsey.

"You did fine, Clarke. It was the first day. This is a process with guys like Whitty. You'll go in and talk with him again this afternoon. We need to get a lead on his partner," Ramsey said.

"You can't let him get the upper hand and disrespect you like he did. Talking to you like you're his girlfriend or something. He gets off on that garbage," Barrera said.

"I know. I was just thrown, I guess. I didn't know what to expect," Cassidy explained.

"You're the authority in that room. You've got to maintain that," Barrera insisted.

"Stay around the station. I'll let you know when he's coming back in," Ramsey said.

Ramsey saw that Cassidy was insecure about questioning Whitty, but certain she'd be able to pull it off. She had the sense that Cassidy Clarke was aiming much higher than being a patrol cop. They shared that ambition, and it would be good for Ramsey to have a trusted protégé to mentor and guide. Janice Sanders had been that for the past few years, but now the detective was embroiled in a harassment lawsuit against the department. Even though she knew Sanders had valid complaints, there was no way Ramsey could speak up and support her. She was a commander now, with her eyes on the top job. She had to protect the department at all costs.

For now, Cassidy had to cut her teeth on a murder interrogation, but Whitty would talk. Ramsey had seen countless guys like him in her career, just bursting in their sociopathic narcissism to show everyone how smart they were. And they always slipped up. They had a much better chance of pushing Whitty with a pretty, young female cop. Even better if she was nervous and he got off on it. She was just the audience losers like Whitty craved, and when he felt confident, he would make the fatal mistake.

"The guy in apartment 4B, did he have a girlfriend or any other regular visitors?" Barrera asked Thuy Pham, a petite Vietnamese woman who lived next door to Whitty in the run-down, motel-style building on Argyle, just above Franklin. She was wearing a demure sundress, but behind her, inside her apartment, Postiff saw a handful of very young women, dressed provocatively in mini shorts and skirts with crop tops. They were clearly sex workers, and Postiff figured that Thuy was their boss, working out of the apartment or nearby streets. They were bored, scrolling through their phones as a television blared a talk show from the VIETV network.

A few streets up the hill, there were expensive vintage homes built in the 1920s, but behind the strip mall that housed Alberto's Donuts and the Lock Ninjas, the scrappy apartment buildings were fortified with iron fencing that enclosed the properties like a cage. There were multiple signs posted warning that they were closed to nonresidents, which meant the buildings were known for drug deals and prostitution. Thuy Pham was so unintimidated by their presence, Postiff figured that she had cover from someone in the LAPD. It wasn't hard to guess what the trade-off was.

Thuy shook her head at Barrera. "No, Mr. Ron don't have no girlfriend. He never has anyone over. No friend, no family."

"No roommate? You haven't seen him with a male companion over here?" Barrera asked.

Thuy was vehement, crossing her arms. "No, no one comes here."

Thuy was the manager of the building and opened Whitty's door when they showed her the warrant. They entered while she stayed in the doorway, keeping a close eye on them. The place reeked of stale marijuana smoke but was otherwise very neat and organized. It looked as if it had been recently cleaned by a professional service; there were fresh vacuum marks on the thin carpet.

"Someone beat us to it," Barrera said.

"Maybe the partner, the guy who this lady's never seen before," Postiff agreed sarcastically.

He turned to Thuy, impatient. "You're sure you've never seen a guy over here? Does Whitty always keep his place this neat?"

"I don't know how Mr. Ron lives. I don't come into his place," Thuy replied impassively.

"She's tough, not giving an inch," Postiff whispered to Barrera.

"You have to be when you're running hookers right in between Gelson's and the Hollywood Bowl. I bet half of them are underage," Barrera muttered.

They opened all the closets and found Whitty's clothing hung properly, his T-shirts and underwear folded inside drawers. The laundry basket was empty; any hope of finding clothes he might have used in the attacks was dashed.

"Has anyone been over here to clean in the past few days? Any service or cleaning lady?" Postiff asked.

"I don't see anyone," Thuy said.

Postiff rifled through the dresser, the storage boxes under the bed. Serial killers often took souvenirs from their victims, macabre mementos to help them recall the crimes in vivid detail. They knew that both Jennifer Dale and Christy Cline were missing jewelry that they never took off: a rose gold charm bracelet and a Turkish gold ring. But there was nothing in the apartment that fit that description.

"This is a waste of time. It's been wiped clean," Barrera said.

"What about the security cameras outside? Do you have the video footage?" Postiff asked.

"They're just for show. They haven't worked in a long time," Thuy said.

She closed the door behind them and locked it. In the doorway of her apartment, several girls hovered, watching in silence. As they passed, Postiff noticed one of them wearing a bracelet that matched the description of the one missing from Jennifer Dale's body. When he stopped to look at the girl, Thuy pushed her inside the apartment and shut the door.

"I'd like to speak to that girl," Postiff said.

"She's busy. Can't talk to you now," Thuy said.

Postiff stepped in closer to her. "I don't know who has your back, but if you think they're going to protect you for interfering with a murder investigation, you're wrong, Miss Pham. You'll be arrested, and then vice will check out this business and speak to these young ladies about the work they do for you."

"They're maids. They clean houses," Thuy said, with fading defiance.

"I bet they do. If I need to go get a warrant to search your place and talk to each of these girls, I'll do it. I'll be back here within an hour, and you'll have to produce every girl I've seen here today or face more charges. Is protecting Mr. Ron worth that to you?"

Thuy Pham glared at him, her animosity simmering. She opened the door and barked an order in Vietnamese to the girl with the bracelet, who quickly jumped up and came outside.

Postiff gently took her wrist and inspected the bracelet. It was a match to the one they had seen in numerous photos at Jennifer's house. He took several photos of it before sliding it off her wrist.

"Who gave you this?" he asked. The girl's eyes darted to Thuy's face. The older woman nodded and looked away.

"Mr. Ron gave me this. A few days ago."

"Ms. Pham, we need to speak to all of the young ladies in your residence," Barrera announced. Thuy Pham went in, closed the door, and then came out a moment later, pushing all the girls in front of her, lining them up along the railing of the second-story walkway.

As Postiff and Barrera began interviewing all the girls, Vithu sat on the floor behind a locked bathroom door in Thuy's apartment. On his lap he clutched a small tackle box. He remained quiet and confident. They didn't have a warrant for his sister's apartment; half an hour ago they didn't even know the name Thuy Pham. If they got a warrant, he'd have more than enough time to take off and hide out. It was stupid of Nonglak to wear the bracelet Whitty gave her. He told Thuy to use only Vietnamese girls, but she had taken on a couple of Thais also, citing some regular customers who preferred them.

Now Nonglak had caught the attention of the detectives, and they would dig for everything. Lucky for him, he had taken Whitty's stash of trophies out of the apartment after Thuy and the girls cleaned up, tossed it in with his own. He opened the tackle box. It was a standard two-tray style, with an open space below and a row of small storage spaces on the upper tray. Whitty's things were in a Ziploc bag. Through the plastic he could see the gold ring he took from the first girl. The chain had broken during the attack, so Whitty just scooped it off the floor as they left.

Vithu's treasures were spread out because he had so many. Each storage space contained multiple items. Some had come all the way from Vietnam, like the mother-of-pearl hair clip from Tuyet in his sixth-grade class, who had disappeared one rainy afternoon. There were rings from two girls in the Philippines, one so hard to get off that he had to cut through her finger. But she didn't know—she was already dead, so it wasn't even very messy. The blood had started to pool at the back of her body, no longer running through her veins. He ran his fingers over the items with a slight smile. So many of them, shiny and glittering. He liked shiny things. He waited for the detectives to finish and leave. He was not worried. No one had even mentioned the girl from the Saint Felix yet. She would be waiting for him to return. He hoped they would be done soon.

Alan Musselman came home to find a dead bird outside his front door. There was no sign that the bird had flown into the door by accident; it looked as if someone had placed it there. Inside, he checked his security cameras. He'd started using them at his last rental in the Hollywood Dell. A disturbed guy lived with his elderly parents up the street, and he'd wander around naked sometimes, using a mirror to catch the reflection of the sun and shine it into the eyes of people in their homes. Who would then see a buck naked guy standing on a hillside, waving at them. Alan had been unpleasantly surprised by him several times.

Now, on the camera footage, he saw his neighbor Bill Clarke approach his house with something wrapped in a paper towel. He bent down to leave it outside the front door. It was the dead swallow. Musselman hoped Chatsworth would be quieter than the Hollywood Hills. He had a deadline for a book that he was stuck on; he just couldn't get the story to work the way he wanted. He'd felt that maybe the naked mirror man had caused him too much distraction, so this quiet street in Chatsworth seemed perfect. But now he had a cop next door who left dead birds at his house, for what reason he couldn't imagine. He'd known the guy was weird yesterday when he came and hung around, asking questions about Alan's life. He picked the bird up in a paper napkin and put it in his freezer as evidence, in case he had to call someone about Bill Clarke. Maybe he wouldn't bother to unpack. Maybe he'd been wrong about how bad it was to have an exhibitionist up the street. Maybe a nutcase cop was worse. Much worse. Because how do you call the cops on a cop?

It was late afternoon when Ramsey tapped Cassidy to do a second interview with Whitty. Barrera and Postiff had just returned to the station and given them the update on Thuy Pham and Whitty's apartment.

"There's something off with it, not just the apartment but with the landlady, who I suspect is running hookers in Hollywood," Postiff said to the group assembled in Carbone's office. It was Ramsey, Barrera, Cassidy, and two other detectives, Jimmy Fort and Nelson Foster, who were working the case.

"She's definitely running hookers, but we might have to go back and get more from her in the next few days, so we didn't move on that," Barrera added. "She's protecting Whitty for some reason. Maybe she has a thing with him, who knows? But the place was all cleaned up."

"The first victim's boyfriend remembered that she had been getting strange phone calls in the weeks before she was murdered. Hang-ups, in the day and at night, silence but someone was on the line," Foster said.

"Christy Cline's boyfriend just remembered this now? Three weeks after she was killed?" Ramsey asked.

Foster shrugged. "According to him they were kind of on the outs, taking a break, whatever that means. Said it made him queasy to think about, and it gave him insomnia. I think he just didn't want to be involved until we circled back to him."

"Great boyfriend. She gets slaughtered, and he doesn't want to 'get involved' because it upsets his tummy and nap time. What are these losers made of?" Postiff said in disgust.

"Bill Clarke's notes said that Jennifer Dale had been getting weird calls as well, same kind of thing," Barrera said.

"How are they getting access to the victims' phone numbers? They can't just be picking them by sight. They have some way into their private information, and Whitty doesn't strike me as some brilliant hacker," Cassidy said.

The older detectives looked at her dismissively; only Postiff engaged with her.

"Not sure. But someone knows how to jam the internet signals. It's made the cameras malfunction at every crime scene. It's deliberate, and someone could do it from a laptop in a car parked up the street. So maybe he's got skills in that area."

"Or his partner does," Cassidy ventured.

"We've checked his phone records. No calls to any of the victims, but he's sharp enough not to use his own cell phone. He probably has those burner phones. But he's getting that information somehow. His work history is all off-the-books handyman stuff, local, word of mouth, paid in cash so there's no record. We got a couple of checks from older people who hired him; we're talking to them tomorrow," Postiff said.

"What's his social media like?" Cassidy asked.

"We gave it the once-over, but we've been focusing on talking to people on the ground," Barrera said. It was obvious he didn't want to include Cassidy and didn't welcome her suggestions.

"I'll send it over to you this evening," Postiff said quietly to Cassidy. Barrera and Fort shot him a dirty look.

Ramsey read the room for a beat, then said, "Gentlemen, you need to keep Officer Clarke up to date on all these developments. Not just minutes before she goes in to talk to Whitty, but over the course of the day as you gain information. She needs to prepare; she needs to know what you know as soon as you know it. This is not a power struggle. Whitty won't talk to any of you, and he will speak to Officer Clarke, so we don't have a lot of options."

"He only wants to talk to her because she's a new boot. He's playing her," Barrera complained.

"For now, but he will make a mistake, and we'll get what we need. The main thing is to keep him talking without a lawyer present. So, all of you, put on your big boy pants and start sharing information with Officer Clarke in real time!" Ramsey ordered, clearly fed up with their pushback. Barrera, Fort, and Foster were silent, but their frustration was palpable. Only Postiff took the commander's directive in stride. He wanted information; he didn't care who got it, like he'd told Cassidy earlier. Right now, he was the only man in the room she respected.

Cassidy looked at Pete Barrera, who she'd known her whole life. He was like a second father to her, but in this moment she saw that he was just a territorial, angry old man who resented her, who could be supportive and kind only as long as she stayed in her place and didn't do anything that threatened his ego. He wanted her to fail at the interrogation. She'd be damned if she'd give him the satisfaction. She had to figure out a way to get to Whitty. It may not happen today, but she would do it soon.

"Are you ready, Officer Clarke?" Ramsey asked.

Cassidy stared hard at Barrera, who kept his eyes averted.

"Bring him in," she said.

CHAPTER TWELVE

Whitty shuffled into the interview room, cocky and full of attitude. His earlier outmaneuvering of Cassidy had boosted his bravado. She entered and took a seat across from him. Now that her suspicions had been confirmed—the detectives weren't on her side—and that Ramsey had twisted them into submission, Cassidy felt a surge of adrenalin. Her competitive nature kicked in, and she wanted to beat Barrera, Foster, Fort, and all the others at their own game, and she didn't care how she did it. She wanted answers from Whitty, but she had to figure out what he wanted, and more importantly, what his idea of winning was.

"Hello, hello, Officer Clarke! They told me it's time for us to chat again," Whitty said.

"That's right."

"I guess all of you've been finding out everything you can about me, right? Digging into my background, my history?"

The background search on Whitty had come up thin. He served briefly in the military until he was discharged, deemed unfit to serve due to his aggressive and antisocial behavior. He'd bounced around the Pacific Northwest and Arizona before landing in California. He had multiple arrests for petty crime, a handful of assault charges, one attempted rape. But it had been woefully empty of anything resembling the violence and depravity of the most recent murders. Either he had recently escalated, or he had gotten away with such crimes for years by picking victims that would not generate widespread investigations.

Cassidy suspected the latter. She looked at him without responding for several beats.

"Yeah, we've looked into it, what there is. Mostly it's just the typical loser stuff: transient lifestyle, constantly moving, a string of bullshit crimes. Not anything very daring or impressive," she said. "Even the military service ended with a crappy little designation: deemed unfit to serve."

Whitty's eyes narrowed. His cracked lips were wet with saliva at the corners of his mouth. Cassidy could feel his fury starting to build. She was surprised that he was so easy to trigger.

"It doesn't say that! I had asthma—that's why they let me go!" he retorted.

"Right. You know the military can't meet its recruiting requirements? No one wants to join, so they'll take anyone. But not you, evidently."

"Sergeant Lewis was unhappy when they discharged me. I was an asset to the army, he said."

"Really? Maybe so. They like people who can't think critically, you know? The dumber the better. Easier to manipulate," she said with a smile.

"Kind of like cops," he shot back.

Cassidy laughed. "Good one. But it doesn't apply to me."

From the observation room, Barrera watched the video feed in dismay.

"What the hell is she doing? She's going along with him, giving him too much power again."

In the interview room, Whitty leaned in toward Cassidy, as if they were meeting for the first time at a bar.

"Why're you acting this way with me, Officer Clarke? You're trying to provoke me again, aren't you?" he asked softly.

Cassidy chuckled. "Maybe I am. I don't know. There's something about you that makes me just want to fight back, you know?"

Surprised, Whitty's eyes sparkled with acknowledgment. "I knew that! I knew that when we were in the alley together. You're the kind that likes a good fight, am I right?"

Cassidy just looked at him, a faint smile on her face. She was figuring out how to push his emotional buttons, but she also needed answers.

"Maybe. Look, Whitty, it's been a long day for both of us. Just give it up. It'll go easier for you if you give us your partner. The girl you attacked near Bronson Canyon survived and confirmed there were two of you."

Whitty's eyes moved back and forth nervously. He hated that the little blond had survived and given them his description. He could see her face, fighting back at him on the floor of that sunny kitchen.

He crossed his arms and said, "I don't know anything about that girl."

"She knows you. She said the other guy held her down while you attacked her. Obviously, you're the main guy, but what's his story?"

Whitty looked away and chuckled.

"You're doing it again, rushing things that should go nice and slow, Officer Clarke. This is the getting-to-know-you phase. What's your favorite food?"

"What do you think he's doing out there now? You told me you're the alpha type, but maybe that was a lie? Or maybe it's the other way around? Is he the one who understands technology, how to make the cameras malfunction? That was pretty tricky. Is he the smart one?" Cassidy prodded.

Whitty looked at her with such unbridled hostility, it felt like a blowtorch coming at her across the table, but he simply shook his head. "You need to answer my questions if you want me to answer yours, pretty lady."

Uncertain, Cassidy stalled for time. She didn't want to give in to his attempts to connect with her personally; she wanted to assert power and control, but Whitty wasn't cooperating. In Carbone's office, Barrera bolted in frustration. A moment later, he burst into the interview. He slapped his hands on the table and leaned across to Whitty.

"Look, asshole, we've got you on this. No way out. DNA doesn't lie. We can proceed to the DA without anything else. This is your chance to tell us who your accomplice is and make it better for yourself in the long run. Enough of this bullshit!"

Whitty sat back, unfazed by Barrera's outburst.

"I know you're all watching us on the camera, you and the other detectives. I like it when people watch. Do you, Officer Clarke?"

"Look at me, Whitty. *I'm* the detective on this case, not Officer Clarke!" Barrera growled at him.

Whitty looked at his nails, began picking at his cuticles. "But I don't want to talk to you, Detective Baloo. Has anyone ever told you that before? That you remind them of Baloo, the bear from *The Jungle Book*? No, I'm not talking anymore. Maybe I need a lawyer to loosen my tongue?"

Cassidy stood up and walked out, leaving Barrera alone with Whitty. If he was going to barge in and play tough guy, let him deal with it. She wasn't sure how much to give and how much to hold back with Whitty, and Barrera busting in hadn't helped. She doubted his strongman tactics were going to work.

She was on her way to Lieutenant Carbone's office when Ramsey came out to meet her.

"I'm sorry, commander. I'm trying to figure out the best way to deal with him, but he keeps getting the upper hand," Cassidy said.

"He has the upper hand. He can call 'lawyer' at any moment, and we're done. Barrera's right—we could go with what we have, but we know there's an accomplice out there. If that guy starts acting alone, we're still chasing down a serial killer. Whitty's not talking anymore. Go home, get some rest. We'll jump back into it first thing tomorrow," Ramsey said, patting Cassidy's shoulder in reassurance.

In the locker room, Cassidy changed into her civilian clothes, frustrated and angry at the way the day had played out. She didn't like failure, at anything. She texted her dad.

I need to talk to you asap about the Whitty thing

She got no response. Where the hell was her dad? The idea of him being out and about made her uneasy; he didn't have a deep bench of buddies to hang out with. He was obsessed with work that was now over, and she didn't know exactly who he would become without it. He needed that routine, the showing up, punching in and out. His mood swings had gotten worse in the past six months. She'd found him roaming around the house in the middle of the night, obsessing over small things. He had trouble concentrating. Without his job to keep the raw edges of his life knitted together, she worried that he might spiral. She'd have to stay on him to keep his appointment with Dr. Baruch next week. If it was CTE at least they'd have a diagnosis and a game plan, a way to get out in front of it, where she always wanted to be.

Maybe Carter was right and she had to step back, let her dad be a grown-up and figure it out on his own. She thought of the annoying Dr. Peterson, who had a point about her parentification and needing distance from her dad. Maybe she hadn't been ready to hear it when she saw him two years ago, but there was no way she could imagine that scenario. It seemed as workable as her riding a bus to the moon.

She still owed her mom a call. She felt a pang of remorse. Her mom always got the sloppy seconds of her attention. Looking back, she wondered how her mom had lived with the crushing loneliness of being married to her dad with a daughter who was a daddy's girl, with no interest in her mom's craft projects or traditional mother-daughter activities. A kid who preferred toy guns and takedowns to Bratz dolls and the Barbie Styling Head, with her strange synthetic hair.

As she left the station, she ran into Postiff, who was obviously waiting to speak with her.

"Detective? Can I help you?" she asked formally. She wasn't in the mood to be told everything she was doing wrong with Whitty.

"Are you free for a drink? I'd like to talk away from the station," Postiff said.

"Sure, where?"

"How's Taix?" he suggested. "Musso's is too close by, might run into Fort or Foster. It's their hangout."

Taix, a classic French restaurant, on a busy corner in Echo Park, had been operating since 1927. It had retained its cool reputation through many shifts in social culture; while other vintage hangouts had gone under years earlier, Taix had clawed its way back to urban hipness by sticking to the basics: great food, classic cocktails, and an ambiance that was more old-time Hollywood than Influencer Chic. Musso and Frank maintained a similar vibe, but it was too well known, too recognizable by tourists and new transplants to the city.

"Okay, meet you there. What're you drinking, if I get there first?" Cassidy asked.

"Manhattan Perfect. House whiskey is fine," Postiff said.

"What makes it perfect? My dad drinks them, but I didn't know there was a difference."

"A Manhattan Sweet tastes like cough syrup. A Manhattan Dry tastes like death in a glass, and the Perfect, is well, perfect," Postiff explained with a grin that made him look like a teenager.

Cassidy walked out, smiling at Postiff's carefully curated persona. She didn't mind; she thought it was kind of cool since he had the goods to back it up. He'd been a patrol cop who responded to a school shooting in Sylmar several years earlier and walked in to disarm the shooter while other Metro cops waited outside for SWAT, afraid to face a fifteen-year-old with an AR15. Postiff had talked the kid down and taken his gun with no fatalities. He was also the only detective on the Hit Men case that seemed to actually want to help her.

As she turned onto Sunset Boulevard, she got a text from her dad.

on my way to coalinga to meet with derby. call me, we can talk about the whitty thing. XOXO binkie!

??? who are you meeting with?

Remember Tyler Derby? The guy we caught years ago? I'm talking with him about the cold cases

Which cold cases?
It's my new passion project! Check out the den, I pulled them all out!
Where'd this come from? I thought you were going to relax and take it easy
I'm not an easy type of guy, binkie. I'm gonna solve those cases, watch me!!

She tossed the phone into the passenger seat in exasperation. This was classic Dad. His mind bouncing around like a hacky sack, each new idea or impulse bursting through like a sun flare and propelling him in a new direction. It had been a few years since he'd gone up north to talk to Tyler Derby, who had terrorized the city with indiscriminate murders that fit no pattern. She knew other detectives sometimes got input from murderers—they'd even made movies about it. But Cassidy was uneasy about Derby; he was the kind of psychopath who thrived on attention and power. She thought he should be put away and forgotten by everyone, to wither in oblivion.

She knew she should call Carter to check in, but she didn't feel like it. She wasn't interested in how the dinner had gone with Doreen and Jim at the Water Grill, and after the day she'd had, she couldn't fake it. She was curious to see what Postiff wanted to discuss, and work was a higher priority to her. She had to face that now that she was actually on the beat. When she and Carter had met, during her gap year, it was exciting. She'd never dated anyone so well to do that he could afford to take her to the top restaurants or to jet off for a weekend getaway in another state. She'd been raised in a middle-class household and dated boys from Cal State who came from a similar background to hers. Carter was exotic and intriguing, not to mention drop-dead handsome. But she was starting to feel a shift away from him, and she wasn't sure how she felt about it, at all. Suddenly, everything in her life was moving so quickly. She was running as fast as she could, trying to catch up. And she hated that.

The sun was low in the sky as Bill drove the endless stretch of highway heading north toward Coalinga. Interstate 5 got you to San Francisco in five short hours, but it was a deadly dull passage through the dusty, forgettable towns where Bakersfield was the crown jewel, and even that was a good hour and a half from Coalinga. It meant driving through miles and miles of flat farmland that was rich with the smell of manure and vegetable crops, pistachio orchards, and the chemical dust from Granite Construction Company that produced tons of slurry seal, hot mix aggregates, and drain rock for the Central Valley.

Bill had made this trip before to speak to Tyler Derby, years after his arrest as the Angel City Killer. Bill and Barrera had hunted him meticulously, finally cornering him in the parking garage of an apartment complex on Sherman Way after he'd attacked seventy-five-year-old Ada Pneff in her living room. Pneff died, and Derby went away for life, no possibility of parole after being found guilty of a string of bludgeoning and stabbing murders.

Stacey Mandel had been one of those cases where everything pointed to Derby. A nice Jewish girl from the Valley, a senior at Northridge State University, Stacey had an active social life, a job in a popular Studio City restaurant. She was also in the wrong place at the wrong time when her killer ambushed her and dumped her body out by the Inglewood Oil Field. Two of his other victims had been taken and killed the same way. There were signature signs on Stacey's body that pointed to Derby's handiwork: the crude branding with a homemade iron tool, the half-moon string of bite marks on her lower back. They'd found the branding tool in his apartment after the arrest. Bill felt he had a shot at a confession since he knew that Derby wanted to transfer down south, away from Coalinga. Life inside was never easy for a rapist and murderer of college girls and old ladies.

Bill knew that for all Derby's posturing and violent misogyny, he was a coward at his core, like most murderers. Losers who had to resort to overpowering smaller, weaker, and sometimes elderly prey to get off and pump up their sense of power. To attack Ada Pneff, who used a walker and an oxygen tank, was the height of self-serving violence. Bill knew Derby had it rough inside, and having no hope of ever getting out must be torture for him. Bill smiled at the thought.

The highway was slowly swallowed up by darkness, the purple shadows falling on the fields until they were invisible, just the pungent scent of the farmland to let Bill know where he was on the route. Within a couple of hours, he'd approach the Harris Ranch feedlot, a stinking, putrid, overcrowded patch of land that housed the cattle that would become Harris Ranch beef and was enough to discourage you from ever eating a burger again. Beyond that, away from the nauseating smell, he would arrive at the Harris Ranch Hotel, the nicest accommodation near the prison. With its classic California Spanish architecture and comfortable rooms, it made a visit to Pleasant Valley State Prison bearable.

Bill felt the adrenaline surging through him; he knew he was going to get something from Derby. He could feel it—his sixth sense was humming. He knew how to play it; he knew what appealed to Derby's ego and how to balance the push-pull dynamic of getting information. He would call Cassidy from the hotel to discuss this with her. Somehow his day had gotten away from him with making the trip up north and reviewing his cold case files. But he knew what he would tell her, to help her deal with Whitty.

There was a game you had to play with suspects, drawing them in like a bee to a succulent flower with comradery and confidence, understanding their plight, just another regular joe caught up in something that was too much for him. And then you hit them with the sting that pinned them to the wall, squirming in futile recognition that they'd been played. He loved the thrill of it, the chase, the hunt, and then what he called the "matador moment," when the sword was driven into the beast's shoulder blades, dropping it to the ground.

Bill had arranged with Eden to drive out and meet up with him. He hoped he'd be done in one visit, but Derby could draw it out over a few days. Bill didn't mind. He didn't have to be anywhere special now that he was retired. When Eden came out, he'd have company and sex, and they could watch *Ice Road Truckers* on the hotel TV. It was going to be a great trip, maybe one of many as he became the Cold Case Closer, solving the open investigations that had haunted him and the department. He came up with that name for himself somewhere between Cholame and Parkfield, en route to Coalinga. Ramsey, McCall, and the others would regret that he was gone from the day-to-day workings of Robbery-Homicide. Barrera was good, but he was no Bill Clarke.

The road was pitch black, nothing visible on either side of the highway. It was like driving in a spectral nightscape, as if time could just open and swallow him whole and no one would ever know. He wondered if that was how Derby's victims felt, how all victims felt in the final moment of life slipping away from them. To do his job, he had to get into the mindsets of the murderer and the victim. Unsettling as it was, it was Bill's special territory. And he loved it.

CHAPTER THIRTEEN

"You're doing fine. Don't let Barrera throw you. He's just pissed and wants to prove himself now that your dad is gone," Postiff said, sipping his Manhattan Perfect cocktail at the Taix bar.

"What does he have to prove at this point? He's been there for donkey years!" Cassidy replied, waiting to drink her Horse's Neck, a Prohibition whiskey cocktail Postiff had suggested and that the bartender, who appeared to be a hundred years old, knew how to make without looking it up in the bar book.

"Your dad was the hotshot of the team. Barrera just has his balls in a twist over Whitty choosing you to talk to. But you need to stop second-guessing yourself. Your instincts are good when you play Whitty and get him off his game. Provoking him with the mild insults about his military service, the ladyboy exchange in the first interview was fire!"

"It just flowed, but I worry that I'm meeting him too much on his turf, like I'm buying into his game. Not maintaining authority as a cop in an interrogation. Like it was kind of a cheap shot."

"This fucker posed a victim at her vanity table with her throat slit. There are no cheap shots with this guy. It's not about authority; it's about information. Short of breaking the law, there's no wrong way to get it," Postiff said.

Easy for him, Cassidy thought. Like most men, Postiff had no idea what kind of shifting standards women faced in every field, but especially in police work. Can't be too emotional, too soft, or you're a weak female.

Can't be too tough, or you're an evil bitch. Can't emasculate your male colleagues, even when you are miles ahead of them in figuring things out. Got to let them save face, or they'll target you.

She had a good feeling about bantering and pulling power plays on Whitty. She felt the shift in him, the way he was on the edge of exploding and perhaps telling too much. He was unstable, with a huge ego, scared of and aggressively violent toward women, a combination that made him easy to provoke.

"But what if I play too much with him, let him get too familiar with me? You saw him, acting like it was a date," she said.

"Who cares? It's not a date. Let him act as if it is. Let him get caught up in how pretty you are, and he might just slip up," Postiff said matter-of-factly. "What I'm saying is, use every advantage you've got. Doesn't matter if someone says you're using your femininity or not being tough enough. That's just bullshit to obscure the fact that it's an advantage in this case. You've got something Barrera will never have, and it's more effective with a psycho like Whitty than all the tough-guy posturing in the world."

Cassidy nodded, feeling encouraged for the first time since the Whitty situation had begun. Maybe she could stop walking on eggshells, worrying if she was being too feminine, too accommodating to a murderer's ego. It didn't matter what Neanderthals like Barrera, Foster, and Fort thought. It mattered what Whitty gave up. It was a game of strategy, of psychological chess, of warfare. She took a sip of her drink; a Horse's Neck was shockingly refreshing, like Judson Postiff, who had just made a crappy day better.

Ethan Acevedo drove the streets of Hollywood, gauging if he had time to stop by Eden's for a quick fix. The hookup with her earlier today had gotten him going—the memory of her yelp of pain and the sound her head made hitting against the wall made him smile, and he felt himself stirring. He remembered a previous girlfriend, Marilise, who lived up the block from Eden. Even if Marilise never considered herself a girlfriend, that was how he defined her. They had met at a barbecue of a mutual friend, and he knew right away that she was exactly that he wanted. Smart, outspoken, pretty in that girl-next-door way. An elementary school teacher. He'd found her address by doing a police and DMV search, even if it was against the law technically, but no one really cared about that stuff. But the first time he showed up unannounced and blasted his siren and lights, she pulled back and got pissed. Said he couldn't show up at her house like that, and how did he know where she lived anyway?

After that, he tried to make her see that he wasn't anyone to be afraid of; he wasn't some creep. He was the kind of guy she wanted and needed. He started waiting outside her gym, which he discovered by following her. He even found a parking spot near her school, so he'd be sure to run into her. It ended badly, with her filing a complaint with the department and him getting a warning from his superiors to stay away from her. Every time he stopped by Eden's he thought of her, wondering if she was a lonely cat lady now, teaching a bunch of brats when she could've been with him, could've quit her job and been a stay-at-home mom. The thought of Marilise always gave him an extra dose of resentment that he worked out of his system with Eden Balcomb, who seemed to like it just fine. She never complained.

He drove past Eden's house and saw that her car was gone. She was probably working. He never really imagined her having any real life outside his hookups with her. He didn't see her as a person with any other function outside his orbit. He drove farther up Beachwood Canyon, toward Cheremoya Avenue, where Marilise lived. He cruised her apartment and saw unknown people through the picture window of her second-story apartment.

The curtains were different. Strangers lived there now. He wondered where she had moved to and why. Maybe she got married? Maybe she met someone she preferred over him. His mood shifted; his anger swelled. He still had her information on his home computer. He'd do a check on Marilise Travers later, to see what he could find out. It wouldn't be at work; no one would know. He turned back toward Eden's place, now annoyed that she wasn't there. Her windows were dark. He considered sneaking in and waiting for her to return, but she could be out with Bill Clarke or whoever else she ran with.

He thought of another woman he had out near Atwater, a divorced single mother who always had time for him, even if her kids were in the next room. Her teenage daughter was something to look at too. He could cruise through Griffith Park, do a cursory check for any drug deals or prostitution, and then swing by Atwater. Unless he made a bust, which had its own kind of thrill, even better if it was a hooker. He could barter for a warning over arrest, and who knew what she'd be willing to give up?

As she left Taix, Cassidy called Bill again. The traffic was heavy on Sunset; she figured there must be some big event nearby. Lately, it seemed like there was always a premiere or a record-release party or the launch of a new gallery. Bill answered in one ring.

"What's up, Binkie?"

"Are you in Coalinga yet?" she asked.

"Just checked into the hotel, Harris Ranch. I'm seeing Derby tomorrow," he said.

"I need to talk to you about the Hollywood Hit Men stuff."

"Pretty fucking amazing that you caught the guy in your first week! I knew you'd be a rock star!"

Cassidy sighed. She wasn't in the mood for his over-the-top projections.

"It was just a random call that ended in an arrest. He'll only talk to me, refuses to speak to the detectives, and I don't know what I'm doing," she said, merging onto the 5 freeway.

"Barrera must be shitting a brick over this!" He laughed.

"He is. Which doesn't make my job easier. I've talked to Whitty twice, but he ends up running the room. Ramsey wants me in there, she's got my back, and she told the detectives to stop stonewalling me. I need your advice. Everyone keeps telling me 'Talk to your dad,' but I haven't had a chance," Cassidy said.

"First of all, Joyce Ramsey doesn't have your back. She's watching out for herself, and that's all. Don't trust her; just play along. Second, you just need to get information out of this guy. Don't let the old dogs like Barrera intimidate you. You get that fucker to talk any way you can—you understand what I'm saying?" Bill advised.

"I gave up playing the tough cop since Whitty doesn't respond to that. The jerk flirts with me when I'm interviewing him."

"Then flirt back! Look at his victims—it's all about power over women. In that room, you have the power, so he has to come at you in a different way. Let him think he's getting away with something, that he's the top dog. Just keep him talking without a lawyer. That's your job. Waltz in there out of uniform and with your hair down. Act like you're friends. He'll pop a piston!"

"Out of uniform? Is that allowed?"

"Who cares? Say it got torn or it's covered in mud. Just make something up. Put it on a personal level with this guy—that's going to be his weakness."

"But how can I make it personal when he's a murder suspect?"

"Because you're a cop. Nothing's ever personal with us; it's a move in a game."

"I feel like all the pressure is on me to get him to tell us who his accomplice is. What if that guy strikes again before we get him? Everything is on me!"

"First off, it's not all on you. It's on the detectives leading the case. You have his DNA; he's been identified. There is nothing this guy can gain except fucking with your head and watching you squirm. That's his whole game. He wants to score a fourth-quarter goal when his team is at zero with one minute left. So, toy with him, make him feel like you're attracted to him, and he'll spill like an overflowing toilet."

"God! Act like I'm attracted to him? That's disgusting!"

"What do you care? As I recall you were a very good actress in that third-grade production of *Alice in Wonderland*. You were the Queen of Hearts, right? 'Off with her head!'"

"How do you remember stuff like that?" She laughed, embarrassed.

"Binkie, I remember your first word. It was *Dada*. And the first time you walked alone across the kitchen. When you scored your first goal in peewee soccer. Shall I go on?"

"Okay! Enough, Dad. I'm just stressed about catching Whitty's helper."

"Let's hope the guy's the beta and won't act without Whitty, but if he does, use that. Play it that Whitty isn't the big dog he thinks he is—the other guy is doing fine on his own. That should set him off. He'll want to impress you, show that he's the boss. You're his new plaything," Bill said.

Cassidy almost gagged. The thought of Whitty looking at her as a plaything was revolting.

"Okay. I'm back at it tomorrow. What time do you see Derby?"

"Ten o'clock, sharp. I think I'll get something."

"I hope so. Be careful, he's a sociopath," Cassidy cautioned.

"Don't I know it? I was at the autopsies of all his victims. Stay safe. That other Hit Man is out there. Text me before bed; let me know the house is locked up tight, Binkie. And remember, we're fighting the good fight."

Cassidy hung up as she headed to the 118 freeway toward Chatsworth. She felt better. Her dad could be infuriating and frustrating as hell, but he was a great detective. And in moments like these, when he was focused and present, he came through like a triple crown champion. She could tell he was resentful and hurt over Pete not keeping him in the loop; it had to sting to be cut off so abruptly. Her dad's advice was right on target. She would come up with her own strategy, push the boundaries to get Whitty to loosen up, use whatever advantage necessary. Barrera could piss off. In the partnership with her dad, Barrera was the anvil, Bill was the scalpel. And as she told Riley, she was her father's daughter.

As Cassidy turned onto her driveway, her phone pinged. Postiff had sent over Whitty's dating profile and social media information. She had a long night ahead of her. As she got out of her car, the new neighbor approached, carrying something wrapped in a paper towel. A tall, gangly guy with a mop of curly hair, he introduced himself.

"I just moved in next door, Alan Musselman. Do you have a moment to talk? It's about your dad."

CHAPTER FOURTEEN

At nine thirty in the morning, Bill pulled into the Pleasant Valley State Prison complex. It was a sprawling institution, housing inmates at all levels of security. There were even some celebrity types. Beyond the property line of all outbuildings and other support structures, there was nothing. Just the flat, hot valley with bone-dry soil that the wind carried off in haphazard clouds of dust, like a crowd fleeing a mass shooter. The dirt was deadly—it carried valley fever, for which there was no cure or vaccine, just a grab bag of treatments to deal with the debilitating symptoms.

Driving in, Bill saw the familiar tall metal fencing and the guard tower, overseeing everything that happened out of doors in the overcrowded powder keg. Inside the walls, in hallways filled with stacked canvas-covered cots, it was a high-octane game of survival for the violent, the mentally unstable, and the victims of traumatic brain injury who spent their lives in and out of incarceration. He was early; he wanted time to prepare. He'd spoken to Derby four times previously, on different cases. Quake Rennison, the warden, was expecting him. He'd reviewed the Stacey Mandel case the previous night. Derby would get news on his appeal in the next two weeks.

At a quarter to ten, Bill walked into the sterile, nondescript building that held the administrative offices of the prison. He passed through the metal detectors easily; he'd left his gun under the driver's seat. First, he checked in with Rennison, a bear of a man who resembled the skipper on the old TV show *Gilligan's Island.*

"Hey, Bill! Great to see you. Glad I can help out with this Derby thing," Rennison said, pumping his hand in a crushing grip.

"I appreciate it. Just retired and I'm hitting the ground running. I think Derby's good for Stacey Mandel, always have."

"Well, I know he's good for way more than he was put away for. I was surprised at how willing he was to speak with you. You know we usually have to play some cat and mouse with him," Rennison said, leading Bill to the interview room.

He'd arranged for Derby and Bill to speak across a table, not through the security glass, a small but important concession. An armed guard would be in the room at all times. Bill settled into his chair and waited. A few minutes later, Tyler Derby was led in. His blue prison garb hung on him; he'd lost a lot of weight since the last time they'd met. His birdlike gaze was the same, darting around the room, looking for any nonexistent way out. The guard stepped silently to the wall and waited. Derby sat down, dark hair turning to gray, his stiff, angular countenance unwilling to reveal anything.

"Hello, Detective Clarke. What a treat to visit with you again. To what do I owe the pleasure?" Derby asked in his signature raspy, almost-a-whisper voice. His skin had an unusual tanned appearance. Bill thought it could be Addison's disease.

"Just going over some old cases. I've retired, you know," Bill replied.

"That's nice for you, after so many years on the job."

"In some ways. But I'm interested in clearing some of these old, cold ones, you know?"

"I'm sure you are. Like maybe the Stacey Mandel case?"

Bill was surprised but didn't show it. Derby knew what he was after. They'd discussed it five years ago during their last visit.

"Maybe. But also Sun Min-Hee, Jerry Oliver, Patrice Scazzina, among others," Bill said amiably.

"That must be hard, isn't it? Leaving those questions unanswered? I would hate that. I like things all tied up nice and neat," Derby said, crossing his legs and leaning back in his chair. Bill noticed that his nails were trimmed and painted a rusty orange.

"I'm the same way. How's the food here these days?"

"Acceptable. They never serve the things I really like, of course. And they only have those dreadful off-brand cookies. I miss real Fig Newtons. I always thought of them like little pillows filled with figs. It's the cake part that sucks in the cheap ones. Too dry," Derby said with a sigh.

"Any decent movies?"

"Nah, just the safe, predictable stuff. I wish we could watch some of the old ones, with Gene Hackman. I like him as an actor. He died, right?" Derby asked.

They were talking in doublespeak, and they both knew what it meant. Rennison could set up a range of privileges for Derby if he cooperated. Fig Newtons, old Gene Hackman movies. The small things that made life in prison a bit more bearable. Maybe even a pack of unfiltered Camel cigarettes. A work detail in the library. But there were big things too.

"Did you ever see him in that old movie *The Conversation*?" Bill asked. "It's about a guy who wiretaps people for hire. And he gets a job that starts to get shady, like he thinks he's working for the good guy, but maybe he's not?"

Derby nodded. "I get that. Sometimes the ones who seem nice are really bad people. Like that Ada Pneff, the day we met in the parking garage. She looked like a nice old lady, but she used to poison the stray cats in the building. Just put it in their food. An evil old bitch but you'd never know to look at her," Derby said.

"You never know, right?" Bill asked.

"That's right. You and I look for different types of things in people. You look for the ones like me. I look for the ones who skate by and do their bad things in secret. We're very similar, and we both know how it feels good when you finally stop one of the bad guys, right?"

"That's right. Best feeling in the world!"

"Stacey Mandel was a cheater. Did you know that? She had a boyfriend at college, and she was cheating with a guy from her job," Derby said darkly.

"I know. I spoke to both of them back in the day," Bill said.

"She was a bitch to do that, wasn't she?" Derby asked.

"I suppose," Bill agreed.

Derby was circling, trying to see how much Bill would offer up if he held Stacey Mandel out like a carrot on a sharp stick. But Bill was in no rush, and he knew Derby was. They'd been going back and forth like that for almost an hour when Rennison ended the interview. Bill was confident; he knew this was a long game. Aside from a potential transfer to a different prison, Derby liked feeling needed and seen by people who lived outside the stone walls of Pleasant Valley.

Despite his penchant for murder, Derby was bright, articulate, and discerning. If they hadn't been on opposite sides of the law, Bill always thought they might've been friends. And Derby was right: Often the people who seemed pleasant and innocent were assholes. They did shit things, like Ada Pneff poisoning the cats. Bill left with a plan to come back and resume their visit the following day.

He drove the short distance back to the hotel. He'd have time for a swim before lunch. Checking his phone, he saw there was a message from Eden telling him she was on her way. He wondered if Alan Musselman had found the dead bird yet. He must've, and it probably caused him some alarm. Like maybe someone was onto him, after all this time.

Bill felt a sharp pain in the center of his forehead, emanating out toward his temples. He took the bottle of Aleve from the glove box; it was almost empty. He'd have to pick up more before dinner, since his headaches always seemed to get worse in the evening. He felt tired, and it was way too early in the day for that. He felt fatigued more and more lately. Probably just winding down to a different gear, now that he was retiring. At least that was what he told himself.

Cassidy woke to the sound of the gardener's leaf blower, like a freight train outside her window. She had fallen asleep sitting up in her bed, reviewing Ronald Whitty's social media accounts. Her neck was stiff from leaning against the headboard, and she was still feeling the effects of wrestling Whitty to the ground at his arrest. She stood and stretched, feeling older than twenty-three. She was going in late today, per Ramsey's order.

Whitty's social media wasn't as revealing as she had hoped. Mostly, it consisted of him following and liking Instagram models who posted half-naked, heavily filtered photos of themselves. He was more active on OnlyFans, where the content was more sexually explicit and pornographic. His subscription allowed him to interact, at a distance, with a range of women, which was lucky for them. He'd had an online relationship with an OnlyFans sex worker named DesiLara that consisted of messages and photo exchanges, but reading through the posts, Cassidy saw that it turned sour when Whitty insisted on an in-person meeting. DesiLara wasn't having it, and he became obsessive and belligerent.

He had no activity on Facebook; it really wasn't the platform for serial killers. Most posts were from boomers showing photos of their cruise vacation or grandkids, a lot of reconnecting with high school buddies. For Whitty, he needed interaction with women to keep his interest. He wasn't posting updates on his Thanksgiving-turkey preparation.

He had registered on several online dating sites, and his history showed that he was completely inept at communicating with women. He couldn't manage the social niceties of engagement, even in the rough-and-ready world of dating apps. He'd posted an old photo of himself, taken in his twenties, and listed his profession as cable/internet tech. She texted Postiff.

> does Whitty have any work history as a cable-internet installer?
> for any of the local companies?

He responded quickly.

no, why?
he has it listed as his job on a couple of dating sites fyi
thx I'll look into it

In the kitchen, she popped a Dunkin' pod into the Keurig coffee maker; with Bill out of town, she could skip the old-fashioned drip Mr. Coffee that he preferred. On the counter, wrapped in tinfoil and inside a plastic bag, she had preserved the dead sparrow. She cringed at the memory of Musselman in the driveway the previous evening, holding the dead bird in a paper towel, his phone with the camera footage of Bill leaving it at his door, like some kind of Mafia warning.

Musselman was exactly the kind of guy that her dad didn't like: educated, nervous, and solitary. He had none of the good-old-boy machismo that Bill identified with, but previously Bill would've stopped well short of actual harassment. He might've made snide remarks or speculated about Musselman's ability to get laid, but her father would never have left a dead bird on his doorstep. Alan Musselman was unnerved and feared that Bill was dangerous. It took over forty-five minutes to convince him that she would stay on top of it and manage the situation from now on.

She owed Carter a call but sent a text instead.

hi honey! Hope school is good i'm under water with the hollywood hit men case. Lots 2 tell u!

He replied immediately.

Great! can't wait to hear all about the bad guys! my folks are thinking of going out on the boat this weekend? My sister is coming up from san diego could be fun a day in newport?

She sighed, wishing that Carter was able to just chill and they could hang out doing nothing in particular. This was something she had only paid attention to in recent weeks, but it had become bothersome. With Carter it was always dinner out with a group of people, or his family sailing on their boat in Newport Harbor. Every invitation had to be accepted, even from people his parents' age that he barely knew, like Doreen and Jim of the hedge funds. Every long weekend meant a trip somewhere, up the coast or a quick flight to some outdoor activity in a nearby state. Mountain climbing in Arizona or hiking in Utah, skiing in Reno. His three sisters were the same way, as were his parents.

It was as if they could not settle and live in their own skin. If they kept busy enough, no one would have to look at or think about anything unpleasant. Or contradictory. Life had to be in perpetual motion, filled with conversation that skimmed the surface of any real substance, everyone smiling and dressed like models in a J.Crew catalog.

But now her real life had begun, and it meant dealing with harsh and serious realities. She had chosen a career in which she did not have the luxury of avoiding unpleasant things. When she tried to imagine them together long term, she came up against uncomfortable realities. She planned to be a patrol cop for a few years and then move up to detective, eventually into management, and perhaps make it to chief one day. That path would be filled with the daily fare served to police officers: inexplicable violence, murders that seared themselves into memory, sexual assaults that defied decency. It was a dark and dangerous place that she knew she could make a difference in.

Carter would get his law degree and go to work for one of his family's business interests. He'd add two days to every three-day weekend; he'd leave at noon on casual Fridays. He'd take two-hour lunches to pick up some new shirts at HUGO BOSS after eating at the Ivy. He would never worry about getting fired or doing well on a job review. She didn't want to think about it today. It was bad enough that doubt had started creeping in when she was with him. She wanted it light and breezy, the way it had been. She sent him a text reply.

That might work, got 2 see how this case plays out and if I can break away

He sent back a thumbs-up emoji. Of course he did. Carter was as uncomplicated as a new hammer from Home Depot.

Vithu carried the take-out bag from Pho 79 up the narrow stairway of the garage apartment adjacent to Thuy's building. She managed this building for the owners, who needed open apartments for the girls they brought over from Southeast Asia with promises of jobs and marriage. It was a transient situation; the girls never stayed long before they were sold off or set up in some kind of sex-for-hire scheme, bound by the debt they owed to the people who transported them. As such, no one noticed Vithu coming and going from the garage apartment. It was just a studio, with blacked-out windows and soundproofing on the walls. It helped having his sister next door to keep an eye on things.

He slipped into the dark apartment. His eyes adjusted, and he saw her, lying on the couch. The Saint Felix girl. It had only been two days, but she wasn't doing well. Getting her had been easy—she jumped into his sedan with the Uber sticker without noticing that it wasn't the car she'd ordered. Her friends had already left; she was the last one to get her ride, and she seemed disoriented. He assumed she was drunk, but she claimed that she was sick with diabetes and her blood sugar was low. He didn't believe her. She had lied about her name, saying she was called Ashley, but on her driver's license it said her name was Noelle. If she was sick with the diabetes, why was she drinking alcohol? Everyone knew it could make you worse. She was trying to make him feel sorry for her.

She had made it so easy for him, easier than he expected. She almost passed out in the back seat, and when he helped her up the stairway to the apartment, she didn't really know what was going on. He had chosen well. He didn't have to resort to any tricks to incapacitate her—she was halfway there when he picked her up. After rinsing her off in the shower, he had settled her onto the couch under a blanket.

He'd put the zip ties on her just for security, but she didn't seem well enough to try and get away. In fact, she had barely moved. He'd turned off her phone and removed the battery; then he tossed it into a trash bin behind a restaurant in Silver Lake. There hadn't been any mention of it in the news—Thuy was following everything now that Whitty was in jail. He felt sorry for Ashley-Noelle; she must have bad friends if no one was looking for her.

Now he had picked up some delicious soup for them, hoping they could have a nice dinner and watch some television. Perhaps then she would be ready to cooperate. He didn't like forcing things unless it was necessary. He pulled back the blanket and smelled the foul odor of urine. She had wet herself; she was groggy and barely awake. Maybe she really was sick with the diabetes, but whatever it was, it hadn't worked out the way he thought. How could he eat pho in a place that smelled of pee? He'd have to wait until dark, but knew he wasn't going to be able to keep Ashley-Noelle.

CHAPTER FIFTEEN

It was late morning, and Eden only had half an hour of driving left to reach the Harris Ranch Hotel. It took her over three hours from Los Angeles, but Bill had suggested her joining him, all on his own. She hadn't had to drop hints or insert herself into his plans like she usually did, which led her to believe that he was beginning to think of her more like a girlfriend again. Getting back with him was her number one goal, even if she kept a couple of other suitors around as insurance.

Ethan Acevedo was an occasional hookup, and she kept open the possibility of something more, even if he had given her no indication of that. Acevedo was like a wild horse, all sweat and hot sex, a good candidate for second position. She'd been through menopause, so she couldn't snare him in the old-school way by getting knocked up, but that might've worked if she'd met him sooner. Her mom, Lavinia, had been advising her to go that route since she was young.

Easiest way to pin a man, she had said, *especially if he thinks of himself as a good guy, and they all do.*

Olive Candle back home had landed a husband that way, and he was as rich as shit with family money. Olive didn't care that he slept around with her daughter's high school friends. She had the house, the new Escalade, and the membership at the Willow Oaks Country Club. But Eden didn't want the mess and bother of kids—she never had. She wanted to be the princess in the fairy tale, to have the undivided attention and affection of her man. When she'd started dating Bill, she'd been jealous of Cassidy until she realized that she was like a little grown-up. Cassidy always did her own thing, and it didn't interfere with their relationship at all.

Bill Clarke was the perfect guy for her, and if she played it right, she could get back with him and even end up living in the ranch house in Chatsworth. Cassidy was going to be moving on soon, now that she'd started her career and had that cute, rich boyfriend. Bill would need company and someone to cook and clean for him. She might even get a proposal if she was patient.

But she had to do something about Acevedo. He was getting too rough and unpredictable. She'd had to go see her doctor after one of his recent visits. He'd left her with a tear in her perineum, and she had to sit in a sitz bath three times a day for a week. Even her psychic, Mama Johanna, told her to get away from him, that he was dangerous and had a dark aura. But that was part of Acevedo's bad-boy appeal.

Maybe it was time to put her whole focus on Bill and do her best to reel him in. Her other boyfriend, Ted Stark, was actually someone else's husband, but that didn't bother her. They had a standing date every Wednesday at her place. She'd cook a fancy meal, and he'd pick movies to watch on Netflix after they'd had sex in her big king-size bed. He always said he would never leave his wife, but if that was the case, what was he doing at Eden's every week? Sometimes he even brought her a gift, a photo he'd taken, or a bottle of spiced rum, which she didn't drink.

Her dance card was full, which was a good thing for any girl. But Bill was the target she'd set her sights on. She pulled into the parking lot of the Harris Ranch Hotel. In her overnight bag she'd packed silk scarves to put over the lampshades, her mango-flavored gel lubricant, and a small bag of weed Acevedo had given her. She smiled to herself. Her mother always said that every girl needs to have a plan.

"Did you ever have any problems with Mr. Whitty when he did work for you here at the house? Any disagreements about the work or the payment?" Barrera asked Stanley Hughes, an elderly retiree with a silvery toupee that made him look like a television preacher. Stanley had hired Ronald Whitty to do work at his condo in Encino and paid him by check, which was one of the only paper trails they had to link Whitty to any recent work history.

"No, no problems at all. A nice fellow, showed up on time and fixed the doors on my kitchen cabinet. Also put in a new faucet in the bathroom," Hughes said.

"Did he have a helper or any other worker with him?" Postiff asked.

"No, came by himself that time. But we met another fellow with him, a little guy when he came to do the cable."

"Did he work for your cable carrier?" Postiff asked, his interest piqued.

Hughes looked embarrassed. "He spoke to my wife, told her he could get us a great deal on the cable and internet if we went directly through him. He said he had the equipment, and we'd have no monthly fee, just pay him $200 cash up front and he'd put it in. So, she hired him to do it. And it worked good too. He came with a helper that day. A small guy who had an accent. Vietnamese, I think. I heard him on a phone call, and it sounded familiar. I was in the service over there for two tours."

"Do you remember anything about his helper? Age or appearance?"

Hughes shook his head. "Not much. I was working from home that day in the back bedroom, so my wife handled it. She can't tell you anything unfortunately. She's over at Saint John of God in memory care. She doesn't even know who I am any longer."

Hughes managed a weak smile, but talking about his wife was hard for him.

"I'm sorry to learn that, Mr. Hughes. Thank you for your time," Postiff said.

As they left, Stanley Hughes followed them to the hallway. "Sorry I can't give you any more information. Am I going to get in trouble with the internet? It works great, and it's a help to me since I'm on a fixed income. With Evelyn out of the house, I watch Pluto most days to pass the time. It has all my old shows."

"There'll be no problem with the internet, Mr. Hughes. Don't give it another thought," Postiff reassured him.

Back in the car, Barrera said, "Bootlegged internet? Maybe that's how Whitty got access to the victims' homes, how they got on his radar?"

"Could be. Cassidy's the one who found it," Postiff said.

"Cassidy Clarke?"

"Yep. I sent her Whitty's social media profiles, and she found it on a dating app. He listed his job as cable-internet installer, and now Stanley Hughes confirmed it," Postiff said.

Barrera looked annoyed but said, "That was good work."

"Good work that neither of us caught. Guess she's a chip off the old block," Postiff added with a smile.

Barrera made a grumbling sound in his throat and hit the gas pedal a little too hard, causing the car to lurch forward.

The only other person who'd paid Whitty by check was a woman named Lilly Siples, who'd hired him to repair a fence to keep her dog from escaping. He'd wanted payment in cash, but she insisted on a check, for her records. Her dog had escaped a few days later and never returned. Knowing Whitty's character, Postiff was sure Lilly's dog had not simply escaped; Whitty probably had a hand in it since she refused to pay him in cash. He couldn't tolerate women saying no to him. But Postiff didn't mention it. Lilly Siples was battling Parkinson's and didn't need the extra distress about her lost dog being taken by a serial killer.

"I think we should talk to Thuy Pham, run a background check on her to see if she has any family here. Maybe Whitty's buddy is related to her and she's not covering for Whitty at all. Maybe it's closer to home," Postiff said.

"Good. Text Carbone to put someone on that. But I want to take a crack at Whitty first," Barrera said, pulling onto the 101 freeway toward Hollywood.

"Ramsey said Cassidy's coming in today at eleven to talk to him again," Postiff said, surprised.

"Ramsey's at a city council meeting, so I'm going to go in and talk with Whitty. We can't waste any more time with Cassidy. She's in over her head," Barrera said.

Postiff said nothing, shifting his gaze out the window. It was a bad idea, driven by Barrera's ego, but he was the senior homicide detective on the case. Postiff couldn't stop him, and if he called Ramsey to alert her, he'd be marked as a pussy and a snitch. He'd get dragged by everyone in Robbery-Homicide. He hated this part of the job. Hated the machismo and the power plays and the territorial bullshit that got in the way of the work. Whitty held the cards; Barrera wasn't going to get anything but trouble out of it, and Postiff would have to take the heat with him.

Whitty stared, not reacting to Detective Barrera's outburst, his attention on the vein in the detective's forehead, which was raised and purple. If he kept this up, he could have a stroke or an aneurism. Whitty thought it would be gratifying to see him collapse to the floor a moment after yelling and slamming his hands on the table.

"We're putting it all together, Whitty. How you got to the girls, access to their houses, information. And we're finding out about your little pal. Vietnamese, right?" Barrera prodded.

Whitty was surprised that they had found out about Vithu, but if they knew his name and identity, Barrera would've said it. Vithu and Thuy Pham were as slippery as anyone he'd ever met. He knew they were lying low and holding the line. If they gave him up, they'd get in plenty of trouble as well. Barrera was reaching.

"Where's Officer Clarke?" Whitty asked.

"Officer Clarke is busy in the field. She's got a regular patrol with her partner. She can't keep coming in here to play games with you."

"I think she enjoys coming in here to visit me," Whitty said.

"She's just a kid, Whitty. Younger than your victims," Barrera said.

If only you knew . . . Whitty thought, a small smile playing around his mouth. Detective Baloo the Bear didn't know about the middle schooler in Tustin. They'd never even found her body. Her photo was probably still up in the entrance to the local Walmart.

"I'm not interested in speaking to you, detective. If you continue with this, I'll need to have a lawyer present," Whitty said.

"Stop fucking with us!" Barrera shouted. Whitty remained stoic.

Joyce Ramsey and Lieutenant Carbone walked in to find Postiff monitoring the video feed from the interview room. He froze; Ramsey was back early.

"What's going on?" Ramsey asked.

Postiff answered stiffly, "Barrera is interviewing Ronald Whitty. I told him Officer Clarke was coming in this morning, but he insisted."

"Goddamn it . . ." she muttered.

"Go tell him we're back and the interview is over," Carbone said.

Postiff nodded and made the short journey to the interview room, feeling like a dead man walking. Ramsey was going to rip them new assholes for this; he didn't even want to imagine how fast it would spread through the detective squad.

He opened the door and stuck his head in. "Commander Ramsey has returned to the station. She'd like a word, detective."

Barrera looked like a kid who'd been caught stealing from the church collection plate. He nodded and stood up. Whitty's eyes followed him in gleeful anticipation.

"Looks like the Big Bear's in trouble! Is that what's going on, Detective Baloo? Let them know that when Officer Pretty Tits arrives, I'll be happy to chat with her, but I might need a day to recover from this," Whitty said with a laugh.

"Her name is Officer Clarke!" Barrera spat at him before he left to face the wrath of Joyce Ramsey.

Cassidy was leaving the house when she got the call from Postiff. She'd put the landline back on the hook and answered one call, but it was another reporter wanting to talk to her, and she hung up. Luckily, there was no voicemail on that line.

"I'm sending you all the stuff we got today. Whitty worked as a bootleg cable-internet guy, most likely with stolen equipment. We're checking to see if any of the victims used him. It would explain how he got access to them, how they caught his attention."

"Okay, thanks. I'll be there soon," she said.

"Check with Ramsey. Barrera went rogue, went in to talk with Whitty today, and it backfired. Ramsey came back early, and we've just been reamed so badly, I don't think either of us will be able to sit without a foam donut for a week," he said.

"Wow, that was vivid, Postiff. Thanks for the visual," she said with a laugh.

"There might be a connection to the Vietnamese landlady at Whitty's apartment. It seems he had a helper on the bootleg cable jobs, possibly Vietnamese, so that could be our guy. We're getting closer."

He hung up. She opened Postiff's message to review his notes. He'd already sent her the whole file as an email attachment. She reviewed the crime scene photos again; they were particularly gruesome. Hard to imagine that smug asshole Whitty had done such horrific things to the three innocent women. She sent a text to Ramsey to confirm her interview with Whitty. Ramsey responded immediately.

You can come in at two. We're letting Whitty cool off after the Barrera incident.

She called her dad, and when he answered, she heard a woman's voice in the background.

"Dad? Are you alone?"

"Yeah, Binkie, I'm on my own."

"How'd it go with Derby?" she asked, ignoring his bad attempt at deceit.

"Good. We're meeting tomorrow morning as well. He brought up Stacey Mandel all on his own," he said.

"Great. You want to tell me what happened with Alan Musselman and the bird?" she asked.

"Oh, you found out about that?"

"He was waiting for me when I got home last night. What's going on with you? You're like Tony Soprano!"

"I think he's got a connection to the Min Sun-Hee case, back from when you were a kid. He looks too much like the neighbor who I always suspected. The guy had a weak alibi, and then he disappeared. This Musselman guy reminds me of him," Bill said.

"Yeah, and you remind me of Billy Bob Thornton, but you're not him."

"You mean the *Sling Blade* guy? He's a pothead!" Bill protested.

Cassidy could hear the manic quality in his voice. She knew that his focus on Alan Musselman had no basis in fact or even real possibility. It was a symptom of his unsteady mental state. She took a deep breath; the conversation was escalating too fast, and he was too far away for her to trust that he would stay on an even keel, especially with the high emotional stakes of another meeting with Tyler Derby.

"Dad, you can't just act on these crazy impulses. Alan Musselman has no connection to that old case. He's a nerdy writer who just wants peace and quiet. He put in cameras and has footage of you leaving the bird, which can be viewed as a threat. Do you want to get a visit from the Devonshire cops? Is that how you want to wind down your career?"

"I'm just trying to solve a cold case!"

"By going after an innocent neighbor? You have an appointment coming up with Dr. Baruch, the neurologist. I'm going to have to tell him about this stuff," she warned.

"What? Like I'm losing it or something? Like I'm brain damaged and don't know what I'm doing?" he said, his temper flaring. "You say you'll have to tell him like I'm a little kid who broke the rules."

"Then stop acting like a little kid and stop breaking the rules!"

In the background, she heard a woman's laugh over the sound of the television.

"Look, Binkie, I don't want to fight. We both have a lot going on. Let's talk tomorrow when I get back, okay?" he said.

Cassidy felt the fight going out of her and remorse moving in.

"Okay, Dad. Drive safely coming back," she said.

"And look at my files in the den for Min Sun-Hee. You'll see what I mean."

As they hung up, she heard the woman again and wondered if they had call girls at the Harris Ranch Hotel. She knew he'd hooked up with some of the glamorous working girls in the hotels in Vegas. A lot of his detective friends did; she'd heard them laughing about it at a poker night several years earlier. She went into the den and surveyed the boxes her dad had brought out to begin his cold case investigations. This was another of his sudden, obsessive projects that he would throw himself into with manic intensity. She knew she'd find him up at two in the morning making notes, reviewing interrogations. There would be exuberant breakthroughs and then sinking disappointments. Dealing with Bill was like riding the biggest roller coaster at Six Flags, but she'd been on the ride her whole life, so she knew what to expect.

The Min Sun-Hee case file was in an open box. Cassidy poured herself a fresh coffee and settled into the couch to review the murder of a teenager fifteen years earlier. She opened her computer and did a background search on Alan Musselman. He would've been eighteen years old when Min Sun-Hee was killed in Los Angeles. He was living in Vermont, attending college at the time. He had nothing to do with Sun-Hee's murder. Her father was losing it.

CHAPTER SIXTEEN

Barrera pulled the Crown Victoria to the curb outside the apartment building of the first victim, Christy Cline. He'd been quiet since Ramsey had chastised him over the Whitty interview. Postiff knew that misstep was driven by his distaste for taking orders that elevated a new, young female officer to do a job that he felt was his. And she was Bill Clarke's daughter, to boot. Postiff saw it as something akin to a Greek tragedy for Barrera. He took a big risk, thinking he would come out like a hero, able to do what Cassidy couldn't and prove his point. Now, he just had humiliation and defeat to carry him through the day. But he'd stepped in it all on his own and had no one else to blame.

Christy Cline's apartment was in a 1930s Spanish-style courtyard with the front doors facing a common walkway separated by garden beds of cactus, agave, and other desert plants. Postiff and Barrera went to apartment G and knocked on the door. They had met the manager, Jettie Redd, when she'd called the police three weeks earlier for a welfare check on Christy. She was a fiftyish woman, petite and wiry, with a mop of frizzy fire-engine red curls that she wore scrunched up on top of her head. She'd vomited when they went inside and discovered the state of Christy's body. Now she opened the door wearing a pair of tiger print leggings and a T-shirt that read *No Uterus—No Choice*.

"Can I help you, detectives?" Jettie asked.

"Hello, Ms. Redd. I hope you don't mind if we ask you a few follow-up questions with regard to Christy Cline. Specifically, we'd like to know if Christy ever used a bootleg cable-internet setup at her apartment?" Barrera asked.

"I saw that you caught the guy, his DNA matches the victims. Is that true?" she asked, squinting at them from behind rhinestone reading glasses.

"We have a suspect who matches the DNA profile, and we think he might've been installing illegal cable-internet boxes," Postiff said.

"We had some of that here. Christy didn't do it, but some of the other residents did. The neighbor next to her, Kevin Butte, had a guy like that come out to put up the box. And I think Jocelyn Kittle, in apartment B," Jettie said.

"Do you remember if Christy had any interaction with the installer? Do you recognize him?" Postiff held a photo on his phone out to Jettie. She bit her lip, looking closely at the image.

"That could be him. I didn't pay much attention. But Christy got annoyed because the guy messed up her internet, and she came out and had some words with him," Jettie said.

"What kind of words?" Barrera asked.

"Asking him when he was going to be done, saying she needed her service back on for her work, that type of thing. She was kind of impatient, and he got a little spicy with her, but it wasn't anything intense. That stuff happens every day in the city, you know?"

"Did he have anyone with him?" Postiff asked.

"Yeah, a small Asian guy. Quiet, very unassuming. He was almost invisible."

"How about the security cameras? Any video from that day?" Postiff asked.

"Our internet was down, here and at a couple of other buildings. That happens a lot up here, nothing new," Jettie said.

They tried Kevin Butte's door, but there was no answer. Jocelyn Kittle cracked her door open with a security chain in place when they knocked.

"Ms. Kittle? We're the detectives working on Christy Cline's murder. We'd like to talk to you about your cable-internet installer," Barrera said.

Jocelyn was a heavyset woman in her seventies. Her face was flushed as she responded, refusing to take the chain off and open the door completely.

"I saw a photo of the fellow you arrested. It was the same man, the one who came to put in the service here," she said nervously.

"Can I show you a photo of him now so you can be sure?" Postiff asked.

She nodded, and he handed her his phone through the opening of the door. She looked at it and handed it back as if it were a burning piece of coal.

"That's him," she said, her voice breaking. "To think he was here in my apartment, and he hurt that poor girl . . . I just can't . . ."

"How did you get in contact with him?" Barrera asked.

"He left a card, stuck into the doorjamb. Offering a deal. We all got one."

"Did he have anyone else with him the day he was here?" Postiff asked.

"He had a helper. He was Asian, I think."

"Do you know his name?"

She shook her head, pushing the door closed even more until there was just a sliver of an opening.

"No, he didn't speak much," Jocelyn said. "I don't feel well, if you don't mind."

She closed the door abruptly. Postiff wandered around the courtyard. He hadn't been to this crime scene, because Christy was the first victim, before he replaced Bill as Barrera's partner. As he ducked under the yellow crime scene tape to inspect the windows, Jettie Redd stepped out to join them. Postiff noted that there was a dirt path and a ravine behind the building, a common feature in the hillside areas. It provided easy access with low visibility for someone who didn't want to be seen.

"Do you all have any idea when this yellow tape will be taken down? It's pretty creepy, and the owner wants to put the unit back on the rental market ASAP," she said.

"As soon as we close the investigation. We have another suspect who has to be apprehended," Postiff replied.

"The little Asian guy? He didn't look like he'd hurt a fly. He was so quiet and polite," Jettie said skeptically.

"Did you catch his name?" Barrera asked.

"Nope. He just skitted about here and there, helping the big guy," Jettie said.

As they walked back to the car, Postiff asked, "I wonder who's going to rent it, knowing that someone was murdered here?"

"I wouldn't. What if Christy Cline's ghost is hanging around, angry and wanting revenge?" Barrera mused.

"You believe in all that stuff? Ghosts and all?"

"Dude, I'm Mexican. Of course I do!" Barrera said.

"Let's hit Thuy Pham again, see what shakes loose."

"I'll text Carbone to put Foster and Fort on following up with the bootleg-internet scam with the other victims. I don't want those two jarheads talking to Thuy Pham. Whitty was probably set off by Christy getting pissed at him. He wanted to get Rosalie McTeer because she didn't flirt with him like he expected. This bastard kills women who don't treat him the way he thinks he deserves," Barrera said.

"Don't a lot of men get upset over that type of thing?" Postiff asked.

Barrera shot him a sharp look but said nothing as he tossed the keys to him.

"You drive this time, hotshot," he said. "How about Cactus for tacos? It's close to Thuy's place."

"Don't you ever eat a salad?" Postiff asked, hanging a U-turn to head toward Cactus Taqueria on Vine Street.

Cassidy read the Whitty update from Postiff, happy that the internet connection was paying off. It would be good to use in her next meeting with Whitty. Even better if they could get the identity of his helper and apprehend him. She texted Carter to let him know she had a free day and Bill was out of town, a rare invitation to hang out at her house. She packed her gym bag to get in a workout and made the long-overdue phone call to her mother in Wyoming. Cathy answered in one ring.

"Hi, honey! How's work? I didn't want to call and bother you," her mom said.

"It's fine, Mom. I'm working on a big case, and it's exciting but also a little intimidating."

"Intimidating? For you? I doubt that," Cathy said with a laugh.

"My partner and I happened to pick up a serial-killer suspect on a routine call, and now I'm the only one he'll talk to," Cassidy explained.

"I don't want you around someone like that, honey," Cathy cautioned. Cassidy didn't share much information; she knew her mom thought of police work negatively. She'd wanted Cassidy to pursue any other career rather than join the LAPD, and they had argued about it.

"It's not bad. And Dad is officially retired now. But he's working on cold cases."

"Of course he is. How's his health?"

"He's doing okay. Still the same kind of obsessive and hyperfocused thing that's happened before. Now he's sure our new neighbor is a suspect in a case from over fifteen years ago."

"Oh, dear. Is he seeing a doctor?"

"Next week. A neurologist at Saint Joe's. I hope he can give us some answers. Maybe medication would help," Cassidy said.

"Good luck getting him to take it. You'll have to go with him to the doctor, you know," her mom advised.

"I can't. I'll be at work. He'll have to go on his own."

"Do you think he will? Or that he'll tell you the truth about the appointment and what the doctor says?" Cathy asked, knowing the answer. Cassidy was silent. Her mother was right. There was no way that her dad would go if she didn't make him.

"I'll change my schedule," Cassidy said, trying to hide her resignation.

"How's Carter?" Cathy asked, shifting the subject.

"He's fine. Busy with law school."

"Give him my best. I know you don't want to hear it, but please consider moving out to your own place, honey. Bill's a grown man. You shouldn't have to do everything for him, and if you're living there, you'll have to," Cathy said.

"I know. I'm starting to see how hard it can be. Is that why you left him?"

Cathy considered the question for a moment, then said, "Yes, and a million other things as well. He's a good man, and he doesn't have a mean bone in his body. But he's all over the place emotionally, and he just doesn't think how his choices affect other people. He needs a mommy, a maid, a chauffeur, a bookkeeper, a cook while he's off chasing down bad guys. He's retired now. You shouldn't spend your youth being all those things to him."

"I know, I know," Cassidy said, regretting that she'd asked. "I should go, Mom. I've got a busy day ahead."

"Call if you need any help with your dad," Cathy said.

They hung up. Cassidy knew that her mom was wary and suspicious of her dad. Their marriage had been rocky and difficult, made worse by his obsessive nature about his work. Cassidy didn't want to hear from another person about how she should step back from her father, stop enabling him, let him solve his own issues. She knew in some deep part of herself that it was the truth, but she couldn't face the realities of it, not yet. As it was, comments like that just got on her nerves. She was locking up and securing the house when Carter called.

"Hey! Have you heard about the podcast?" he asked.

"No, which one?"

"The big one, *LA Murder Now* with that cool host. I listen to it all the time. Her name is Zelda Zed. She's huge, tons of followers, and she's covering the Hollywood Hit Men!"

Cassidy wondered if Zelda Zed was one of the people who'd been calling her phone incessantly all morning.

"I've never heard of Zelda Zed," Cassidy said.

"Are you shitting me? She's very big—lots of people follow her show. I've sent you a photo from her website."

A text arrived with a moody photo of a young woman with blue-black hair in a pixie cut. She looked like countless girls who frequented the nightclub scene in Hollywood.

"What's she saying about the case? How does she get her information?" Cassidy asked, her wariness growing.

"She must have an informant. She even mentioned you in yesterday's episode. It was way cool. I told everyone that you're my girlfriend."

Cassidy felt her gut tighten. The idea that a hipster podcaster with a made-up name like Zelda Zed was talking about her involvement in the Hit Men case made her feel queasy. Even worse that there might be an informant in the department.

"Thanks for letting me know," Cassidy said. "I'll check it out."

"You should be a guest on the show," Carter suggested.

"Right, and get fired in the first week of work," Cassidy replied.

"And yeah, I'm good to come out to Bonanza tonight. I'll pick up some Thai food, and we can Netflix and chill?" Carter said.

Cassidy smiled. "That was the plan."

An uncomplicated evening with Carter would be good. An easy movie, Thai food, and some sexual release would set her up nicely for the next day's work with Whitty.

As Cassidy pulled out of the driveway, she didn't notice a silver Tesla heading toward her. She didn't see the driver, with her blue-black pixie cut hairstyle, park outside Alan Musselman's house with a clear view of the Clarke home. Zelda Zed let the engine idle while she confirmed the information she had gotten from her source inside the LAPD. She had the right house. She cut the engine and took a long sip of her Starbucks London Fog specialized tea. She would just wait until Officer Cassidy Clarke returned so she could ask her a few questions about the Hollywood Hit Men.

CHAPTER SEVENTEEN

Thuy stood in the shadows of Vithu's studio apartment, the windows covered with foil, the air stuffy and foul smelling due to the state of the girl unconscious on his couch. The girl her brother called Ashley-Noelle was near death. Her body was clammy and cold; she was barely breathing. She had urinated on the couch and soaked it through, but Vithu was afraid to move her. He'd have to get a new one once they got rid of her, and Thuy would have to pay for it.

"Why didn't you drop her somewhere when she told you she has the diabetes?" Thuy whispered harshly at him.

Vithu stood in the doorway to the tiny bathroom, just a toilet, a shower attachment on the wall, and a drain in the cement floor.

"I didn't believe her. She looked drunk. I thought that was all," he whined.

"She's going to die here if we don't get her out," Thuy said.

"But what if they find her and she tells them everything?" Vithu cried.

"Then you do what you and Whitty did to the others. End it quickly," Thuy said. She didn't even blink. She was as steady as a level, not one bubble off.

Vithu nodded. Thuy always knew what to do. The cops had not been back to talk to her. Ashley-Noelle had turned into a disaster. She fell sick so fast, he wasn't even able to spend time with her, to see if she might be the one who stayed. She was sweating and vomiting and peeing herself and making a mess of everything. Thuy was putting a blanket on the girl when she got a text, and her expression turned sour.

"Nonglak says the police are at my apartment, the ones who came before," Thuy hissed at him.

They went to the window and pulled the tinfoil back ever so slightly. There was no movement in the alley that separated their two buildings, but then Barrera stepped out on the stairway and scanned the area. He didn't notice Vithu's apartment. It had a chain and padlock on the door, the windows blacked out. There was no sign that it was occupied. No one knew of his existence.

Thuy silently cursed the day she had given in to her parents and agreed to bring Vithu over with them. She had come to the US legally and had filed the necessary paperwork. Vithu had a serious criminal record in Haiphong. He'd been committed to a mental hospital. She had to get fake documents for him to come with them.

Now he lived in Los Angeles in a no-man's-land with no traceable identity. He had no Social Security number, no driver's license, no lease agreement. Thuy kept him afloat, and he got small jobs in the local community, working for cash. He helped to take care of an elderly Armenian lady with dementia, and he ran errands for the AP 13 gangsters. But he was always getting into some mess of some kind. The same kind of stuff he did in Haiphong with the girls. The things he did with Whitty.

Thuy managed several apartments on the block for the owner, Avi Bierman. Vithu lived in the tiny apartment over the garage of the building next door. Avi Bierman didn't know he was there; it was used for storage. If the cops went to see Bierman at his big house in Hancock Park, he might talk and tell them everything. He was a weak, stupid, fat fool, and he'd confess about how she brought the girls from Thailand to be maids, about the sex work and all the rest. Avi just wanted the money from the operation in exchange for the apartment space. She'd go to jail; she could lose everything she had built. Now Vithu and Whitty had led the police right to her.

She seethed with rage but kept vigil at the window, watching the detectives talking with the girls outside on her walkway. They all knew to keep their mouths shut or there would be big trouble, but Nonglak couldn't help herself sometimes. Thuy watched and waited. Tonight, they would get rid of the sick girl. The police would not find Vithu, and everything would be fine if they just stayed quiet and out of sight.

Cassidy showed up at the station ready to talk to Whitty, but Ramsey corralled her in the hallway.

"I would've called you sooner if I'd known, but Whitty won't talk today. He says he's not feeling well. The medical staff just went in to treat him," Ramsey said, exasperated.

"Is he really sick?" Cassidy asked.

"I doubt it, but we can't ignore it. He knew we had an interview scheduled. I think he just wants to mess with us, to keep us off balance."

"Okay, I'll check in with Postiff and Barrera," Cassidy said.

"I'll let you know if something changes."

Cassidy went to the detective division, where she found Postiff and Barrera digging into Thuy Pham's background.

"Hey. I guess you found out that Whitty isn't feeling well enough to be interviewed today," Postiff said.

"Lying son of a bitch," Barrera muttered.

"We're not finding much on Thuy Pham, the landlady. She came from Vietnam over twenty years ago, all aboveboard. No brother, son, or nephew that could be Whitty's helper."

"We spoke to the owner, a guy named Avi Bierman, lives in one of those mansions in Hancock Park where it's all Hasidic. He says he knows nothing about Thuy, just collects the rents from her. He was sweating through his white shirt, but that might be normal. He's as big as the Michelin Tire guy," Barrera said disagreeably.

"Well, you're not exactly John Cena," Postiff said. "Foster and Fort got something. The second victim, Elise Mannard, had a bootleg cable box at her place, and they found Whitty's card in a kitchen drawer."

"So, we have a clear link to two victims, right?" Cassidy asked.

"Yeah, but nothing on Jennifer Dale yet."

"I need a coffee that's better than the garbage we have here. I'm doing a Starbucks run. Want anything?" Barrera asked, standing and stretching his rotund body.

"A venti iced lavender-cream oat milk matcha," Postiff said.

"What the hell is that?" Barrera asked.

"I'm just fucking with you. Get me a hot mocha, the biggest one they have," Postiff said with a small laugh.

"Cassidy?" Barrera asked.

"Nothing for me, thanks," she said.

Barrera walked off, muttering to himself about coffee drinks and piss-ass detectives.

"Is your dad home?" Postiff asked Cassidy once Barrera was gone.

"He's up north, in Coalinga."

"But he's on his cell, right?" he asked, dialing Bill's number. "I need his input on something with the Hit Men."

"Clarke here," Bill answered, out of habit.

"Hi Bill, it's Postiff. I wanted to check with you about Jennifer Dale. We've found a link that ties Ronald Whitty to two victims through a cable-internet scam. But there's no tie to Jennifer Dale. Any thoughts?"

"You sure you can talk to me? Barrera shut me down when I called for an update," Bill said.

"I don't have anything to do with Pete's ego bullshit. I just want to solve it, and you were there when she was found."

"You're sure?" Bill asked.

"Don't make me jump through hoops, man. What do you think?" Postiff asked.

"You said it's a cable-internet scam?"

"Yeah, they pay him a flat fee; he hooks it up illegally to the pole. No monthly charge. Probably with stolen equipment. We think that's how he got inside to case their homes, got their phone numbers."

There was a heavy pause on the line, then, "Try Paxton Sparks."

"The country-western guy? With the Taco Bell song?" Postiff asked in surprise.

"She worked as a chef for him. I went to his place, a lot of people coming and going. Service people, tech types. Whitty could've worked for him and noticed Jennifer," Bill said.

"You think a guy with money like that would put in a bootleg-internet hookup?"

"Paxton Sparks may live high on the hog, but he's a grasping little jerk. He's got the big house, the cars, but it's all for show. There's no there there, as someone said."

"It was Gertrude Stein," Postiff said.

"Whatever. I know it was some famous writer type."

"Does he have people? You know, the firewall I have to get through to talk to him?"

"Try his assistant. A gal named Laci Hughes. She's a nervous little kiss ass, but she might know. His child bride might, also. Her name's Kellie."

"Okay. Thanks."

"And it'll be best to talk to his wife if he's not there. He's a controlling bastard, didn't want her talking to me or anyone else."

"Will do. Thanks for the tip," Postiff said, then hung up.

"That was nice of you," Cassidy said.

"I'm not being nice. I need answers, and your dad's a genius detective. You sticking around?"

"No, I'm heading home if Whitty won't talk. Keep me posted, okay?"

Postiff watched her leave, knowing how hard it had to be walking in her dad's shadow every day. One of Bill Clarke's strengths was that he always looked one or more degrees beyond what was obvious. If a guy's wife provided an alibi, Bill would dig into their relationship to see if she was covering for him and why she might. For all his bluster and overbearing ego, he understood human behavior and, more importantly, the human frailty that can push people to make bad choices. Unlike

Barrera, he understood why people did the bad things they did, and that was how he drew confessions out of them.

In the interrogation, he seemed like a tough uncle that had your back if you just told him the truth. Of course, then he'd turn it all over to the DA and celebrate another criminal going down, but he knew how to play it. Postiff had observed him in several interrogations and tried to learn what he could and fit it into his own investigation style.

He called Laci Hughes, but it went straight to voicemail. He was tired and hungry. He didn't want to have to drive up to Paxton Sparks's house in person, but most likely he would. He'd hoped to get out in time to visit Millie Grace, to give her an update on the case. To check up on her progress and show his support, maybe lay a little groundwork for a posttrial coffee date at the appropriate time. It was a long way off, but he was a patient man when he found something that he liked.

Half an hour later he was at Paxton Sparks's big house on Mulholland, ringing the bell at a tall iron gate. A woman's voice came over the intercom, and he announced himself. A moment later the gate swung open, and he pulled in. A young blond woman stepped out to meet him as he approached the house.

"I'm Kellie Sparks. Pax isn't here—he's in the studio. But maybe I can help?" she asked.

"Thank you. I just wanted to know about your cable-and-internet service. Do you have the records or statements from the carrier?" Postiff asked, following her into the house. She led him to the kitchen, where she put an electric kettle on.

"Would you like some tea, detective? I'm having some," she said over her shoulder, her long blond hair spilling down her back like a silken waterfall.

"Sure, thank you."

"I bet you all work some crazy hours, catching criminals," she said, preparing two mugs. "Green or black tea? I like chai the best, but Pax won't allow it. I have to sneak the sugar too," she said, pulling out a brown bag from the back of a drawer.

"Why do you hide the sugar?" Postiff asked.

"Pax doesn't eat sugar, and he doesn't want me to either. But I get the packets at Smart & Final and hide them," she said with a conspiratorial grin.

She took several packets out and slid them across the counter to him, leaning over in a way that exposed a good portion of her cleavage in a tight tank top. If he didn't know better, he would think she was flirting with him. But he did know better, and he was being looked at like a Ring Pop.

"About the internet service. Do you have those billing statements?" he asked.

She sat on one of the barstools and spun around in a circle with a giggle.

"It's kind of embarrassing to say, but Pax put in that under-the-table kind of internet. It was a guy he met somewhere who said he'd do it, and the company wouldn't know, so Pax would only pay him that one time. It was kind of white trash, but that's what he wanted," she said.

Postiff pulled up Whitty's photo on his phone and held it out to her.

"Was this the guy?" he asked.

She took his phone, her fingers brushing the back of his hand.

"I think so. He was in the house for about two hours. And his little helper was with him. He sent the little guy up on the pole while he wired the inside," she said.

"Was the helper Asian?"

"How'd you know that?" she said, looking at him as if he were Einstein.

Postiff stood to leave. "Thank you for your help, Mrs. Sparks. I can find my way out."

"But your tea?" she asked.

"I have to get going. Thank you again," he said.

They had the link that connected Whitty and Jennifer Dale. As he walked to his car, the gates opened, and he saw Paxton Sparks drive his Corvette in. Postiff flashed his badge at him and got into his car without a word. He drove off before Sparks could ask him anything or discover that his pretty, young wife had been showing him the forbidden sugar packets.

Cassidy rolled off Carter, who lay in her bed, his head thrown back and his eyes closed. They were both sweating from a rigorous round of lovemaking that left the sheets in a tangle and half off the bed. Their clothing was scattered hastily across the floor. She had practically jumped him when he arrived, and the Thai food still sat unopened on the kitchen counter.

She flopped onto her back, pushing the remaining covers away with her feet, exposing her skin to the cool night air that filtered in from the open window. Outside, it smelled of California sagebrush and the sharp, peppery scent of wild mustard that covered the hillside behind the house. Carter reached out his hand to take hers and breathed a contented sigh.

These were the moments she liked him the best. Sex was the place where she was able to draw closer to him emotionally. The distance she always maintained fell away in the sensory interaction of skin on skin, the meeting and rhythmic locking of their two bodies. Carter was a good lover, if not the most adventurous or daring. He was fun, willing and had the stamina of an athlete. They were a good fit in that way.

"That was . . . great," Carter said, not moving.

"You know what I like? When we're right in the middle of it and you reach under my back and pull me into a different position without losing a beat," Cassidy whispered.

Carter laughed. "You like that I'm-the-man stuff, I see."

"Yeah, I do . . . sometimes."

"That's probably because you're so tough, most men are scared of you!"

Cassidy sprang out of bed like a gymnast and walked to the window, looking out into the darkness at the back of the yard.

"Be careful, a coyote might see you naked," Carter warned, slipping into his jeans.

"I'm hungry. Let's eat," Cassidy said, brushing past his shirtless body and into the kitchen. She began unpacking the pad thai and *tom yung koong* soup while Carter looked out to the street.

"It looks like she left. I can't believe Zelda Zed was staking out your house to try and talk to you," he said.

"I hope she doesn't return," Cassidy said.

She'd come home from the gym to find Zelda Zed waiting in her car; luckily she had recognized her from the photo Carter had sent and bolted toward the house. But not before Zed had cornered her in the entryway and grilled her with questions about the Hit Men and Whitty.

Was he acting alone?!

Is there a connection and discernable motive among the three murders?!

Does he have a criminal history similar to these crimes?!

Is there an accomplice still at large?!

Cassidy replied that it was an ongoing investigation, she had no comment, and Zed was trespassing, so if she didn't leave immediately, she would be arrested. Even with the warning, Zed persisted as Cassidy slipped into the house and slammed the door. Afterward, she felt breathless, and her heart was pounding wildly. Zed remained outside, shouting questions until Alan Musselman came out to investigate and she finally left.

"So, where's your dad tonight? Not with Eden, I hope?" Carter asked.

"He's up in Coalinga, talking to a convicted murderer. It's a guy he put away years ago, Tyler Derby. He was the Angel City Killer. My dad is hoping to close some cold cases."

"He can't leave it behind, can he?" Carter said, avoiding the hot peppers that came with the food.

"At least it will keep him busy. He thinks our neighbor was involved in a case from years ago and freaked the poor guy out. He was waiting to talk to me when I got home last night," Cassidy said.

"Oof, that must've been uncomfortable. Maybe dealing with this guy up north will shift his focus. I don't think you should have to run interference, that's all. He's a grown man," Carter said, then took a gulp of ice water. "This food is spicy!"

"How's school going?" she asked.

"It's fine. My dad says that when I pass the bar, they'll slide me into the legal-counsel role that handles the real estate side of the business, so it will be pretty dry. I'll be in the Westside office, so I won't have to commute to the downtown building."

"That'll be nice. You can avoid the 10 freeway."

"I know, right? I won't have to change gyms. I can still shoot down Sunset to the beach for a run. You're going to stay at my place this weekend, right? After we get back from going out on the boat?"

"Don't know if I can make it. I have to interrogate the Hit Men suspect, and I have to be there when Lieutenant Carbone and Ramsey want me there. It's not my call," Cassidy said.

"Can't you tell them you're going out boating? That it's a family thing and you have to be there?"

"They know my dad; they'll know there's no way that Bill is out boating in Newport Harbor. But family gatherings don't count anyway. I can't miss work for something like that," she said, with a twinge of exasperation that Carter could be so clueless about the realities of being a cop. "I saw Kylie, and she asked me to stop coming to visit her so often."

"Really? Did she say why?" Carter said, then swallowed a glob of white rice.

"No. It was weird, just came out of nowhere."

"Well, she probably understands that your life is going to get really busy with work and everything. She doesn't want to be a burden to you any longer."

"She's not a burden to me," Cassidy said, feeling a flutter of indignation.

"Come on, Cassidy. Of course she is. You feel guilty that you survived unscathed, you have a great life and future, and she's trapped at that place forever. It probably brings her down to see you."

"I don't believe that. You don't understand the relationship that we have," Cassidy said defensively.

"You're right, I don't. You're a lot more noble and self-sacrificing than I am. So, about Newport, I hope you can make it. We're going to Joey for dinner when we're done on the boat. Oh, I have something I want to show you. My mom sent it to me today, and it's really funny. It's a video—I can hook my phone up to the TV to play it."

Carter grabbed the remote and synced the TV to his iPhone. He sat back down as a video filled the screen. It was of a group of teenage boys cavorting around a dormitory setting, wearing funny masks and roughhousing.

"This is part of the initiation ceremony when I was elected head boy at my prep school. It's all these crazy stunts and things they make you do, and everyone is in a mask. It's wild!" He laughed, watching his younger self running around with a group of equally wealthy, privileged white boys, behaving like buffoons in their little rarefied corner of society. She looked at his smiling, handsome face, totally unaware of how ridiculous this head boy video would make him seem to someone from any other social class or background. It was then that she realized he had no idea what world she lived in. He didn't see her, or understand her, at all.

Vithu wanted to take Thuy's car, but she refused. He couldn't risk using his own, so he hot-wired a Nissan Sentra that was parked in a deserted industrial area off San Fernando Road. It had been ticketed for being left over seventy-two hours, so Vithu thought it might be abandoned. Now it was parked with the headlights off and the engine idling halfway up a dirt access road in Glassell Park. On the street below were small Craftsman homes. The access road led to the more affluent residents of the area, with their remodeled mid-century homes that had views to the ocean on a clear day. The car was hidden from view, tucked into a stand of pepper trees. Thuy wore a short blond wig; Vithu wore his hair tied back in a bandanna like a gang member. She helped him pull Ashley-Noelle's limp body from the back seat and carry her to the base of a tree. He turned to hurry back to the car, but Thuy stopped him.

"You're going to leave her like that? You think they'll believe she died of diabetes out here under a tree?" she asked.

"No? Should I just do it?" he asked calmly.

"Make it look like she was attacked by someone. You know what to do," she said, handing him the knife she had brought from her kitchen. "Girls get killed like this every day." She locked her eyes on the dirt path, refusing to look at him.

"Okay," he agreed, deftly taking the knife from her.

"You'll stay in Anaheim. I'll drive, and we'll ditch this car along the way. Just do it." She didn't look at him again. She was right. He'd stay in the back bedroom of his parents' apartment. They never went out; his mother suffered from agoraphobia. He'd be safe there until everyone moved on and forgot.

Vithu crept close to Ashley-Noelle's body, her head hanging down onto her chest, her breathing barely audible. He propped her head back and opened her eyelids, then posed her arms, crossed over her legs as if she were waiting for a friend at Starbucks. He slashed the knife quickly across her throat, making a deep cut. He jumped back to avoid the spurt of blood that ran down her neck and shoulder. Her eyes were glassy, but they flickered with a faint light of recognition that she was dying. Vithu watched for a beat, his heart fluttering with the excitement that death always triggered in him. He plunged the knife into her torso several more times. He couldn't resist dipping his finger into the thick blood at her throat and drawing a heart on her cheek. He liked that little detail that Whitty always left behind, marking them as his prey, like a wild animal spraying his scent on a kill. He jammed the knife into his waistband as he jumped into the passenger seat and curled himself into a ball over his knees so no one would see a passenger in the car.

Thuy said nothing as she put the car into reverse and sped down the narrow streets, past the houses with their bright, happy café lights hung on the porch. Neighbors who would be horrified come daylight to find their jogging path cordoned off by yellow police tape, the quaint cul-de-sac crowded with the coroner's vans. And the city would be shaken by another young woman found dead.

CHAPTER EIGHTEEN

Bill and Derby sat across from one another in the meeting room at Pleasant Valley Prison. It was always easier the second day, like two old friends falling into step after a long break. They'd discussed politics and movies, fishing and women, but the conversation had hit a lull.

"Do you know anything about prison transfers?" Derby asked, trying to play it cool, but Bill could sense his anxiety.

"No, they don't talk to me about stuff like that. But I'm sure they would be open to reconsidering your location, if you gave them something significant," Bill said.

"Really?"

"Sure, why not?" Bill mused. He knew it was a long shot, but the California Department of Corrections and Rehabilitation sometimes looked kindly on confessions and other displays of cooperation from prisoners, as did the governor. Derby sat with his legs crossed, his foot tapping nervously at nothing.

"Rennison says I might get moved down south to Donovan. That Manson guy, Tex Watson, is there," Derby said. "If you tell them something new, do they put you on trial again?"

Bill remained impassive. "If you're already serving a life sentence, they usually don't go through the expense of a trial for a new case. It's all about money, you know."

"Ain't it, though?" Derby said.

Bill sat back and waited. Derby was nervous today. He must've been going through some extra hard shit with the other inmates, but Bill wasn't going to reassure him. Derby was sweating, despite the chilly temperature of the room.

Finally, he spoke. "I have some information that could be important. To certain people."

Bill's pulse quickened. "Showing remorse and taking responsibility are major components of these cases. You know that, Tyler. Especially if it's something that hasn't been properly closed and solved."

Derby nodded. "You know, Stacey Mandel had spoken to me at that Argentine restaurant where she worked. I'd been there a few times, and she'd seen me."

Bill didn't say anything; he just waited and listened for what might come next. Derby sat with his shoulders hunched, his hands clenched between his knees.

"I killed her on the fourteenth of May in 2007. I waited for her after work. I hit her with a hammer from behind as she got to her car. And she collapsed. I put her into my van, where I indulged in . . . her physical person while she was unconscious . . ."

"You mean you sexually assaulted her?" Bill asked bluntly. Derby squinted and squirmed in distaste, nodding his head.

"After that, I had to use the brand on her because once they'd been mine, I had to mark them. I didn't really want to do it because I hadn't really enjoyed it. She was so far gone from the hammer that she was like a mannequin. But I did the brand. It was all in the van."

"And the teeth marks on her lower back? That's another signature of yours, isn't it?"

"That happened . . . during the . . . sex part. I washed her in bleach after that. You didn't get no DNA from her, right?" Derby asked.

"Right." Bill nodded.

"I stashed the tarp I used in the van. You all never found it, but I can tell you where I put it."

Except for a mild disgust when he recounted the branding, Derby was expressionless and calm as he confessed to Stacey Mandel's murder. It was as if he were talking about what he'd bought at Costco that day. Derby sat back and tugged at the cartilage of his ear, a longtime stress habit.

"And then there was a girl in Escondido, a minor. She was never found, but I put her in the Cleveland National Forest out at the base of what they call Pilot Rock."

"Do you remember her name?" Bill asked.

Derby smiled. His teeth were a pale yellow, and his upper lip pulled up to reveal too much of his gumline. His gaze was an odd combination of dead-eyed excitement; there was no emotion behind his eyes but for an unsettling sense of perverse glee. Bill held his stare, unflinching and composed.

"Remedios Carson. It was on her backpack," Derby said. "I kept it for a few days, but then I got rid of it, out near San Ysidro. I thought of going into Mexico, but I don't speak the language, and I don't like Mexicans anyway."

Bill nodded. He knew that Rennison had to be running the name Remedios Carson through the system to find a report on her disappearance. With the location at Pilot Rock, they might find her remains. That would be the kind of slam dunk Bill hadn't even allowed himself to dream of, right out of the gate with his cold case work.

"This is really helpful, Tyler. I'm sure this will carry weight with the Department of Corrections."

"Might even get some help from Pretty Boy Newsom, right?" Derby asked with a brittle laugh, referring to the glamorous governor of California.

"Maybe. Where's the tarp you used with Stacey?" Bill asked, his heart pounding.

"I left it under the house of a lady who lived in my street. Her name was Lucille Washington. Her kids might still live there. I used to do yard work for them. I crawled into the area under the house and hid it there."

"This will be really useful, Tyler. If it all pans out."

"It will, detective. And it'll help you to stay relevant now that they've kicked you out of your job," Derby said with an edge, just to let the detective know that he was no patsy; he knew when he was being used, but that game could be played both ways. Derby had gambled and played his best hand. He had nothing to lose. Now he would see if Bill Clarke could deliver.

Barrera and Postiff stood beneath the drooping branches of the pepper tree in Glassell Park, a gentrifying hillside neighborhood northeast of Hollywood. On the street below, a crowd of terrified residents huddled together, in shock at the discovery of a young woman's dead body propped and posed against a tree. The victim, yet to be properly identified, had been taken by the coroner's office for an autopsy. The forensic team was scouring the scene for any DNA. There were vague footprints and tire tracks in the dry, dusty soil, but they were blown out for the most part.

An unknown number of cars had driven the path since the body dump. Two early-morning joggers had run right over the tire tracks and missed the girl against the tree until they were on the way back and could see clearly beneath the shadow of the branches. Ed Minot, a reporter from the local KTLA station, was hovering, microphone in hand.

"I'm here in Glassell Park at the scene of what could be another murder by the Hollywood Hit Men. One of the alleged murderers, Ronald Whitty, is in custody, but police suspect there are two killers working together, and if so, this new murder could be the work of his partner. Much like the serial-killer duo of the eighties, Buono and Bianchi, the Hit Men have been terrorizing Hollywood neighborhoods with a string of murders of young women . . ."

Barrera turned his back toward the reporters, annoyed. They would say whatever they wanted to fuel the panic that already had the city in a headlock of fear.

"It might be Whitty's partner, acting on his own," Postiff said.

"Or a copycat. The others were found at home; it bugs me that this one was dumped out here and posed. Big shift in the MO. And the heart on her cheek is in blood—that's a new touch."

"Maybe without Whitty he couldn't get inside her house as easily. The posing is so similar and the slit to her throat. He could've lost the lipstick or forgotten it. I think it's him. No one outside the investigation knows about the heart," Postiff said.

"I heard that podcast broad has a source inside the department—that's how she gets her info. Could've been leaked."

"I think it's the partner," Postiff asserted.

"The possible Vietnamese partner that we can't find?" Barrera said, his frustration bubbling over.

Zelda Zed of the *LA Murder Now* podcast was there with a handful of true crime junkies, all trading snippets of information and speculation. Zed was filming herself on her iPhone with a lighted selfie stick as she walked the perimeter of the police tape, the dry hillside behind her.

"A steep, dusty road deep in the rapidly gentrifying area of Glassell Park. On the streets below, a working-class, heavily immigrant neighborhood, but up above, the luxury homes of the wealthy who still want the cultural flavor and diversity of Northeast LA. Both united today by the gruesome murder of a young woman, a likely new victim of the Hollywood Hit Men!" Zed said dramatically, straight into the camera.

"I wish these idiots would get lost," Barrera said, signaling to an officer to move Zed and the others back. "Get these jerks out of here. They're in the way! And be sure we get all the home-security and Ring-camera footage from the people on this street. There are only two ways to this path; we need to check the video from every house on the route to see what cars passed by."

"He'll have to show up on something. I'm going to check with the houses up above," Postiff said, pointing to a platform deck on a huge modern house that jutted out over the dirt road. The house appeared to have three lots, all fenced and enclosed, with the house sitting at the top like a cherry on a banana split. On the deck, two men stood watching in bathrobes, holding cups and looking down in horror at the scene below.

"I just know those two are a couple. I can sense it from here," Barrera said. "The house from *Architectural Digest*, the plushy robes, the curiosity over coffee . . . I bet they drink some special free-trade blend grown by a tribe that hasn't yet made contact with the civilized world, or some shit like that!"

"Since you're steeped in every outdated, homophobic trope, I guess I should be the one to talk to them," Postiff said with a smile, heading up the path to the paved street above.

"Good thing you've got the booties on to protect those pricey mules, Mr. Gen Z!" Barrera shouted. Postiff was secretly glad for the coverage provided by the forensic booties; his Belvederes cost way too much money to get ruined walking in the dirt.

When he reached the street above, he was breathing hard. It was steeper than it looked. He had barely knocked on the door of the house with the huge deck when it swung open, one of the men standing there with his steaming coffee cup.

"Are you one of the detectives? I'm Jack Tufts. This is my husband, Jeffrey Cortez."

Cortez stood behind Tufts, now wearing slacks and a dress shirt. He was tying a purple patterned necktie.

"I'm running off to work. I have to catch the train over by the museum. Do you think it's what everyone is saying? Another murder by the Hollywood Hit Men?" Cortez asked nervously.

"We're not sure yet. Did either of you see anything yesterday or last night?"

Tufts shook his head. "Not a thing. Jeffrey was at a work event until late, and I was here with our cat, Didot. He's not doing well, so I was sitting up with him, watching Hulu. But I did check the security camera footage." He handed Postiff a flash drive. "There was a car down there.

It was some type of older sedan, but the license plate wasn't clear. The time stamp is on there. It pulled up, idled for a few minutes, and then it drove away, The bushes blocked everything else."

Postiff took it. He wished every neighbor was as diligent as Jack Tufts.

"And what time did you get home, Mr. Cortez?" Postiff asked.

"It must've been about eleven. Jack came to get me at the station. I didn't want to wait to take an Uber; it's kind of sketchy over there. And then we both went straight to bed."

"Was the body put there on the Goat Path? That's what our neighbor said," Tufts asked.

"What neighbor?" Postiff asked.

"He calls himself Wombat, but that's not his real name. He's a performance artist," Cortez said. "He lives next door. He might've seen something."

Postiff thanked them and went next door to speak to Wombat. He wondered what kind of performance artist the guy had to be to afford a house in that neighborhood. He was about to knock when Wombat stepped out, closing the door behind him. He was in his early thirties. His hair was dyed an unnatural cornmeal yellow and cut in an elven style. Postiff mused that all he needed were the pointy ears to be in the next *Lord of the Rings* movie.

"You're one of the cops, right? I saw something down here late last night. More like early morning," Wombat said, dropping his voice for effect.

"What did you see, Mr. . . . ? What is your name?" Postiff asked.

"Getty. Henry Parker Getty, but I go by Wombat in my work."

Postiff jotted it down on his phone. Henry Parker Getty. A performance artist with a hefty trust fund.

"And what exactly did you see?" Postiff asked.

"I couldn't sleep. I have major issues with insomnia. And I was on my deck, must've been close to two in the morning. I think there was a car down here by the tree. The lights were off, but I heard an engine idling," Wombat said.

"Did you see any people?"

"It was total darkness, man, just black, no lights. I thought I saw some movement, and then I absolutely saw a car back out, with the headlights off. It disappeared down one of those streets."

"You didn't hear any voices? A woman screaming, any shouting?"

"Nah, it was quiet. I think they must've dumped the body."

"And what did you do then?"

"Went back inside to smoke some weed. I'm in the middle of a project, and my head just gets all wound up, you know? But there were people out on the Goat Path earlier in the evening, walking back from dinner and stuff. Nothing was there, no body or nothing. It's scary as shit!" he said, his voice rising.

"Okay, I'll leave my card. If you remember anything else, don't hesitate to call me."

Postiff tried a few other doors, but no one answered. He began the walk back down to the crime scene. He was certain that Henry Parker Getty had seen the killer's car, and the victim had been murdered someplace else and brought to Glassell Park. They had hoped that Whitty's partner was a follower who needed Whitty's guidance to strike. But now he had proved that he was ready to go out and kill all on his own.

CHAPTER NINETEEN

At the Harris Ranch Hotel, Bill tossed his clothes into a duffel bag, his mind spinning up and down like a WHEE-LO on crank. He hadn't expected Derby to give up Stacey Mandel so easily, or that he would confess to a different killing, far outside the LAPD jurisdiction. If they could locate Remedios Carson's remains, it would be like hitting a triple at the bottom of the ninth with a tied score. Two cold cases closed, with confessions from the killer. Eden came out of the bathroom in her bathing suit, preparing to go for a swim in the pool.

"Hey, babe, I gotta go. I've got to get back to LA to deal with this Derby stuff. This is big, really big!" he said.

Eden cocked her head to the side and puffed her lips into a pout.

"But I thought we could hang out by the pool today," she said.

"We'll do it next time, okay? I think this guy Derby is going to be a gold mine for me. So, we'll come back in another week or so, and we'll go all out. Steak dinner, cocktails, maybe go to a real movie in a theater. But I've got to get back to LA now. So, baby, go for your swim, have lunch and relax, charge it to the room. We'll talk this week, okay?" he said, racing out the door.

Eden looked around the room, with her silk scarves on the lampshades, the scented candles she had brought to set the mood. Now Bill was gone like hotcakes, and she was alone. But leaving her here meant he trusted her, like a girlfriend or wife. He wouldn't leave just a casual fling to stay in his hotel room. Once her disappointment lifted, she decided that it had worked out well. It meant that they were on track to get back together, making plans for another trip. She had her phone ringer turned off, and now she saw that Acevedo had called several times, which was out of character for him. She flopped back onto the bed and dialed his number.

"Hey, baby girl!" he said.

"Hey Acevedo, the Tomato! Have you missed me?" she asked.

"I came by to see you, but you were gone. Where you at?" he asked.

"Wouldn't you like to know?" she teased, with a flirtatious giggle. Acevedo was silent. Eden waited for a response, but he didn't say anything.

"I'm just out of town for a day or two. With a friend," she explained.

"I bet you're with some guy, right? I came by your house twice, and it was dark," Acevedo complained.

"I'm with a pal who actually made plans with me, not like you who just drops by unannounced. That's not very gentlemanly," she teased.

"Who said I'm a gentleman? That's not the kind of thing we have, is it?" he said, his voice low and flat.

"You're just kind of a wild man, aren't you? Not into the nicer things, like staying in a hotel and taking a girl out to dinner?"

"And you're kind of a whore, aren't you? Running with different guys?" he said angrily.

Stunned, Eden replied, "What kind of thing is that to say to me? Just because I wasn't there when you came by for an easy fuck?"

"Watch how you talk to me!" Acevedo warned her.

Maybe it was because she was hours away at Harris Ranch or because she began to believe that the romance with Bill was back on track. Or she was tired of Acevedo treating her like a blow-up doll. She did something she had never done. She talked back to him.

"Well, you watch how you talk to me! You don't own me, and it's not okay to treat me like trash just 'cause I'm not home waiting for your call. I have a life and other relationships, just like you!"

"You better stay in line with me and be there when I come for you," he growled before hanging up.

Eden sat up on the bed, her heart pounding. She had never spoken that way to a man in her life. She was too worried about losing their interest to ever speak up. But it felt good. Acevedo was mean and rough, even if he was sexy as hell. It wasn't worth it, not now that things were heading in the right direction with Bill. She didn't like to admit it, but part of the reason she had flirted with Acevedo at the station was to make Bill jealous. It hadn't worked, but it did lead to some hot sex.

She waited for a moment, wondering if Acevedo would call her back, but he didn't. She slipped into her flip-flops. He could stew over it for a day or two. She was tired of putting him first. She skipped down the hallway to the elevator and rode it to the main floor. The water would be perfect at this time of day, and who knew—maybe she'd meet one of the Harris Ranch owners at the pool, they'd have a whirlwind romance, and she'd end up living on a big hacienda, like in a Hallmark movie.

Joyce Ramsey stood behind Deputy Chief of Police Gary Hunsaker outside Parker Center in downtown Los Angeles. All the LAPD top brass were there, including Hollywood Division Robbery-Homicide Lieutenant Lisa Carbone, along with Barrera and Postiff. Hunsaker was addressing a large group of reporters from all major local and national news outlets.

"We are committing all police resources to apprehending the individuals responsible for several murders of young women in the Hollywood area of Los Angeles. The most recent victim has been identified as twenty-three-year-old Noelle Gerrard from Angeleno Heights. We have discovered evidence that could point to the same perpetrators, but we are awaiting the final DNA results from the crime scene. We have had one suspect, Mr. Ronald Whitty, in custody since before Ms. Gerrard was killed, and we believe he was working with a partner who is still at large and might be responsible for Ms. Gerrard's death."

The reporters began asking questions, jockeying for position in the crowd.

"When will it be confirmed that the latest victim was killed by the Hollywood Hit Men?"

"Was Ms. Gerrard murdered at home like the previous victims?"

"Have you figured out how the Hit Men targeted their victims?"

"Has the woman who survived an attack been given police protection since she identified suspect Ronald Whitty?"

Hunsaker answered their questions, giving as little information as possible. Again, no mention was made of the knife wounds to the body or the heart drawn on Noelle's cheek. He did not disclose that the coroner had already determined the time of death was between two and three in the morning. The autopsy found that Gerrard was in a dire state of diabetic ketoacidosis prior to the fatal knife wound that severed her carotid artery. She had started to slip into organ failure by the time her throat was cut; both were factors in her death. Ramsey shifted her weight uncomfortably. She didn't even want to imagine how the poor girl had suffered.

With Ronald Whitty in custody, the public had started to relax, just a little. This new victim would ignite not only a citywide firestorm of terror, but Ramsey could also come under fire for going along with Whitty's demands to speak only to Cassidy Clarke. Luckily, that detail had not been leaked to the press. Ramsey didn't think Barrera or any of the other more seasoned detectives would've done much better. Whitty was a wily, seasoned criminal; he was only going to talk when he was ready. But there would be forces in the department who would try to use it against her.

She could turn the blame to Cassidy and put it squarely on her shoulders. Clarke had been unable to get any information out of him before another murder occurred. A young, inexperienced officer who couldn't deliver would be a convenient scapegoat if it came to it. Cassidy had another meeting with Whitty scheduled in the afternoon. Ramsey would wait and see how it played out before leaking any information about her to the press. Whitty had them in a stranglehold, and Ramsey was over it. Something had to break today.

The press conference ended after Barrera and Postiff spoke to the crowd, assuring them that Whitty's accomplice would soon be in custody; a major break was expected with the final DNA analysis. As they headed back into Parker Center to regroup, Barrera's phone rang. It was Bill Clarke again. He had ignored three calls from Bill previously, but he answered this one. He knew Bill would not stop until he did.

"Hey, what's up, brother?" Barrera said.

"I'm on my way back from Coalinga. I've been looking over cold cases, and I drove up to talk to Tyler Derby. He gave up the information on Stacey Mandel's murder, a confession and where he stashed hard evidence. And he admitted to another cold case in San Diego. It's over, man. I left messages for Ramsey and Carbone, but we can finally close it!"

Barrera stood still for a moment in the crowd of cops and other city officials gathered in Parker Center. Damn Bill Clarke. He couldn't just retire quietly; he had to keep running down these old cases like a cattle dog. Barrera knew that the day he left the force he had no intention of ever looking at a murder book or case notes again in his life. He'd sit in his big backyard drinking a Michelada, watching the gardener mow the lawn and plant new flower bulbs each autumn, complaining about the way he cut the roses. He wouldn't be thinking about dead people. But Clarke was a different beast, and Barrera had to admit that closing the Mandel case was good news the department needed right now.

"That rocks, man! I can't believe you did it. I'm at Parker Center; we just did a press conference on the Hit Men. We got a new victim, but I'm gonna grab Ramsey before she goes into another meeting. Call me when you get home. Great work, partner!" Barrera said. Then he hung up and pushed through the crowd to Joyce Ramsey.

He knew the department would give the Mandel case a lot of attention. They'd get a story in the *Times* and every other major news outlet, probably even the broadcast news stations. The department would want to highlight the success of the Hollywood homicide detectives to detract from the reality that they had four young women dead, one guy in custody who refused to talk, and no idea as to the identity of one who was still on the loose, dumping dead bodies like Noelle Gerrard's.

Driving through the flatlands of the San Joaquin Valley, Bill hung up from Barrera and pounded his fist against the steering wheel. He was still the best; no one could touch him. He'd have the LAPD detectives on the hunt for Lucille Washington's house with a warrant within twenty-four hours. The detectives in San Diego were arranging a search of the Pilot Rock area with the cadaver dogs, forensics, the whole circus. They'd even asked him to come down and be part of it, complete with local news coverage. He called Cassidy to tell her the good news.

"What's up, Dad?"

"I got a confession in the Stacey Mandel case! I think we'll get full-court press coverage on it. Barrera just told me you've got a new victim?"

"Postiff let me know. They're all at a press conference. It's on me, Dad. I have to get something out of Whitty today."

"Don't worry. Go in there and play dirty. Manipulate the guy—hit his ego. He's doing this to stall and hang on to power as long as he can, but his weakness is women. He hates them; he loves them. Use it against him," Bill advised.

"Okay, thanks. And I think . . . I'm going to take a little break from Carter," she said, surprising even herself to say it out loud.

"Good. He's a nice kid, but he's not in your league, honey."

"What do you mean? He's a catch to a lot of people."

"Here's the thing: A guy like Carter thinks he's as smart as you are, as driven as you are, as disciplined. But he's not—he's never even been tested. And in time, he'll realize that being with you doesn't make him the same as you. Then he'll resent you and do shit to make you smaller, like cheat with some girl who isn't half of what you are, bring down your confidence in a thousand small ways. You're way better than that, Binkie."

Cassidy was silent, taken aback at her father's blunt assessment of Carter. It was everything she felt but couldn't put into words. Her dad was right. In the midst of his own excitement, he'd cut right to the heart of the matter, like a surgeon with a scalpel. She could sense that underneath Carter's polished exterior was something else, something petty and perhaps even unkind.

"Thanks, Dad. And congratulations on the Mandel case. You've done a great job," she said.

"Thanks, Binkie. I'm going to be going down to San Diego in the next day or so. It's going to be big news. Maybe you'll be able to join me?"

"Maybe. I'll see you at home later. Drive safely."

Bill hung up. He was glad she was stepping back from Carter Sims. He'd known guys like that before, who take an amazing girl and turn her into a shadow of herself, just to build himself up. Bill had screwed up his marriage to Cathy, but it wasn't for those reasons. She was a great wife, and he told her so; he just couldn't get away from his job enough to make it work. Bill liked women; he liked everything about them. The way they smelled, with their pretty perfume, the way they hung their fancy underwear on the shower door to dry. He didn't even mind when they shaved their legs with his razor, dulling the blade.

But he knew plenty of men who didn't like women at all. They weren't gay—they just harbored a resentment and fear of women. The pathological ones became like Tyler Derby or Ron Whitty. But there was a common garden variety of that guy, and they were everywhere. He suspected that Carter might be one of those types. He was a punk, no matter what his family pedigree was. Cassidy could do much better. He knew she'd kick it with Whitty also. She'd show them all up, leave them breathing her dust. Today, the Clarkes were unstoppable.

Whitty sat in the interview room waiting for Officer Pretty Tits to arrive. He'd recovered from his feigned illness and signaled he was ready to talk to her again. He loved holding them all over the fire this way. In the old days, they would've beat the crap out of a guy like him, kept him awake all night, handcuffed to his bed in his own shit and piss. Now they were trying to pretend that they were the good guys, because there were cameras everywhere, and they couldn't hide it any longer when people ended up dead in custody. They'd even agreed to have Pretty Tits talk to him when she had no idea what she was doing.

He held all the cards, and he loved watching them flounder and chase their own tails. He'd keep it up for another day or so; then he'd lawyer up, and they'd get nothing from him. But he'd get to sit across from that pretty girl and watch her struggle to get control of the situation. If he couldn't be out in the world catching them like butterflies in his net, he would get what he could in here. It made his dick hard just to have her so close to him, the uncertain look in her eyes when he didn't say what she wanted. He loved that, more than anything else. Seeing them weak against his prowess, unable to get the upper hand.

The door opened, and she came in, all buttoned up in her police blues, shoes so shiny he was sure she could see her reflection in them.

"Hi there, Officer Clarke! I've missed you!" he said brazenly.

She slid onto her chair and cracked a smile at him. "I kind of missed you, too, Whitty."

He felt a hot flush in his groin. "Really? I thought you were a little scared of me."

She smiled again and leaned back in her chair. "A little. I'm a new cop, you know. Not an experienced tough guy like Detectives Barrera or Postiff. I felt a little in over my head, if we're telling the truth."

"Are we doing that?" he asked coyly.

"Maybe and maybe not," she said, slowly raising her eyelids, the way she might when meeting a good-looking guy in a bar. Whitty imagined himself as that guy with her sending him all the green lights to go ahead.

"So, what've you been up to?" he asked.

"Waiting to get the chance to talk to you. That's all I do now. No more patrol, just wait until they tell me it's time to see you," she said with a little laugh.

"An easy gig." He laughed in response.

"Oh, there's nothing easy about you, sir!" Cassidy said, and Whitty smiled, licking his dry lips, brushing his palm over his face in feigned embarrassment.

In her office, the lieutenant watched in confusion with Ramsey.

"What's she doing?" Carbone asked.

"I don't know. Barrera and Postiff are out in the field—maybe they advised her to take this approach," Ramsey replied, but she had to admit, Whitty was more talkative than he had been previously.

Back in the interview room, Cassidy reached up and pulled the claw clip out of her hair, letting it fall over her shoulders.

"You look way prettier with your hair down, officer," Whitty said.

"Thank you, Mr. Whitty. It's almost quitting time, and I'm getting ready to unwind," she said.

"What does a cop like you do to relax?" he asked.

"I go to the shooting range and blast a few rounds of an automatic, and then I beat up some homeless people for kicks," she replied.

Whitty burst into laughter. "Good looking and funny, that's what you are!"

They went back and forth, engaged in seemingly meaningless low-level flirtations for a long time, but Cassidy saw how Whitty relaxed into it and began to lead with his emotions, letting go of his strategic, calculated responses to her. When the interaction felt smooth and uninhibited, she shifted gears.

"Actually, it's been kind of busy out there. They found another body, a girl who they think fits the Hollywood Hit Men pattern," she said casually. "But I don't think it is."

Whitty sat up and tapped his fingers on the table between them.

"Where did they find her?" he asked.

"Out near Eagle Rock. She was dumped, killed someplace else."

"They know who she is?"

"Yeah, a social media influencer and gig worker, like so many people these days. Making ends meet," Cassidy replied.

"One of those leeches, right? Living off the laziness and stupidity of the wannabes and the rich shits who don't know the meaning of a hard day's work!" he said, his mood shifted to seething resentment. Cassidy marveled at how quickly he switched gears emotionally, indicative of his mental instability. But this was the first mention of the victims being leeches and Whitty's perception of women who worked in the modern gig economy.

"Yeah, I get it. They have no idea what it is to work a real job, right? Out on the streets, in construction, plumbing, dry wall. Let them spend a day doing that stuff rather than sitting at a computer with an espresso!" Cassidy goaded him on.

"Exactly. They don't know what real life is. Sitting in their nice apartments, with their fancy laptops, doing useless crap that has no value. And then acting all high and mighty!" Whitty said, rubbing his hands together.

"I agree. Let them try being a cop for a day—then we'll talk," she said.

"I respect that about you, Officer Clarke. You're a hard worker, and you're tough."

"Thank you, Mr. Whitty. So, some of my colleagues think this girl was killed by that partner that we talked about the first day. But I doubt that."

"Me too. I can't see V doing anything like that. He doesn't think things through," he said impulsively. Cassidy ignored his mention of a person named V and continued as if she hadn't heard it.

"I just don't see it. I think it's a copycat, trying to make us think that it's the Hit Men," Cassidy said.

"It's a damn copycat trying to do all the same wild shit. The posing, the knife work. Just a fucking copycat trying to keep up with the real thing!" he said with bravado.

She hadn't mentioned knife work or the posing of the bodies. Those details had been kept from the press so as not to freak out the public any more than they already were. Whitty had made several mistakes in this session, and she held back the desire to let him know that she'd caught them. Instead, she played dumb and smiled at him.

"So, we'll see. I'm sure they'll catch the copycat pretty soon. I heard he left a lot of clues at the scene."

Now Whitty's expression changed. His eyes grew furtive, and he leaned across the table toward her.

"Like what?" he asked, almost a whisper.

"Not sure. I just heard that he wasn't too careful. It seemed like a rush job. They'll get him," she said.

Whitty leaned back in his chair, crossing his arms over his chest. He rocked back and forth for a minute and then said abruptly, "I need to go back to my cell. I'm not feeling too good."

"Are you sure? I'm enjoying our little talk."

Whitty grinned. "I bet you got a good-looking man at home who treats you right."

"No, I'm a free agent at the moment," she said, dropping her gaze at him again in a slightly provocative way. He smiled, forgetting his sickness.

"Do you live in an apartment or a house, officer?"

"Just an apartment, a studio right here in Hollywood. One of those courtyard-style places," she lied.

"I been to places like that with my work. They're nice. Garden-like," he said.

"I know. Easy in and out, the way I like it," Cassidy said.

Whitty felt a tingling rush up his leg, hitting his groin like a heat bomb. He was getting too aroused. He shifted his weight uncomfortably.

"I need to go back to my cell," he said.

"All right. I hope we can get together again soon," she said.

The guard came to take him back. He just needed a break to regroup, make a plan now that they'd found a new body. He didn't think it was Vithu—he wouldn't do anything on his own. But he was excited to talk to Pretty Tits again, now that she was coming around to him. He was starting to like her. A lot.

CHAPTER TWENTY

After talking to Whitty, Cassidy felt like she needed a shower, but she had another twenty minutes before she got home. It had taken all her self-control not to throw up when he looked at her suggestively across the table. But she had gotten good information out of him, and more importantly, she left him wanting more. She could see it on his face when she stood up to leave.

Ramsey and Carbone had praised her, and she knew she had bought at least one more day of their patience and goodwill. She let go of any discomfort she might have felt previously about letting the interview take on an intimate tone with a sexually violent criminal like Whitty. She wished she could go back to patrol with Sean Riley and just be a new boot. Barrera, Postiff, and the rest of Robbery-Homicide could figure out who the hell "V" was. She had done her part, and she was exhausted after being in that freezing, cramped room with a disgusting predator.

She decided she would speak to Carter in a day or so, suggest that they take a break while she was on this case. Then she could see how she felt without him around. Maybe she'd miss him and rediscover what she liked about him to begin with. When she got home, she saw her dad's car in the driveway. Inside she found him going over his cold case files in the den, a Coors Light in his hand.

"Hey, Binkie! How'd it go today?"

"Good. I took your advice, and it worked," she said, flopping down onto the plaid couch that they'd had since she was born, but he refused to part with.

"What'd he do?" Bill asked.

"I let my hair down. I flirted with him. I thought I would throw up, but we went back and forth for over an hour that way. Then I started talking about the new victim, and he mentioned someone named V, who he said was too reckless to do it on his own. And he talked about the stuff that hadn't been released to the public: the posing, the knife wounds. He was all excited and talked too much," she said happily.

"Now they're tracking down V, right?"

"Yes. It's more than we had before, and his admission about the knife wounds and the posing will help make it a slam dunk with the DNA. I'm hoping we can leverage that. You were right—he was never going to say anything if I questioned him directly or played tough."

"It's different with every perp. They all have a weakness; you have to find it. Good job, Binkie."

"Thanks. I heard they got a warrant for a house out in Sylmar, for evidence in the Mandel case?"

"I just heard from Ramsey. We're doing a press conference tomorrow to announce the Derby confession. The deputy chief spoke to the family today, and they're getting their DNA. When they locate the tarp at the Washington house, if it's a match, it will be closed. And then I go to San Diego for the other case. Pretty exciting, huh?" he asked, grinning broadly.

"Very. Don't forget you have the appointment with the neurologist in a few days, so you need to be here for that."

Bill grimaced and took a swig of his beer. "I can't miss this for a doctor's appointment. There's nothing wrong with me anyway. I'm only going to shut you up about this brain stuff," he said.

"I shifted my schedule to go with you, so make sure you're available," she insisted.

The doorbell rang. Cassidy stood up to answer it.

"You don't need to come with me to the doctor like I'm a little kid," Bill protested as she walked away.

Cassidy peered out the peephole, afraid it might be Zelda Zed again. But it was Eden Balcomb holding a large Domino's pizza.

When Cassidy opened the door, Eden smiled and said, "Get it while it's hot! Do you remember that scene from *Sex and the City*? When Carrie shows up at Mr. Big's house with a pizza like this? It was so cute!"

"No, I never watched that show. C'mon in," Cassidy said.

"I just wanted to check in with your dad about next week. I'm on my way back home from Coalinga," she said with a grin and a wink.

"Were you with my dad at Harris Ranch?" Cassidy asked.

"Sure was. He said we're going to go again next week sometime. I could've called him, but I kinda felt like seeing him again, and I figured after the drive, he wouldn't want to cook."

Cassidy walked into the den with Eden following her.

"Dad, Eden wanted to know about your next trip to Coalinga?" she asked pointedly.

Bill looked up, and his face flushed when he saw Eden. She wasn't supposed to show up at his house unannounced.

"What're you doing here?" he said brusquely.

"I just wanted to see you, babe. And I brought a pizza!" Eden said with a smile.

"We have an understanding, okay? This is not it."

"I just wanted to see if you had any idea when we're going back to Coalinga again. I had a great time at the pool today," she said, sitting on the couch. Bill moved to her and took her arm, pulling her to her feet.

"Sorry, this is not cool. I'm working right now, and Cassidy just got home from work as well. This is not the time for visitors," he said, ushering Eden toward the front door. She pulled back, the hurt and confusion clear on her face.

"But I thought we could hang out a bit. You know, after we had such a good time—"

"No. You have to go!" Bill insisted, his temper flaring.

"Dad, it's not a big deal. We can have the pizza. I like Domino's," Cassidy chimed in, hoping to defuse the growing tension.

"Don't get involved in this, Cassidy. It's between me and Eden, and she knows better, okay? This is the same old shit, pushing the line, trying to turn this into something it isn't!" Bill snapped at her.

Now Eden's eyes teared up, and she pulled her skinny arm away from his grip.

"I don't know why you're being so mean! I just brought a fucking pizza over 'cause I thought you'd be hungry and I wanted to see you!" she cried.

"You just saw me at Harris Ranch! We hung out; we ate dinner; we watched a movie! That was enough!" Bill shouted.

Cassidy saw that his reaction was too big, and his emotional state was escalating. He was embarrassed about Eden, that he'd lied when they spoke on the phone from Coalinga, saying he was alone. Now that she'd shown up uninvited, he was exposed and furious.

"It's not a big deal, Dad. We can just eat the pizza," Cassidy said again, but Bill blew up, grabbing the pizza and tossing it across the room.

"We're NOT EATING THE PIZZA! I want you to leave, Eden! Now!" he said, opening the door and pushing her outside.

In the driveway, Eden erupted into tears, screeching, "You're an asshole, Bill! Just a fucking asshole!"

She got into her car and sped away. Cassidy looked around the cul-de-sac and saw that Alan Musselman was watching from his window. She turned to Bill.

"What was that? You went ballistic on her over nothing," she said.

"It wasn't nothing!" he shouted. "She always does this. She thinks this is some big relationship when it isn't."

"Then why do you keep leading her on? If you know she's wanting more, then stop seeing her. You're half the problem," she said.

"I'm not the one with a problem, okay? It's Eden and her bullshit!" he shouted, banging his hand against the front door. Cassidy remembered all the times she had tried to calm down the same type of eruption when her parents were still together.

"Your reaction is too big—don't you see that? You escalate way too quickly over minor things. That's why I want you to see Dr. Baruch," she said.

"I'm not going to see that doctor when I have so much work to do on these cold cases!" he shouted, storming off to the den.

"You're not working anymore! You're retired! And I'm not cleaning up this pizza!" she shouted after him, immediately regretting her outburst. She needed to stay calm when he got like this, but it could be so difficult. She never knew what to expect from him. Everything could change in a split second.

Her mom was right—she needed to get a place of her own. There was no way this situation was healthy for her. She looked at the pizza slices scattered around the room, dripping cheese smeared on the sofa cushions. A moment later, Bill burst out of the den and grabbed a trash bag from the kitchen. He began tossing the pizza into the bag and then threw it out the back door.

"I'm heading out to cool off," he said, slamming the door behind him.

He got into his car and peeled out, leaving black skid marks on the concrete. Cassidy followed and saw that Alan Musselman was still peering out his window. This was all she needed after walking a tightrope at work and bearing the weight of a new Hit Men victim that she might've been able to prevent. Her phone rang; it was Carter. She let it go to voicemail. She wasn't in the right frame of mind for that conversation.

Postiff had clocked out, but when he was working a big case, he was never really off work. Barrera was better at disconnecting and coming back fresh the next day. But he had a wife and family, even if his kids were grown. All Postiff had was a well-decorated house in the Ranchito area of Burbank, close to the studios. It was quiet and safe, a gathering of low-slung smaller ranch homes with big lots, some still retaining the original stables out back. Most people had converted them into ADUs to use as rental property in the popular area, close to the Equestrian Center.

Postiff still had a small two-stall barn and a turnout at the back of his property but no horses. He considered renting them out to horse people, but he didn't want the insurance liability, nor did he want teenage girls in riding breeches developing crushes on him, as a single man who lived alone. Or lonely, rich housewives who obsessed over their horses to fill the void in their lives. He'd been invited to a few events at the Equestrian Center by his neighbors, and those horse women had scared him, with their Barbie-blond hair and Botox, their eyes like sci-fi tractor beams, pulling any young, virile man into their orbit. They loved cowboys and cops, and Postiff had no interest.

He was heading home on Cahuenga when he decided to swing by Thuy Pham's apartment building and take another look at Whitty's unit. He double-parked with his flashers on and found the main door to the building unlocked. He took the stairs two at a time and ducked under the police tape to unlock Whitty's door. Inside the apartment was still neat and orderly; there was no sign of anyone having been there. He flipped on the light and sat on the couch. He knew in his gut that Thuy was the link to Whitty's Vietnamese helper. The proximity made it too easy, and it explained Thuy's hostility.

Postiff heard a noise outside the front door and instinctively unholstered his firearm, standing up and moving quietly toward the sound. A moment later the door was slowly pushed open, and he stepped forward to confront one of Thuy's girls, Nonglak, the one who had Jennifer Dale's bracelet.

"Sorry, so sorry, sir . . ." Nonglak whispered, bowing and stepping back. "I saw the light and your car in front. I want to tell you something—"

"What? About Ron Whitty?"

She nodded, but before she could speak, they both heard heavy footsteps on the stairway and Thuy chattering loudly in Vietnamese. Nonglak turned as Postiff jammed his card into her hand, and she hid it inside her shirt.

"Call me when you can talk. And I'll come back," he said.

She nodded and said, "Miss Thuy cannot see me . . ." as she slipped back into the adjacent apartment.

Postiff made no effort to hide his presence, and when Thuy Pham saw him, she froze. She was in the company of a young Vietnamese woman carrying grocery bags.

"I came by to take another look at Ron Whitty's unit," he said, locking the door behind him and pushing past her without any further explanation. He knew that Thuy Pham was more involved than she seemed to be, and he was determined to find out how.

Bill drove over the speed limit on the 101 freeway with no real destination in mind. His heart was pumping after the confrontation with Eden and Cassidy. He was mortified that Eden had shown up at the house with Cassidy there, and she'd discovered that he'd lied about being alone in Coalinga. He didn't even know why he was embarrassed; he was a grown man, and he could do what he wanted with whomever he pleased. But Eden always came across as so needy and neurotic, and she wasn't the kind of woman he wanted to parade around and show off. She was more like a guilty secret that he couldn't quite let go of because she made everything so easy for him. Except tonight, she'd arrived and pushed him right over the edge.

He felt bad for the way he'd run her off, and as he drove past West Hills, Sherman Oaks, and Studio City, whizzing by the sprawling neighborhoods of the San Fernando Valley, he found himself exiting the freeway at Gower, just a few blocks from Eden's place on Beachwood. He wanted to smooth things over with her, but he also needed her to understand that she couldn't just change the terms of everything whenever she wanted. They had an understanding that things between them were casual. He pulled up to her fourplex and saw her car in the carport. He sat for some time, deciding whether to stay or go. He went to her door and knocked, then jammed his hands into the pockets of his bomber jacket. She opened and stared at him for a beat.

"What d'you want?" she asked, her eyes still red from crying.

"I'm sorry for the way I acted. It was out of line—you just caught me off guard," he said stiffly. He'd never been good at apologies, but over the years with Cassidy, he'd learned that it was sometimes the best and simplest way to fix things when he'd screwed up.

"Okay. You want a drink? I have Jack Daniel's and vodka," she said.

"JD would be great," he said, following her into the apartment.

They sat and made small talk while scrolling through old shows on Pluto TV. Eden made a bowl of popcorn.

"You didn't need to be such a meanie. It was just a pizza," Eden said.

"Yeah, but you know we don't hang out at my house with Cassidy there," Bill said.

"We used to all the time."

"But things were different then. We were in more of a boyfriend-girlfriend thing."

"I just thought it would be nice to visit you," she said, pouting.

Bill sighed. This was exactly why he'd stopped seeing her a few years earlier. The childish moods, the overstepping boundaries in the hope that he'd let it go, and she could take it as tacit approval that the lines had shifted. It was a constant game of manipulation, of Eden wanting more than he wanted to give.

"I don't want a repeat of the fridge situation, okay?" Bill said, referring to an incident five years earlier when his refrigerator had broken, and Eden offered to give him one to replace it. He had agreed, not realizing it was her fridge from her apartment, and she took his acceptance that she had the green light to move in with him. They'd had a big fight in the driveway about that when she showed up with the fridge and a U-Haul of all her stuff.

"I was just being nice back then, helping you out when yours broke," she said.

Bill was silent. It had been a mistake to come see her. She would never accept the boundaries that he needed; she would just pretend to go along with them until she pushed too far, again and again. Cassidy was right—he was simply leading her on by spending time with her. Part of him wanted to tell her that it was over, but he knew that would trigger another crying meltdown. He wished he had never drifted back into any type of involvement with her. After they finished the popcorn, he stood to leave.

"I've got to get home," he said.

"When are we going back up to Coalinga?" she asked.

"Not sure. I'll let you know."

"But we are going back again, right?" Eden pushed.

"Sure, sometime in the next few weeks," Bill lied.

He left, annoyed that he'd driven all the way to her place only to end up in the same spot they were earlier. He just wanted the whole thing to go away; he didn't want the mess of breaking it off and the shit show that would provoke. He climbed into his car and sat for a moment, wishing Eden would just disappear so he wouldn't have to deal with her ever again.

Eden drew the curtains and cleaned up, taking the popcorn and cocktail glasses to the kitchen sink. She was happy that Bill had come by to patch things up. She had overstepped a little; it was just her excitement that they might get back together that made her bring that crazy pizza over with no warning. As she headed to the bathroom to start her skin-care routine before bed, she saw that Bill had left his bomber jacket on her purple velour chair.

There was a knock at the door, and she assumed it was Bill, returning for his jacket.

She opened it with a wide smile and said, "Back so soon, babe?" as a metal bar struck her in the face and knocked her back.

Blood spurted from her nose, and she stumbled onto the floor, her eyes adjusting to the dizzying lights overhead as she regained her vision. A hand gripped her around the neck, and she heard the front door click shut behind her assailant. She fought back, but she was no match for him as he straddled her. His hand was like a steel claw, fingernails digging into her flesh as he cut off her air supply. She saw the flash of a blade and lost consciousness, her mind and body showing her one last act of mercy before her life ended.

CHAPTER TWENTY-ONE

Bill stood with Barrera outside Parker Center for the early-morning press conference announcing the new information in the Stacey Mandel murder case. Lieutenant Carbone spoke to the gathered reporters from a podium bearing the seal of the LAPD. The marine layer still hung over the city like a damp doily.

"After eighteen years, we have a confession and significant new information in the Stacey Mandel murder case from 2007. The lead detectives on the case, Peter Barrera and William Clarke, had long believed that Tyler Derby was responsible for her death, but without enough evidence to take to trial, they did not include her case in the serial-murder case that charged Derby with five other crimes and ultimately put him behind bars for life. William Clarke is recently retired and took it upon himself to travel to Pleasant Valley State Prison to speak to Derby and succeeded in getting a confession from him for Stacey's murder and another cold case in San Diego, which is being investigated. Derby also gave Mr. Clarke information regarding the location of physical evidence in Ms. Mandel's murder that will be tested for DNA. The dedication of our detectives in the Hollywood Division of the LAPD is unmatched. This is another example of their excellence and dogged determination to bring criminals to justice."

She stepped back and ushered Bill to the microphone. He looked out at the faces of the assembled press corps and took a moment to bask in the satisfaction of his moment.

"I'm relieved that we finally got a confession from the man we always felt was responsible for Stacey's murder, and I hope the police in Escondido are successful in closing the case of Remedios Carson as well. This is a great day in law enforcement in Los Angeles. Thank you!" he said.

As the conference broke up, reporters drew near to the staging area, trying to get close to Bill and get a sound bite from him. Joyce Ramsey made a point to shake his hand as did several other LAPD officials.

Despite his low-grade jealousy of Bill, Barrera slapped him on the back and leaned in. "Good job, brother. We need this shot in the arm right now. You're making us all look good."

Bill beamed, relishing the attention. A tall, red-haired woman in a dark suit pushed her way forward and put her business card into Bill's hand.

"I'm Ainsley Wright, Mr. Clarke. I'm an agent representing sports and media figures on the speakers' circuit. I think you and I could have a very beneficial working relationship. A lot of people will want to hear what you have to say," she said, as a young man elbowed in front of her.

"Hi, Mr. Clarke! I'm Johan Barry. I'm a producer for KTLA, and we would love to be in touch with you about appearing on one or more of our news shows about this case," he said, handing Bill another business card.

This jockeying for position among reporters wanting access to him went on for the next half hour, until the crowd melted away. The police representatives had dispersed; Bill found himself face to face with a young woman sporting a blue-black pixie cut and big green eyes.

She extended her hand. "Mr. Clarke, my name is Zelda Zed. I host one of the top crime podcasts here in the city, called *LA Murder Now*, and I would love to talk to you about your career and the many cases you've worked on. I'm thinking we could devote several episodes just to your story, if you're interested."

Bill shook her hand and said, "I'd love that! I started listening to crime podcasts about a year ago."

"Do you have time to talk now? There's a great little coffeehouse nearby where we could lay out some plans for the show," she said.

"Let's go!" Bill replied, thrilled at the idea.

Postiff sat in Millie Grace's sunny kitchen helping her to prepare two cups of green tea. A uniformed officer stood outside her front door; she'd had police protection ever since she was released from the hospital and had identified Whitty.

"We're getting closer to apprehending Whitty's partner. We're following up on some strong leads today, so I hope you'll be able to rest easy once we have him," Postiff said.

"That would be good. I'm on leave from work for the next few weeks, and Rosalie set up a GoFundMe to help cover expenses. A lot of very kind people have contributed to it. When they say that people in LA are phonies and jerks, they don't know what they're talking about. Everyone, even our neighbors, have been wonderful," she said.

Her head was still wrapped in bandages. She wore an eye patch and would require further surgery to repair her vision in that eye. She needed a walker to get around, she had a cast on each arm, but she was making her best effort to perform her daily tasks.

"I was wondering if you might have any further recollections of the second assailant? Sometimes it takes a little time for those things to come to the surface," Postiff said.

"I do. He was smaller in stature than Whitty, and slender. I think he had longer black hair. He wore a ski mask, but I remember seeing tufts of black hair where the mask ended on his neck. And he had a scar, a rather long, narrow scar on the back of one of his hands. It didn't look new."

"Those are terrific details, Ms. Grace. This will help us a lot."

"Please, call me Millie. Your first name is Judson, right? I saw it on the card you left."

He smiled. She'd looked at his card, which gave him a little boost of confidence.

"Yes, Judson is my first name. I've been a police officer for six years and just moved up to detective in Robbery-Homicide."

"You seem to be doing quite a good job," she said, with a faint smile. Her facial bruises were beginning to turn from purple to yellow, and she still had significant swelling around her jaw. She carefully took a sip of her tea.

"Are you a California native?" Postiff asked.

"Oh, gosh no! I'm from Missouri. My dad's a farmer, but I just wanted a taste of big-city life, so I came out here after college. I studied art history, and I'm hoping to get a job in one of the museums. I had an interview to be an intern at the Getty just before this happened, so I'm hoping I can follow through with that."

"The Getty is beautiful. I've been there a few times. I really liked the exhibit on Mayan art a few years back. I'm sure you'll get that job, and then you'll be on your way," he said.

"They have really good programs for kids, if you're interested," she said.

"Oh, I don't have kids. I'm not even married," he said, enjoying the little dance they were doing.

"Me either. Obviously. And Rosalie is just my roommate—we're not a couple or anything like that. We're both straight. Out here, I feel like I have to clarify that since everyone is so open about all that." She laughed nervously.

"I didn't get that sense at all, when I met you both."

"Good," she said, then added, "not that there'd be anything wrong with it if we were a couple. I don't mean that . . . I just meant . . . we're not . . ." Her voice trailed off, and she gave him a shy, sheepish look, which he found immensely charming. She took another sip of her tea and recovered her composure, looking him dead in the eye.

"They have a lot of great things coming up at the Getty. Maybe when I'm put back together better than Humpty-Dumpty, we can go check out one of their events," Millie said.

Postiff was grateful and relieved at her frankness. As a detective, he couldn't really make the first move, but now this pretty farm girl from Missouri had opened that door. He liked that even in her banged-up condition, she had the confidence to suggest a future date.

"That would be terrific," he said with a big smile. "Let's stay in touch when this is over."

Cassidy slept until nine and prepared to hit the gym before work. She had another meeting with Whitty scheduled for the early afternoon, and she hoped it would be the last one. Or that Barrera and Postiff had a lead on his accomplice. If she could break free of the high-stakes nightmare Whitty had put her in, she could resume life on her own terms.

She hadn't heard her dad come home last night, but she could see signs that he had been back. She caught the press conference and hoped that the positive attention would help settle him down, calm his restless, explosive energy. Maybe he could segue into private investigations of cold cases and reestablish some structure in his life, without spending too much time untethered or day drinking with Eden.

She dialed Carter. Every time she thought of the head boy video, she knew she needed a breather from him. Her call went straight to voicemail, and for a moment she wished she could just send him a text or an email, but she knew that would be too much. She might approach certain aspects of their relationship the way men do, but the change-in-relationship-status text was beyond the pale. She was still a woman after all, and as such, she had certain standards to maintain. Breakup by text was far beneath her sense of propriety and self-respect. But it would've been so easy.

Postiff and Barrera stood outside Thuy Pham's apartment, where she leaned against the doorjamb, wrapped in a cotton robe.

"I saw you last night, looking at Mr. Ron's place. I have nothing more to say to you," she said.

"We're trying to track down a fellow that Whitty calls V. Do you know anyone like that? Anyone who's been around here with him named V or Victor, Vikram, Vinnie?" Barrera asked.

A slight shiver ran up her spine. She couldn't believe that Whitty had talked or admitted anything, but if he did, she couldn't let him pin it all on Vithu. She didn't trust the detectives. Most likely they were on a fishing expedition, hoping to hit something.

She shrugged. "No, I don't know of anyone named V or Victor or any of that."

"Several people who used Whitty to install bootleg cable TV said he had a helper who was perhaps Vietnamese. Does that ring any kind of bell for you?" Barrera asked.

Thuy fixed him with a scathing look. "Just because I am Vietnamese doesn't mean I know every Vietnamese person in the city. Why should I know who Mr. Ron works with?"

Postiff reached into his jacket pocket for his phone and realized he didn't have it.

"Be right back. I left my phone in the car," he said, excusing himself.

Out on the street, he retrieved his phone from the glove box and saw Nonglak hiding in the narrow walkway between Thuy's building and the one next door. She waved him over.

"You have to look at Thuy's brother, Vithu. He's crazy. He lives back there," she whispered, pointing to the garage at the back of the driveway. Postiff looked at the locked storage room, the stairway landing filled with empty oil canisters and trash bags.

"Someone lives back there?" he asked, his heart racing.

"Thuy's brother. He helps Mr. Ron."

Thuy Pham had a brother named Vithu, who worked with Ron Whitty. Postiff felt the snap in his gut that came when he knew they'd broken the case.

"Show me where," he said, and Nonglak pointed to the storage room.

"I can only show you if Thuy's not here. She'll kill me if she knows I told you," Nonglak said, shaking her head.

"Okay, stay away from her place. We're going to move on this right now. Go get a coffee or something," he said, handing her a ten-dollar bill.

She hurried away, and he raced up to Thuy's apartment, where he found Barrera still engaged in a game of back-and-forth with her. Postiff took her by the arm and snapped handcuffs onto her before she knew what was happening.

"We're arresting you on suspicion of prostitution and human trafficking, Ms. Pham. We also need to speak to you about your brother, Vithu Pham, in relation to the recent murders of young women in the Hollywood area. You have the right to remain silent . . ." Postiff began Mirandizing her as she pulled against the cuffs in protest.

"I don't know what you're talking about!" she shouted.

Barrera looked at him in utter surprise, and Postiff said, "We need a warrant right away for the building next door, including the garage and storage room above. Any building that she manages for Avi Bierman."

The color drained from Thuy's face. She hadn't had a chance to clean up Vithu's place with bleach yet. She'd been waiting until the girls were in for the night and there was no risk of being seen. Nonglak was nosy and always stirring the others against her. There were still signs of Noelle Gerrard in the apartment; even her purse and ID were in the trash under the sink. Thuy's legs were unsteady as Postiff led her down the stairway; still, she cursed them loudly in Vietnamese.

"What the hell happened?" Barrera asked.

"A little bird spilled a secret," he whispered. "She has a brother."

Back at the Hollywood station, Postiff was digging deep to find anything on Vithu Pham while Barrera researched every inch of the buildings that Thuy managed for Avi Bierman. Ramsey had reached out to the INTERPOL US National Central Bureau to search for any criminal history of Vithu in Vietnam. Postiff texted Cassidy that they might have identified V, and Ramsey had decided to stall the Whitty interview until they knew more.

Thuy Pham sat in a jail cell, awaiting her initial interview. She hadn't asked for a lawyer yet, but they expected her to. Unlike Whitty, she didn't have any interest in anything besides her own survival, and she knew playing power games wouldn't help her. She was stoic, her mind working feverishly to find a way out of the corner she was in. She had a lot of information they would be interested in, from Whitty and Vithu's activities to Avi Bierman arranging the visas for the girls back home who thought they were coming to work as domestics, only to find themselves in the sex trade. Avi Bierman even kept their passports locked up at his Hancock Park house. If she was going to go down, she would take as many people with her as possible, and maybe this would be the end of carrying her good-for-nothing brother on her back. She wouldn't get life in prison; she'd give them information in exchange for a lighter sentence, and then she'd be free. She'd start over and build her life up again, just like she always did.

Cassidy arrived at the station and found Postiff and Ramsey in Carbone's office.

"What's the latest on V?" she asked.

"We're hoping to get some information from the USNCB for Vithu Pham, Thuy's brother, who doesn't show up on any of her family immigration records," Ramsey said.

"Do you think he came in with false documents?"

"If he came with the family, it's likely, especially if he had a serious criminal record back home and they had to cover it up. He's probably been living under the radar since then, with his sister's help," Carbone said. "Which makes her liable as an accessory in the murders."

Ramsey's cell phone rang. "It's the USNCB," she said.

She listened intently and took notes on the call. Then she hung up and said, "I think we've got him! He was arrested multiple times in Haiphong for violent sexual assault and crimes against women and girls, starting when he was in school. Put in a mental institution for several years. There's been no activity from him or any sign of life in Vietnam since Thuy and her parents immigrated. They live in Anaheim, so we need to get out there. We have to find him within the next twenty-four hours."

Postiff jumped up. "We have him! Let's get a team ready to head to Anaheim and talk to the parents. I'll bet he's there."

Ramsey turned to Cassidy. "Just sit tight. I want you to go into that room with Whitty armed with everything. We'll stall the interview for a few hours. We're going to get a confession today."

Barrera and a small army of police officers fanned out to search the three buildings that Thuy Pham managed. When they stepped inside the garage apartment where Vithu lived, the rancid smell of stale bodily fluids hit them. It was a disgusting mess, with food wrappers and moldy leftovers strewn around the floor. There were dark, damp stains on the couch, and it reeked of urine. Under the sink, they found her purse and wallet, with her identification.

From a shelf made of cinder block and boards, Barrera picked up a family photo of what appeared to be Thuy, Vithu, and their parents. Vithu was slight and slender, with thick, shoulder-length black hair. He had a wide, youthful face and dark, almond-shaped eyes. Postiff arrived and stepped into the foul-smelling unit. Barrera handed him the framed photo.

"I'm sure that's him. He fits the description," Barrera said.

"What the hell? This is where Vithu Pham lived?" he asked, covering his nose with a handkerchief.

"Yeah. I'm sure this is where he kept the Gerrard girl and where she went into diabetic shock. Hard to imagine this being the last place you live before it's over," Barrera said with a sigh.

"Once we get this enlarged and out to the public, someone will recognize him and we'll have him within twenty-four hours," Postiff said.

"Maybe we'll get lucky and it'll be a citizen takedown."

"Have you seen the girl who had the bracelet, Nonglak? The one who tipped us off to Vithu Pham?" Postiff asked.

"All Thuy's girls are waiting in a downstairs apartment with a police guard. It's Sean Riley, Cassidy Clarke's partner."

"I bet he'll be happy to have her on patrol again," Postiff said.

"Won't we all?" Barrera grumbled.

A forensic technician came out holding a plastic tackle box and handed it to Barrera.

"I think you should see this, detective. It was on a shelf in the closet," she said.

Barrera opened the box. Inside there was a pile of baubles, from hair clips to necklaces and rings, earrings, and scarves. One blue plastic rosary. He recognized Christy Cline's ring from photos provided by her family. They were souvenirs that had belonged to the victims of both Whitty and Vithu. Postiff felt suddenly sick, a wave of nausea hitting him in the gut.

"There are so many," he whispered.

CHAPTER TWENTY-TWO

"You mean a breather or breaking up?" Carter asked over the phone as Cassidy sat in her car in the parking lot of the Hollywood station. She was on hold until Ramsey gave her the go-ahead with Whitty, and she couldn't have this conversation inside the station.

"I mean a breather, a short break. This case is weighing so heavily on me, and I have the stuff with my dad. He's going to the neuro in a few days to see if he has CTE, and everything is just . . . too much."

"And you think the solution to all that pressure is to take a breather from me?" he asked. She could hear the hurt in his voice.

She knew Carter had never been on the letdown side of a relationship. He'd always dated girls who dreamed of getting him to the altar with that big trust fund attached. He was the one who ended things and determined everything.

"I can't take a breather from any of the other things. And you're so busy with law school, it's not like we have the same kind of time we did when we first met. I feel bad that I can't come to things like the boating trip with your family. I don't want to feel like I'm letting you down," she explained.

"But you could take a step back from your dad. I've told you a hundred times, he's a grown man and you shouldn't be managing so many things for him, taking care of the house stuff, all the rest. And if he has CTE, it's all the more reason for you to get your own place or move in with me," he pushed.

"What're you talking about?"

"If he has CTE and he's going to have more degeneration in his brain, he'll need someone to come in and help him, eventually to take care of him. You can't do that with your work. And people hire someone to do that; they don't do it themselves."

Cassidy was silent. This was the disconnect that Carter would never understand. In his world, the messiness of life, anything that was difficult or inconvenient, could be farmed out for a price. He thought his money could insulate him from life in a way that was a privileged pipe dream.

"That's not workable for me. I can't do that, not when he might need help dealing with a diagnosis and some kind of transition. It's not who I am," she said.

"Okay. You're a good daughter, but don't let this drag on. I'm here for you, Cassidy. I want you to know that. However long you need, whatever. I'm here and I'm waiting," he said.

Her phone pinged with a text.

"Thank you. I appreciate it. I just got a text from Detective Postiff. I have to call him back."

"Okay. We'll talk soon, right?"

"Yeah," she lied. A wave of relief washed over her as she hung up and dialed Postiff.

"What's up? Do you have him yet?" she asked.

"Not yet. We're finishing up with the search at Thuy's place. We found his treasure box. It has items from the three victims and a lot of others. I'm sending it over to the station with your partner, Riley. You should look at it before you talk to Whitty. We're heading out to Anaheim now."

"Okay, thanks."

She hung up, shaken by the idea that she would examine the macabre keepsakes that serial killers took from their victims. It was one of their twisted behaviors that she could not get her mind around.

Her dad had done it many times, but she was not ready to see what the treasure box held.

Ethan Acevedo stopped at the flower section of Pavilions market on Melrose and Vine. He was on his way to the station, but he wanted to pick up a little something to drop off for Eden. Flowers were always nice. His workload had been heavy, too many high-risk situations that he and the other Metro cops had to step up and take care of. He'd gotten into a rut in many areas of his life. It was rise early, eat a keto breakfast, hit the gym, visit the chiro twice a week for an adjustment and his epidural steroid injection to help the back pain from an old injury. And twice a week to see Dr. Vosgerchian, who took care of his anabolic steroids to keep him in top performance shape.

Then it was work a twelve-hour shift, six days a week, broken up by visits to his ladies to help release tension and stress. It seemed he needed that more and more these days. His moods were more intense, and he got pissed at situations all the time now. One of his buddies recommended therapy, but after one visit to some limp-dick shrink in Sherman Oaks, he'd given up. He didn't need to talk about his emotions. He needed his women, wet and ready, to help him chill when everything built up too much.

All his regulars were single, except for one who was married to a guy twenty-five years older than she was. Her name was Teresa; she had come from the Philippines, popped out two kids, and was biding her time until she could leave the geezer. She loved Acevedo, they spoke Tagalog, and he was her type, brown skinned and athletic. Not pasty white with a bulging gut and watery, pale eyes like the *matanda* she was married to. She was cool; she didn't expect anything more than a few good fucks every week when her husband was at work. Sometimes she sent him home with *lumpia*, which was a treat.

He didn't care about Eden; she was just a fuck buddy. It didn't matter to him who she hooked up with or if she was out of town with another guy. It just made him think of Marilise, and his feelings got all twisted up, so he'd acted like a jerk. He pulled up to Eden's house and walked to the front door to knock. There was no answer, but her car was there. He knocked again and tried the door. It was firmly locked.

A wiry older man with a shock of thick graying hair approached him.

"Can I help you, officer?"

"Yeah, I'm dropping these flowers off for Eden, but she's not answering. Her car is still here. Have you seen her this morning?" Acevedo asked.

"I'm Michael Lyman, the landlord. I haven't seen Eden today, but she might be asleep. I can take those and give them to her later. I'll put them in water, so they don't wilt," Lyman said. Acevedo handed him the bouquet.

"Thank you, sir."

"Any message?"

"Just tell her that the Tomato came by. She'll know who you mean," Acevedo said with a grin. His teeth were perfectly straight and as white as a Kleenex.

"That's cute! I'll be sure to give them to her," Lyman said, turning back to his apartment. Acevedo watched him go, the bouquet clutched firmly against his chest. It was good he'd run into Lyman. Everything was going to be just fine.

Bill stood with a group of officers in a cordoned-off area of the Cleveland National Forest, which spanned out into three counties: San Diego, Riverside, and Orange. The police had brought in cadaver dogs and digging equipment to the area at Pilot Rock, where Tyler Derby said he'd buried Remedios Carson. Her family had given DNA samples in case any human remains were found, and one of the cadaver dogs had alerted next to a twisted tree stump. The forensic anthropologists from the University of California at San Diego and the University of California at Riverside were at work, managing the recovery.

Bill's coffee meeting with Zelda Zed had been productive. She had a lot of ideas about how to build several podcast episodes around his career and the many cases he'd worked for the LAPD. She even knew that his daughter was a new boot, and Zelda was interested in the early days of the Hollywood Hit Men case, when he was on it with Barrera. They had another meeting scheduled the following week to decide which cases they would focus on.

Bill was elated. It was just what he needed to bridge his past and his future. He could become a cold case closer; people might even pay for his services to help them find answers in the cases that the police weren't working any longer. The department always maintained that all the cold cases were open and ongoing, but everyone knew that they were as dead as dogmeat.

He loved the idea of Zelda's audience following his story. He could even become a kind of folk hero to the true crime fanatics out there in the millions. Maybe he could do a podcast of his own, with Zelda's producers. When he was on the force, he couldn't talk to the press unless it was sanctioned by the department, but now he could talk as much as he liked with no repercussions.

One of the university anthropologists put her hand up, signaling that they had found human remains. Tyler Derby had told the truth, it seemed. Bill took a deep breath. It was just a matter of time now.

Cassidy waited for the box of Whitty and Vithu's souvenirs that Sean Riley was bringing to the station. She was in Carbone's office, dressed in a cotton sundress and flip-flops, her hair loose, when Riley walked in, gingerly holding the gray tackle box. A plastic envelope with Jennifer Dale's bracelet sat on top of the box.

"You're interviewing Whitty out of uniform?" he asked.

Cassidy nodded. "It's part of my plan. My dad gave me great advice to let Whitty feel like he's putting the interview on a personal level, that I'm naive and easily manipulated in my Pollyanna sundress."

"You've got a guard in there with you, so I guess it's safe," Riley said. "Here's the box. It's got a lot of stuff in it. There's things that came from Vietnam, so I guess this Vithu guy's been at this for a long time."

She opened the box and saw there were several layers of trinkets. Christy Cline's gold ring was visible on the top. As she dug through the trinkets, she saw a silver onyx-inlaid cross, like the one Elise Mannard wore. She searched for something with Vietnamese writing on it. She found a leather bracelet with the words *kí nghi* embossed onto it. She googled it and found that it meant *vacation*. She wondered if an unsuspecting young tourist was taken in by Vithu and ended up dead.

"It's creepy, isn't it?" Riley asked.

"Yeah. I'm hoping this is over today so I can go back on patrol with you."

"Same. Good luck in there," he said before leaving.

Cassidy didn't want to handle the items; it felt like a violation of some sort. Things that the victims wore or used regularly, part of their everyday lives. When they slipped on a ring or fastened a necklace on that final day, they never knew what awaited them. She felt like a thief to be touching them. But she knew they would be helpful in the room with Whitty, so she steeled herself to the task at hand and stashed several in the pocket of her dress.

It was two hours past the original time for the interview when Ramsey came in and announced, "We're going to go ahead. The detectives and backup should be getting to Anaheim within the next half hour. We're going to find Vithu Pham today—we've released his photo to the public, and we're already getting calls. Just tell Whitty that we have him and he's talking. Lying to a suspect in an interview is legal. We've got so much on him now, he's trapped."

Cassidy watched the video feed when Whitty came in, completely relaxed. He took a seat as if he were at a neighborhood café where he knew all the waiters. She had a game plan. This would be the last day of talking to him. After a few minutes, she came in, and Whitty's eyes lit up.

"You're looking mighty fine today, Officer Clarke," he said, with a whistle.

Cassidy giggled and languidly took her seat across from him. The sundress had a fitted bodice and a full skirt. She could see Whitty's hungry eyes staring at her breasts as if he might suddenly develop x-ray vision.

"Hey there, Mr. Whitty. How'd you sleep last night?" she asked.

"Pretty good. They got me in my own cell for my protection, they say."

"I couldn't sleep a wink, tossed and turned all night," she said. "My air-conditioning broke, and it was so hot in my apartment. I had to keep all the windows open."

"That's not too safe. Someone could get in."

"But I'd hear them, and I have a gun in the house."

"They can get in anyway, and you'd never hear them till it was too late," he insisted.

"I guess you would know, right?" She smiled.

He grinned back at her. "I'm just looking out for you, Officer Clarke."

"Thank you. You're quite the gentleman," she said.

She followed the same strategy as their last interview, spending close to an hour in flirtatious banter with him, gauging his responses as he relaxed. He told her off-color jokes, and she burst into laughter. They leaned in close to tell each other about strange dreams they'd had. At one point she saw that he almost reached out and laid his hand over hers.

Finally, she checked her watch and said, "I should get going soon. My friend's expecting me at her house."

On her wrist, Jennifer Dale's rose gold bracelet jangled against her steel watchband. She saw Whitty recognize it, and his expression shifted.

"Where'd you get that?" he asked.

"The watch? It was a gift from my dad," she said innocently.

"No, the bracelet."

"It belonged to one of the victims, Jennifer Dale. You remember her? The pretty girl who lived in the Hollywood Dell? I think you saw her up at Paxton Sparks's house on Mulholland. And then you gave it to Nonglak, one of Thuy Pham's girls, right? She gave it to Detective Postiff."

He blanched for a moment but said nothing.

"And I have this too," she said, pulling out Christy Cline's Turkish gold ring with the double gemstones. She set it on the table between them. His eyes darted back and forth between the pieces, his mind working.

"It's heavy, isn't it? Christy Cline always wore it on her right ring finger. She had a tan line there when they found her, so they knew something was missing."

"How'd you get those things?" he asked warily.

"We got them from your friend, Vithu Pham. He had them in his garage apartment next door to your place. I got this from him too," she said, taking out the leather bracelet.

"I guess he got this from a victim in Vietnam. He kept busy over there!"

"I don't know who you mean," he said.

"I think you do, Ron. Little Vithu Pham, with the long black hair? Your apartment manager's brother? We have them both here right now. And you know how Asians are, family first before everything. They have a lot to say," she said, leaning back in her chair.

"Like what?"

"We know that you targeted the women with your cable-internet TV scam. You even did it for that older couple out in the Valley, right? We found your card in Elise Mannard's kitchen drawer, and Christy's neighbors identified you from a photo. I bet you liked Paxton Sparks's wife, too, huh? I heard she's young and pretty, with big knockers. Fake, but still, you like that type. Big boobs but built like a fourteen-year-old boy from the waist down. Certain types of guys who don't like women love that sort of thing."

"What d'you mean? Don't like women? I'm not a faggot!"

"I don't mean that, Ron. I mean the ones who don't like that women have their own money; they control their own lives now. But you did say that thing about the tight fit with a ladyboy the day we met, remember? So maybe you do like a little bit of that action . . ."

She saw his eyes flash with sudden rage and betrayal. She continued, "I bet none of these girls gave you the time of day, right? When you tried to talk to them, they brushed you off. Or they were just annoyed, like Christy was over the internet being off while you worked. I heard she got kind of hot with you."

"She was an uppity bitch! Like she owned the place. Getting in my face about how long I was taking, like she had something important to do!" he snapped.

"But she did. She made bank, handling social media for her clients. She pulled in way more than you did. She drove a new BMW, just like Jennifer. Those apartments aren't cheap, right in Hollywood."

"And I'm not into guys, so shut up about that!" he said.

"Really? That's not why you chose Vithu as your helper? He's small, very good looking with that long hair. You might think he was a girl from behind," she said.

He slammed his hand against the table.

"Why're you talking shit like this? You said yourself those types don't know what it is to do real work. Those women were parasites, just living on the backs of people stupid enough to pay them! And they thought they were hotter than fuck, didn't they? Oh yeah, they just blew me off like I was trash!" He was shouting now.

"Shhh, it's okay, Ron. Don't get all worked up, sweetie . . ." she said softly.

He was breathing hard and thrown off by her sudden change in demeanor. She smiled kindly at him, leaning across the table as if they were two old friends having a heart-to-heart. She could see his emotions were ricocheting back and forth like a pinball.

"This is where it's at, Ron. Four witnesses have identified you at the places you encountered the victims. We know you had possession of their personal property that ties you to the murders. We have your DNA under Jennifer Dale's fingernails and on a victim who survived and identified you as well. And we have Thuy and Vithu Pham in this station, talking to detectives right now, throwing you under the bus. I like you. We have a nice rapport, don't we? I want to help you any way I can, but you have to come clean with me. Tell me why you did it, how it went down. I know you had your reasons," Cassidy said.

His breathing was hard and fast. He looked at her, trying desperately to reel his emotions back in after they'd been released in a tsunami of rage and confusion.

"They were bitches," he finally said quietly. "And they acted like they were better than me . . ."

Cassidy sat back, nodding in agreement, encouraging him to unburden himself. She maintained her sympathetic composure, fighting the urge to scream, while he confessed how he butchered Christy Cline, Elise Mannard, and Jennifer Dale to death.

CHAPTER TWENTY-THREE

Bill sat in the makeup chair at the local San Diego news station SD Today for a live interview on the six o'clock broadcast. The search at Pilot Rock had uncovered the remains of a female, under the age of fourteen, and dental records had confirmed it was Remedios Carson. Her grieving family chose not to speak publicly. The reporter at the scene had done a brief interview with Bill, but the producers wanted a three-minute segment on the evening news.

Bill had brought his black suit, just in case something like this developed. Zelda Zed had suggested it. He knew this was just the beginning of something big. He had hit the jackpot with these first two cases. He'd already discussed the questions the news anchor was planning to ask, highlighting his dogged determination to solve these cases after his stellar career as a Los Angeles homicide detective.

The makeup artist patted light foundation over his skin, evening out his sunspots and brightening his skin tone with a bit of blusher. He thought he looked at least five to seven years younger. But he needed to start working out at the gym again, especially if he was going to be running down these cold cases and managing all the attention that would bring him. His head was throbbing, and he had no Aleve left, but the production assistant had brought him four extra-strength Advil caplets.

He had already made a plan to drive back up to Coalinga again. He was sure Derby could offer him insight from the killer's perspective, to help him move in the right direction on several cold cases. He especially wanted to run the whole Alan Musselman and Min Sun-Hee theory past him.

Bill knew he and Cassidy needed to talk when he got back home; he didn't like the way they'd left things. He'd gotten too riled up over Eden's unplanned visit to their house. He'd dodged the neurologist issue a few times, but now that he wasn't working, he knew his daughter wasn't going to let it go. She was just like him in that way. Maybe she was right, but he didn't think it was the kind of thing that needed a diagnosis from a head doctor. He had become more volatile with age, but didn't everyone? Wasn't part of getting older that you didn't have the patience for bullshit any longer? He'd read that many times. He'd have to go in soon to see this Dr. Baruch that she had found. He couldn't stall forever, but he couldn't see how to fit it into his schedule now. He had cases to close.

A young production assistant stuck her head into the makeup trailer. "We're ready for you, Mr. Clarke."

Vithu sat shivering in the upstairs bedroom of his parents' stucco tract house in West Anaheim. It wasn't cold—he was unable to control his anxiety knowing that there were six police cars outside, waiting for him with the detectives from Los Angeles. Hs parents had already been taken from the house. They walked out willingly, and now his mother was calling his phone again to convince him to give himself up. He refused to answer; he'd already spoken to her twice.

Everything had gone smoothly after they dumped Ashley-Noelle. Thuy had dropped him off in Anaheim, but he had been unable to settle down. After his parents went to sleep, he'd taken their car and driven back to the city. He wanted to be caught up in the traffic, the throngs of people hitting the clubs and restaurants, moving through the crosswalks en masse, like a wave of seawater breaking on the shore. He drove through Hollywood, down the busy boulevards, up the narrow, winding streets of the hillside neighborhoods. He liked seeing people through their windows, the blue light of a television set behind a thin curtain. They had no idea what might be outside. He had come back as dawn was breaking.

Now he banged his palms against his forehead, wondering how he ever let himself get caught up with Ronald Whitty. Why he'd helped him with his crooked business. Why had he broken into the house by Bronson Canyon and held that little blond girl down while Whitty tried to strangle her. Or the others, the ones they'd posed and drawn lipstick hearts on their faces. He'd been caught up in the thrill of the killing, like always. With Whitty it was easier, and he did most of the work.

But Vithu wasn't as driven as Whitty, who was like a grenade, always on the verge of exploding in amped-up sexual rage. Vithu could manage his impulses, and so far, he'd done just fine and never been caught. He chose the women that no one would miss, and the cops wouldn't try hard to find. And he spaced them out and moved around the vast city. Whitty was set off by those white women who dismissed him, and he struck in quick succession, gaining way too much attention and even a nickname for them. The Hollywood Hit Men. Vithu liked that, though, just a little.

Working with Whitty had made him reckless and in need of that rush—that was why he'd chosen Ashley-Noelle. If he had never picked her up, never seen her stumbling in the crosswalk, his prey drive wouldn't have been triggered. If she hadn't been out drinking late at night, also. She put herself in a vulnerable position. She should've been home if she was sick. He reassured himself that it wasn't completely his fault.

He heard the police calling again for him to surrender. He was afraid to peer out the window to see where they were, but he was sure he heard footsteps and movement all around the perimeter of the house. They would come in by force, and then they might just kill him and say he fired first and plant a gun on him. He didn't stand a chance if they burst in. He stood up, his legs shaking, and he was afraid he might pee himself. He wished he could talk to Thuy to find out what she knew, but she wasn't answering, and the cops said they had her in custody. No one was coming to save him this time. He began to whimper as he walked down the stairs and opened the front door, his hands held high over his head.

Ramsey breathed a giant sigh of relief when she got the call from Barrera. They had Vithu Pham in custody. A press conference would be held within the hour to let the frightened residents of the city know that the Hollywood Hit Men were behind bars and the killings were over. Cassidy Clarke had come through and gotten a confession from Whitty, which would mean a slam dunk with the district attorney. Since Cassidy was a woman half Whitty's size and no one had conveniently turned off the interrogation-room camera, he couldn't claim he was coerced or forced to confess with threats or intimidation.

And once Thuy Pham started talking, she didn't stop. She told them about Whitty's exploits, how he'd threatened her if she spoke to police, how he'd coerced her disturbed brother into helping him. She even gave up Avi Bierman for his part in the trafficking of girls from Southeast Asia for sex work. The Hollywood Hit Men were locked up, and a sex ring had been exposed, with some high-value players, which always went over well with the public. They liked seeing Avi Bierman being arrested outside his big mansion.

Ramsey could leverage this win with the police commission and other city officials. Chief McCall would be retiring in two years, and she wanted to line herself up as the obvious choice to replace him. The media department sent over a clip of Bill Clarke on the evening news down in San Diego. He'd done a great job closing two cold cases, but Bill had always been obsessive and driven by his huge ego to outshine everyone.

He'd crossed the line a few times, especially when there weren't cameras everywhere, and once he was sure of someone's guilt, he would not stop. Even when new evidence came out that proved a suspect's innocence. He went by the old cop adage that even if the guy wasn't guilty of this crime, he'd done something similar, so nailing him was just fine. Too many attorneys in the DA's office felt the same way. They were the top cops, after all.

Ramsey had her issues with Bill Clarke. He'd been a brash young officer when she joined the LAPD. He was already making a name for himself on the street. He and the other officers weren't happy about having so many women on the force, especially ones with ambition beyond the detective division. A couple of them thought it was a big laugh to leave maxi pads lying around the station and ask the female boots of they'd lost something. Bill was never directly involved, but he didn't give up any names when the department finally investigated it.

Bill Clarke held up that blue wall of silence for his male colleagues; they all did that. There would always be the predators, like Acevedo, who'd had so many complaints against him she'd lost count. But they'd received several calls from a representative in Sacramento, asking them to fix it with Acevedo, so they had buried those reports, and he was still on the force, in good standing.

But she was certain that Bill Clarke was not a good choice to represent LAPD detectives after retirement. If the press wanted to do stories that supported the police and their lifetime commitment to solving crimes, there were other former cops they could talk to. Bill Clarke was too high strung, too quick to anger, and too problematic in many ways. She dialed Mary Zanetti, the media liaison, to let her know to reach out to their news contacts and quash any interest in a story on Bill Clarke. They also needed to shut down interest from the online creators, who were building a whole new, younger generation of people obsessed with crime in the city. She'd call Zelda Zed personally, since Zed had featured her on an episode of *LA Murder Now*. Joyce Ramsey didn't want to see Bill Clarke's face on her office television set again, anytime soon.

"Here's to another psycho behind bars! The streets are safer tonight!" Postiff said, clinking his beer bottle with those of Cassidy, Foster, Fort, and Dykstra at the Casting Couch bar, where the Hollywood freeway meets the 101. It was a cozy place, just far enough from the high-priced, trendy spots that now filled the neighborhood near the station. And it was frequented by actors and studio workers as well from nearby Universal and Warner Brothers, so the crowd was mixed, which made for interesting social dynamics: cops and people who played them on television.

Barrera left after one beer; he had a long drive to Simi Valley, and now that he was older, he no longer spent several hours unwinding from work with his cop buddies. In the old days, it had been impossible to flip the switch from finding dead bodies to hearing about the stresses of the PTA meeting and the candy-bar fundraiser. Now he walked away at the end of each day and looked forward to watching his Netflix shows on the couch with Gloria, coasting along until he had his own retirement party at the Moose Lodge in Burbank.

The group at the Casting Couch celebrated a win, and now they could relax and breathe without wondering what else they should've done that day to find the Hit Men. Ron Whitty and Vithu Pham would never see the outside of a prison again, once their trials were over. Postiff didn't know how their public defenders would even mount a defense, with all the evidence against them and Whitty's confession. Vithu Pham had lawyered up immediately, but his sister's statement was so incriminating against him, it was almost as if she wanted him locked up forever.

Cassidy was pleased to be included with the detectives, and she could sense that their grudging acceptance of her was loosening. She had proven herself and accomplished what was asked of her. She was no longer just a new boot, finding her way on the force. She could sense that the men were on their better behavior with her present and could guess what their conversation would be if she weren't there, especially with the way Fort and Dykstra kept eyeing a pretty, young woman playing pool in a tube top and torn-up jeans.

Postiff's phone rang, and he stepped away to take the call. Cassidy saw his face change, his body language slumping inward as if he'd been punched. He ran his hand over his eyes and made another call before returning to the table.

"I've got to go. I just called Barrera. It seems Vithu Pham struck again, after Noelle Gerrard and before we picked him up. A new victim, found in her home with all the signature markers of the Hit Men. I'm heading over there now," he said.

The celebratory mood of the group dropped faster than a greased pig. Everyone went silent. Then Cassidy's phone rang. She saw it was Montoya calling.

"Hey, what's up?" Cassidy said. She could hear street noise behind Montoya and assumed she was on duty.

"I'm out here in Hollywood, and we did a welfare check on a woman who looks to be another victim of the Hit Men," she said, her voice clearly distressed.

"I know. I'm with Postiff and the other detectives. He said he just got the call."

"I just wanted to give you a heads-up, so you're not caught off guard. The victim is your dad's ex-girlfriend, the one who's always around."

Cassidy's mind blanked for a moment as she tried to comprehend what Montoya was telling her.

"I don't know who you mean," she said.

"It's Eden Balcomb. She's been murdered."

CHAPTER TWENTY-FOUR

Tyler Derby sat in his cell at Pleasant Valley State Prison, pulling on each finger to crack his knuckles hard, waiting for the popping sound and the quick jolt of pain in his hand. Then he'd have some relief until the tension started building once again, seizing his hands up like a Gorgon's hair. He'd messed his hands up when he was young, digging ditches and clearing rocks back in Henryetta, Oklahoma. He'd been so eager to earn that shitty pay that he kept working when his cheap tools broke, using his hands to get the job done. He'd worked on bigger crews out at Lake Eufaula and some near the Arkansas border, but he'd had to leave the state after an incident required him to disappear for a while. Now the cracking was a habit when he felt his anger flaring up.

Quake Rennison had called him into his office hours earlier, and Derby had been expecting some good news about his transfer request.

Instead, Rennison had looked at him across his desk, his intertwined fingers resting on his bulging gut, and said, "Your request for a transfer was denied. You need to accept that you're never moving out of here, Derby."

"They just rejected it outright? No hearing, nothing? What about the stuff I gave Bill Clarke? He said they look favorably on those things," Derby asked.

"Favorably if you didn't commit a bunch of murders years ago and just admitted to one that no one even knew about. You're stuck here, buddy," Rennison said with satisfaction.

"What about Donovan down in San Diego? I've got to get out of here. Presley and Pimentel are making my life hell," Derby implored. The two inmates and their group were on him every day, roughing him up, stealing his shit, and making sure he paid for every rape he committed.

"You can put in another request and see what happens," Rennison said, standing up to dismiss him back to his cell. Derby shuffled to his feet and left feeling defeated and used.

Now he sat brooding over Bill Clarke, who was an asshole and a liar. Clarke had come sniffing around for something to build himself up, and he'd talked like Derby had a chance of getting transferred if he just gave them something. Talked like they were old friends with a lot in common. Made him feel that someone on the outside took an interest in him and might help him to make his dismal existence better. Bill saw the need in him and took advantage of it.

But Derby could see needs in people too. That's how he was able to kill so many victims, beyond the few they knew about and prosecuted him for. He knew how to read people, to gain their trust, to get them to open up their lives just enough for him to get his elbow in the door and pry it open a bit further. He worked slowly—that was how he got to the old bitch who poisoned the cats. He helped her with simple chores around her apartment, used a drill to hang some shelves in her kitchen, chatted with her over a cup of instant coffee. Then he killed her when he got the urge.

He saw needs in Bill Clarke, to be important, powerful in ways that were slipping away from him. He wanted attention, validation, to be at the helm of a destiny that was built on the age-old questions of good and evil. He saw in Bill the grandiose desire to be bigger than just an average Joe, and he knew how to exploit that. No, now that his request for a transfer had been denied and he had lost the thing he wanted most, it was time for Bill Clarke to pay. Time for him to lose something also, and if Derby couldn't break out and take it from him in the external world, he could take it another way.

Cassidy tried calling Bill, but it went to voicemail. She didn't want him to hear about Eden's murder on the news. She wanted to go to the crime scene, but she felt it wasn't right for her to show up with no reason to be there. She remembered Eden crying and yelling at Bill in their driveway just the night before, and she felt an overwhelming sadness and shock. Eden wasn't a woman Cassidy could relate to easily; she found her annoying and desperate, but she didn't deserve to die violently in what should've been the safety of her own home.

Cassidy wanted to talk to Montoya or Postiff and get more information. What were the chances that Vithu Pham would've crossed paths with someone who was a volunteer at the Hollywood station? That in the small window of time between Noelle Gerrard's death and his arrest, in a gigantic, teeming city, he struck someone known to her?

She left the bar and got into her car, not even certain of where she was going until she turned onto Franklin Avenue and found herself at the intersection with Beachwood Canyon. She turned left, and within a few blocks, she saw the flashing police lights. An officer was diverting traffic onto a side street away from frightened onlookers, and yellow tape had cordoned off the scene. She knew the building where Eden lived; she had picked Bill up from there a few times. A Ford Explorer from the forensic investigation team was parked in the driveway. Cassidy saw Barrera on his phone, under the big avocado tree outside Eden's living room window. Seeing him there, with all the activity, made it real for her. She hung a U-turn and headed back to the freeway, hoping she would find Bill home and break the news to him before someone else did.

Postiff walked through the neat, well-appointed apartment, the victim propped up against a large vintage trunk that served as a coffee table. She looked like a Barbie that had been carelessly tossed aside, except that her clothing was drenched in blood from the gash in her neck. She had been killed like the other Hit Men victims, left with a lipstick heart drawn on her cheek, leaving no doubt that her killer was Vithu Pham.

The fact that he managed to kill another victim after Noelle Gerrard hit Postiff like a personal attack.

The coroner had determined the time of death as twenty-four to thirty-six hours earlier, so while they were celebrating Vithu's arrest and he was meeting with his court-appointed lawyer, Eden Balcomb was dead and waiting to be discovered. Her landlord had made the call for a welfare check. When the police arrived, he reported that he usually saw Eden coming and going in the morning, and she worked for another neighbor up the street, Adina Howard, who, in her eighties, needed help with her grocery shopping and getting to and from appointments. Adina had called him to let him know Eden hadn't shown up with her prescription refill as planned. He had knocked and considered going in to check, but he thought better of it and called the police.

They found business cards and letterhead for Eden's business, Jill of All Trades, and her client list, mostly older and handicapped people who lived alone, with no family. Like previous victims, she had carved out a job in the gig economy, but Postiff was mystified as to how Vithu could've known to target her. Unless he and Whitty had scoped her out previously, since she lived squarely within their killing zone. Officer Montoya had alerted Postiff that Eden was a volunteer at the Hollywood station and had been at Bill Clarke's retirement party. He didn't recognize her, but that was mostly due to the state of her body after being attacked.

He needed a formal statement from Michael Lyman, who remained bustling among the terrified neighbors like a man hosting a block party. He even brought out Chinet paper cups of coffee and water to those gathered at the perimeter of the crime scene. Postiff found Barrera, looking every bit of his sixty-six years, talking with members of the coroner's team. He approached as Barrera reached across the yellow line and took a steaming cup of coffee from Michael Lyman.

"That old guy is an odd bird, isn't he?" Barrera said. "He even put fancy creamer in my coffee."

"I'm going to get a formal statement from him. What'd the coroners say?" Postiff asked.

"It's going to be another hour or so. The photographers need to finish, and they want to be sure we have everything before they take her. This one hits hard, man. She used to be Bill's girlfriend. Gloria and I have had dinner with her a bunch of times," Barrera said.

"She dated Bill Clarke? You're shitting me!" Postiff said. "Montoya told me she was at the Smoke House, but I thought it was just because she was a volunteer."

"Nah, they dated after he and Cathy split up. They were kind of in a casual, no-strings-attached type of thing," Barrera explained.

"So, we're going to have to interview him?" Postiff asked.

Barrera winced. "Yeah, but Bill didn't have anything to do with this. It's another Hit Men murder."

Postiff nodded. They had a ton of work at the scene and then had to arrange an interview with Vithu and his lawyer to discuss this new murder. It was going to be a long night.

Ramsey was out to dinner with her husband, Jim, at the California Club in downtown LA when she got the call from Postiff. The club was one of the oldest social clubs in the city, established in 1888 for the wealthy and well connected. It was old school and old money, California-style. While there were other, hipper social clubs for trendsetters, the California Club was an old-fashioned establishment type of place, a stepping stone for anyone in the conservative world of law enforcement to show that they were staunchly committed to maintaining the status quo among the city's power brokers. Now, seated in the dining room, she puckered her lips in distaste for seeing Postiff's name come up on the call.

She answered in a quiet, subdued voice, "Yes, detective?"

"We have another Hit Men victim. Pham must've killed her in the past day or so before we caught him. She has the signatures that only the killers would know. And she was a volunteer at the station. Eden Balcomb," he said.

Ramsey looked at her veal cutlet and lost her appetite. Another victim, bearing the signatures of the Hit Men murders. One last "fuck you" to the police and the city, from Vithu Pham. Ramsey had a vague recollection of Eden Balcomb, among the women who volunteered at the Hollywood Division. Most were over forty, divorced, and bought into the whole hero-on-a-white-horse fantasy. They didn't know anything about the millions spent on court settlements over officers who beat up their wives. The ones who had to be moved to desk duty because they couldn't control their aggression or predatory behavior against civilians.

She signaled the waiter for the check; Jim didn't even look up from his steak.

"We have another Hit Men victim. I have to go to the scene," she said.

He nodded. "Of course. You don't mind of I stay and finish my meal?"

"That's fine. I'll probably be home late," she said, standing.

"I'll leave your teacup prepared," he said, then gave her a quick kiss.

Jim always left her a cup with a green tea bag in it on the kitchen counter for her to have before bed. She could easily have put the bag in herself, but it was a nice gesture after twenty-five years of marriage. It was a kindness that she welcomed because she knew that Jim would spend the next two hours at the California Club bar, drinking gin and tonics, and then visit the downtown apartment of his mistress, an English teacher at Immaculate Heart High School in Los Feliz.

Ramsey had known about the affair for years; she had stopped demanding that it end or threatening to leave him if it did not. They both knew that the social and political fallout would be destructive to both of them. Jim was a founding partner of one of the biggest advertising companies in the city. They had come to an understanding about it. If it did not interfere with their social commitments and it was kept secret to avoid any embarrassment, she tolerated it. She wasn't happy, but she had agreed to the arrangement. She needed a successful husband with the right education, in the right profession, if she wanted to advance in law enforcement.

As a woman, she had to have everything lined up to conform perfectly with the establishment expectations. She had worked hard to pour herself into the narrow mold required of women in the LAPD, and having come this far, she wouldn't allow anything to rock the boat, even her husband's affair.

But now, as she stood on the street waiting for the valet to bring her car around, she wasn't thinking about Jim or the trials of a long-term marriage. She was figuring out how to minimize the damage of a new Hit Men victim, killed before the police apprehended Vithu Pham. It made them look inept, that they were chasing down a killer who managed to strike right in a busy neighborhood, not half a mile from the Hollywood station. The fact that Eden was a volunteer made it even worse. He had killed one of their own, right under their noses. She only hoped that when she got to the crime scene, the body would be gone. She had her veal cutlet in a to-go bag, and she was hoping to eat it later at home with a strong glass of Cabernet.

CHAPTER TWENTY-FIVE

Postiff sat in Michael Lyman's cluttered kitchen, drinking a third cup of coffee with Italian Sweet Crème. Lyman moved back and forth, offering a cinnamon roll and then a tin of butter cookies to him.

"I'm fine, Mr. Lyman. I just need you to sit here and tell me exactly how you came to call the police for a welfare check, and if you can describe anything or anyone strange that you saw around Ms. Balcomb's apartment in the past two days."

Lyman sat awkwardly on a wooden chair, like a schoolboy called to the principal's office.

"I've known Eden for decades. She moved in back in 2001. Always a good tenant, always paid her rent on time. You know she does quite well with that business of hers. It's a shame so many older people are left on their own. She was good at that, always had time for a little chat with them. She was a good egg," he said, his voice shaking.

"Did you know anything about her personal life? Family or relationships?"

"She had no family, just a crazy mother in a nursing home out in Mississippi. They haven't spoken in years."

"Boyfriends?" Postiff asked.

"Eden had . . . a few. She was quite a nice-looking woman, you know. Not my type, of course, I swing the other way. But I was involved with a girl when I was in the navy. I like women—I even had a fiancée once—but you know, nature calls and one must answer!" Lyman said with a nervous laugh.

"Can you tell me about Eden's personal life?" Postiff asked, steering the conversation back on point.

"Eden was married years ago and divorced. She had those cop boyfriends, and then the other guy, the chubby one."

Postiff perked up and leaned in. "Cop boyfriends? They were actual police officers?"

"Yeah. The older one was a detective, I think. His name was Bill or Bob. He always came in his own personal car. He used to come around a lot. She introduced him to me once as her boyfriend a few years back. The other one was more recent. He always came in uniform, in a police car. He'd blast the siren and the lights when he pulled up. He's a jerk, if you ask me," Lyman said. "But he did drop off flowers for her earlier today. I've been knocking on her door to deliver them, but she never answered."

"He was here today? What did he look like?"

"Medium height, very muscular, short dark hair. He looked Latino or maybe Filipino. He usually treated her like crap."

"How do you mean? Was he violent?" Postiff asked.

"Not exactly. But he would just show up here whenever he wanted. It was obvious they didn't have a date or anything. He'd just come in the middle of the day, get laid, and leave. Like she was just a fuck-girl. No respect."

"How did you know they had sex?"

Lyman rolled his eyes and leaned across the sticky kitchen table.

"Believe me, the way that barbarian did it, everyone in the building could hear. The last time, he just pushed the door open, and he was on top of her, right in the entryway. Up against the wall, like a streetwalker or something! I was going out to the store, and I saw them, with the door open. No respect at all," Lyman said, shaking his head.

"When did this man bring her flowers today? Morning, afternoon?"

"He came in the morning. He was at her door with a bouquet, you know, the cheap kind you get at the market. He asked if I'd seen her, and I took the flowers to put them in water so I could give them to her later. He said to tell her that Mr. Tomato came by, that she would know what that meant."

"Did you see him here on the night she was killed?"

"The older one was here. I didn't notice when he left. Then I thought I heard her door open, and she was talking to someone. I didn't see who it was. There was a thump, like something hitting the wall, and then nothing," Lyman said, tears spilling over his ruddy cheeks. "That must've been when it happened."

"And you said there's another guy?"

"Yeah, the chubby guy. I don't know what he does; he comes every Wednesday. I think he's married, because he wears a wedding ring. She seemed to like that one a lot. She was always rushing home with a bag full of groceries from Bristol Farms to make him fancy food. She cooked for her clients, you know. She was quite good at it," Lyman explained.

"Do you know his name?"

"Maybe Greg or Ted? He drives a car from a dealership in the Valley. He always looked furtive, just rushing inside, looking around."

"Did Eden or any other tenants ever get bootleg internet or cable service?" Postiff asked.

"Oh, no! I would notice if they did, and I don't go for that type of thing. It's not right. And a lot of people get ripped off—they have service for a month or two, and then it's gone. And there's no one to complain to."

"Thank you, Mr. Lyman. I'll call you if we have any further questions," Postiff said, standing to leave.

"You might want to talk to the fellow next door to Eden. His name is Arturo Blanco. He's disabled, and he's usually home. He might've heard or seen something," Lyman suggested.

"Thank you, I'll try him now," Postiff said. He headed out the door and bumped into Barrera.

"Anything?" Barrera asked.

"He says she dates three guys—two cops and another guy, a civilian, but he was only ever here during the day. He described Bill Clarke, who was here the night she died. Then he thought he heard her talking to someone at her door."

"So, maybe Vithu was watching and waiting until Bill left?" Barrera suggested.

"Maybe. He doesn't know the name of the other cop. The guy brought her flowers earlier today. He said he's medium height, muscular, short black hair," Postiff said.

"Any guy on the force could fit that description. No, Vithu Pham is good for this one. The details fit," Barrera said.

Postiff nodded and headed to check with Arturo Blanco. He knocked on the door, certain he heard a television on inside, but there was no answer. He tried again, but Blanco wasn't answering, or he wasn't home. Barrera was probably right about Vithu, but Postiff was bothered by Lyman's information about the uniformed cop in Eden's life. Possibly Filipino, the aggressive attitude, the blaring siren and lights. He knew one cop who fit that description perfectly. It was Ethan Acevedo.

Cassidy pulled into the driveway to find Bill's car, which was a relief. It was well after ten p.m.; she hoped he was still up and she wouldn't have to wake him to deliver the news about Eden. She stepped inside and found him in the kitchen, sitting at the big round table with Zelda Zed.

"Hey, Cassidy! I want you to meet Zelda. She hosts that big podcast, *LA Murder Now*, and she's doing a few episodes about me and my career," he said.

Zelda smiled at her. "We met but just briefly."

Cassidy didn't know what to say. She couldn't believe that her dad had invited Zed into their house when she was trying to avoid her. She had no doubt that Zed was using Bill to try and get information about the Hit Men case.

"I'm sorry, Ms. Zed, but I can't talk to you, and my dad shouldn't, either, regarding any open investigations," she said tersely.

"I didn't say anything about the Hit Men. She wants to know about my talk with Derby and the cold cases. She saw my news interview in San Diego," he said.

"That's fine, but you'll have to do it another day. I have something very important to talk to you about, and it's a private matter," Cassidy said.

"But Zelda . . ." Bill protested, but Cassidy cut him off.

"I'm sorry, Dad. But this is a big deal, and it's just between us."

Zed stood up and extended her hand to Cassidy. "I understand completely. Thank you for your time, Mr. Clarke."

"We're meeting again, right?" he asked.

"Of course," Zed said, taking her leave.

Cassidy turned to Bill, wanting to know how on earth a bottom-feeder like Zelda Zed had ended up in their house, but she had more pressing news to deliver.

"Did you catch my spot on the evening news in San Diego? Zelda says we could even branch out and do our own podcast together," Bill said.

"We'll discuss Zelda Zed later. You need to sit down for a minute," Cassidy said.

"What's up?" Bill asked, grabbing a handful of chips from a bag of Lay's on the counter.

"I think you'll need to sit down, Dad."

"Okay, what's the big news?" he asked, taking a seat at the table.

"Someone has been hurt . . ." she began.

"It's not your mom, is it?" he asked.

"No, Mom is fine. But I got a call from Montoya tonight. She was out on a welfare check and—"

"It's not Pete, is it? Does he have a new case? You guys got the Hit Men, right?"

"No, it's not Pete. It's Eden, Dad. She's dead," Cassidy said.

Bill stared at her for a beat; his face was as white as milk. He blinked his eyes several times as if trying to see through fog.

"Eden? She was here just last night. Did she have an accident? Driving?" he asked.

"No, she was murdered. In her apartment. They think it was Vithu Pham, before they arrested him."

Now Bill bolted out of his chair, then paced back and forth.

"How? When was this?" he asked, his voice hoarse.

"Montoya said they think it was in the last twenty-four hours. The night she was here," Cassidy said.

"But I was over there! She was fine. I left late after watching TV for a while," he said.

"You were at her house last night? Why?"

"I felt bad after I ran her off that way. I just got too worked up—you were right. So, I went over to apologize. We made some microwave popcorn and watched TV. I left about eleven thirty."

Cassidy stared at her father for a beat, with the hard realization that he was perhaps the last person besides the killer to see Eden alive. She remembered how he'd exploded at her, throwing the pizza and storming off. She knew it was an insane thought when it came to her, but in a small corner of her mind, she wondered if he had been angry enough to lose control. Perhaps his rage intensified, until he showed up at Eden's door in a fury. She shook the idea away. She was just rattled by the news of Eden's death and the heavy task of letting Bill know.

Bill walked back and forth, running his hands through his hair, mumbling to himself.

"Who's on the case? Is it Pete and Postiff?" he asked.

"Yeah, because they think it's a Hit Men murder, they're the leads. I was out with Postiff and the other detectives when he got the news."

Bill suddenly grabbed his car keys from the cigar box on the counter where they were stored.

"I've got to go. I'm going over there to see what they're doing," he said.

"Dad, you can't. You can't show up there. You know what it's like," she cautioned him.

"But what if they miss something?" he asked, his voice anguished.

"They know what to do. I know it's hard for you. I'm sorry to give you this news."

"I've got to get out, just to drive around or something. I can't sit still here at home!" he said, unable to settle in one place. He hurried out the front door, leaving it open behind him. Cassidy followed, watching as he drove away, his taillights disappearing down the quiet suburban street.

Bill drove aimlessly along Ventura Boulevard. He couldn't get his mind to accept that Eden had been murdered. He tried to imagine how it had happened, when the killer had shown up. He called Barrera a third time, but it went to voicemail again. He left no message. Cassidy said they thought it was a Hit Men murder, done by the helper since Whitty was locked up. Eden was careful; she wouldn't open the door to someone unknown to her. He needed to see the case notes, to see how the man had gotten inside her apartment, what her time of death was. If Bill had stayed over, it wouldn't have happened. If he had let her hang out and eat the pizza with them, it wouldn't have happened. His sense of guilt knocked the air out of him.

Cassidy was right. There was something off in his brain. He was tired more than usual; his headaches had gotten worse. He'd always been quick to anger or get excited, but it was all more intense now. He had trouble relaxing and settling down. He had to keep moving sometimes, and his thoughts would race, chasing after one that lit up like a spark only to vanish. Sometimes he felt like there was a darkness at the edge of his mind, a ring of shadows pushing in on him.

He wondered if he could've blacked out, as he sometimes did lately. He'd had a few instances when he didn't know how he had gotten from one place to another. He remembered being in his yard with a bad headache, followed by a sensation that everything was getting dark and then, nothing. He'd become aware later that he was in his car in the driveway, but he had no idea how he'd gotten there. He never mentioned it to Cassidy or anyone else. He told himself it was something like sleepwalking.

The motorcycle accident years ago had hit him hard; he'd had a brain bleed and a serious concussion. It left him with a broken nose and two black eyes. He wasn't supposed to drive for several weeks, but he did. He also went back to work, even if he had trouble with short-term memory recall at first. But he got better with time, went back to being his old self, more or less.

He drove through a McDonald's and got a black coffee. He finished it in three gulps, burning his tongue and throat a bit, but it felt good in a strange way. He started to cry as he drove into Sherman Oaks, passing the old Sportsmen's Lodge. The restaurants on Ventura Boulevard were all different from what he remembered, the businesses had new names. Everything had changed. His whole world was disappearing before him, and even the stable standby girl he could always count on was gone now. The one who would always look at him like he was someone important, like he was the sun and she just wanted to orbit around him for a little while. He hadn't realized that Eden had played that role in his life. Until now.

CHAPTER TWENTY-SIX

The next morning, Barrera and Postiff sat with Vithu Pham and his attorney, Carol Korn, in the interview room at the Hollywood station. Vithu looked ragged, as if he hadn't slept in days. His long hair was greasy and pulled back in a ponytail. With his slight frame and quiet demeanor, it was hard to imagine that he could've taken part in Whitty's killing spree and murdered two more victims on his own. He had signed a statement admitting to Noelle Gerrard's murder and claimed that the others were Whitty's doing; he only helped by keeping a lookout and jamming the internet signals with his laptop, seated in a car near the victims' homes.

"We'd like to ask you about Eden Balcomb, the last victim. In Beachwood Canyon," Postiff said.

Vithu looked at them blankly, then turned to Ms. Korn. "I don't know what this is."

"We're aware of the charges in the killings of Ms. Dale, Ms. Cline, Ms. Mannard, and Ms. Gerrard. Is this a new case?" Korn asked.

"Don't play dumb, Vithu. We know it was you, same MO. What we want to know is when did you do it and how did you choose her? Was it just by chance, like Noelle, or was it targeted? Had you and Whitty seen her before?" Barrera asked.

Vithu shook his head. "I have no idea who you're talking about."

Annoyed, Barrera slid a stack of crime scene photos across the table to him. They showed Eden's body propped up against the coffee table, her shirt drenched in blood. Korn glanced at them, then looked away. Vithu stared at them but shook his head again.

"I don't know who this is! I didn't do this!" he protested.

"Right. No one knows about the lipstick heart that you and Whitty used on the victims. We've kept that information under wraps, but some random guy on the street decides to do it also? Does that make sense to you, Vithu?" Barrera asked, his impatience clear.

Vithu grabbed Korn's arm with his hands, locked tight with cuffs.

"It wasn't me! I admit to the Saint Felix girl, Noelle. But I don't know anything about this woman! Who is she?" he shouted, squirming in his chair.

Postiff leaned in. "We discovered her body last night in her apartment in Hollywood. Right in the area where you and Whitty worked. She was stabbed, and her throat was cut, exactly the same way as your victims, with a lipstick heart drawn on her cheek. So, what would you think if you were us?"

"You found her last night? I was here last night!" Vithu protested.

"You were free and out in the city when Eden Balcomb was murdered. Just stop with the bullshit and come clean. We want to hear your side of the story. I understand things get out of hand sometimes," Barrera said.

"But I was in Anaheim. I was there the whole time! My mother can tell you. She never leaves the house!" Vithu cried.

"Your parents go to sleep early, and Ms. Balcomb was killed between midnight and one a.m. You could easily have driven to the city and gone back home before they woke up," Postiff said.

Vithu was quiet. It was as if they knew he had left his parents' home. He wasn't going to mention his late-night drive through the streets of Hollywood. He wondered if maybe someone had seen him.

"Do you have anything besides guesswork that ties my client to this murder?" Korn asked.

"You won't find anything. I was never there!" Vithu insisted. He started to cry.

"Do you have any DNA or fingerprints?" Korn insisted.

"They haven't come back from the lab yet, but we will have them this morning," Barrera said.

"Then call us when you have something concrete. You have nothing to indicate that Mr. Pham had anything to do with this, and you can't just sit here badgering him. We're done here," Korn said, standing up.

Barrera and Postiff watched as Vithu was led away by an officer and Korn walked briskly out of the station, her high heels clicking on the linoleum.

"Well, round one is over. We'll pull him back in when we have forensics. Working on his own, he might've left something behind," Barrera said. They were getting fresh coffee from the kitchen area when Fort stuck his head in.

"The lab results are back. I left them on your desk," he said to Barrera.

"Good. Maybe we can catch Ms. Korn before she drives away and finish this," Barrera said.

"There's no match to Vithu Pham at Eden's apartment. Nothing. No prints, no DNA," Fort said.

Postiff and Barrera looked at each other, stunned and dismayed.

"Who else would know about the lipstick heart?" Barrera asked.

They both knew the answer, but neither wanted to say it out loud.

Finally, Postiff said, "A cop who's familiar with the case and works in this station."

"I got to call Bill Clarke," Barrera said quietly.

"And we have to find out who the other officer is," Postiff added.

"The guy with the flowers, right? But why would he bring flowers if he did it and knew she was already dead?"

"To make it look like he had no idea," Postiff said. "Be seen by the landlord, showing up, nothing to hide."

"That's a ballsy move, but yeah. I can see it. You have any ideas?"

"I have one. Ethan Acevedo."

Barrera took a swig of his coffee. "Shit."

Cassidy got to work early. It was her first day back on patrol with Riley, and she was eager to step into her normal routine. The station was abuzz with the news of Eden's death, and a quiet, heavy pall hung over everyone. The other volunteers were organizing a small memorial for her. As Cassidy headed to roll call, Barrera tapped her arm and pulled her into an empty conference room. He held a plastic grocery bag, which he handed to her.

"I want you to keep this. It's your dad's jacket. It was at Eden's crime scene last night. I saw it before forensics and the photographer arrived, so I grabbed it. You should put it in your car, someplace outside of the station," he said.

"He said that he went over there and hung out with her. He's not a suspect, is he?" she asked.

"No, nothing like that. But there are no fingerprints or DNA from Vithu Pham anywhere in Eden's house. So, we have to look at other people as well."

"Like my dad?"

"It's just protocol. He was involved with her in some type of relationship. We have to talk to him, but we all know Bill had nothing to do with this," Barrera reassured her. "I've got to run. Just put it someplace safe." He hurried back to join Postiff in Carbone's office.

Cassidy looked in the bag and saw her dad's bomber jacket. It smelled of Old Spice cologne; the collar was frayed. She knew she shouldn't have it. It was a piece of evidence from a murder scene. As much as she wanted to believe Barrera's assurances, she knew that if he took Bill's jacket, it was a precautionary move to protect him, and that was terrifying and wrong in so many ways.

She tucked the bag under her arm and got her car keys from her locker. She knew she should give the bag to Postiff and tell him what Barrera had done, but that would cause a giant mess of trouble for everyone. She felt as if all eyes were on her as she hurried out to the parking lot and stashed the bag in the trunk of her car. She'd had to make a split-second decision, and she chose complicity. She leaned on her car, breathing deep to calm her racing heart. She knew the station security cameras had recorded everything.

She wondered if this was how it began, how a cop could be turned to do something they knew was wrong to protect someone else. Was this the slow slide into covering up excessive force and unprovoked shootings? Racial profiling? All the things that the new LAPD was supposedly trying to eradicate. Last night, she'd had vague, improbable suspicions that Bill might have lost his temper and gone too far with Eden. But they were the worst-case-scenario speculations of a hypervigilant mind, not actual, realistic fears. She knew her dad could not have killed Eden, but the jacket, and the furtive way Barrera had handed it off to her, gave those suspicions weight, and she didn't want to consider what that might mean.

She left Bill a voicemail as she and Riley pulled out onto Wilcox. They drove in silence for a few blocks. Cassidy was distracted, unable to think of anything except the jacket in the trunk of her car and how that seemingly small act had shifted her world dramatically in a matter of minutes. And there was not another soul she could discuss it with.

"How's your dad taking Eden's murder?" Riley asked.

"Not so good. He was really upset when I told him last night."

"Even if they weren't in a serious thing, it's still a shock," Riley said.

They pulled up outside a new, modern apartment building. They rode the elevator to the third floor and knocked on apartment 3G. It was opened by a pudgy, pale man in his sixties. He had a round face and straw-colored hair cut in a Dutch-boy style.

"Mr. Szabó? You called regarding a poisoning?" Cassidy asked.

Szabó ushered them into his apartment, which was filled with books, LPs, and VHS tapes. He spoke in a quiet voice, as if someone in the next room were listening.

"It's Debbie. She's putting it in the food," he said.

"Have you been tested for toxins?" Riley asked.

Szabó shook his head. "Not yet. But I feel awful all the time. I looked up my symptoms on Google, and they all match the ones for poisoning. So, I looked at what I eat the most of each day, and that's when it pointed to Debbie."

"Is Debbie your roommate? Your wife?" Cassidy asked, curious about Szabó's odd demeanor.

"No, she's just always here," Szabó said.

"Can we talk to Debbie?" Cassidy asked.

Szabó nodded. "She's in the kitchen, but she won't tell you anything."

"How do you feel now?" Riley asked.

"Not good, not good at all. I feel sick to my stomach all the time. I had a fever yesterday."

"I can call an ambulance for you, Mr. Szabó, but we really need to speak to Debbie so we can find out what's going on," Cassidy said, taking Riley aside.

"What do you think?" Riley asked her.

"I expected to find him writhing on the floor, vomiting. This guy looks fine, but I don't want to take a chance," she whispered.

Riley turned back to Szabó. "I'm going to speak to Debbie. You can wait here or come with me."

"I'll go with you. She's hard to find if you don't know where to look," Szabó said.

Puzzled, Riley and Cassidy entered the small retro kitchen, filled with boxes of crackers and cookies on the countertops. There was no one in the room. Szabó stepped onto a footstool and reached up to the highest cabinet and pulled out a box of chocolate Swiss rolls. He handed the box to Cassidy with a self-satisfied smirk.

"Go ahead, ask her why she does it. She won't say anything, but it's all there in black and white!"

Cassidy looked around the room and at the box. "Who are you talking about?"

Szabó pointed to the drawing of the girl on the box of cakes, a vintage depiction of a smiling auburn-haired girl in a white cap. The snack brand was Little Debbie.

"That's her! She makes these things that are so hard to stop eating, but they're filled with crap! Look at the ingredients! Soybean oil, palm oil . . . it's like eating a bar of cholesterol for someone my age! Does she care when she puts that stuff in? Not at all!" Szabó shouted.

Cassidy and Riley exchanged a look, realizing Szabó was delusional. Cassidy set the box down on the counter.

"Mr. Szabó, do you believe that Little Debbie, the girl on the box, is poisoning you?"

"What else could you call it? Why are Americans all obese? Because of people like her!" he said.

"Okay, Mr. Szabó, do you have any thoughts of hurting yourself or other people?" Riley asked evenly.

Szabó looked at him with disdain. "What? Of course not, I'm not crazy! I just wish she'd stop putting all that bad stuff into the snacks! I tried to reason with her, but she never responds!"

Cassidy picked up the box of Swiss rolls.

"Can I take these? That way I can contact her myself and ask her to stop," she said.

"Be my guest. Maybe she'll listen when a cop calls her," Szabó said.

As they left the building, Cassidy said, "As weird as that was, I needed it. It was a good distraction."

"Is the Hit Men case still hanging over you?" Riley asked.

She looked at him, weighing if she could confide in him, but decided against it.

"In a way, yes. Want a Swiss roll?"

Alan Musselman opened his morning paper over a double espresso and a piece of raisin cinnamon brioche. On the front page, he saw the article about another possible murder by the Hollywood Hit Men. Like everyone, he'd been relieved when they announced that they'd caught both killers. From the article, it looked like there was one last unfortunate victim. There was a photo of her; her name was Eden Balcomb. Musselman looked closely at her. He'd seen her somewhere. The story said she'd been killed in her apartment by someone suspected to be one of the Hit Men. It described her as a divorcée and small business owner who lived alone in Hollywood. He tried to think if perhaps he'd seen her at the gym, or maybe she worked at the local Whole Foods? She was pretty in the photo; he would've noticed her. He was sitting down at his computer to work when he suddenly remembered where he'd seen Eden Balcomb.

She was the woman having a screaming match with his neighbor Bill Clarke a couple of nights ago. With the high-powered lights in Clarke's driveway, Musselman was able to see her clearly from his front window. Their fight had been bad, with Clarke yelling at her and cursing while she had a full-blown meltdown before driving off. Clarke had taken off shortly after she left and hadn't come back for several hours. Musselman worked late every night and saw him return after midnight. He checked the news article again. It said Eden Balcomb had died late on the night of the fight with Clarke. Someone needed to know about that important detail.

Musselman dialed the Hollywood Division of the LAPD and asked to speak to the detective quoted in the news story, a Judson Postiff. He chuckled to himself. After the way Clarke had nosed around his property, harassing him, trespassing to leave the creepy dead bird, this call was going to be sweet.

CHAPTER TWENTY-SEVEN

Bill sat across from Tyler Derby at Pleasant Valley State Prison. When he'd gotten the call from Rennison that Derby was willing to talk again, he tossed his stuff in an overnight bag and headed out. He'd have to see the head doctor another day, and he knew that Cassidy would be mad, but it was his life, and getting Derby's input on some old cases was more important. He wanted to have all his material lined up, with new cold cases solved, so he and Zelda Zed would have a lot to talk about. He'd left a few messages for Ainsley Wright, the speakers' agent, but she hadn't gotten back to him. She'd seemed so eager at the Stacey Mandel press conference, but after that first phone conversation, she went silent.

He'd spent a sleepless night unable to stop obsessing over Eden's death. He wished he were still at work and could pore over the evidence, go through it a hundred times to be sure he hadn't missed anything or to discover the missing piece. He would ask Barrera to let him know what was going on; Pete would do that for him. After all, he and Gloria had met Eden a number of times.

But now, he and Derby sat across from each other in the chilly, drab meeting room. Bill had given him his notes on the Min Sun-Hee case and the connection to Alan Musselman. Derby scanned through it.

"What d'you think, Tyler? I just have that detective's sixth sense that this guy is part of it somehow," Bill said.

"Well, you got to listen to that, Bill. You know a lot more about this than other people. He could be the guy you suspected from the start.

It's easy to get a new identity. You should talk to the guys in here. They know people who can get you Social Security numbers, new ID. They can make the old you disappear," Derby assured him.

"The day I met him, it was a trigger. I felt it right away. It's in the set of his shoulders, his gait. Just like that neighbor, Tom Britt, who had a shit alibi and seemed too nervous when we spoke to him. And then the guy just dropped off the face of the earth! My daughter is a cop, and she says it's crazy, that the guy might've moved or died, but I didn't find any signs of that," Bill said.

"Your daughter is a cop too? You must be proud," Derby said with a grin.

"Oh, yeah. Her name's Cassidy. She's a new boot in the same division I just retired from. She just helped crack a big serial-killer case, right out of the gate," Bill bragged.

Derby nodded, filing that information for future use. Bill Clarke had a daughter, a cop no less. Now he even knew her first name. Clarke was reckless in his need for validation.

"It's a bitter pill, isn't it? When the guy you know is bad, gets away with it? I hated seeing people like Ada Pneff kill those cats. But there were plenty of other bad ones I wasn't able to stop," Derby said.

"You're right about that. I've had a few cases that fell apart when they went to court or the DA refused to file charges, saying we didn't have enough evidence when I knew we had the right guy. I knew it in my gut, and it made me so damn furious when we couldn't put them away," Bill agreed.

"You know, Bill, we both hate to see bad people get away with bad things. We just have a different way of dealing with it," Derby said with a small laugh.

"That's why I became a cop. I wanted to take the bad guys down, and I've gotten in trouble sometimes for stepping outside the lines, as they say. Going too far in an interrogation or what they call profiling someone, but when you've been in the game this long, you just know," Bill said.

"As a cop, of course, you must stay inside the lines. But when you're on the edge out here with guys like me, you don't have to do that. You can trust your gut. You can make your move and get it done. And then you just gotta stay under the radar, knowing you did the right thing."

Bill nodded, taking notes in one of his binders. Derby was right in some ways. It felt good to talk to someone who understood. He couldn't talk to Cassidy this way; she was a fresh, new boot who still believed that the system worked the way it was supposed to. He couldn't let her know how it really was; she'd have to find that out for herself. People want to believe that life is fair and there is retribution for those who deserve it. But guys like Derby and him, they knew how the rules worked and how they were broken.

For his part, Derby knew Bill was completely off base with his theory about Alan Musselman. The guy was too young by over fifteen years, and he'd been nowhere near LA at the time of the Min Sun-Hee murder. He was just a poor jerk unfortunate enough to live next door to a crazy cop who decided that he had to be guilty of something, a cop who had to be right when he believed he was.

Derby could tell there was something wrong with Bill, the way his eyes popped. He sat up as if a jolt of electricity had hit him when you said what he wanted to hear. He hadn't been that way when they first met years ago. Back then, Bill was tough as old boots and a skilled detective who kept a cool poker face. Now, he was like a kid eager for validation, letting you hold his prized toy if you gave him a turn on the swing. And when he was high up in the air, he wouldn't notice that you had run off with it.

Derby knew he could push Bill Clarke further than he ever intended to go, and he was going to enjoy doing it.

"So, what're you going to do when you get back home and confront this Musselman? You'll have to get evidence against him, get inside his house, go through his stuff. He must have the information somewhere safe but where he can get a hold of it right away," Derby said.

"I think I can do it," Bill agreed. He was already forming a plan.

Zelda Zed saw several calls from Bill Clarke on her cell phone, but she was waiting to return them. After speaking to Joyce Ramsey about Bill's past and his propensity to push the limits, she was reconsidering doing a series of episodes about him. Online sleuths were ruthless, and if there was dirt on Bill somewhere, they'd find it, and it would reflect badly on her. But a series of podcasts about a cop who goes bad might be the perfect thing. She knew there had to be a different side to him, apart from the earnest, dedicated detective persona that he presented. She knew he had a failed marriage, and from what Ramsey said, he'd gotten into trouble more than a few times.

Ramsey had described him as a dinosaur, and that might be Zelda's angle for the story. An older detective, out of touch with the world, stuck in his dysfunctional ways. She could hit the issues that have affected the LAPD for years, the racism, the misogyny, the paramilitary mindset, pitting them against the civilian population they're supposed to serve and protect. Bill Clarke could be a great subject and, unwittingly, give her a ton of information.

Joyce Ramsey didn't want a podcast that glorified Bill, but she also didn't want one that made the department look bad, in the past or the present day. A story about a rogue cop who ran around violating people's civil rights or manipulating confessions wouldn't be good for the department. But Joyce Ramsey couldn't have it both ways.

Postiff hung up the phone with Alan Musselman, who described himself as Bill Clarke's neighbor. He seemed like a normal guy. He didn't say anything crazy or show any sign of having a grudge against the police. He recognized Eden's photo in the paper since she and Bill had a screaming fight in the driveway the night she was killed. He said it happened around nine o'clock, that she drove off crying, and then Bill followed. None of that looked good for Bill, and Postiff hated that the investigation might be turning in his direction.

The forensic team found blood DNA that didn't match Eden's on her upper body; the killer cut himself on the blade as he stabbed her. It didn't match Vithu. Postiff would have to get DNA from Bill and positively identify the other cop Eden was involved with.

He asked around about Acevedo, but it was hard to get the Metro cops to talk—they took the blue wall of silence to a new level, and even within the department, they thought they didn't have to answer to anyone. That was why a lot of them were on the list to be phased out. Postiff went to college with one of the attorneys who worked solely on cases against the Metro cops who had grossly overstepped their duty and broken the law. He shared the list over drinks one night at the Blue Room, and Acevedo was on it.

They'd gone through Eden's phone records and identified her clients, Bill, Ted-the-married-lover, and repeated calls from a burner phone that wasn't linked to any cell phone carrier. Knowing that Eden's other companion was a cop who drove a patrol car, Postiff had been dialing the burner phone number at random times in the station, just to see if it rang. So far he'd had no luck with that strategy. Barrera also wanted to visit her apartment again and talk to the neighbors they had missed. They needed to see video coverage from every Ring camera on the street, but people were wary of getting involved. If he and Barrera had to, they'd push for a subpoena. Ted-the-married-lover was avoiding Postiff's messages, and if he didn't call back soon, Postiff would show up at his house with Barrera, who he knew would particularly enjoy that type of thing.

CHAPTER TWENTY-EIGHT

Cassidy arrived at home to accompany Bill to his appointment with Dr. Baruch to find the house empty. There was a note on the kitchen counter explaining that he'd driven up to Coalinga to talk to Tyler Derby again. She crumpled it up in frustration and tossed it in the trash. It had taken over a month to get the appointment with a specialist, and now they'd have to wait again. She dialed his phone; it went straight to voicemail. She realized the idea that he would be home waiting and willingly go to a neurologist was ridiculous. She would probably have to trick him—tell him they were going to the shooting range for practice and then head to Saint Joseph's.

She was annoyed that she'd taken the afternoon off for nothing, but she couldn't stay mad at Bill. He was struggling with Eden's murder, and he didn't even know yet that he'd have to be interviewed by his old partner or his replacement, which would hit him hard. Carter had called her twice since yesterday. She didn't have anything to say to him, and she hadn't really missed him, she'd been so busy with the Hit Men case. She felt vaguely bad about it and dialed his number.

"Hi, how's it going?" he asked, sounding chipper and upbeat.

"It's been a crazy week. My dad's ex, Eden, was murdered a couple of days ago, so that's a hard thing to deal with," she said.

"Oh my god! I didn't realize it was her! I just scanned over the paper and saw that there was a new victim, but you've caught both of the killers, right?"

"Alleged killers. But yeah, we have them both in custody."

"So, that means that things are calming down for you. Maybe we can stop this nonsense of taking a break?" he asked.

Cassidy waited to respond. Her need to step back from their relationship was not nonsense. Taking a break was to reassess where they were at and if they had a real future together. It seemed like every time Carter opened his mouth, he made it more evident that they did not. She knew that she had changed; now that she was in her real life, not a freewheeling postcollege detour, it was defined by things that simply didn't fit with his world, which was like one big, extended vacation. He didn't know what hardship was, or the unfair, capricious way that life can take everything from you, as it did for Kylie and countless other people. The cruel, random way that misfortune can strike, destroying your sense of security. He never would, most likely. And he wasn't reflecting at all on the differences between them; he was just waiting for her to come to her senses and realize how great he was.

"It's only been since yesterday, Carter. I'm still in the thick of it, with Eden's murder and all. My dad is having a hard time."

"Then he should get counseling and get past it. Nothing good comes from focusing on difficult things," he advised.

"His girlfriend was murdered in her own house. It's not like he needs a new bumper on his car," she said.

"I know, but this stuff is just too intense, right? Who deals with stuff like this? It's murders and interrogations and dead bodies. What happened to cops giving speeding tickets and stopping shoplifters?" he asked.

"There's more to being a cop than that. We deal with real things like murders. The big problem of the day isn't that they changed the parking passes at the country club," she shot back at him.

He was silent for a moment; then he said, "That was uncool, Cassidy. I deal with much bigger problems than that, okay? And I have to go to a class right now. Let's talk later."

He hung up in a huff, and she felt both angry and sad at the same time. Angry at how clueless he was and at herself for not seeing sooner how ill suited they were. Or pretending not to see it. Sad because she realized they were going through the inevitable steps that would lead to the end. This wasn't a breather—it was the beginning of a breakup. She knew they would never work together long term. She wondered why she hadn't just ended it quickly, with one sharp, surgical strike.

It was because she felt guilty doing that; she felt that she needed to go through the requisite suffering to show that she'd cared at one point. Facing that she didn't really care was unsettling. She didn't want to consider what that might mean. Maybe she wasn't meant to fall in love, get married, and have a family. Maybe she wasn't wired for that type of traditional life. It was too much to consider at twenty-three. She knew she shouldn't have made the snarky country-club remark. She shouldn't have been annoyed by his narrow, privileged view of life. She should have understood that her world was all new to him.

But she was tired of the shoulds and shouldn'ts in her life. Tired of walking the line to keep everyone steady and on track. She'd come home early from work to make sure a grown man went to a doctor's appointment. She'd called Carter when she really didn't want to because she felt she owed it to him. She'd smoothed everything over with Alan Musselman when her dad made a mess of it. She'd hidden his jacket in her car, despite her misgivings. She'd sat across a table from a murderer who scared the hell out of her because Joyce Ramsey made it clear she had no choice but to do it. She suddenly felt overwhelmingly tired of everything and everybody. She went to her room, stripped off her clothes, and climbed into bed. She was asleep within seconds.

Barrera stood on the cement walkway outside Eden's apartment while Postiff spoke to Michael Lyman. He had left a message for Bill, but he hadn't said what it was about. But Bill had been a detective for years; he knew the drill. They had to speak to those closest to the victim. When Postiff told him about the call from Bill's neighbor who witnessed the loud scene with Eden, he wished for once that Bill had been able to keep himself in check, and not just give in to his "big feelings," as his daughter-in-law would say.

In his heart, Barrera knew that Bill Clarke could not have killed Eden. He'd seen him shoot suspects, killing two of them. He'd been there when Bill slapped a suspect during an interrogation hard enough to make his nose bleed. He'd done the same things himself. But to brutally kill a woman that he'd been involved with? It wasn't possible, no matter how loudly Bill had shouted at her in the driveway. He'd done the same with Gloria now and then.

Postiff approached with Michael Lyman. "Mr. Lyman doesn't have any kind of security cameras here in the common areas, but three of the residents have Ring cameras. The only one that would show someone coming or going from Eden's apartment is Arturo Blanco's, and he's not answering his door."

"Not answering, or he's not home?" Barrera asked.

Lyman shrugged. "Not sure. He doesn't drive, so there's no car to see if he's here. He's disabled. He's quite a good singer, also."

Postiff looked at him for a beat, confused. "A singer?"

"Yes, he comes to the senior center over by the Hollywood Bowl sometimes. He's not really old enough, only in his late forties, but he's really good, so we let him in for Broadway Show Tune evenings, every Tuesday. He does a great rendition of all the Streisand songs."

"Have you spoken to him about Ms. Balcomb's murder? If he saw anything or his camera picked up anyone coming or going?" Postiff asked.

"No, that's the funny thing. He's usually out and about, chatting with everyone, especially about something like this! When they had the fire up by the Hollywood Sign, he was like the Red Cross, but he has been silent and out of sight. I think he saw something," Lyman said ominously.

"Has Mr. Blanco had any problems with Ms. Balcomb? Did they argue? Any jealousy?" Barrera asked.

Lyman shook his head. "No, Arturo and Eden were buddies. They went grocery shopping together; they went to the Korean facial spa together. He adored Eden, and they were on very good terms."

They tried Blanco's door again but got no answer.

"What d'you think?" Postiff asked Barrera.

"I agree with the landlord. The guy saw something, and he's afraid. Maybe the killer saw him. Or he's our guy."

"Could be. A neighbor who's fixated on her or resents her for some reason. Or jealous of her other boyfriends. Let's give him until later today to get back to us, then get the warrant for his security camera. When do you want to talk to Bill?" Barrera asked.

"I'll handle it. It's kind of weird for you to do it," Postiff said.

"Yeah, but I can if I have to. Any updates on Acevedo?"

"I'm going to make the request later today. We'll have to have everything in place to make any move on him," Postiff said wearily.

"I don't look forward to that. He's a slimy son of a bitch. I checked out his record. He has three serious stalking complaints against him, all credible. And other harassment reports as well."

"So that burner phone could belong to him. If you had a history like his, would you call women from your own phone that could be traced?" Postiff asked.

Barrera tossed him the keys and climbed into the passenger seat.

"I don't feel like driving anymore today," he said grumpily.

He stared out the window in silence as Postiff hung a U-turn on Beachwood Canyon Drive. Why couldn't it have been Vithu Pham's blood at the scene? Why hadn't someone seen him clearly leaving her place after the murder? When they'd caught Vithu, Barrera thought it was over. He hoped it was the last serial-killer case of his career. But nothing could ever be easy. He felt Postiff was onto something real, that Acevedo could be involved in Eden's murder, but it would turn into a major shit show if they started down that path. Investigating a senior member of the Metro Division had risks, and he didn't want to end his career embroiled in an all-out interdepartmental war. He was not going to give up on the idea of Vithu as the killer until someone could give him definitive proof that it was someone else. And he refused to believe for one minute that it was Bill Clarke, no matter what anyone thought.

CHAPTER TWENTY-NINE

It was late, too late for anything to be open in Coalinga. After his meeting with Derby, Bill had a quick dinner, and then he drove around for several hours. He was having trouble concentrating; he felt restless and exhausted at the same time, which drove him crazy.

He kept going over Derby's words again and again. How sometimes you had to step outside the lines. He knew that. He'd known it when he and Barrera had roughed up suspects to get them to come clean. That used to be standard procedure. Sometimes you had to bend the rules, but he began to wonder how far you could go. Sure, Derby was a murderer operating within his own twisted logic. Bill knew that no one in their right mind would kill someone over cheating on their boyfriend or poisoning cats, but who was to say what was immoral or not? The older he got, the more that line became blurred. And lately, it was harder than ever to see it clearly.

Everything was shifting inside him. He wondered how he had ever been so certain about who the good guys and the bad guys were. And if someone had hurt a lot of people—done things that caused them to lose their lives or their homes, or hurt their kids—didn't they have a debt to pay to someone? He thought of suspects over the years that he knew were guilty but they'd gotten off on a technicality or the DA had declined to press charges. Was it right that they just got away with it? Didn't people like him have a responsibility to make sure they couldn't hurt other people again? He wanted to talk to Pete about it. They'd worked so many cases together back in the day. He'd missed two of Pete's calls, but it was way too late to call him back now. Zelda had left a message also; he looked forward to talking with her about Derby.

He drove aimlessly until he found himself back in the Harris Ranch Hotel parking lot. He went in to find the hotel quiet. Everyone was asleep at that hour. He walked out to the pool area and laid down on a chaise longue. The night air was cool, the dry, earthy smell of the soil mixed with the fragrant night-blooming jasmine. He looked up at the sky. He could see the stars more clearly out here, far from the city lights. There were so many stars; the sky was huge and infinite. He felt so small, and he realized how little the things we do in this life matter. We are all so puny, just toiling away down here in our messy, paltry little lives, trying to make sense of ourselves and our world. In the big scheme of things, it really didn't matter what we did down here on earth. There were no real good guys or bad guys. We could do what needed to be done to set the system right, to put life back in balance. It really didn't matter.

Ramsey hung up the conference call with Chief McCall and Joe Werner from the DA's office. It was past midnight, but the issues with the Eden Balcomb murder were getting complicated. With no forensic evidence implicating Vithu Pham, everyone's rush to call it the final Hit Men murder had been a mistake. If it wasn't Pham, it was a civilian copycat or a cop on the inside. The lipstick heart drawn on her cheek, the posing of the body both pointed clearly to the latter, which was a nightmare for everyone.

They'd all been alerted to the fact that Eden was Bill Clarke's ex-girlfriend, and she still had some kind of involvement with him. Dykstra had seen Ethan Acevedo being way too familiar with her at Bill's retirement party, and there were rumors that they had something going on as well. The DA was planning to bring charges within the next two days against both Whitty and Pham for the three Hit Men murders and Pham alone for Noelle Gerrard. But they needed more to charge him in the Balcomb case.

Public trust in the LAPD had never been good. The department had a long history of people of color being shot under suspicious or downright indefensible circumstances. A one-hundred-pound, elderly homeless woman holding a screwdriver fifteen feet away from officers, shot and killed on a major boulevard in broad daylight. A man on his front porch, holding his wallet, was deemed a threat to officers' safety and shot to death. Cops in the Rampart Division caused a national scandal for selling drugs and planting guns on people they shot. Every time they took a step forward, there were problematic cops pushing them back to the starting line. In the past few months, three officers had been fired for beating a suspect who was handcuffed to a bench, immobilized.

Ramsey knew a number of the men who became cops had psychological and emotional issues. They loved the power that came with a badge and a gun but lacked the temperament and self-control to manage them. And the good ones, who became cops for all the right reasons, were often compromised into being lesser versions of the bad ones. The pressure to conform, to hold the thin blue line, was huge, and the consequences of not doing so could be lethal out in the field.

So many who started the job full of vigor and idealism had it knocked out of them systematically over the years. Ramsey had been one of those officers, and now she had been climbing the ladder, pushing against the glass ceiling for so long, she couldn't turn back or upset the status quo. She was a success story for women in the LAPD, but it had come at a cost. The callous, look-out-for-number-one types who acted as if that price were insignificant compared to the gains were lying. She knew that the loss of integrity, of belief in the system and in oneself, turned a person into a hollow husk of a human being. She had to face that she didn't have the strength or the character to do anything differently.

And now, the idea of a rogue cop murdering Eden Balcomb was bad enough, but that he'd drawn a lipstick heart on her like the other Hit Men victims was macabre and meant to mislead. It would cause a ripple effect, and every arrest that officer had made, every court proceeding that he had testified in would be questioned. The department would face a crisis of confidence that it might not recover from.

Sitting in her Hancock Park home, looking out at her big backyard with the saltwater infinity pool glimmering in the moonlight, she knew they had to launch a clandestine, internal investigation. The chief and Werner agreed that it had to be low-key; they didn't want the Feds involved yet. The department spent over a decade under federal oversight due to police abuse back in the early 2000s, and no one wanted to return to that situation. Because Bill Clarke was now a suspect, she'd have to remove Barrera from the case, and that would cause the old-timers in Robbery-Homicide to get all hot and salty. They'd murmur and mumble about how a woman couldn't be trusted to make decisions, how she was too emotional, how it was personal, despite it being a decision made by Chief McCall.

She didn't care. They needed to find out who'd killed Eden, and if it was a cop, he needed to be made an example of. They had to show that he was an aberration. They could purge the bad cops from the department on their own; they could be trusted. She knew she'd never get to sleep, and Jim wasn't home yet; given the hour, he had to be with his mistress. She would've welcomed someone to talk to, just for the human connection and dialogue, but she was alone in the big Tudor-style house. She found the bottle of prescription hydroxyzine her doctor had given her and cut a pill in half, then washed it down with a glass of water. She checked the alarm system and padded up the winding staircase. Each heavy step felt like she was scaling a mountain.

Cassidy spent a sleepless night tossing and turning, unable to stop thinking about Eden's murder. It seemed that it was always the middle of the night when her worst terrors struck. With nothing else to distract her or keep her from spinning into wild speculation, her fears multiplied like grotesque shadows on the wall. She couldn't stop seeing Bill's rage when he'd exploded at Eden for showing up unannounced. The way he'd gone outside to yell at her, white with fury that was overblown and out of proportion. In that state he could be dangerous. Despite the late hour, she called her mom. Cathy answered on the second ring.

"Is everything okay? Are you hurt?" Cathy asked, sounding groggy and slow.

"I'm fine, Mom. Sorry to call so late, but I'm freaking out. I need to talk to you," Cassidy said, her knees drawn up under her covers.

"Do you need me to come out there? I can get a flight in a few hours," Cathy offered, and Cassidy felt an immediate pang of guilt. Her mother was across the country and ready to jump on a plane to come out and help her, even when Cassidy had clearly chosen Bill over her when the family split up.

"I want to know about Dad. A woman he'd been seeing was murdered a couple of days ago. He had a big fight with her here at the house earlier that night. His reaction was crazy, way over the top. Then he left for a few hours—"

Cathy interrupted her. "Are you asking if I think he's capable of hurting someone?"

Cassidy paused before answering. "Yeah, that's what I'm asking."

"I never spoke to you about this, but when I finally decided to leave your dad, it was because of an incident that happened when you weren't at home. He'd been getting more and more volatile since the accident, but he hid it well, you know? He'd always had such a big personality. We were home one afternoon on his day off, and he lost it over his LP collection. I had been cleaning, and I put them in a different cabinet, and when he looked for them, they weren't there. He began screaming and throwing things across the room. I got upset, of course, and said they were just records, but he came up to me and grabbed me by the shoulders. He shook me so hard I felt a snap in my neck. I had to wear a brace after that," Cathy said.

"I remember that. You said someone rear-ended you," Cassidy said.

"I said that so you wouldn't know. You thought your dad hung the moon, and you were only fifteen. I knew he would never hurt you, ever. And of course, he apologized and promised it would never happen again. But that was it for me. I was scared of him. And it's been eight years since then, I'm sure his mental health is worse now. How did the appointment go with the neurologist?"

"He skipped it. And went up to Coalinga to talk with a convicted murderer again."

"I'm sorry for the poor woman who was killed. I'm sure it was someone else. But if you even have to ask yourself if your dad could be capable of that, you already know the answer. I think you should take a leave of absence and come out here until this is sorted out," Cathy suggested.

"I'd love to, Mom, but I can't. I just started work, and I'm back on patrol again. I'll be fine. I just wanted to get your input. I should go. It's late."

"I'm sorry I couldn't reassure you that Bill could never do anything like that. Check in with me this week, okay? And try to get some sleep."

Cassidy hung up the phone and checked her dad's location. He was at Harris Ranch Hotel. She walked down the hallway to his room and stood in the center of it for a moment, taking in his collection of vintage cigarette lighters on the dresser, the model of a Harley-Davidson motorcycle. She opened his closet and ran her hand along his row of dress shirts, still in plastic from the dry cleaner's, his out-of-style suits hanging neatly. She leaned in and buried her face in them, smelling his familiar scent of Dial Gold bar soap and Old Spice cologne. And she began to cry.

CHAPTER THIRTY

"What do you mean you're taking me off Eden Balcomb's murder? Postiff and I are just waiting to pull the security camera footage from her neighbor," Barrera said, standing in Ramsey's office before morning roll call.

"I have to, Pete. Bill Clarke is a suspect, and after so many years as his partner, it just doesn't look right to have you investigating him," she replied.

"What? You think I'm gonna give him special treatment?" Barrera protested.

"No, I don't. But it will look that way to people on the outside, especially the OIG. I need you to deal with this quietly, just step back and be reassigned for the time being. We've got enough to deal with right now," Ramsey said.

"Fine. But this is bullshit!" he said, slamming the door behind him.

He didn't care if people thought it was unprofessional—he was furious. To be sidelined at the end of his career—as if he couldn't be trusted to stay impartial while investigating his former partner—was a kick in the head. He wondered if Cassidy had told Ramsey about the jacket; that might explain this sudden move. He did it to keep attention off Bill until they had real evidence against him. Barrera was planning to get his DNA sample when he took his statement. Now it would be someone else. As hard as it would've been to interview him as a suspect, he knew it was going to be even harder on Bill to have someone else do it. He was on his way to roll call when he bumped into Cassidy.

"Hey, did you tell anyone about yesterday?" he asked her.

She glanced around to be certain no one was paying attention, and said quietly, "Of course not."

"You sure? Because Ramsey just took me off the Eden case because your dad is a suspect, and she thinks I can't be trusted!" he said.

"I had nothing to do with that. My dad is a formal suspect?" she asked.

"I know he couldn't have done it, but he was there; he saw her regularly. We have to retrace her steps, and some of them lead to Bill," he said.

"Thanks for letting me know. I didn't mention it to anyone," she assured him.

He disappeared down a hallway as she went in for the roll call. She needed to see Barrera and Postiff's notes on the case or the murder book. She had to figure out what they knew about Bill, if they had hard evidence against him. Now that Barrera was off it, she couldn't ask him, and she doubted Postiff would give her anything. She thought of asking Riley for help, but she couldn't compromise him. She had to get access to the notes before she spoke to her dad. She would ask him directly if he had anything to do with Eden's murder. She might catch him off guard, and he'd tell her the truth, one way or the other.

During roll call there was no mention of Barrera being taken off the Balcomb murder, and Postiff wasn't present. Cassidy saw him enter Ramsey's office. She weighed the probability that she would be successful in getting a hold of any pertinent information about the investigation on the sly. It was too risky, and if she was caught, it would look even worse for her dad and jeopardize her career as well. Her best approach was to ask Postiff directly and put all her concerns on the table, letting him know about Barrera and her dad's jacket. She would leave that in his hands; the weight of it was too heavy for her to carry in secret.

Ramsey moved to close the blinds on the window of her office and turned to Postiff.

"If you interview Acevedo or any other member of the department, we have to take all the proper precautions, and that will take a few days to get in place. We'll get pushback from the union; he'll have to have a lawyer present. We'll have to find a neutral location. We need a separate investigative agency to do the interview, and we don't want to get the Feds involved yet. Chief McCall wants this to be an internal investigation, to keep it under wraps for as long as we can."

"Okay. I'd like to use Detective Sandra Moody from the Hollenbeck station and Officer Montoya. I know you've taken Barrera off the case because of Bill Clarke being a suspect. I've got a few ideas about who to bring on. I can give you a short list within the hour. Is that okay?" he asked.

Ramsey nodded in agreement. Postiff was smart and meticulous. She knew in a few years' time he would be the star of the Robbery-Homicide division. She trusted his instincts as well as his honesty. Postiff left her office and bumped into Cassidy, who had clearly been waiting to speak with him.

"May I talk to you privately, detective?"

He nodded and led her into an empty conference room.

"What's up?"

"Barrera told me he's off Eden's case since you have to interview my dad."

"Yes, I just found that out."

"He gave me my dad's bomber jacket. It was in Eden's apartment when you guys were called out, and he grabbed it before forensics got there," she said.

"Are you kidding me?"

"I know my dad's a suspect. I wanted to know if you can let me know what evidence you have that points to him. I don't believe he's capable of something like that, but I'm sick over this," she pleaded.

He looked at her for a beat. He hadn't considered her for the internal investigation team, but he now saw that she could be a good source of information on Bill Clarke, who he knew would not be easy to deal with. He'd get indignant and push back. But Cassidy was earnest and idealistic, committed to doing the right thing. He knew he could convince Ramsey to go along with it.

"I appreciate this information. It seems you want the truth above everything else," he said.

"I do," she said quietly. "Whatever it is."

"Ramsey just told me to put together a team to quietly investigate Eden's murder and to look into your dad and others in the department that I suspect. I'd like to have you on that team if you're willing, without mentioning the jacket or Barrera. I don't want his career to end on that note, and you can just turn it over to me. It won't come to light unless it has to," he said.

"I'd like to do that. Thank you for asking me," Cassidy said.

"Go out on your patrol. I'll text you later, and we'll get everyone up to speed," Postiff said.

She was halfway across the room when she realized he'd said *others in the department that I suspect.* It meant there was someone else on the inside who could be the murderer. She turned back to ask him who it was, but he was gone.

Ethan Acevedo was at the Hollywood station to drop off paperwork for Lieutenant Carbone. He had fabricated an excuse to be there so he could get a sense of what was happening with the Eden Balcomb case, which was now all over the news. He knew he would be a person of interest since he had a relationship of sorts with her. He had a lot of buddies who worked out of the Hollywood station, even though Metro was based in the remodeled Rampart Division. He'd seen Barrera storm out of Ramsey's office before roll call. He'd seen Postiff go in and how Ramsey had closed the blinds. Something was going on. He'd asked around, and Fort told him that there was no DNA match at the scene to Vithu Pham.

Acevedo had been at Eden's apartment regularly; his DNA was bound to be all over the place. He didn't want to be subjected to any questioning and have details of his sexual escapades come to light. He was due for vacation time—he'd skipped taking it for several years. Maybe now would be a good time to get away until everything settled down.

He called George Rollings, a level-three captain and the head of the Metro Division at Rampart.

"Captain Rollings, Metro."

"Hello, sir. This is Acevedo. I'm at the Hollywood station right now, but something has come up rather suddenly."

"What's up?" he asked.

"I wanted to know if I could take my vacation days, starting immediately," Acevedo asked.

Rollings laughed. "You never take vacation days, Acevedo! You're the most driven guy in Metro. What's going on?"

"It's my dad. He's got Alzheimer's, and it's getting worse. My mom really needs help in making some decisions about his living situation, and I don't want her to have to visit those assisted living places alone. It'll be really hard for her," he said.

"No problem. I'll do the paperwork today and give it to Danner this morning to process. Take care, and I hope it works out well for your parents. It's hard. I've been there with my old man."

"Thank you, captain," Acevedo said, then hung up.

He was tight with Josh Danner, the second-level captain who was the assistant commanding officer of Metro. They'd been buddies since the academy. It was good to have those guys on the team who understood the need to hold the line and protect each other.

The press conference announcing the charges against Ron Whitty and Vithu Pham ran on the local morning news. Whitty heard about it from a guard at the jail. It looked like Vithu and Thuy had given him up, tried to blame him for the three Hit Men murders, and Vithu had killed one on his own. He could imagine Thuy Pham acting like she didn't speak perfect English, telling them how he intimidated her into covering for him. She wouldn't mention how she'd confiscate the passports of the young women she brought here to work as maids. Or how she'd whip those new arrivals from Thailand or Myanmar with a leather strap when they realized they were supposed to have sex with strangers and resisted.

But he could throw a wrench into the whole thing if he recanted his confession and gave them more information about Vithu's crimes and Thuy's hookers. If he made up some crazy shit about other victims or invented another accomplice. They'd go off chasing their own tails while he stalled and bought more time. And he'd get a chance to talk to Officer Pretty Tits again. She'd looked so good the last time he saw her, in that cotton sundress, all cute and fresh smelling. He'd thought of that many times in the solitude of his cell.

He was playing a game against time; that was all he had at this point. The longer it took for him to get that life sentence, the more he'd feel he won. The more money he made them waste on a big, sensational trial, the better. He relished the idea of photographers taking his photo going in and out of court, of it being on the front page of the *LA Times*. He knew he'd get jail groupies, those sad, desperate women who were so easy to manipulate. That would be something. He'd get to see them on visitation day, get them all worked up to find a lawyer to defend him, promise the great life they'd have together if he could just get out. Maybe he could wrangle for conjugal visits. He could string this out and take control of the story. That was what he wanted most, stuck in the hellhole of the Hollywood jail: control.

Bill stepped into the Coffee Bean & Tea Leaf in Canoga Park, scanning the room for Zelda Zed. He saw her seated at a window table and hurried to join her. He'd just returned from Pleasant Valley, where his session with Tyler Derby had been productive. He completely supported Bill's theory about Alan Musselman, and he had some interesting ideas about Eden's case as well. He agreed that Bill had to get the notes and case files from Barrera to review and that he should be included in the ongoing investigation, since he had known Eden personally. That was not standard procedure for a retired detective, but Derby said he was not a standard-issue detective, and he had earned the right to extra access. Bill agreed.

His head was pounding, and he was beginning to see a shadow creeping in at the periphery of his vision; he knocked back four Aleve tablets as he sat down.

"Detective Clarke, it's so nice to meet you again," Zelda said with a broad smile.

"Great to see you too. I've just gotten off the road from Coalinga. I saw Derby again," he said.

"How'd that go?"

"Really productive. He's giving me input on an old case and a new one, also . . ."

He shared his suspicions about Musselman and his plan to uncover his real identity. She nodded and took notes. Then he elaborated on Derby and their shared ideology about justice and retribution, the gray area between right and wrong.

"That's really interesting, Bill. It raises so many big issues. Do you mind if I record this? It's pretty deep, and I don't want to miss anything," she said.

"No problem. This thing with Derby really makes me think, you know? And then there's the new case, the final Hit Men murder that's going on," he said. "You know my daughter did the interrogation of the first suspect, Ron Whitty. He refused to talk to anyone but her, and she went in and aced it like a pro!"

Zelda covered her surprise at this information; Joyce Ramsey hadn't said anything about a new boot talking to a major suspect in a serial-murder case. It had not been mentioned in any news update from the LAPD. She wondered how the citizens of Los Angeles would feel to know that the police let an untried, inexperienced officer, rather than a seasoned detective, interview a serial killer.

"How'd she do it?" Zelda asked.

"She asked me for some advice, of course, and I told her she had to get into the mind of a guy like Whitty. Find his weakness and exploit it; it's always a mental game with these fuckers," he bragged.

"And the new murder? The victim in Beachwood Canyon?" she asked.

"Well, that's a strange one. I knew her personally. I dated her a couple of years ago. And actually, I was at her place the night it happened . . ." Bill began.

Zelda took a sip of her lavender tea and nodded, encouraging him to keep talking. She checked to make sure her iPhone was recording everything he said. With his views on the muddy line between good and evil, his presence at the home of a murder victim the night she died, this was going to make for a stunning episode of her show.

Ethan Acevedo sat in a window seat on the plane to Puerto Vallarta, sipping his in-flight margarita. It felt good to be getting away. He had gone way too long without a break, just hitting the Metro grind every day like a warrior. He'd booked the flight on his way home to pack a bag, then headed straight to the airport. His dad did have Alzheimer's, but with his mom and a live-in caregiver, Acevedo didn't really need to help out. It was an easy excuse to use with Rollings. He didn't want to voice his concerns about the Balcomb interview and having his personal life exposed, especially since he often hooked up with women when he was on the clock. If Postiff wanted to speak to any of them, it could cause a lot of trouble for him.

He was glad he'd dropped the flowers off with her swishy landlord. He knew he shouldn't have gotten angry with her on the phone, but he did think she was kind of a slut. What business did she have with several boyfriends? His other women, the married Filipina in Los Feliz and the single mom in Atwater, didn't have time to be hanging out with other guys—they were busy with their kids the way women should be. They made time for him since he could give them what they wanted without a lot of strings attached. Eden was looking for something different. She actually thought she might have a real relationship with the guys she ran with. She had tried a few times to push for him to take her out or to go with her to some event she had tickets for, but he never did. He didn't want a girlfriend—he just wanted an easy, uncomplicated hookup when he needed it.

After Marilise, he had given up on women. He wondered about the guy she married, some limp-dick dentist. When he got back, he would drive out to Santa Clarita one night to see where they lived, what kind of cars they drove. His head felt light as his body relaxed into the seat. He signaled the flight attendant for another drink. A getaway to the beach in Mexico was just what he needed until all the bullshit blew over.

CHAPTER THIRTY-ONE

When Cassidy returned from patrol with Riley, Postiff corralled her into a conference room, where she saw Montoya and a tall thirtysomething brunette in a suit.

"This is Detective Sandra Moody. She used to work at this station before being transferred to Hollenbeck. We're borrowing her for this investigation, which Commander Ramsey wants to be kept under wraps. We have two members of this department under suspicion in the murder of Eden Balcomb. One is Bill Clarke, and the other is Ethan Acevedo. We're getting the security camera footage from her neighbor later, and we're doing a photo lineup with her landlord. Her cell phone records show calls to both Bill and a burner phone that we have not yet identified who it belongs to. We have to tread lightly given the requirements for investigating officers in our own department. I'll speak to Captain Rollings regarding Acevedo today, but be prepared for a lot of pushback on this."

"What about DNA?" Moody asked.

"We have blood DNA, most likely from the murderer, on Eden's body. There is DNA from a different male on a drinking glass on the coffee table and in the bathroom. Since our department doesn't keep DNA on its employees, we need to run both suspects against our evidence."

There was a pause as this information sank in; then Cassidy asked, "Should I bring in something with my dad's DNA on it?"

"That would be easier. I know this is very hard for you. I appreciate your help," Postiff said.

Cassidy wondered if Postiff included her in the investigation to get easy access to evidence that might hurt her father, since they lived in the same house. It felt like a betrayal on one hand and an effort to save him at the same time. She recognized that she was now crossing her own personal Rubicon. There was no turning away or turning back at this point. If her dad's DNA was simply on glassware at Eden's, there was an explanation for that. If it was his blood DNA on her body, it would be the worst scenario she could imagine. But she had to know.

Postiff gave them copies of the murder book that contained all photos, notes, the coroner's report, et cetera.

"Moody and I are heading over now to the apartment to do the photo lineup and pull the camera footage. We need to get Acevedo's DNA. Diana and Cassidy, you'll have to collect his trash. He lives in a guesthouse behind his parents' place. Trash day is tomorrow, so you need to get it tonight," Postiff said.

"Do you think we could get a warrant for Acevedo's DNA if he shows up on video footage on the night of the murder?" Montoya asked.

"Maybe if it lines up with the time of death," Postiff said. "But I'd rather get a public domain sample. The lawyer for the officers' union is going to fight this. I hate that two of our guys are even suspects. I hope the DNA doesn't match either of them, but it's best to get it in the least aggressive way. I'm going to call Rollings, just to start getting acquainted with what we have so far."

As Montoya and Cassidy settled in to review the murder book, Postiff stepped out to call the Rampart Division. Rollings's phone went straight to voicemail. Postiff dialed Josh Danner, the second-in-command of Metro. Danner answered immediately.

"Captain Danner, this is Judson Postiff in the Hollywood station. We need to interview one of your Metro officers, Ethan Acevedo."

"What is it in regard to?" Danner asked.

"The Eden Balcomb murder case. It is a routine interview. Officer Acevedo had a personal relationship with the victim, so we're talking to everyone. I know the protocol for the interview; I'll be arranging that within the week."

"All right, I'll let the union know as well so they have a representative there. But you'll probably have to wait until he comes back from vacation."

"Acevedo is on vacation? Since when?"

"He filed for it a few weeks ago; it came through today. He has family things to deal with. His dad has Alzheimer's," Danner said.

"Okay, thank you. I'll let you know if anything changes," Postiff said, dismayed at the delay.

Josh Danner hung up the phone and went back to reviewing the threat assessments in the downtown area. He didn't give Postiff's request a second thought. Acevedo was one of his best Metro cops, always ready to go above and beyond. When he'd called earlier to ask him to change the date of his vacation request to a few weeks earlier, Danner had been happy to do it. The young detective would catch the creep who killed Eden Balcomb, and Acevedo didn't need to be dragged into it. If anyone held firm on the thin blue line, it was Metro.

Bill tossed his overnight bag into his room and stood at the entryway window watching Alan Musselman's house. His car was there, and a light was on in a first floor window. Bill was determined to get inside Musselman's house when he was out and find something that pointed to him having created a new identity for himself. Derby said it was possible, even likely; that once you entered the criminal underworld, it was easy to find people to do such things. Bill knew that for years there had been a thriving trade in false Social Security numbers and fake IDs in MacArthur Park, a few miles from downtown LA.

He'd left a message for Postiff. After steering him toward Paxton Sparks, he figured the young detective wouldn't mind giving him some updates on Eden's case. He wanted to go over the case files and look at the murder book as soon as possible so he could weigh in. Zelda agreed that he should be given access, with his track record as a homicide detective. He saw his gym bag in the corner, but he hadn't been able to get back to Brickhouse for a few days. His schedule with the cold cases had taken all his focus. He also needed a checkup at his regular doctor to get something stronger for his headaches. He'd cut down on his drinking in recent years, but he stopped for a twelve-pack of Foster's Lager at the nearby convenience store. Sometimes a cold beer helped his head for a little while. He was sitting in a chair, watching the window when his phone rang. It was Barrera.

"Hey! What's up, brother?" Bill asked.

"Not much. I thought you were gonna be on the KTLA news for the Stacey Mandel case? Gloria's been watching for it, but she hasn't seen anything," Barrera said.

"Yeah, the agent I spoke to, Ainsley Wright, has been super busy, but I think we're going to do it in the next week or so," Bill lied. Wright hadn't returned any of his calls nor had the KTLA producer that showed up in San Diego. It was like all that initial interest from them had just evaporated overnight. He'd decided not to call them again; after all, he was the one who had a story. He'd find someone else to run with it, like Zelda Zed.

"I just wanted to let you know Ramsey took me off Eden's investigation," Barrera said.

"Why? It's a Hit Men murder, isn't it? That's what the press said."

"That's what we thought. She had the lipstick heart on her cheek, the whole MO was almost the same, but the DNA wasn't a match to Vithu Pham."

"So, you got DNA?" Bill asked. "But they didn't leave any at the other crime scenes."

There was a pause, and then Barrera said, "Hasn't Cassidy spoken to you about this?"

"No, I've been up in Coalinga, talking to Derby."

Barrera was silent. Bill waited until he thought the line had gone dead.

"Pete? You there?" he asked.

"Okay, I know this is going to be hard, man. And I shouldn't be saying anything, but I'm so fucking furious at Ramsey, I'm just going to do it. You're a suspect, man."

Bill felt as if he'd been gut punched, the air knocked out of him.

"A suspect? I'm a suspect?"

"Yeah, you left your fucking jacket there. I grabbed it before forensics arrived. I gave it to Cassidy."

"How can I be a suspect? I'm a homicide detective!" Bill said, his voice rising.

"I know you didn't do it, but Ramsey said I can't be on the case since we worked together for so long," Barrera said bitterly.

"Of course I didn't do it! Jesus Christ, how can they think it could be me?" Bill shouted.

"I think Postiff is running it, but it's all very hush-hush. The DNA doesn't match either of the Hit Men suspects, so they're looking at other people," Barrera said.

"Fucking hell," Bill said quietly.

"I'm working with Fort and Foster, which is like working with Beavis and Butt-Head. I hope they wrap Eden's case up soon. Have you heard anything about a funeral or a service?"

"No, nothing. She has no family except a crazy mom down south someplace," Bill said.

"Kind of sad, to go that way," Barrera said.

"If you hear anything in the pipeline, let me know. I'm going to ask Cassidy about it also. Ramsey has to be on crack to make me a suspect!"

"I get it, man. I still think it's gonna be Vithu Pham; he and Whitty left nothing at the earlier crime scenes either. But Eden didn't have anything under her fingernails. She didn't fight back, so she must've known the guy and didn't see it coming or he incapacitated her immediately."

They hung up, and Bill went to the kitchen to get a cold beer from the fridge. He popped it open, the familiar whooshing sound of the pressure releasing from the tab reassuring him. The first cold swallow of beer hit his throat and traveled up to his head, giving him a momentary brain freeze, which was what he wanted. Numbness, forgetting, everything suspended, progressing no further.

How nice it would be to stay in that space, he thought.

Knowing that he was a suspect in Eden's murder, he suddenly remembered all the different places his DNA would be found in her apartment. In her bedroom, on her sofa, on items in her kitchen. And since she was killed the night they returned from Coalinga, her rape kit could contain his semen.

But he had proof that they were involved in a relationship to explain all that. The Harris Ranch Hotel had a record of her joining him voluntarily, but he hadn't put her name on the room register. Someone there would recognize her from the dinner they had in the dining room. Or maybe not. Surely, a lot of people had seen her at his retirement party, seated with him in a booth. He felt a rising sense of panic, for the first time in his life realizing what it felt like to be innocent but to have been in the wrong place at the wrong time.

He thought of the suspects who had insisted upon their innocence, claiming the same things he was claiming now. He had ridiculed them, pressured them to confess, never once believing their explanations. He could imagine how trapped and helpless they had to have felt, how much he would hate to face a guy like him now that he was on the other side of the divide, a place he never expected to be. He considered that he might need a lawyer but refused to believe that the department he had given his life to would turn on him this way.

The worst part was that Barrera said Cassidy knew about it. She hadn't mentioned anything to him, hadn't called him up immediately to let him know. He was struggling with the weight of that betrayal when he heard her car pull up in the driveway. He opened the door before she stuck her key into the dead bolt.

He confronted her. "I just spoke to Pete. He said I'm a suspect in Eden's murder and you knew about it."

Cassidy carried her duty bag and the Eden Balcomb murder book along with a bag of groceries. She didn't want Bill to see the murder book. She knew he'd insist on looking at it, and she couldn't allow that. She pushed past him and headed to her bedroom.

"It's not the way it seems," she said, entering her bedroom. She stashed the murder book with her duty bag in the closet and closed the door as Bill stepped into her room.

"He said he found my jacket there and gave it to you," Bill said.

"Which he shouldn't have done. Everyone knows you were involved in a relationship with her, so your jacket or your DNA being at her place is normal. He's the one who acted as if your jacket was some big piece of evidence," she said.

"Where is it now?" he asked.

She couldn't tell him she gave it to Postiff, so she stalled.

"I took it to the dry cleaner's," she said.

"You took it because you think it might hold evidence that points to me? Do you think I killed Eden?" he asked.

She stared at him for a long beat. He held her gaze, never flinching.

"Did you?" she asked.

The color drained from his face, and when he spoke his voice was barely audible. "Do you really think I'm capable of something like that?"

"You shook Mom so hard, something in her neck snapped and she had to wear a brace. And that was eight years ago. You're more volatile now," she said.

"How did you know about that? It was an accident!" he insisted.

"No, it wasn't. An accident is when a car blows a tire and spins out of control. Or when a bridge suddenly collapses. A man grabbing his wife in a fit of anger and hurting her is not an accident!" she said.

Bill sat on the bed, his eyes averted. "I wasn't myself that day—" he started, but Cassidy interrupted him. She felt as if a tsunami of frustration were breaking free, and she could not hold back her words.

"You were exactly who you are. It's not having a 'big personality'! It's not about being 'passionate'! It's hotheaded, low impulse control, reactionary. Acting out and making everyone else adjust . . . or clean up after you. You've always been that person, and it's only getting worse. That's why I want you to see a doctor."

"Fine! I'll go see the damn doctor. But you think I could've killed Eden?"

"Didn't you act like a crazy person the night she dropped by? You screamed at her; you threw a pizza all over the room; you followed her out into the driveway. Your reaction was way over the top. And then you left in a rage. So, step outside yourself and think like the detective that you are. Would you be a suspect?"

Bill stared at his feet, shaking his head.

"As hard as it is for you to hear and for me to say it, I'm not positive that you couldn't lose control and do something like that. Mom decided to leave that day because she was scared of you."

Now he looked up at her, pained and confused.

"She said that?" he asked.

"She did. I don't want to believe that you killed Eden, Dad. I'm sure your DNA will clear you. They have blood DNA on her body; they think the knife slipped and the killer cut himself. That's what they want a match to," she said.

"How do you know that?" he asked.

She stared at him for a beat before replying, "I can't talk about that with you."

He looked down; then he nodded and asked, "Do you have a DNA collection kit in your bag? I think I still have one somewhere."

"I have one. Are we doing this now?" she asked.

"The sooner the better. I didn't kill her, Cassidy."

"Then your DNA will prove it."

"And my word is not enough?" he asked, his voice cracking.

She looked away from him. To see him hurting was more than she could manage without breaking down.

"I'm sorry, Dad. It's not."

She went into the closet and took the DNA collection kit from her duty bag. She opened it and handed the swab to Bill, who traced a circle on the inside of his mouth and handed it back to her.

"Never thought I'd be doing this in a million years," he said.

"Me either."

She put the completed kit back into her bag in silence and carried the groceries to the kitchen. Bill sat on her bed, remembering the years when her room was filled with toys and stuffies, fan photos of boy bands. Cathy had painted a blue sky on her ceiling, and her trophies from school sports were displayed on the bookshelf. As a little girl, she thought her daddy could do no wrong; she was a child, and she saw the world as a child does. Now she was an adult, and it pierced him like a hot iron between the eyes to know that she didn't trust him.

He knew the fault didn't lie with her. He'd been acting out and making excuses for a long time. He was avoiding the appointment with the neurologist because he was afraid of what they might find, and in his usual way, he hoped to bluster and boom his way out of it. He had so many muddled thoughts lately, so many mood swings and obsessive loops that he'd get stuck in, it felt good to have clarity for a moment, even if it was painful. He'd been making Cassidy act like his parent for a long time while he carried on like a rowdy adolescent. He went to the kitchen, where he found her preparing dinner.

He hung in the doorway and asked, "Can you text me Dr. Baruch's number? I'm going to reschedule for the soonest possible appointment."

"Good. I can call his office," she offered.

"No, it's my responsibility. I'll do it."

CHAPTER THIRTY-TWO

Ethan Acevedo sat at the hotel bar, listening to the ocean rolling in and out, like a lullaby.

He pondered the Eden situation, and it had actually worked out well for him. Their relationship wasn't going anywhere, and after she'd spoken to him so rudely on the phone, he realized that she might get it into her head to cause trouble for him. She might get vindictive that he didn't want to be her boyfriend. She could've contacted the department and made a complaint. He'd seen how things had changed in recent years, how women were speaking up and people were listening. Men could lose their jobs, or worse. It had gotten dangerous for guys like him. He had the assemblyman in Sacramento to watch his back if it went that far. He'd kept the evidence from his kid's attempted murder case, in the event he ever needed to use it. But having Eden out of the picture was better for everyone.

Bill Clarke might take the fall for it since he had a history with her. He'd been kind of off kilter in recent years; everyone knew that. He was unpredictable, and he could well be blamed for her death. And the second Hit Man, Vithu Pham, wasn't completely in the clear. Who else would've known the details about the bodies? The biggest problem was the blood DNA. That's what Fort told him. Whoever did it made a big mistake leaving that evidence behind. He finished off his margarita and ordered another one. He'd met a cute little senorita at the bar when he arrived, and they'd gone straight to his room. He'd figured she was a pro since she knew all the dirty tricks he liked, and when he'd tossed a hundred bucks at her when it was over, she didn't flinch and stuck it into the pocket of her flimsy sundress. She was meeting him again in the next half hour. She was a beauty, with jet-black hair and eyes like coffee-colored saucers. Her name was Maria, but weren't all of them called Maria?

Paul Pineda checked himself in the restroom mirror at the Rampart station before heading home. He'd gotten a fresh cut the day before and had his nails trimmed and buffed. He liked looking good in uniform, and making Metro was his dream. He was grateful that Ethan Acevedo had taken him under his wing and was helping him navigate the department when so many changes were happening. He liked that the other Metro cops saw him as Acevedo's protégé; it gave him an extra boost that made him stand out.

Standing out had always been important to him. He was barely five foot eight and was fortunate that the LAPD had lowered their height requirement. He'd wrestled in high school, but wrestlers never got the same kind of adoration and respect that the football players did, and that had always bothered him. The girls he liked were blond cheerleaders, and they didn't give him the time of day. His parents had money. They hoped he would be a doctor or lawyer, but he didn't have the discipline for that. They'd even sent him to a pricey private university, but that was mostly so they could brag to their friends at Saint Brendan's Catholic Church near their Windsor Square house.

He knew his dad was disappointed that his only son had chosen to be a cop. That was for working-class kids without a lot of options, but it suited him just fine. He didn't have to struggle to keep up with the smart kids, he got the automatic respect that came with the uniform and the gun, and he could flex that power whenever he wanted. He would never say it out loud, but he hated Blacks and barely tolerated Latinos; the only thing he liked about them was their food. And he felt that as a Filipino, the other Asians looked down on him, so he loved to patrol K-Town and jack up any young guy in a nice car who needed to be taken down a few pegs.

He'd married his perfect match, a blond, blue-eyed bank teller who quit her job when they got married, and now she was seven months pregnant. Acevedo kept pushing him to hook up with other women since she had gained sixty pounds and felt exhausted and nauseous all the time. He hadn't crossed that line yet; it felt wrong to cheat on his wife, but Acevedo made it seem like it was required. That all the guys did it, and he'd look like a simp if he didn't. He was relieved that Acevedo had taken a sudden vacation to Mexico. He'd been ramping up the pressure for Pineda to hook up with a little actress who did a couple of car-insurance commercials and was a freak who loved men in uniform. He'd even arranged for them to drive patrol together so Pineda could spend time with her while Acevedo was out covering for him. With him gone for a few weeks, Pineda got a reprieve from having to go through with it because saying no wasn't an option.

It bothered him that Acevedo left the burner phone with him. They'd spoken a few times, mostly about the murder in Beachwood Canyon; Acevedo wanted updates since he had a thing going with the woman who was killed, and he didn't want his affairs exposed. He assured Pineda that they would catch the killer before he returned, and it was just easier this way. Pineda was uncomfortable with the whole thing, especially since that phone had been ringing at odd times, but Acevedo told him not to answer unless it was from his international number.

Pineda knew he was into a lot of under-the-table stuff; he'd brag about it when the Metro guys were alone, about an unarmed guy he'd shot in a house raid in Echo Park, a drunk girl he'd banged on the freeway in exchange for not issuing a DUI. There were moments when Pineda was afraid of him, of the weird, shiny-eyed look he'd get when talking about his exploits. He considered leaving the burner phone in his car, but he knew that if Acevedo called, he'd have to explain why he hadn't answered.

The phone buzzed in his pocket. It was the same number, the one he didn't recognize. He didn't answer it.

It was almost eleven p.m., and the city traffic was still flowing. Cassidy and Montoya sat in an unmarked car up the street from Acevedo's house in Windsor Square. It was his parents' home, and as Postiff had described, there was a guesthouse in the back of the large property. They could see Acevedo's truck parked behind a wrought iron fence. Cassidy and Montoya were both out of uniform, dressed in grubby clothes and sneakers, in case they had to act like they were homeless scavengers going through the trash.

Montoya pulled out a vape. "You mind?"

Cassidy shook her head. "No problem. How're we going to know if it's his trash or his parents'?"

"There are separate trash cans back there by the guesthouse, see?"

She handed Cassidy a pair of night vision binoculars.

"These are cool," Cassidy said. She saw trash and recycling cans next to Acevedo's truck.

"My dad gave them to me when I graduated from the academy."

They sat in silence watching the house.

"Shouldn't they have put the trash out already?" Cassidy asked.

"You never know. Some jerks put it out really late so no one can steal their recycling," Montoya replied. "Like anyone's going to get rich on old soda cans."

"Doesn't it all go to the same place anyway?"

"Yeah, but some people are assholes who don't want anyone to get anything for free. How's your dad doing? He knows he's a suspect, right?" Montoya asked.

"We talked about it tonight. I dropped his DNA sample with Postiff when we picked up the car," she replied.

"How's he taking it?"

Cassidy shrugged; she didn't want to discuss it. The evening with Bill had been so upsetting that it took all her self-control to pull it together and come to stake out Acevedo.

"He insists he had nothing to do with it. He was over there watching TV, and then he left. Whoever killed her showed up after he was gone."

"He'll be cleared. There's no way he did it," Montoya said.

"Do you believe that? Or are you just saying it to make me feel better?"

"I believe it. So does everyone, all the detectives, the patrol cops. No one thinks your dad is a murderer. An egomaniac perhaps but not a murderer!" Montoya chuckled.

Cassidy smiled. It was good to know that his friends weren't throwing him under the bus. Yet.

"What do you think about Acevedo for Eden's murder?" Cassidy asked.

"I think he would kill someone without breaking a sweat. I think he'd go have a big piece of pie afterward and sleep like a baby. He's a freak," Montoya said with disgust.

"Did he ever bother you?"

"Yeah, right when I started. He would hang around, looking for me. He'd move in real close, no personal space. Always asking me out, like it was a given that I would go since he's Metro. I'd been warned, so I always made up an excuse. Then he showed up at my gym, parked outside, and wanted to go get a drink. So, I asked my cousin, Emiliano, to act like he was my boyfriend the next day when we went to the gym together, and I saw Acevedo's truck up the block. So, Emiliano put his arm around me and acted all lovey-dovey. We did that for a couple of weeks, and then I started wearing a fake diamond that looked like an engagement ring and said I was getting married, so Acevedo left me alone. See?"

She held out her left hand, where she wore a big, flashy diamond-ring set.

"That looks real. Where'd you get it?" Cassidy asked.

"At a CVS in Whittier. Cubic zirconia. I call it my flyswatter. When Acevedo asked about it, I said my fiancé was a lawyer, and that was it," Montoya said with a laugh.

The side door of the house opened, and a young woman stepped out wearing hospital scrubs. She grabbed the heavy trash cans and pushed the wrought iron gate open, dragging the cans to the curb.

"She looks like a caregiver, right?" Montoya asked.

"Yeah. Postiff mentioned that Acevedo's dad isn't well," Cassidy said as they watched the woman walk to the guesthouse and pull Acevedo's trash cans out.

"Bingo!" Montoya said.

The woman closed the gate behind her and hurried back inside. They watched as the lights in the dining and living rooms went out; just a lamp light was left on in a side window. They waited a long time, but she did not come out.

"She must be a live-in. It's a big house," Cassidy mused.

"It's probably worth a fortune in this neighborhood! His folks have money. I think he's the only kid, so that creep will inherit all of it when they go," Montoya said, drawing on her vape. "How long d'you want to wait?"

"Until everyone's asleep. We'll just look like we're homeless, digging for cans and stuff."

They watched and waited until almost midnight, when the neighborhood became quiet. Up the street, they saw several homeless people with shopping carts descending on the trash cans on the curb. They fanned out to hit different houses, making quick work of rummaging through the garbage.

"Let's go when they get a little closer, so we blend in," Cassidy said, cracking open the door of the car.

"Right. You're gonna blend in looking like Nicole Kidman going through the trash. Okay, now!" Montoya said, throwing the driver's door open and springing out.

She and Cassidy scurried to Acevedo's trash cans and grabbed the plastic bags that were inside. The other trash pickers on the street shouted at them.

"Hurry! They'll beat us up!" Cassidy whispered.

"We're cops! They're not going to beat us up!" Montoya said, tossing the trash bags into the trunk and then jumping into the driver's seat. Cassidy slid in as Montoya pulled away, slamming her door when they were in motion.

"That was like a real getaway exit!" Cassidy said.

"All I know is we've been on the clock since this morning and if they want this garbage sifted through, they can do it," Montoya said.

"Postiff is the last person I can imagine going through trash. He's so stylish and classy," Cassidy said.

"True. We're gonna end up doing it. Do you think Postiff is gay?" Montoya asked.

"I never got that vibe. He's kind of . . . hot, in a way. He has good taste in clothes, he'd know what wine to order in a nice restaurant, but he's also tough as shit. Remember that school shooting when he walked in alone and stopped it?"

"I know. I think I love him," Montoya said wistfully.

"And he probably thinks you're engaged to your cousin," Cassidy said with a laugh.

"Thanks, Acevedo . . ." Montoya muttered.

At the Hollywood station, the detective bureau was quiet, except for Postiff and Moody sitting at side-by-side desks, poring over data.

"You know, the complaints against Bill Clarke were all for selective enforcement, demonstrating bias, two excessive-force incidents when he was on patrol. Nothing specifically related to aggression or sexual impropriety with women," Moody said and took a sip from a chipped coffee mug. "Clarke doesn't have anything in his file like that, and Acevedo's is filled with them."

Postiff leaned over to look at Moody's computer screen and perused the complaints against Acevedo.

"He's got issues with women, clearly. He's harassed several new boots when they started working. He's got a lot of complaints for sexual harassment."

"And two from women who said he stopped them late at night on Laurel Canyon and pressured them to give him a blow job to get out of a ticket," Moody said. "How has this guy not been fired?"

"I heard some shit went down with a state assemblyman and the guy protects him," Postiff said.

"So, he's got coverage from up top. That explains it and his impunity. Anyone else would be afraid of getting caught," Moody said. "What time do you think Montoya and Clarke junior will be back with Acevedo's trash?"

"Any minute now. Cassidy handed over Bill's DNA earlier. I thought she would swipe a toothbrush or something, but he gave her a sample willingly," Postiff said.

"That's rough. When do you want to interview him?" Moody asked.

"Since he's retired, we don't need all the protocol to do it. I left him a message earlier to see if we can talk to him tomorrow. I don't think he did it, but Ramsey is pushing him as the main suspect," Postiff said.

Moody scoffed. "She must have something against him. She's like that—it's all about her personal favorites or scapegoats."

"Tell me about it." Postiff sighed.

Moody sat up suddenly. "Hey! Look at this! Did you know Acevedo has an ex-wife? She lives out in Alhambra. Anne Choi."

"Did you find a divorce decree?"

"No, annulment. After three months of marriage. The cause listed is fraud," Moody said pointedly.

"Let's set up a time to talk with her, in person," Postiff said.

A young uniformed officer walked into the detective bureau holding a piece of paper.

"We just had a call on the main number, asking for the detective working the Eden Balcomb case. It was a man. He spoke really low—I could barely understand him. I put him on hold so I could transfer the call to you, but he hung up before I could."

"Did he give you his name?" Postiff asked.

"I wrote it down for you. It's Arturo Blanco."

Cassidy pulled her MINI Cooper out of the Hollywood-station parking lot. She and Montoya had dropped off Acevedo's trash with Postiff and Moody, who were still working. She was exhausted from the day but restless at the same time. She didn't relish going home and dealing with her dad when their earlier conversation had been so difficult and painful. She drove through the twenty-four-hour McDonald's on Vine Street for a large coffee and decided to head west.

She and Carter hadn't spoken much, just a few scattered, brief conversations in the past week, but she thought it might be good to drop in on him. It could turn into a booty call, she knew, showing up after midnight, but that would be fine by her. She needed something to pull her out of the emotional spiral she was caught in. Everything had been too much for her to manage. She still felt a pang of resentment toward Ramsey for making her the point of contact with Whitty, regardless of his conditions. She suspected that she'd been used as a lightning rod, to take the fall if things had gone badly. Then the horror of Eden's murder and her dad falling under suspicion. She wished she could climb into a hole in the ground and stay there.

Perhaps Carter had been a casualty of her being so overwhelmed. He'd told her again and again that he wanted to make it work, that he was there for her if she needed him. She drove Sunset all the way, enjoying the decompression that came with watching the gritty streets of Hollywood give way to the excess and glamour of the Sunset Strip. The winding curves of the boulevard as it traversed into Beverly Hills, where the streets were silent, the houses safely perched behind tall gates and long driveways. She passed the sprawling UCLA campus and the outskirts of Bel Air, crossing the 405 freeway and heading into the wooded, exclusive enclave of Brentwood.

Carter's condo was on Barrington, one of the main thoroughfares into the small, wealthy neighborhood. She found a parking spot and punched the security code to open the heavy glass doors of the building. She rode the elevator, her SKECHERS sliding on the polished marble floor. She sighed in a certain kind of relief, the relief of luxury and safety. The sense that nothing bad would happen here, in this cocoon of wealth and protection. Carter provided her that comfort; she hadn't realized it before. Perhaps that was something she needed, not to see him as a partner to share in her daily struggles with crime and the vagaries of human experience, but as an escape from it. Maybe he could be a safe harbor, where all that mattered were four-star dinner reservations and boating trips, fancy holidays and exotic vacations.

She rang his doorbell; he was probably asleep. But the door was opened immediately by a petite blond girl in sweats and a USC hoodie. The television was on in the living room.

Cassidy stepped back, surprised as the girl asked, "Are you from GRUBHUB?"

"No, I'm not," Cassidy said as Carter emerged from the kitchen holding two bottles of beer. He blanched when he saw her.

"Cassidy! Is everything okay?" he asked. The blond looked at him, uncertain and questioning.

"Yeah, I'm fine. I was working near here. We were called in as backup for the Westside station," she lied.

"You should've called," he said.

"Yeah, I can see that. I've got to get going. I was just stopping by to say hi. Nice to meet you," she said to the blond, who had crossed her arms and planted herself firmly in the doorway.

"Amber's a classmate of mine. We were just studying for an exam," Carter stammered awkwardly.

"Sure, good luck with that," Cassidy said, turning and hurrying to catch the elevator.

"I'll walk you out!" Carter offered, pushing past the blond and following Cassidy, who got into the elevator and hit the button to close the doors as he approached. The shiny gold doors drew together as Carter tried to put his hand out to stop them.

"Don't do that," Cassidy said sharply; he pulled his hand back.

"It's not what you think . . ." he said as the doors closed and the elevator began its descent.

She rode down, her heart racing. Her surprise had turned to embarrassment and then anger. Not at him but at herself. He had nothing to apologize for; she was the one who had called for time apart. She'd shown up unannounced and uninvited. She jogged to her car and got in, her face flushed. She sat for a moment, watching as Carter stepped out of the building, scanning the street for her. A giant SUV pulled into the space in front of her, blocking his view. She hung a U-turn on the now quiet street and sped back toward the freeway. It would be a short drive home.

She upbraided herself for thinking a visit to Carter was a good idea. It was a symptom of how unsettled and unhappy she felt about her life at the moment. Carter was easy and uncomplicated, and she had fallen back on him as a quick fix to help her forget for a little while. But had she stayed, she knew in the morning she would've felt the same tightening sense of claustrophobia at his expectations of her and how she fit into his life. A quick stress hookup wouldn't have changed that. She had been saved from making a misstep that would've complicated a simple breakup. She texted him,

we're done for good. don't call me

She blocked his number. She laughed quietly at the image of Amber, with her arms crossed territorially, glaring at her in the doorway. She could have Carter Sims, his fat trust fund, and his tiresome family with their dull-as-dirt world of attending the regatta and society events at the California Club. The good thing was that now they didn't have to go through the torturous final dance of their relationship's demise. She could play at being upset, and that would be the end of it. She decided to ask Montoya to pick her up a fake diamond ring at the CVS in Whittier. And the next time she bumped into Carter Sims, she'd be wearing it, just to rock his world and make him wonder. She definitely needed a flyswatter.

Bill sat in the shadows of the Red Line Gentlemen's Club in Reseda. His head was pounding, and the discomfort made his thoughts muddy. Cassidy had left after a tense dinner, without telling him where she was going. He knew he'd acted like a jerk, but he didn't have a quick fix for it this time. He felt the sting of his daughter's suspicions like a throbbing ache in his body. How had he fucked everything up so badly that she could think him capable of murder? He would never forget the look on her face when she asked him if he did it. Hurt, anger, confusion. His little girl would never see him the same way again.

He signaled the barely clad waitress for another drink while a blond Slavic-looking beauty did a pole dance in nothing but a tiny sequined G-string. She had shed the glittery bra she had come onstage with, and now her perfectly shaped silicone breasts held their form as she contorted and twisted her lithe body around the metal pole, twerking to the delight of the men assembled in the dimly lit club. She smiled at him; it was the third time she had paid him special attention, and he'd slipped a handful of bills into her G-string. He heard her name was Mila and that she was Hungarian. He knocked back his drink, the warm, swimming sensation rising up from his gut to his forehead.

He'd heard the message from Postiff suggesting that he come to the station to be interviewed and give a statement regarding Eden's death. It would be Postiff and Sandra Moody, a detective he'd worked with a few years earlier. Now she was back and interviewing him as a suspect, which was an unforgivable trespass against him, as far as he was concerned. He knew it was standard procedure, but he had earned the right to be above suspicion, hadn't he? He would show up and answer all their questions, and he'd leave with his head held high. Fuck them. He wished it were earlier; he would've liked to call Derby to discuss it with him. Even though he was a criminal, Derby had a lot of right ideas about things. He certainly saw Bill as he was, and appreciated him too.

The stripper came to the edge of the stage, where the light hit her in such a way that he could see everything.

The waitress came by and whispered, "Would you like a private lap dance with Mila? I can tell Ciro, the manager."

Bill considered for a moment. A private lap dance would be innocent enough. She looked like a nice girl; maybe he'd discover why she was working in this type of place to make a living. Maybe he could help her. He downed his drink and followed the waitress to the back room.

CHAPTER THIRTY-THREE

Cassidy slept in an extra hour after the late-night evidence grab. They would start searching through it first thing when she got to the station. The house was quiet when she padded into the kitchen to start the coffee. Her dad's car wasn't there, and she stuck her head into his room to see that his bed hadn't been slept in either. She felt a pang of concern, but it passed. Her father was an adult; he didn't have to check in every evening at curfew. She walked out to the driveway and waved at Alan Musselman, who gave her a terse nod in response. She grabbed the *Los Angeles Times* and went back inside.

After a quick breakfast, she prepared for work. There was still no sign of her dad. She went into his room and saw his overnight bag from Coalinga hadn't been unpacked, and she unzipped it to toss his laundry into the washer. Tucked in between his clothing, she saw two notebooks. She knew she shouldn't open them, but she couldn't resist. She had never known her dad to keep a journal or notes of any kind, other than the murder book for each of his cases. She flipped through them, his uneven script scattered across the pages in a way that seemed frenetic, disconnected.

Who determines and decides what is GOOD or RIGHT when evil persists and goes unchecked . . . how does the required price and PENANCE get paid? . . .

An EYE for an EYE, what goes around MUST come around!!!

Is retribution only for god . . . or the government to decide . . . Morality is a HUMAN construct . . .

Who exacts the punishment when the EVIL EVADES JUSTICE . . .

How can a good man let it go UNPUNISHED . . . how little all of this matters on this small blue ball floating in space . . . insignificant lives . . . BREAK FREE of the false parameters invented by man . . .

Troubled, Cassidy closed the notebooks and put them back into his bag. If these were the thoughts swirling around in his head, he was moving closer every day to acting upon his personal ideas of crime and punishment. Under the illusion of his own righteousness in an unjust world, he could be capable of anything, she feared. She knew he had to be impaired.

After a quick shower, she texted Bill but got no response. She checked his location on his phone and saw that his phone was at the Best Western Garden Lodge in Reseda. She knew she shouldn't drive over there, but she wouldn't be able to focus on work if she was wondering where he was and if he was safe or not. Twenty minutes later, she pulled up at the Best Western and saw his car in the lot. The hotel was next to the Red Line Gentlemen's Club, and she knew he had been there in the past, with his detective buddies. Her anxiety dissipated. He could well have had too much to drink and decided to sleep it off. Uber was still a newfangled thing to him, and he didn't quite trust it. Relieved, she backed out of the lot and headed for the freeway to Hollywood.

Postiff pulled up at Eden's apartment building to find the trauma cleaning service was at work in her unit. He knocked on Arturo Blanco's door, certain that he heard movement inside, but no one answered. Postiff was cranky; he'd slept only four hours and wasn't in the mood for a skittish witness holding up his investigation.

"Mr. Blanco? This is Judson Postiff of the LAPD. You called yesterday for me?" he shouted loudly, knocking again. Michael Lyman came out from his apartment wearing a flowing Japanese robe and a pair of old Levi's.

"You saw the cleaners are here? I'm glad they've come, but it's so . . . final. Like they're erasing any sign of Eden," he said.

"Have you seen Mr. Blanco in the last twenty-four hours?" Postiff asked impatiently.

"Yes, he was out and about yesterday, and I can tell you . . . he looked shaken! Positively shaken!"

The door to Blanco's apartment swung open, and a heavyset Latino man in his forties stood there.

"I'm Arturo Blanco. Are you the detective?" he asked nervously.

"Yes, you called me yesterday?" Postiff asked.

"Come in. Go home, Michael. Nothing's going on here." He waved his hand dismissively at Lyman, who flipped his robe and turned on his heel.

Postiff stepped inside a compulsively neat apartment with every wall covered in Garfield memorabilia and collectibles.

"I assume you have some information, since you reached out to me?" Postiff asked.

Blanco nodded and opened a bottle of water.

"Yes, I saw Eden's boyfriend arrive—you know the one who's a detective? His name is Bill, I think."

Postiff nodded. "Yes, I'm aware of Mr. Clarke's relationship with Eden. What time did he arrive?"

"It had to be close to ten thirty or eleven. They spoke in the doorway for a bit. He seemed like he was apologizing or something. Then they went inside. He left about an hour and a half later."

"Did he return?"

"I don't think so. I heard someone ring her bell just after he left, and she opened it. It didn't seem like a stranger, and then suddenly there was a loud thump, and the door closed. When I looked on my Ring camera, I saw him. He left about half an hour later," Blanco said.

"Who was it?"

Blanco moved to his front curtains and peered outside fearfully.

"It was the other guy. The one who comes in uniform, with the sirens. The creepy one," he said.

"Do you have that video saved?" Postiff asked, all tiredness gone as his adrenaline kicked in.

"I saved it. It's on this flash drive. But last night, a guy came over knocking really late. I didn't answer, but I was afraid it was him."

"I have a photo of the officer I think you're talking about. Do you think you would recognize him?" Postiff asked, holding out his phone with Acevedo's photo.

Blanco pulled back when he saw it and nodded, covering his mouth with his hand.

"That's him. He's the one who came over after the other guy left. He did it, didn't he? What if he knows I saw him?" Blanco asked in rising panic.

"I'll have extra patrols here on your street, and I'll keep you updated when we are in touch with him," Postiff said.

"I don't want extra patrols! He's a cop—they'll be his friends! Can I go to a hotel or something?"

Postiff knew he shouldn't do it, but he felt sorry for weird Arturo Blanco and his sad Garfield collection. He drew three hundred-dollar bills out of his wallet and handed them to him.

"Just keep this between you and me, okay? Take it and go stay someplace else for the next day or so. I'll be in touch."

"Thank you, detective. I'll be gone in half an hour!" Blanco said, relieved.

Postiff texted Cassidy, Montoya, and Moody.

The neighbor at Eden's apartment saw a man arrive after Bill left. It was Acevedo. Let's get that DNA asap!!

Cassidy and Montoya had the trash from Acevedo's garbage spread out on a sterile plastic tarp in an empty meeting room at the station. With rubber gloves, they sifted through the trash, discarding frozen food boxes, empty milk cartons, and food scraps. When Postiff's text arrived, Montoya gave Cassidy a high five.

"What'd I tell you? Your dad is going to be in the clear," Montoya said.

"I just want the DNA so they can run them both," Cassidy said. "Doesn't this guy use Kleenex or plastic cups?"

They were rooting through a plastic bag containing bathroom trash when Montoya shouted, "I've got it! Discarded toilet paper with blood on it! And a disposable razor!"

They bagged the evidence and put the remaining trash back into the bags for storage. As they worked, Moody stuck her head in.

"You got Postiff's text, right?"

"Yeah, and we just found some stuff that should have DNA on it," Montoya replied.

Cassidy remained silent, her mind still on Bill's notebooks.

"I just came from talking to Acevedo's ex-wife. She says he's a nutcase. Addicted to violent pornography, into really scary stuff. She left after three months, and had to go into hiding," Moody said.

"When is my dad coming in?" Cassidy asked.

"I'm hoping later today. But it's not pointing toward him right now," Moody said.

"And the DNA?"

"They've had some accident at the lab. Everything is delayed. Hang in there," Moody reassured her.

"It's going to be fine, Cassidy," Montoya said.

"We'll know when the DNA is back," Cassidy said, leaving the room.

She walked outside to the parking lot for fresh air. She felt on the verge of hyperventilating. Her hands were clammy, and sweat was creeping up her neck, staining her white T-shirt. She realized she was having a full-blown panic attack, which hadn't happened for many years. She'd had them regularly after the Keyes-family tragedy. She wished she could go visit Kylie, but she had promised to stay away. These were the moments when she needed their friendship the most, to tether her to something solid. She bent over and put her head between her knees, taking deep breaths.

Staring down at the cracked asphalt of the parking lot, the exhaust from passing cars filtering into her nostrils, she wondered if she had made the right choice in becoming a cop like her dad. She was barely a week on the job, and she was already coming apart. She had to consider that maybe she wasn't tough enough for it. Maybe it was time to think of something else to do with her life, but she had no idea what that might be.

Postiff arrived back at the station, energized by the meeting with Blanco. He wanted to let Rollings know that a witness had seen Acevedo at Eden's apartment, but he didn't want to tip his hand too soon to Metro. As he walked in, he saw a group of Metro officers that he knew must've been preparing for some action on the streets of Hollywood. There were political protests, and with the new laws criminalizing homelessness, sometimes Metro came in to help clear out the many encampments located under the freeway overpasses.

They were planning to talk to Eden's other boyfriend, Ted Stark, later that day to see if he could be cleared as a suspect. Postiff had been dialing the burner phone since they'd found the number in Eden's records. He tried it again and heard the faint buzzing coming from the group of Metro cops. He moved closer to them and saw Paul Pineda take the burner phone from his pocket and check the number. As they broke up to head out, Postiff tapped Pineda's arm.

"I need to speak to you before you leave, officer," Postiff said.

"We're just leaving, detective. Maybe when we get back, I can do it."

"We'll do it now. It will just take a minute," Postiff insisted, leading him toward a conference room.

Bill had been home from the Best Western for several hours, watching Musselman's house from a back bedroom window. He was there and hadn't gone out all day. Bill was impatient for him to leave so he could put his plan into action. His phone rang, and he answered it immediately. It was Derby calling collect from Pleasant Valley.

"Hello, detective, how's tricks?" Derby asked jovially.

"Not great, Tyler . . ." Bill replied, filling him in on all the developments since his return from Coalinga. Derby listened sympathetically.

"That's awful, Bill. Really, how can they think you're a suspect? You're above that, you know. It's a sign of their disrespect for you. I would file a serious complaint against the department," Derby said.

"I'm considering it," Bill agreed, "but I'm thinking of going into Musselman's place today when he leaves. I'm going to find the stuff we talked about."

"Good idea. I'm sure you'll find exactly what you're looking for. You're right about him being connected to the Sun-Hee murder. Everything you told me points right to it," Derby goaded him.

"I'll call you when I find something. We can go over it together before I present it to the cold case detectives. We're going to have another slam dunk, case closed," Bill said. "I see Musselman leaving. It's time to make my move!"

Bill hung up and stuck his mini flashlight and lock jimmy into his pocket. He pulled a dark baseball cap down over his head and waited, watching Musselman's car drive off. He slipped out and crossed the empty street, opening Musselman's side gate and darting into the yard unseen by any neighbors. A gardener worked at a house two doors down, his leaf blower making enough noise to cover the sound of Bill working his jimmy into the doorjamb. There was no alarm system; he had made note of that during his initial exploration of the yard. The back door finally gave, and he pushed it open, then stepped inside.

He would find the proof that Alan Musselman was involved in the murder of Min Sun-Hee, one way or another.

CHAPTER THIRTY-FOUR

Pineda left the interview with Postiff, sweat soaking his white T-shirt beneath his wool uniform. He'd learned that while Postiff might look like a hip, metrosexual type of guy, he was a tough motherfucker of a detective. Pineda had walked right into all his traps, didn't even see them coming. He was forced to admit that Acevedo had given him the phone while he was away, that it was used primarily to communicate with Acevedo's various female friends. He'd been tricked into revealing that Acevedo hooked up with his women while he was on the clock.

From the way Postiff talked, it seemed like Acevedo could be a suspect, which freaked Pineda out most of all. It was one thing to bullshit with the Metro guys about all the crazy stuff he'd done, but they all knew most of it was just grandstanding. Pineda didn't really believe all the things Acevedo bragged about; he'd have to be nuts to have really done it. Now Postiff was making it seem like Acevedo could be a murderer.

And worst of all, Postiff had put him on the spot to report back all conversations he would have with Acevedo in the coming days. He said if Acevedo was involved in the Balcomb murder, Pineda could be charged as an accessory for giving him information if he didn't cooperate. At that, Pineda almost shit his pants. He'd worked hard to get into the LAPD. He was moving up, with a baby on the way. If he was charged, he'd lose his job and his future, and he could go to prison. His whole life would go up in smoke; his wife would divorce him; his parents might disown him for the shame he brought them. He walked out to his car, his eyes averted to avoid meeting anyone's gaze. He was afraid he might burst into tears from the anxiety of it all.

Why did he always choose the wrong guy to side with? In high school, he'd become the best friend of a kid on the wrestling team who sexually assaulted a girl at a party and then tried to cover it up. Pineda had been dragged into it for helping the guy get rid of his semen-stained clothing and giving him a false alibi. When it came out, it was only his parents' big donation to Saint Brendan's School that saved his ass and didn't get him kicked out. And the girl's father didn't want to press charges, to spare the family humiliation.

In college, he hung out with a trio of guys who falsified their grades, hacking into the computer system. He'd gone along with it, like he always did. Because they hadn't changed his grades, he wasn't held accountable, but he was questioned by the dean and had to give evidence against the others, which branded him as a snitch. He hated to admit it, but he was just a beta. He wasn't the shot caller, the alpha who made the decisions and took the risks. He went along and never seemed to get it that he was running headlong off a cliff until it was too late. Now, he had Postiff expecting him to deliver information on Acevedo. He was terrified of what would happen to him if Acevedo found out. He'd done it again. He'd found a way to put himself into the worst possible position.

Ted Stark, Eden's married boyfriend, sat in the interview room with Postiff and Moody. He was sweating profusely, wearing a carefully curated outfit of ripped jeans, bowling shirt, and porkpie hat perched on his head. A pair of large Harry Potter–style glasses rested on his nose. At fifty-eight, he looked like he was dressed up as a teenager for a costume party.

"Thank you for finally coming in today, Mr. Stark. I was beginning to think you were avoiding me," Postiff said.

"I was just so upset by the whole thing. Eden was such a nice girl—woman, I mean—I can't believe something like this happened," Stark said, his voice shaking.

"How long have you known her?" Moody asked.

"About seven years. We're friends, kind of . . . friends with benefits, I guess," Stark explained with a sheepish smile.

"You mean you were involved in an intimate, sexual relationship with Ms. Balcomb?" Postiff asked.

Stark squirmed in his chair. "I mean . . . it sounds so . . . involved . . . when you put it that way. It was casual. She knew it wasn't serious. I'm married for fifteen years. I have two kids."

"Married fifteen years, a family man with children, yet you were carrying on with Eden, no strings attached, no expectations. Is that what you're saying?" Moody prodded him.

"Yeah. Eden was cool with it, most of the time. Except she got all depressed on holidays and stuff. You know, the whole 'Why are you with your family all day?' thing," Stark said, trying to muster a laugh. It sounded like he was choking on a piece of meat.

"You were never serious with her?" Moody asked.

"No, I told her I'm not leaving my wife, ever. It was just a fun thing with Eden."

"Fun, how?" Postiff asked.

"I mean, she was great. She loved to do the stuff I like to do. We'd watch movies on Netflix. I'm a huge movie buff; I know all the background stuff about the directors and all. She loved to cook, so she made killer food every time I came over. It was the perfect escape."

"Did she ever threaten to tell your wife? Did you ever fight about that?" Postiff asked.

"A couple times she got mad and said she'd call Laura and tell her everything, which really pissed me off. Like, she knew the rules when we started, and then she'd say shit like that!" Stark said with indignation.

"How pissed off did you get, Ted?" Postiff asked, leaning in.

"Pretty pissed off! I mean, wouldn't you?" Stark said, slowly realizing Postiff's meaning. "But not mad enough to hurt her or anything. No way!"

"Would you be willing to give a DNA sample? We'd like to clear you as a suspect," Moody said.

Stark's eyes narrowed. He resembled a frightened piglet.

"What if I don't?" he asked.

"We'll get a warrant for it, and I'd be more than happy to come by your house to get it, so you don't have to make another trip over here," Postiff said with a smile.

"You guys really like to fuck with someone's head," Stark said, suddenly petulant.

"Not like stringing your side piece along for seven years, having her cook for you, fuck you, and let me guess, I bet when you'd watch movies you'd explain them to her. I'm sure your wife had no patience for that, but Eden did, right? Maybe I could ask Laura in person when we come with the warrant?" Moody asked.

Stark turned bright red and laid his sweaty palms on the table.

"I'll do the DNA," he said, all indignation gone.

Bill moved quietly through Alan Musselman's house; piles of unpacked boxes were stacked along the wall in the hallway. He hoped the proof he was searching for wasn't in one of them. He focused on the office, flipping through a tall file cabinet filled with neatly labeled folders. They were related to publishing contracts and health insurance, investment documents and appliance maintenance manuals. He found one marked *Birth Certificate / Passport / Naturalization* and removed it. He was sure there would be something incriminating inside and began pulling each document out and quickly scanning through it. He took photos of each page with his phone.

Alan Musselman was born in Prague and immigrated to the US as a child. He was thirty-seven years old. He became a naturalized American citizen when he was ten years old, with a US birth certificate issued from the state of Vermont. Annoyed and impatient that he was not finding what he was looking for, Bill began pulling out more documents, photographing all of them and tossing them aside. In one folder he found two Social Security cards and knew he'd hit the jackpot. He snapped a quick photo as he heard Musselman's car pull up outside. Bill dumped the files he was holding and hurried toward the back door of the house but not in time to avoid Musselman, who collided with him.

"What the fuck are you doing here?" Musselman shouted, startled.

Bill said nothing but pushed past him and ran out into the yard. Musselman kept shouting and cursing as he followed him, catching up and grabbing the back of Bill's hoodie, pulling him off balance. Bill turned and swung on him, hitting Musselman in the face before bolting through the gate and sprinting to his car. He jumped in and drove off, his heart pounding. In his rearview mirror, he saw Musselman standing in his driveway, blood running down his face, screaming. The gardener was at his side; several other neighbors had come out to see what the commotion was.

Bill knew he'd face breaking and entering charges, but he was sure they would dismiss them when they saw that he was getting vital information to solve a long-dead cold case. He knew the two Social Security cards were going to expose Musselman as Tom Britt. Cornered like a rat, Alan Musselman would have to admit to killing Min Sun-Hee and explain how he'd gone off the radar and become someone else. Bill couldn't wait to tell Zelda—it would make a thrilling episode for the podcast. But first, he wanted to let Derby know that he'd succeeded. He dialed Pleasant Valley State Prison. He heard police sirens in the area. He wasn't worried. He would be hailed as a hero, again.

Joyce Ramsey found Cassidy reviewing phone records in the Balcomb case.

"Officer Clarke, I'm going to need you in the interview room. Ron Whitty wants to make some kind of further confession, only to you," she said.

Cassidy grimaced and hung her head. This was the last thing she wanted to deal with. The DA had filed charges; they had the confession and the evidence they needed. She didn't know why she had to be offered up to Whitty like a sacrifice, to appease his twisted ego.

"Commander, I'm right in the middle of the Balcomb investigation. I told Detective Postiff I would have these phone records done this afternoon," Cassidy said.

"This takes precedence. I'll see you there in five minutes," Ramsey said, waiting for her. Cassidy stood up, hiding her annoyance, and followed her.

"This is a no-stress interview. We don't need anything from him. He wants to talk, so we'll listen. We would love to get information on other victims, but the priority is going with cases we have already filed. If he's playing games, just shut him down," Ramsey said.

They watched Whitty being led into the interview room with his usual nonchalant attitude.

"Thank you, commander," Cassidy said, before heading in.

When she entered, Whitty grinned at her and tapped the table. "Nice to see you, Officer Clarke. You can sit right here with me. Have you missed me?"

"Not at all. I'm very busy with work," Cassidy said.

Whitty licked his dry, chapped lips. "I bet you've missed me a little bit. I have some new information that I think you're gonna want. But first I want to know how you've been doing."

"Just tell me what you want to say, Mr. Whitty. I'm ready to listen."

"I might have some more information about some other cases. You know, you guys didn't find out about all my victims, and I had another helper besides that little shit, Vithu Pham."

Cassidy slid a pad of paper and a pen across the table to him.

"Please write down the names of the victims and the date and place of their deaths. We will investigate, and if you're telling the truth, the judge might look favorably on that when you go to trial," Cassidy said.

"You're doing it again, moving right to the main course without any appetizers! Why aren't you in that pretty dress today, officer? I liked the way it fit you real nice," he said suggestively.

Cassidy sighed. She was sick and tired of Whitty and Ramsey and the whole charade.

"If you have other victims to reveal, this is the time to do it. If you want to use this interview to play games and jockey for position, you have nothing to gain. We have your confession, Vithu's and Thuy Pham's statements; you've been identified by the victim in Bronson Canyon; we have your DNA at the crime scenes. The charges have been filed. Discovering other victims would be good, but the DA is ready to proceed."

Whitty laughed softly, but she could see that he was rattled that his game wasn't working the way he had hoped.

She continued, "To be clear, Mr. Whitty, I wore that pretty dress that fit me 'real nice' because I know your weakness is women. I knew it would get you all excited if I flirted with you and acted like I thought you were interesting. And you'd talk, eventually. I was doing my job, which was to get information, and I got it. I wouldn't look twice at a loser like you, just like those poor women you murdered. You're a pathetic coward. So, if you have something to say, then say it. I don't have to play these games because our main priority is to make sure you are locked up for the rest of your life. And with the evidence we have, you will be."

The veins in Whitty's neck bulged as he kicked his chair out from underneath him with a guttural howl. The police guard lunged for him, pinning him face down on the table.

"You're just a bitch! A lying bitch like the others!" he screamed in uncontrollable rage.

Cassidy leaned down until her face was inches from his.

"I'm not like the others, Mr. Whitty. They're dead, and I'm the one who caught you."

Vithu Pham sat in an interview room, waiting for Thuy to be brought in. His lawyer told him that there was no match to his DNA at the last victim's house. He was relieved; he didn't know that woman at all. He wondered if they would run his DNA against evidence from other victims, from before he ever met Whitty. They were mostly prostitutes and street people, and he hoped no one was trying to solve those cases. Like back home, there were certain women that no one bothered to look for.

Korn had told him he would face life in prison, and he'd probably never be eligible for parole. He didn't want to be in the same place as Whitty, didn't want to be reminded of his worst mistake. His parents hadn't called or come to see him. He couldn't see a way out of his situation, but maybe Thuy would have a plan. She always did.

After a few minutes, a guard brought her in. Her orange jumpsuit was too large, her neck looked like a chicken's, and her face was washed clean of makeup. She looked older than he remembered her, just a few days earlier.

"Hi, Thuy," he said.

She sat down without greeting him. The police had asked her to talk with him while they monitored the conversation. After seeing the tackle box filled with personal items, they wanted to know what other murders he could be connected to. If she could get information out of him, it would help her human trafficking case. She needed all the help she could get; Avi Bierman had hired a topflight criminal-defense attorney and left her swinging in the wind, all on her own.

"Have you talked to Mom and Dad?" he asked.

"No, they are too ashamed. They will never speak to us again," she lied.

They were afraid to come by the jail and to call, but she had spoken to them. They were staying in their house, hiding from everyone in their community. She imagined a different life, without carrying her disturbed brother like a boulder on her back. Maybe Nevada, where she could set up shop with new girls and have a place with breathing room. She'd change her name legally. A clean slate. But for that, Vithu needed to talk.

"Why did you do it? Why can't you stay out of trouble?" she asked him.

"I don't know why. I never knew why. It just . . . comes over me . . ." he stammered.

"How many?"

"No one missed them."

She slammed her palm against the tabletop. "How many, and where did you find them?"

"There was one in San Pedro, by the port. And a homeless girl out in San Bernardino . . . they were prostitutes, so it didn't matter . . ." he said.

"When? I need to know. If you don't tell me the truth, I will never have anything to do with you again. You'll have no family, no mother or father. No one!"

"Okay, okay . . . I'll tell you everything I remember . . ." he blubbered.

In the observation room, Postiff, Barrera, and Ramsey watched and listened, taking notes as he detailed the murders he had committed against the women he decided didn't matter, whose only purpose was to fulfill his bloodlust. They'd already sent his DNA to Vietnam so the police in Haiphong could run it. With his quiet demeanor and boyish appearance, Vithu Pham was turning out to be the most prolific serial killer they had ever seen.

Cassidy clocked out after her interview with Whitty. She told Ramsey that she had a migraine, which was a lie, but she didn't care. She couldn't sit in the station any longer, with the weight of Eden's investigation hanging over her. She was drowning in doubt about everything. Her father's innocence, her career, her flagging fortitude. She was near home when she made a detour to the New Day facility. She pulled into the far side of the parking lot. She didn't go in, honoring Kylie's request to stay away for a little while. She felt as if everything she had believed in was shifting underneath her.

She sat in her car, wishing she could go in and flop down on Kylie's bed, chatting about nothing and everything. Her phone rang with a number she didn't recognize. The caller had been trying her for the past few hours, and she'd ignored the call, thinking it was a reporter or some other scam. This time, she answered it.

"Cassidy? This is Nima Zenovich."

Cassidy remembered Nima from the academy. She was a new boot, assigned to the Devonshire Police Department in the West Valley.

"Hey, Nima, what's up?"

"I just wanted to let you know, your dad was arrested and brought in earlier. He broke into someone's house, and he says he's getting evidence for a cold case. But he's in our jail right now."

CHAPTER THIRTY-FIVE

Cassidy pulled into the Devonshire station after spending an hour in traffic. A big rig had overturned on the freeway, trapping drivers at a standstill. She raced inside and asked for Zenovich. A few minutes later, she emerged.

"I got here as fast as I could. I need to post my dad's bail," Cassidy said.

"He's out. His bail was posted, and he left."

"Who posted it?" Cassidy asked, baffled.

"Let me see. It was just in the last half hour," Zenovich said, checking the computer. "It was a woman named Zelda Zed."

Cassidy walked to her car in a daze. Her father had called Zelda Zed to bail him out. Cassidy had no idea what was going on. She drove back home, hoping to find him there. When she arrived, the sun was going down and the purple shadows had begun to blanket the hillside around their house. Bill's car wasn't in the driveway. She stepped inside to find the house dark. She flipped on the lights in the living room and saw Bill sitting alone on the couch. In his hand, he held a .38 revolver.

"Dad?" she asked.

"Turn the lights off; my eyes are bothering me," he said quietly.

She turned them off and moved slowly toward him. She kept her eyes on the gun and sat across from him in the dark.

"What happened?" she asked.

"I went into Musselman's house when he was gone. I knew he was the guy, the one who killed Min Sun-Hee. I just knew it . . ." he said, his voice trailing off.

"And then what?"

"He came home and I ran. He grabbed me by the fence, and I hit him. Then I took off. I found two Social Security cards, Cassidy. I knew he'd gotten a new identity, to hide after killing her," he said. "Even Derby said people do that all the time."

"Did Derby encourage you to do this? I saw your notebooks, all that stuff about good and evil. They were in your bag from Coalinga. Did he say those things?" she asked gently.

"He did. He and I are similar, you know? We both want to stop bad people from doing bad things. He gets it, and he said I should try to find evidence, that Musselman probably had something to do with it. So, I did, but it went all wrong. The other Social Security card was for his dad, who died years ago. How can he not be Tom Britt? It all made sense to me," Bill said, confused and uncertain.

Cassidy moved next to him on the couch. She reached out and took the gun from him, then set it out of reach.

"Daddy, I need you to listen to me, okay?"

Bill looked at her in surprise. "You haven't called me that in a long time, Binkie."

"Alan Musselman had nothing to do with Min Sun-Hee, but your brain played tricks on you. It made you believe things that aren't true. You're nothing like Tyler Derby. He's a murderer and a liar. You're not like him at all. You're one of the good guys, okay?"

"But you don't believe me, do you? About Eden?" he asked.

"I do believe you. I was wrong and I was scared. I said some stupid things that I regret. I believe you, one hundred percent."

Bill reached out and took her hand. "I know a lot of people don't like me. I've made a lot of people mad over the years. But when you said you didn't trust my word, it broke me. You're the most important person in my world, Binkie. I promise you, I didn't hurt Eden."

She pulled him into a hug. "I know, Dad. We're going to find out who did. And we're going to get help for you."

"I'm so tired all the time . . ." he said quietly.

He put his arms around her, and she laid her head on his thick shoulder, the way she had as a little girl. They sat that way, without speaking, as the sun went down completely, enveloping the room in darkness.

Zelda Zed sat across from Joyce Ramsey at Alcove, in Los Feliz. It was far enough away from the station and expensive enough that Ramsey knew she wouldn't meet any cops there.

"So, what happened after you bailed him out?" Ramsey asked.

"He said he was sure that this neighbor was involved in a cold case from years ago. And the best part, he's been talking to a convicted killer up in the Central Valley whose been feeding him all of this craziness. He's really off his rocker!" Zed said with a laugh.

"He's crazier than I thought. You know his ex-girlfriend was killed this past week, and he's a suspect," Ramsey said, adding sugar to her black coffee.

"He was at her house that night! He admitted it to me. It's going to be a great episode; it might even be two or three installments. But he says he didn't do it," Zed said.

"Of course he says that. It could be another cop, but I'd prefer it to be Bill Clarke."

"Why?"

"The other guy is active duty. Clarke is retired. If we're going to have a rogue cop who kills someone, it's better if he's no longer working for the LAPD. We can make him into a lone-wolf bad guy. It's easier to distance the department from that," Ramsey explained.

"I'll keep that in mind," Zed said. "I'm talking to his neighbor today, to hear what happened inside his house with Clarke."

"Good. I want to bury him," Ramsey said, then took a bite of her salade Niçoise.

Ethan Acevedo finished his fourth margarita and felt his brain swimming in a strong tequila buzz. He was restless. Pineda hadn't returned his calls to the burner phone. His hot little hookup, Maria, had given him a hard time the night before. After they went for late-night street tacos and drinks, she didn't let him do it the way he wanted. She even pushed him off her, bucking her tight little ass into the air and knocking him off balance. He'd landed hard and twisted his ankle.

So, he got a little heated with her, pushed her around, and made her do it his way, even if she didn't like it. Afterward, she cried and said some choice words to him in Spanish. He'd slapped her a few times for that also, but she had called him earlier, wanting to meet tonight so he'd been right. She liked it rough. But the whole thing was too complicated. He didn't want any drama or emotional garbage with women. He might just change hotels and find something new to spend his money on.

But for tonight, he could have one last hookup with her. She would probably cry when he told her it was over. Maybe he could go to Acapulco next. Or Playa del Carmen. Maria said she wanted to meet on the beach, which suited him fine. He liked pounding in the sand, with the breeze and the waves all around. He walked unsteadily down the stairs to the beach. It was dark and empty. He could hear the waves breaking on the shore. She wanted to meet by a rock jetty, where it was private and no one would be able to see them. He liked that.

The wind picked up, and he felt a spray of salt water on his face. As he got closer to the rocks, he saw her. She was wearing an embroidered sundress, her dark hair falling loose over her shoulders. In the shadows, her smile was like a beacon. He approached, hoping she wasn't wearing anything underneath that dress.

"Hi, Papito," she purred as he drew near.

She pulled him in for a kiss, and as he pushed his tongue into her mouth, she reached her smooth hands into his waistband, pulling his bathing suit down to his knees. He smiled in expectation. Then he felt hands grab his arms, pinning them behind his back. He pulled away, but they were too strong, immobilizing him. In the dark, his eyes adjusted, and he saw several men gathered around Maria, who looked at him with disgust. There were three more behind him. As they held his arms tight, one of them kicked him hard, hitting his solar plexus with precision. The wind went out of him, and his legs buckled as he struggled to breathe. His bathing suit tangled around his ankles, leaving him naked.

"How do you like it, *pendejo*? You're the big tough guy now?" one of the men said, kicking him hard in the ribs with steel-toed cowboy boots.

Acevedo felt his ribs crack, and a stunning pain shot through his torso. He tried to curl in on himself, but they pulled him to his feet and took turns beating him with their fists, landing heavy punches about his head and neck. His lip split open, and his nose spurted blood, which ran into his mouth, choking him. All the while, Maria watched with smug satisfaction. She handed one of the men a steel rod, which he slammed against Acevedo's shins, cracking them with the force of the blow. Acevedo fell to the ground, and the men pushed him over onto his stomach.

"You like making girls do things they don't like? You like hurting them, *cabrón*?" one of the men hissed into his ear, jamming his face hard against the sand, clogging his nostrils.

"Let's see how you like it, gringo . . ."

Acevedo was jolted with a searing pain that felt as if he were being split in two. They dragged him to the water's edge as he was on the brink of losing consciousness and pushed his head into the water. He struggled weakly against them, and he heard Maria's voice through the gurgling of the water filling his ears and his lungs.

"And my name is Lupita . . . *hijo de puta* . . ."

He lost consciousness. They left him and disappeared up the beach, the lights from the hotels twinkling as the waves rolled in and out, pulling his motionless body into the ocean.

CHAPTER THIRTY-SIX

Cassidy sat in Carbone's office, holding a piece of paper, waiting for the lieutenant to return with a fresh coffee. She saw Postiff and Moody heading out while Montoya worked on a computer in the meeting room that had become their central command post for the internal investigation. Carbone entered with two cups and placed one next to Cassidy.

"That wasn't necessary, lieutenant. Thank you."

"I figured you might need a caffeine boost after the week you've had," Carbone said.

"I've thought a lot about it, and I want to hand in my resignation from the LAPD. I thought I could do this, but it's too much for me," Cassidy said, sliding the paper across the desk that separated them.

Carbone looked at the resignation and stuck it in a desk drawer.

"I'm not accepting it, Officer Clarke. You've been through a trial by fire. You're new and you're young. We asked a lot of you, and I understand that you need a break. We can work with that, but I know I speak for Commander Ramsey and Chief McCall: We don't want to lose someone like you."

"I don't think I'm cut out for this," Cassidy protested.

"Take a couple of weeks off, effective immediately—get away from all of it, and then come back to me. New boots like you are the future of this department, Cassidy. Don't give up on us yet."

"I don't know, lieutenant. This really opened my eyes, and I don't know if it's for me. I'll take the time off, and maybe we'll talk about it again in a few weeks?"

"That will be fine. Take all the time that you need," Carbone said.

Cassidy left her office and went to clean out her locker. She saw Riley preparing to go out on patrol.

"Hey Mini Clarke! When're you coming back out with me?" he asked.

"Mini Clarke? Is that my new name?"

"I just made it up. I think it suits you. Boon Nam wants to give you a free massage at her place. I'm going to pick up some *luk chup* from her today; I asked her to get you a box."

Cassidy smiled. She'd missed Riley and the small considerations he paid her. Man-Bun in the park and the Little Debbie delusions seemed so peaceful and pleasant compared to what she had gone through in the past week.

"Thank you. I'll be sure to get it from you. Be safe out there," she said.

"Don't worry. I'll be back," he said in his best Terminator impression.

She watched him saunter off to roll call, happy and at ease with himself. There were a lot worse things than spending every day with a partner like Riley. Maybe there was a way back. She got a text from Postiff as she was walking to the parking lot.

DNA IS BACK NOT YOUR DAD ITS ACEVEDO!

She froze, stunned at the news. Then she hurried out to the parking lot, holding herself together until she burst into tears of relief. She cried big heaving sobs, leaning against the hood of her car. She didn't care who saw her. She dialed her father.

"What's up, Binkie? The doctor's appointment is still on, right?"

"Yes. The DNA from Eden came back. It was Acevedo, Dad. He killed her," she said.

There was a long silence on the line.

"If I hadn't gotten so mad at her—" he began, but Cassidy cut him off.

"It's not your fault. She was involved with him, and he's a psycho. He was going to do what he was going to do."

"I can't believe it's over," he said finally.

"That's right, Daddy. It's over."

Postiff, Moody, and Montoya moved through Acevedo's guesthouse with a team of officers. His parents stood in the doorway of the main house, watching in disbelief. A police technologist worked, extracting the video footage from Acevedo's security cameras and loading it onto a laptop. They found a cache of violent pornography as well as videos he shot secretly of women he had sex with at his home. In a duffel bag behind a false wall in the laundry room, they found a knife and bloody clothing; it was the same type of knife used to kill Eden. Postiff had no doubts it would have DNA from both Acevedo and Eden.

"As soon as this gets out to the public, I have a feeling the phone is going to be ringing off the hook from women calling with horror stories about him," Postiff said.

He glanced over at Acevedo's elderly parents. His father was in pajamas, the caretaker helping him stand up. They had no idea what was happening.

Postiff approached them. "I'm very sorry, Mr. and Mrs. Acevedo, but your son is going to be charged with a very serious crime. I don't think your friend in Sacramento will be able to help, and that situation will be exposed. You may want to hire an attorney as soon as possible," he said. Then he turned and walked away. He had a stop to make at the Rampart Division.

Cassidy sat with Bill in Dr. Baruch's office, reviewing his test results. He'd been given a CAT scan, an MRI, and a PET. The doctor had done a spinal tap as well; the results would be back in two to three days.

"Unfortunately, none of these tests can definitely show CTE. The only way to accurately determine the changes in the brain tissue is during an autopsy," Dr. Baruch said.

"So, I have to kick the bucket to see if I have it," Bill said with a nervous laugh.

"You suffered a brain injury about ten years ago, right?"

"He had a motorcycle accident and had a serious concussion with a brain bleed. And he's been boxing for years, as a workout," Cassidy said.

"I did them all when I was young. The Aleman Boxing Club bouts, Cupid's Rumble, Golden Gloves up in Fresno. And I just kept it up. I'm a homicide detective. It's a great release," Bill said.

"And you got hit in the head a lot, I imagine," Baruch said.

"Well, yeah. I've been hit pretty hard, many times."

"CTE has a lot of the same symptoms as Alzheimer's and frontotemporal dementia, so you might be experiencing headaches, short-term memory loss, aggressive behaviors, obsessive thoughts, cognitive impairment. There can be poor impulse control, an increase in anger, that sort of thing," Baruch explained.

"Well, I have all those things now. What happens when it gets worse?" Bill asked.

"There can be trouble with balance, speech, executive functioning. Sometimes people engage in self-harm," Baruch said.

"Wow. What a lot to look forward to," Bill said.

"You may not have CTE, Mr. Clarke. You may just be experiencing normal brain aging. There's no way to be certain."

"Is there anything we can do to keep it from getting worse?" Cassidy asked.

"The basic things that are good for everyone: a healthy diet and exercise. And there are medications; physical and occupational therapies can help with certain activities. There's even cognitive rehabilitation and sometimes TMS, which involves magnetic pulses to stimulate brain cells. It's best to live a healthy lifestyle, minimize stress. I can put together a packet of information for you so you can come up with a plan," Baruch offered.

He left the room, and Bill turned to Cassidy. "Honey, if I get as bad as he says, just shoot me, okay?"

"That's not going to happen, Dad. We're going to come up with a game plan. Healthy diet, exercise, all of it. You should start meditating also, maybe take up tai chi," she suggested.

"Oh crap, that's for old ladies in the park!" he said.

"Whatever it is, I'll be there with you. Don't worry. We're a team," she assured him.

"Right. Like Tom and Jerry," he said.

"Or Ricky and Lucy," she added.

"How about Binkie and Bill?" he suggested.

Tears welled up in her eyes; he took her hand and patted it gently.

"It's okay, it's going to be okay. You don't have to cry," he said.

"I'm not crying; you're crying!" Cassidy said with a small laugh.

CHAPTER THIRTY-SEVEN

Postiff rolled into the Rampart station to speak to Captain Rollings in person. He found him in his office. Ramsey had kept the DNA and the search warrant on Acevedo a secret, not wanting any interference from Metro until they had hard evidence. Rollings greeted Postiff with a thin smile, his eyes cold.

"What can I do for you, detective?" he asked.

"Captain, I wanted to let you know that we have DNA confirmation from the crime scene at the murder of Eden Balcomb. The blood DNA is from your officer, Ethan Acevedo. It was found on the victim's body where she was attacked with a knife, which we found when we executed the search warrant at his home earlier," Postiff said.

"When did all this go down?" Rollings asked, his face pale with shock.

"They're finishing up the search of his residence now. I was told by Captain Danner that he's on vacation and put in the request a few weeks ago, but he is not at home, and his parents' caretaker said that he went on a trip."

"Acevedo just asked me about it. He said his mom needed help with his dad, who had Alzheimer's!" Rollings said, his voice tight with anger and embarrassment.

"We checked with customs and border patrol, and they confirmed that he traveled to Mexico from LAX. Perhaps Danner or someone else in your division knows where he is? We're filing an extradition request with the Mexican government so he can be picked up and sent back to be charged," Postiff said evenly. He enjoyed seeing Rollings squirm.

"We'll track him down; you can count on it. I'll get back to you the minute I hear something," Rollings assured him.

"Thank you, captain. Also, Acevedo left a burner phone with one of your other officers, Paul Pineda. He might be implicated as well," Postiff said, turning on his heel and leaving without another word. He smiled as he walked out; he hated the Metro cops.

Behind him he heard Rollings shout at his assistant, "Get Danner in my office now!"

Cassidy knocked on Alan Musselman's door, noticing a big box from Chewy had been delivered. Musselman cracked the door open, a big mixed-breed dog behind him.

"Mr. Musselman, may I speak to you for a moment?" she asked.

He gave her a wary look. "What is it, Ms. Clarke?"

"I want to apologize for what my dad did. I'm sure he does also. He's not been himself lately. He's suffering from some kind of brain degeneration, perhaps CTE. His behavior has been really erratic, and I'm sorry that he focused on you with no cause whatsoever. He's going into therapy, and we're coming up with a plan to help him deal with this condition," she explained.

Musselman's shoulders slumped, and his eyes softened. "I'm sorry to hear that. My dad had dementia. I know how hard that can be. And how crazy they can act. That changes things."

"Thank you for your understanding," she said.

"You should know, that woman Zelda Zed? She's planning to do a podcast about your dad as a rogue cop who loses it. 'A cop gone bad' is what she told me. She wanted my side of the story, and she gave me the creeps. You should warn your dad not to talk to her."

"Thank you for letting me know," Cassidy said, keeping her fury in check as she headed toward home. Inside the house, she moved quietly. Bill was asleep in his room, having taken his new medication from Dr.

Baruch. She found Bill's cell phone and Zelda Zed's number in his contacts. She dialed, her hands shaking with rage.

"Hello, Bill, what can I do for you?" Zed asked.

"This is his daughter, Cassidy Clarke. I heard you're planning a podcast about my dad, making him look crazy and dangerous. He's not well. He saw a neurologist this week. If you malign his character or damage his reputation, I'll expose you as a low-life bloodsucker for trying to profit off a man suffering from a brain disease. How do you think that will play to your Gen Z followers? How quickly do you think you'll be canceled?"

She heard Zed's surprised intake of breath as she tried to recover.

"Okay, whatever. I didn't know. It was Joyce Ramsey who really pushed it. She has it in for him for some reason. I can easily do a different story. I like your dad. He's a cool guy," Zelda said.

"Forget you ever met him," Cassidy said and hung up.

Arturo Blanco watched as Michael Lyman hammered a **For Rent** sign into the grass outside their apartment building. Eden's unit had been cleaned up, all signs of her violent death erased. Blanco remembered the day she moved in. She had a little dog back then that had escaped, and Blanco had run up the street to catch him. They'd been friends ever since. Detective Postiff called to let him know that they had identified Eden's killer; it was the cop who showed up late at her place that evening, He was out of the country, but they would have him in custody soon, so Blanco returned home from the 101 Motel.

He moved to Lyman, then helped him to steady the sign.

"It's a sad day, Arturo. A sad, sad day," Lyman said quietly.

"At least they know who did it."

"I never liked that guy, never. He had a bad energy. I wish she'd never taken up with him," Lyman said. "Women have to be so careful these days."

"Is anyone arranging anything for her? A service or something?" Blanco asked.

"I might do it. She had no family. I'm sure some of her clients would come, don't you think?"

"I can help you with that."

"Okay. Are you coming to the Broadway Show Tunes on Tuesday at the senior center?" Lyman asked.

"Maybe," Blanco replied.

"I think you should. I'm doing 'Don't Cry for Me Argentina.' Oh, and I picked up a new Garfield statue for you at a garage sale over on La Granada Drive. I have it inside," he said, turning toward his apartment.

"Thank you," Blanco said, following him across the lawn, the big white magnolia flowers blooming in the branches overhead.

Tyler Derby had called Bill Clarke twice but received no reply. He wanted to know how it all went down, the breaking and entering at Alan Musselman's house and the aftermath. Derby wanted to hear about his arrest and the shitload of trouble he had gotten in. He figured he could keep Bill spinning as long as he could keep feeding his paranoia. He liked having power over a detective like Clarke, the cream of the crop who everyone looked up to. It felt good to bring a guy like that down a few notches.

Derby had pulled prison library duty and was hoping to stay there. It was safer and quieter than the laundry detail, where Pimentel and Presley were the ruling thugs who controlled everything that went down. Guys were always getting shanked down there, and they could easily push you into the dryer room, with the big rumbling machines, and no one would hear anything. He was reshelving books when Warden Rennison showed up.

"They closed the Stacey Mandel case in Los Angeles with what you gave them. Clarke told me they found DNA on the tarp you used in the van where you killed her," he said. "So, you got some brownie points for that."

Derby just nodded, making no reply, pushing the cart down the quiet aisle of bookcases.

"And the DA in San Diego might try you for the murder of Remedios Carson. She was just a child, and you know what happens in here when the inmates find out you killed a kid," Rennison added.

Derby froze. He never thought they might try him for that murder, not when he was already put away for life. Clarke had made it seem like they would look favorably on any cold case admission he gave them. He hoped for that transfer to Donovan, not another trial that would rain a whole new level of misery down on him at Pleasant Valley.

"Bill Clarke's daughter called also. She said if you contact her dad again, she'll file a complaint against you with the Department of Corrections, and there'll be consequences for harassing the detective who arrested you. You need to stop causing more problems for yourself, Derby!" Rennison said with a laugh, turning to go. "And you're going back to laundry detail tomorrow," he added as he walked out of the quiet, peaceful library.

EPILOGUE

Bill, Cassidy, and Postiff stood with Barrera at the Hollywood Forever Cemetery, behind Paramount Studios. Montoya and Moore were there, as well as Michael Lyman and Arturo Blanco. A few of Eden's elderly clients had come, one in a wheelchair. Eden's ashes were being put into the columbarium; several funeral wreaths were set up on stands. Bill had hired a small trio of musicians, who played the Bach *Trauerode* as her urn was placed inside.

"She liked this place," Bill said. "We used to come here and watch the outdoor movies."

"She was a good egg," Lyman said.

"She and I liked going to K-Town for dumplings and facials," Blanco added.

The cemetery was filled with headstones and crypts of old movie stars from the early days of the film industry. Judy Garland was there, along with Rudolph Valentino. The traffic on Santa Monica Boulevard was busy; the clanging sounds from nearby auto body shops carried over the street noise. Two swans floated in the small lake that surrounded the large marble crypt of Douglas Fairbanks Jr.

Cassidy slipped her arm through Bill's; they stood in silence. Postiff held a bouquet of freesias, which he stuck into the small vase attached to the plaque that bore her name: Elaine Eden May Balcomb.

"Why don't you sing a song, Arturo? She loved it when you sang those old show tunes," Lyman suggested.

Blanco looked around at the others and asked timidly, "Should I? She did have a favorite that we used to sing in the car. It's really old, from the Ziegfield Follies in the 1920s."

"Sing it. She'd like that," Lyman insisted.

They all nodded and agreed. Blanco cleared his throat and smoothed his plaid suit jacket self-consciously. His voice rang out, a sweet tenor, amplified by the marble walls of the mausoleum.

"Nightshades falling, lovebirds calling; what makes the world go round? Nothing but love. When whippoorwills call and evening is nigh, I hurry to my blue heaven. A turn to the right, a little white light will lead you to my blue heaven . . ."

ABOUT THE AUTHOR

Photo © 2024 Paul Gregory

Michele Domínguez Greene is a Southern California native with a long-standing career in the arts. As a working actress, she has appeared in numerous television, theater, and indie film productions, including *The Kill Floor*, a 2023 festival favorite. She received an Emmy nomination for her work on the groundbreaking NBC series *L.A. Law*.

Greene's debut novel, *Chasing the Jaguar*, was nominated for an American Library Association Award. Her second YA title was *Keep Sweet*. Her first novel for adults, part of a three-book series, is slated for a May 2025 release in the UK. *Hollywood Hit Men* kicks off the author's Cassidy Clarke series in the US.

Greene lives in California with her family and serves as artistic director of Adelante Arts Collective, a performing and language arts program for at-risk youth and underserved communities. She enjoys cooking, hiking, art, and roller-skating. She has too many rescue pets but will stop for stray dogs, yard sales, and weird stuff by the side of the road.